OUR LADY OF THE SCYTHE

DO WHAT THOU WILT

Cover art and design by Soares Artwork
https://www.facebook.com/SoaresArtwork

Punk AF logo by Caelan Stokkermans Arts
https://www.caelanstokkermansarts.com/

Interior Formatting by Lori Michelle
http://www.TheAuthorsAlley.com

# Our Lady of the Scythe
## Demon Academy

# B.J. Swann

For FREE stories, reviews, images, and more,
visit B.J. Swann's website,
www.aeonofchaos.com

# Table of Contents

# CHAPTER 1:
## FUCHICIDE

**RAZA STEPPED OUT** of the cab and onto the curb. The city was ablaze with neon light that polluted the sky with a ghostly blue glow. The cool air of midnight lashed her bare arms and legs, feeding the excitement that thudded in her blood.

*It's happening,* she thought. *It's totally happening!*

She'd hit the club about an hour before midnight. Her sexy black dress had done its work well. Almost too well. She'd had to fend off a dozen scrubs before she'd finally encountered a suitor who'd been more to her liking—James, the handsome young man who was presently leading her away from the cab and towards his apartment.

He smiled as he ushered her through into the lobby of his building and led her up the stairs. She took the opportunity to ogle his arse as he ascended above her. His tight buns alone spoke of many, many hours spent sweating in the gym. Did he say he was a personal trainer? Or an IT consultant? She couldn't quite remember. Their conversation in the club had been nothing but window-dressing anyway. The real communication had been encoded in the things in-between— his smile, his gaze, the brushing back of her long black hair, the flirtation in both of their eyes.

She felt another surge of excitement as she entered his apartment. He gestured her graciously into the living room, where a set of half-shut Venetians gave them a segmented

1

view of the city. The apartment was clean and stylishly furnished, decorated with reproductions of antique French ephemera. There were Mucha-esque advertisements for perfume and cognac. Mixed in with those were posters from a bunch of cult movies she'd never even heard of. One was called *Legend of the Overfiend,* another one *Class of Nuke 'em High.*

Of course she wasn't really focused on the posters, but on her host. He was tanned and naturally blond. He smiled at her again and waved her to a couch.

"Take a seat," he said.

She sat down and crossed her legs. Her short dress rode up, giving him a view of her thighs. He smiled again, clearly luxuriating in the spectacle. He looked tipsy, though considerably less drunk than she was. She'd been nervously pounding drinks at the bar, waiting for someone like James to arrive. And when he finally *had* arrived, she'd downed all the drinks he'd bought for her as well. Now all that booze was swimming and singing in her blood, feeding her excitement like oil on a fire.

"Would you like another drink?" he asked, licking his lips.

"Okay," she said. "Do you have any Bacardi Breezers?"

James paused for a second.

"'Fraid not," he said. "But I've got some whiskey. It's pretty good stuff . . . "

"Ugh," she said, making a disgusted face. "I can't stand straight liquor."

"I could mix it up with some Coke for you?" he suggested.

"Okay!" she said with a smile.

He grinned at her and hurried to the kitchen, where he fetched some cola from the fridge and a bottle of Talisker from the cupboard. The Talisker was quality stuff, brought back from his recent tour of the distilleries of Scotland. He felt a tinge of horror as he poured it into a tumbler and diluted it with cola. It seemed like blasphemy.

"Sorry, old buddy," he whispered, addressing the bottle as he held it in his hand. "But if you saw this girl, you'd understand. Still, I guess you'll get to see her in a moment. And if things go right, pretty soon we'll both be inside of her!"

He grinned at the bottle, poured a dram for himself, then headed back toward the living room with a drink in each hand. He paused at the threshold, taking in the sight of her as she sat there unawares. She was gorgeous, with dusky skin and a Middle Eastern look. Her body was toned, supple. Not just from exercise, it seemed, but from the natural robustness of youth. Just how old was she, he wondered? He'd met her in the club, but he wasn't a hundred percent sure she was old enough to legally attend such a venue. He made a firm decision not to ask.

*If there's grass on the field, play ball,* he thought to himself, as he strode over to the couch.

She smiled as he sat down beside her and handed her the drink. She downed it. Her face blushed red and she coughed from the coarseness of the liquor.

They both laughed, then sat there for a moment, their gazes meeting in a flicker of mutual excitement. Raza leaned forward and placed her glass on the table. He waited for her to draw back, then pulled her into an embrace. She leaned into him eagerly, pressing her lips against his.

She kissed like a virgin, all fervent lust devoid of technique. Her tongue roved hungrily, darting and swirling in his mouth. He matched her pace, sliding a hand up her leg as they kissed. Her skin was smooth, flawless, damp with sweat from their earlier dancing.

He decided to wow her with his skills. If this girl was as sexually inexperienced as she seemed, he thought, it'd be a simple matter to blow her tiny mind. He pulled back from the kiss, knelt down before her, and started kissing his way up her long slender legs. A jolt of excitement carried through her body and into his lips. She opened her thighs to accept his advance.

*She's definitely keen!* he thought as he kissed his way closer to his goal. Her body twitched; her breaths began to quicken in a mounting a crescendo of excitement—and he'd barely even started!

Her skin smelled of sweat, with a hint of something sweeter from inside of her legs. He worked his way higher and slowly started peeling off her panties. They bunched up, flimsy and damp from perspiration, but more from desire. He caught a glimpse of her pussy, topped by a glossy black bush.

*Definitely grass on the field,* he thought to himself as he leaned in closer.

Raza reclined on the couch as his tongue went to work. Gently, teasingly he lapped at her lips, drawing ever closer to her clit. Her blood was rushing and hot now. She could hear it in her ears, throbbing, like water through some underground aqueduct. She thought of the high-pressure storm drains that lay close to her home, roiling and thundering underneath the streets. It'd recently come to light that some unknown maniac had been tossing dead bodies down those storm drains for years. The fury of the water had torn them apart, smashing the bones into powder and dispersing them out into the sea. The authorities only found out what was happening because one of the bodies got lodged in a bottleneck of garbage midway down one of the pipes and created an overflow. Was her own churning blood so relentless and terrible, she wondered?

*Weird thoughts like that must be caused by the liquor,* she decided.

She put them aside and focused instead on sensation. James had upped the ante now. His mouth had made a seal atop her clit, and his tongue was now flickering across it like that of a serpent. She muttered and bucked on the couch, wrapping her thighs around his head.

*It's totally happening,* she thought again.

Soon she'd be rid of her virginity. She was already getting teased by her peers for having kept it so long. Most of the girls at her school had lost theirs by sixteen at the latest, and yet here she was, eighteen years old and still inexperienced. Not that she hadn't tried to pop her cherry before. She would have succeeded, too, if only that horrible *thing* hadn't happened . . .

*Don't think about it,* she thought. *Tonight's the night!*

She stayed positive, feeling the waves of pleasure roll out from her clit as he plied it with his tongue. A climax was approaching, hovering on the edge of sensation, like breakers whipping up as a prelude to *tsunami*. It felt much like it did when she fingered herself, only hotter. Not just more erotic, more insistent, but physically *hotter*. Her thundering blood, burning as with fever, grew louder and louder as it raced through her temples like a military band. Her mind began to fall into delirium.

*Oh no,* she thought, even as her very thoughts began to fracture. *That THING is happening again!*

James was ensconced in her thighs, his mouth on her pussy. Gushing juices slathered his lips and poured down his chin, carrying a vaguely metallic, bittersweet flavour. Her thighs were wrapped around his head, locking him in place. It seemed like his skills were definitely making an impression!

He kept up his ministrations, waiting for the tell-tale signs of a climax. All the while he steadily grew more and more aware of the pressure encompassing his head. Her thighs were squeezing him like a vice. His skull started aching. He tried to pry apart her legs, but the action was impossible. Trapped and blinded by the pressure of her thighs, his searching hands told him that those thighs had somehow grown bigger. Bigger, stronger, and heavily muscled, like the flanks of a body builder.

The timbre of her voice had changed too, from a delicate moan to a bestial rasp. He could hear the racket she was making even through the deafening seal formed by her thighs around his ears. She sounded like a she-wolf in heat getting fucked by some rough lupine lover.

James' hackles stood on end. Cold waves of terror shot down through his spine. His cock had previously been hard enough—at least in his own imagination—to smash through a stack of wooden planks, like some Karate master's fist in a public demonstration. Now it was withering from fear.

He gave up the cunnilingus and tried to pry himself loose. His hands remained helpless, her giant thighs unyielding. He twisted his head, smearing her skin with the juices that clung to his mouth, spreading just enough lubrication to pull himself free.

His head shot out from in-between her thighs like a stubborn cork popping loose from a wine bottle. He stumbled backwards and quickly looked up, frozen with terror by the presence before him.

At some point the lights had exploded, leaving the living room dark. Deafened by the pressure of her thighs, he hadn't heard the POPS! that had sounded overhead.

Now she loomed before him in the shadows. Slivers of glass clung to her skin, like jagged bits of dance-party glitter. Her dress was gone, torn to shreds. Her naked body was as big as a bear's, though still distinctly feminine.

Aspects of her anatomy had burgeoned and multiplied. Four giant breasts hung from her chest, splitting open like the muzzles of hounds, laying bare their wet beds of saliva and teeth. Those breasts weren't puppies—they were junkyard dogs!

Four massive arms shot out towards him, dragging him

close before he could flee. He caught a glimpse of her head before she pulled him to her chest. Her locks were long and writhing like serpents, hiding most of her face in a frenzy of black. He caught a glimpse of the eyes that shone through the locks like ruby-red lanterns, a glimpse of the teeth that glinted like steel.

Then he was clutched to her bosom. Her breasts bit his flesh like a wolf pack. He screamed, then wheezed as her talons stabbed into his back and skewered his lungs like a pair of pitchforks.

He coughed out blood between her massive, two-fold cleavage. Hot breath blasted his head. Jaws clamped down, encompassing his skull, building up pressure like a hydraulic vice. He felt another, *inverse* sensation as her fingers flexed inside of his torso, gripping the curves of his ribcage and pulling them outwards.

The pressures mounted, edging him closer to oblivion. She paused, holding him in place at the brink. A gigantic tongue slithered down from her mouth and into his, carrying the same artless kiss as before. He bit it reflexively as it plunged down his throat, tasting blood that crackled like sherbet on his tongue.

Then she chomped his head in half like a soft-centred candy, and pulled him apart like a statue of popsicle sticks.

Raza woke up a few minutes later, naked and covered in blood. Her mouth tasted bitter, like metal. The room looked like the inside of an abattoir that needed to be closed for numerous health code violations. Bits of what once had been James were scattered all over the walls, ceiling and furniture.

She stood up and hastily inspected her body. It was a matter of instinct. She ran her hands up her chest, recoiling for a moment as they slathered through the gore that coated her breasts. Her body was littered with bits of broken glass.

7

Glancing upwards she saw the busted lights that were the cause of her injuries. Otherwise she seemed fine, save for an ache in her tongue.

She glanced around again. The room was dark but for the light that came peeking through the blinds. The gallons of blood looked black in the mixture of neon and moonlight. She could just make out a piece of James' face—the lips—sitting in a puddle of gore. They seemed to be voicing some frozen accusation.

Raza started crying. The last thing she could remember from before she blacked out was James giving her head. There'd been a growing feeling of heat in her body, a sensation she'd mistaken at first as being purely derived from the approach of an orgasm. Then it had felt like a fever, a blossoming fire in the depths of her veins, consuming her thoughts with its bright incandescence. Then that *thing* had happened again, just like it had the two times before.

As she stood there sobbing, her short and unfortunate sexual history flashed through her mind like a personal horror movie.

She remembered her first kiss. She been fourteen at the time. She and a boy called Emiel had spent a lot of time flirting at school before they finally worked up the mutual courage to sneak off behind one of the portable classrooms in the yard and make out.

Raza was almost breathless with anticipation. Even now, years later, she still remembered the dizzying excitement, the butterflies careening in her stomach, the heat and the hunger underneath.

That first kiss was awkward, with plenty of sloppy tongue, but she liked it nonetheless. As they kissed Emiel started feeling her up. She didn't have a problem with that. She started feeling hot, as though she were succumbing to a fever. She closed her eyes—and fell into darkness.

The next thing she knew Emiel was screaming. She opened her eyes and saw his arm was broken. Not just broken, but mangled, with a piece of shattered bone poking out. He looked at her in terror, then ran off with blood dripping down from his fingers. Raza stood there for a second, wondering what the fuck was going on. What had she missed in that moment of darkness? Had Emiel tripped over and injured himself in his eagerness to feel up her thighs? Had a meth-addled junkie leapt out from the bushes and given him a brutal Chinese Burn? Had a monster emerged from the shadows with a hunger for blood, only to retreat when she'd opened her eyes?

A medley of screams cut through her thoughts as the kids in the schoolyard got a look at Emiel's injuries. Raza rushed out from behind the portable and saw Emiel being tended to by Mr. Willis, her hated science teacher.

"What happened?" she heard Willis say.

"Raza," said Emiel. "Raza tried to rip my arm off! Her eyes were red. She looked like a dog!"

Students looked at her in shock. The awful Mr. Willis peered at her coldly, as he always did, like a scientist studying a microbe.

The police and paramedics were called. Raza was seated in the principal's office while her parents were summoned. Her blood pounded. She was so afraid of getting in trouble! What could she do? When the questioning began, she panicked and told them Emiel had groped her against her will, and she'd snapped and fought back. The lie was accepted, even though Emiel fiercely denied it. His claims that Raza had somehow "changed"—that she'd had "red eyes," and had "looked like a dog"—were taken as evidence of his dangerous instability, perhaps of incipient psychosis. He was sent to a school for troubled teenagers. Raza was sent to a therapist who spent hours telling her the incident wasn't her fault, that she'd just been defending herself, that she was a very brave girl, etcetera. By the end of the therapy sessions Raza had spent so much time lying about the incident that she almost believed her own bullshit. Maybe Emiel really was a crazy pervert? Maybe he really had attacked her, and she'd acted instinctively to protect herself? Maybe she'd blocked it all out? People could do that, right? She'd seen stuff like that in movies—repressed memories, amnesia, secret traumas. But a part of her knew that wasn't true. A part of her knew Emiel was innocent and she was to blame, even though she didn't really understand what had happened.

Others were suspicious as well. No-one could truly explain how a slender girl could all but detach a boy's arm. Many of Raza's peers opted to believe Emiel's version of events, and Raza ended up being shunned by most of the student body. "Creepy Raza," they called her. "Bloody Raza," "Raza the Bone-Breaker." She got stuck on the fringes of the school with the weirdos and the nerds. Luckily she wasn't totally alone; she ended up making friends with a pair of shy girls called Lilly and Fatima. But the boys would have nothing to do with her. To them she was like a poisoned flower—they didn't dare to touch her, even if they happened to think she was hot.

Years passed in this manner. Raza got stuck on the sidelines, watching other students fall into puppy love, hearing all the gossip about who was making out with who, who was getting blowjobs, who was giving them, who'd gone all the way, who'd had to buy the morning after pill, which was the best brand of condom, did cherry-flavoured lube actually taste any good?

The whole situation made her sick with envy. Of course her friends told her not to worry, that she should just chill out, that she'd find a boy one day who wasn't scared of her, maybe when she went to uni or something. But Raza didn't want to wait that long. She wasn't like Fatima and Lilly. She was *hungry*. In sex education class, the teacher said boys think about sex nineteen times a day on average. A lot of the girls in the class gasped, thinking that was a lot of sexy thoughts, but Raza didn't gasp at all. She thought about sex *at least* that much, probably more. But with her reputation as a dangerous weirdo, there wasn't much she could do to put all those thoughts into action. Until . . .

Until during her sixteenth year, when she finally found a boy who didn't care about her grim reputation. He wasn't a boy from her school. He was a seventeen-year-old dropout called Zach who lived in her neighbourhood and seemed to spend most of his time smoking weed and working as an apprentice panel beater. Kids at Raza's school said he was a dropkick, a loser. So when he and Raza started flirting at the local shopping centre, she decided to keep their connection a secret. She didn't tell anyone about it—not her friends, and definitely not her parents. She was worried they would judge her. Hell, she was already judging herself. Zach was definitely a bogan. He wore tracky dacks and wife beaters and had a sort of vacant, permanently-stoned look in his eyes. But his body was toned from all that panel-beating. And Raza was oh so desperate . . .

It wasn't long until she ended up at his house, making out with him on his bed while his mother was out. Again she was almost breathless from anticipation. Her heart hammered. Butterflies careened in her stomach. She gasped with delight as his hand went between her legs. She got hot, as though she were succumbing to a fever. She closed her eyes. The world went dark. She woke up –

And found herself surrounded by his organs. The guy had been eviscerated and torn into pieces. It was worse than anything she'd ever seen, even worse than those online gore videos that creepy kid had posted on all the school computers that time. There was so much blood. Somehow it smelled sort of sweet, like syrup. Raza didn't know what to do. Her instinct told her to run.

She cleaned herself up and sprinted back to her house. Luckily almost no-one saw her, and those few who did didn't notice the splatters of blood she'd been too frantic to clean off her face. She got home and cleaned herself up even more. A few hours later it was all on the news—how a young panel-beater's apprentice had been gruesomely murdered in Glenroy. The police had never seen anything like it. They thought perhaps an animal was responsible, something big and powerful, like a bear or a lion, which perhaps had been smuggled into the country illegally, then somehow set loose in Melbourne's northern suburbs. The local media speculated, even more wildly, that a lion had escaped from some drug lord's private petting zoo, hopped up on the steroids and meth it had ostensibly been fed by its Scarface-like owner.

When Raza saw the news reports she didn't know what to think. On the one hand, there were some similarities with what had happened to Emiel at school. In both instances there had been excitement, heat, darkness—and ultimately, blood. She couldn't help but wondering—was she somehow responsible? Then again, maybe it really had been an animal attack. Maybe she'd seen it, but had blocked it all out because it was just too traumatic to remember?

In the end she wasn't sure what to believe. So she clung to the explanation that exonerated her, telling it to herself over and over, even though a part of her was sceptical, and was always whispering from the back of her mind—*You did it, Raza. There's something wrong with you . . .*

After that she stayed away from boys for a while. It was agonizing. Because by this point, pretty much everyone at her school seemed to be having sex. Even her shy friends Lilly and Fatima had boyfriends they'd met through extracurricular activities. She was happy for them, of course, but she couldn't help being envious. Here they were falling in love while Raza was stuck all alone. Night after night she lay in bed caressing herself, wishing her fingers belonged to someone else, wishing there was another tongue—another body—to give her delight.

By the time she turned eighteen she couldn't take it anymore. She told herself those earlier events were nothing but freak occurrences, accidents. That nothing like that would ever happen again. On one level she believed her self-talk. On another level she was bleakly anticipating the same awful cycle as before—heat, darkness, blood, perhaps even death. That voice at the back of her mind had warned her again—*Don't do it, Raza. There's something very wrong with you . . .*

She did her best to shut that voice up. She went to the pub and drank enough to smother her fears. She met James, drank even more, then went home with him. And yet, despite how drunk she was, she still kept feeling those hints of foreboding, those ominous cues that things weren't okay. She felt them even when she was following James from the taxi. At the back of her mind his sexy walk up the stairs took on the likeness of a death march. But she wanted to believe, more than anything, that things would be different this time. And she was just so horny! She couldn't keep herself contained anymore.

And so here she was again, surrounded by the pieces of another mangled carcass. What could've happened this time? Could a slasher movie maniac have burst through the window and hacked James to death with a machete, Jason Voorhees-style? Could Raza have seen it all, and once again blocked it out to protect herself from the trauma? Could this all be just a string of unfortunate coincidences with Raza at the middle?

*Yeah, right*, said that voice at the back of her head. *And maybe all those unexploded landmines in Africa will start shooting out confetti and Reese's peanut butter Pieces.*

This time there was no denying it. This time that voice in her head was definitely right. Two mutilated males might've been a coincidence, but three was a pattern. Every time she tried to get busy with a boy, they ended up looking like roadkill, and Raza was the common denominator. But why? Raza's mind started racing, grasping for some explanation.

Perhaps the answer lay in her background? Her parents were from Iraq, but they weren't very traditional. They'd never even warned her off sex before marriage. In fact, whenever she went to ask them for advice, they always gave the same enigmatic response—"Do What Thou Wilt Shall be the Whole of the Law." She'd Googled the phrase, and found it attributed to some guy called Aleister Crowley, who'd run some kind of creepy old-person sex cult in Sicily, until he'd been kicked out by Mussolini for perverting public morals. He'd adopted the maxim from the writings of some medieval French guy called Rabelais. Now that didn't sound very Middle Eastern at all!

Still, maybe there was some kind of familial connection with the killings? Like maybe some deranged, obsessive patriarch had followed her parents from Iraq, and was secretly stalking her, trying to keep her pure for some secret, prearranged-marriage. Maybe he was honour-killing all of her lovers, before they could stretch out her hymen!

It wasn't impossible, she thought. The stalker could've shot her with some kind of dart gun, knocking her out while he despatched her would-be lovers with a scimitar. She glanced over at the window, looking for a sign that a high-powered dart had been shot through the glass to puncture her skin. Part of the window had indeed been shattered, but only by a piece of James' flying ribcage.

Okay, so maybe the stalker theory was a bit far-fetched. But what other options were there? Was she like one of those mutants from the *X-Men* movies, exploding with terrible power whenever she got close to popping her cherry? Was she firing lightning bolts out of her pussy?

She didn't have time to think about this stuff right now. She had to make a getaway! The last thing she needed was *this* fucked-up shit derailing her existence.

She found the bathroom and took a quick shower, scrubbing herself hard to wash off all the blood, then towelling herself dry as she returned to the living room. There she searched through the gore for her handbag. The cheap, faux-leather exterior was wet with gore. Gingerly she opened it, withdrawing a bag of vacuum-sealed clothing. She'd brought it to wear the next day, after her successful sexual experience had finally been consummated. She'd told herself the bag was necessary, both to keep the outfit fresh, and to shrink it down enough to be carried in her diminutive purse. Still, perhaps a part of her had been planning for the bloodshed all along, taking steps to insulate her clothing from the carnage she knew was likely to occur. She spared another guilty glance at James' disembodied lips.

Sirens started blaring in the distance. Were they coming for her? It sure felt like it. Hurriedly she opened the bag and took out the crisp high school uniform that had neatly been folded within.

She quickly got dressed and escaped into the night, walking a couple of Ks before she dialled up a taxi. She bid the driver drop her off a few blocks from her house, then made her way through the dark suburban streets until she finally arrived at her home, where she tiptoed to the door and slowly inserted the key so as not to wake her parents.

In the void of silence that filled the front yard the clicking of the tumblers sounded like gathering thunder. Her heart raced with fear at the thought of discovery. As liberal as her parents might be, she didn't want them intruding on her private, hidden life.

She hesitated as the lock clicked over, waiting for any telltale signs that her parents had awoken, like a flicker of light on the upstairs landing, or the shuffling of feet on the stairs.

But the house remained silent and dark. She quickly stepped inside and shut the door behind her. She shut her eyes, too, and slumped back against the door, letting her exhausted body slide down to the linoleum below.

She let out a sigh and looked up, finding her mother and father waiting in the darkness.

"Shahrazad," said her father, using her full name. "There's something we need to talk to you about."

# CHAPTER 2:
## WE NEED TO TALK

**F**OR A MOMENT Raza sat frozen with her back to the door. The expression on both of her parents' faces looked ominous. Silently they walked towards the kitchen, beckoning for Raza to follow. She sat there for a few more moments, heart pounding nervously. Then she stood up and followed. She found them sitting at the kitchen table with one of the lights on, a warm, soft light that spread soft shadows over everything. It was a quaint suburban kitchen—boring, prosaic. Her parents were quaint suburban people, similarly boring in her eyes. Both of them were dressed in their department store dressing gowns. Her father had dark hair and a bushy black beard. Her mother, like many of her people, had straw-blond hair and bright blue eyes.

They were Kurds from Iraq. Specifically they were Yezidis, a religious and ethnic minority that seemed very poorly understood. Even Raza herself didn't know that much about them. Her parents didn't seem to practice their religion, and had never told her much about her people's beliefs. Everything she'd learned about the Yezidis had come from the internet. The info was scant, confusing, and often contradictory. It seemed that their religion was in some ways very similar, and in other ways very different, to that of the Christian Gnostics or the ancient Cathars. They believed that the world had been made not by God or Allah, but by an entity known as Melek Taus, a Demiurge who reigned as the lord of all matter, and the steward of the physical realm. The Yezidis prayed to him, accepting his temporal dominion. And yet Melek Taus was often equated by outsiders with another, far more famous entity, widely known in western cultures as Satan. Thus the Yezidis were often persecuted by Muslims, who believed them to be in league with demons.

This was but one of the reasons why Raza's parents had been granted a humanitarian visa by the Australian government around the start of the Iraq war. They'd come to the country with dozens of other persecuted minorities, including thousands of Iraqi Christians, otherwise known as Chaldeans. Baby Raza had come over with them, but she remembered almost nothing of that time. All she knew was the placid beige world of Melbourne suburbia, a liminal zone between the excitement of the city and the desolate vastness of the bush.

To some people Raza's parents might've seemed exotic. But they didn't seem exotic to her. Nor were they exotic in the suburb of Glenroy, which had a large population of Middle Eastern migrants. There were so many, in fact, that the Skips—the Aussie kids—jokingly referred to the place as "Glenroy-istan." Of course Raza was basically Aussie too, having grown up there. And she was also partly American, culturally, at least, having been raised on a diet of American movies, music and pop culture, to the point where her accent was part Aussie strine, almost part valley girl.

She sat down at the table opposite her parents.

"Shahrazad, we need to talk," said her father, repeating his earlier statement, as if to delay what actually needed to be said.

Raza nodded silently, while the blood kept on nervously pumping in her veins. She waited for her parents to speak but they were silent, awkward, clearly unready for whatever momentous discussion was supposed to take place. Her mum tried to put her at ease with an artificial smile. It didn't work. Her dad lit a cigarette and started smoking it so fast the ash seemed to be chasing the butt toward his yellowed fingers. He'd clearly been smoking a lot, even more than usual; the ashtray on the table was jam-packed with butts and the whole house stank.

Raza's blood kept pumping. Something weird was going on.

*Could they?* she thought. *Could they possibly know?*

Unable to bear their awkward glances anymore, Raza looked away. Her eyes fixed on the only unusual object in the room, a fat candle that burned with a dim blue flame atop one of the kitchen counters. She hadn't seen it before, she'd been too focused on her parents and their ominous words. Now that she did see it, it only made things seem even stranger. Her parents weren't the sort to burn candles unless the power was out. And this candle was odd. It was jet black, with strange-looking symbols inked down the sides. It looked like something the goth girl at Raza's school might have kept in her bedroom for her weird Wiccan rituals. But Raza's parents weren't goths or Wiccans. They weren't even the type to use candles for a romantic evening. As far as she knew they didn't even have romantic evenings.

Raza sniffed the air. Over the heavy scent of tobacco smoke she could smell the candle's scent; it smelled like burning pork fat, with a twist of something strange.

"What's with the candle?" said Raza, unable to bear the tension of the silence any longer.

"Oh," said her mother with another artificial smile that was supposed to be reassuring, but ended up being disturbing instead. "That candle, that's actually the reason— well, one of the reasons—why we need to talk to you. It's a special candle. A magick candle."

"A magick candle?" said Raza, dripping with scepticism.

"That's right, dear," said her mother. "A *magick* candle. Someone gave it to us long ago. It's supposed to start burning when you come of age."

"Come of age? But I turned eighteen months ago . . . "

"That's not what I mean, Raza. It's supposed to start burning when you truly come of age. When you go through the change. When you taste human meat."

Raza's eyes went wide. Was this really happening? Her heart pounded in her chest as though she were running a five-minute mile. She felt hot. The heat seemed to crawl on her face and her skin like a thousand tiny insects. She was so shocked she couldn't move, couldn't talk, couldn't think, could only just sit there as her mum smiled another try-hard smile and let out a nervous little laugh.

"It's quite a relief, really," she said. "I was starting to think the bloody thing was broken! The candle, that is. I was starting to think it was a dud. I mean, we were pretty sure you'd already manifested your birthright years ago, at sixteen. That was you, wasn't it, with the panel-beater's apprentice? That boy Zachary?"

Raza gulped and trembled, still too shocked to process events. Her mother's words washed over her like a scalding wave, but didn't yet sink to the marrow. She said nothing.

"That's okay, Raza," said her mum. "It doesn't really matter. But the candle is burning now. It's been burning for hours. Which means you've probably killed someone. Right?"

Raza's breaths came deep and fast. A part of her wanted to spring up and defend herself, but she still felt paralysed, not just by shock, but by a terrible feeling that her mum's words were true.

Her mother caught the fear in her eye.

"It's okay, dear," she said. "We're not judging you. It's perfectly natural, considering what you are."

"What . . . what I am?" stammered Raza.

"We're not your biological parents," said her dad, speaking for the first time in minutes. "Your mother died in childbirth, back in Iraq. And your father . . . "

For a moment Raza's dad looked away. Was that a glimmer of terror in his eyes? Her mum picked up the thread of conversation.

"Your father was . . . your father is . . . " she paused. "Maybe it's best you just see for yourself."

Her mother got up and started pottering around in the cupboards. Her father lit a cigarette and sat there smoking, unable to look her in the eye. Raza sat there reeling. She was adopted? Her birth mother was dead? She couldn't believe her parents had been lying to her all this time—that they weren't her real parents at all! And who the fuck was her actual father? Who the fuck—*what* the fuck—was *she*? She sat in a whirl of confusion as her mother made a series of strange preparations.

First she set up a series of incense burners. Soon the room was whirling with aromatic smoke. The restless and nebulous substance seemed to match the pace of Raza's own thoughts. Then Raza's mother went off into another room, and returned with a slab of black onyx, which she placed between two of the burners, so that its inchoate surface was bathed in the smoke.

"You'll see your real father soon," said Raza's mother. "Just don't look at him too closely, or things might go badly . . . "

Raza had no idea what to think at this point. All she could do was sit there nodding. She was too confused—too shocked—even to wonder how the fuck an onyx mirror and incense sticks were going to show her who her father really was. The whole thing was like a dream, and like a dream, it seemed to make sense deep down, even if it didn't on the surface. She felt an electric tingle in the back of her neck, as if she knew something was coming—something momentous. Her father felt it too, and seemed to be afraid, the way he shrank into his seat and took gigantic drags on his cigarette, so that the ashes spread quick towards the filter again, and fell like a toppling grey tower.

Raza's mother knelt down and started chanting in front of the mirror. The words she spoke were strange. They weren't Kurdish or English or any other language with which Raza was familiar. Some of the accents were guttural, some of them sibilant, like the growling of beasts mixed up with the whispering of snakes. The words sounded sinister, and sent a chill down Raza's spine. Slowly she noticed that there was one word—or one phrase—that kept being repeated. It sounded like "*Axe Kill Gore.*" Eventually her mother kept repeating it over and over, like some kind of mantra.

The smoke in the room started whipping up wildly. The smell of ozone entered the air, along with a faint electrical current that made some of her hairs stand on end. She noticed her father was shielding his eyes. So was her mother as she blindly stepped back from the mirror and huddled in the corner of the room. Both of them looked scared—or awed. Or both.

"Your father is coming now," whispered her mother. "Your father the demon . . ."

Raza's sense of shock and paralysis deepened. The word 'demon' resounded in her head like the clangour of some titanic, shattering bell.

Suddenly the shadows in the mirror were no longer the shadows of the living room, but the shadows of elsewhere. The sleek onyx surface was no longer offering a reflection of the world; it was beaming an image from somewhere else entirely, like some sort of igneous television screen. At first there was nothing but roiling darkness, some sort of cosmic static. Then a being took shape from the blackness, a being whose body seemed to roil and ripple like fire and smoke. It hurt Raza's eyes to look at him. The onyx cracked. She got the impression it wasn't strong enough to convey the fullness of his form, only to suggest an outline of his terrible majesty.

From his bull-like head arose a coiling crown of horns. Myriad horns, resembling those of the bull, the goat, the ram, and the stag. His eyes were yellow fire, piercing outwards from the crude coalescence of blackness that made up his image. His teeth glittered like steel. Behind him hung thousands of blades, as if a whole entire warehouse of daggers had been split from their ricassos and sent floating in the air. Looking closer she saw they were the feathers of terrible wings. Between his legs something slithered and coiled, like a pair of great serpents intertwining.

That was all she saw before the pain in her head compelled her to quickly look away. She remembered her mother's warning: *Just don't look at him too closely, or things might go badly . . .*

She heard her mother speak the demon's name in that same peculiar language that definitely wasn't Kurdish, and definitely wasn't English, the name that sounded like *"Axe Kill Gore."*

The demon answered, ignoring the mortals and focusing on Raza.

"Hello, childe," he said.

His voice was booming. From somewhere behind him came the great rhythmic grinding of a blade on a whetstone.

For a moment Raza stood there in terror and awe, lost for words.

"Hi," she managed to mutter at last. "Dad . . . ?"

The word felt strange on her lips, but nonetheless rang true. She dared another glance at the mirror. This one gave her a migraine. She could just make out the swivel of his eyes as he examined her.

"Your adoptive parents tell me you're maturing quite nicely," he said. "They've done a good job so far, but it's time you got a proper education. Besides, you need to be around your own kind. Beings that aren't so . . . fragile."

"Am I coming . . . am I coming to live with you?" she asked, hardly knowing what she was saying, feeling excited and terrified all at once.

"No," he said curtly. "I'm way too busy. But don't worry, you'll be sent to a very fine boarding school. It's called *Our Lady of the Scythe.* Some of the greatest demon-spawn in the cosmos have received their education there. Perhaps one day, should you do very well, I might even ask you to join me in the family business."

"The family business?" she asked.

Her father ignored the question. "Pay attention to your studies, Raza. Or don't—the choice is yours. Remember to always follow your heart, and your loins, wherever they may lead you. Do What Thou Wilt Shall Be The Whole of the Law. From time to time, I'll be watching."

With that the mirror exploded, and the demon was gone. Perhaps the poor earthly object had no longer been able to take the strain of conveying such a powerful image. Either that, or it had just been her father's brusque way of hanging up the telephone.

Raza sat there shaking as the room returned to normal. Silently the woman she'd always called "mother" made her a cup of hot cocoa. Raza sat in the steam of it until it went cold, then drank it without tasting the sweetness. Eventually her father started talking, telling her more of the story of her birth.

Raza's real mother had died in childbirth, just as she'd already been told. Her father, the demon, took her up in his claws and gave her to her mortal foster parents. His instructions to them were simple: raise her up, watch over her, and educate her with the demon's own doctrine of absolute freedom: "Do What Thou Wilt Shall Be The Whole of the Law." They watched her grow up, waiting for a sign that her heritage was starting to manifest. When they learned about Zachary's death on the news they suspected it was her, but couldn't be sure, so they waited for the candle to burn before telling her the truth—that her murderous episodes were caused by the awakening of some inherent power in her blood, a terrible power Raza would have to learn to understand, not within human society, but in the halls of some strange demonic boarding school, far from the squishy mortal bodies that inhabited Melbourne.

Raza was shocked that her *X-Men* theory had been somewhat close to the mark!

She felt like she was dreaming, but she knew it was all true.

Slowly things began to sink in. Slowly things began to make sense. Not all at once, but in a stuttering, fragmentary way, the way you might make sense of a car crash, once the concussion starts to clear. Raza's parents had always been distant, aloof. Their parental advice was limited to endlessly quoting the demon's only dictate. In a way they'd been preparing for this day her whole life.

"So what now?" she asked. "I have to go away, to this—this demon school?"

Her mother nodded. "First thing in the morning," she said.

For a moment Raza sat there, eyes filled with shock.

"In the morning?!" she shouted. "But what about my friends—my life!"

"I'm sorry, Raza, but it's all for the best. You need to go someplace where you can learn more about yourself. You can send a text to say goodbye to your friends, but you can't talk to them. No phone calls, and no sneaking out—or something very bad might happen."

Raza sat there for yet another moment of shock and paralysis. Then she let out a miserable groan and rushed up the stairs to her room.

She threw herself down on the bed and took out her phone. She needed to message her best friends, Fatima and Lilly, and tell them she was going. But what could she say? She bit her lip. She couldn't tell the truth. Eventually she wrote to them, telling them her parents were sending her to boarding school, and she didn't know when she'd be back.

Perhaps they'd already been awake. Perhaps her message had woken them up. Either way they replied almost immediately, their words full of sadness and shock. This was so sudden, they said! Why was this happening?

What could Raza say? That her parents weren't her parents at all? That her father was a demon? That she herself was some kind of monster that tore people to pieces whenever she tried to have sex with them? She just wrote that her parents were dicks.

Her friends sent a series of commiserating messages, saying how sorry they were, how much they loved her, and how much they'd miss her. Raza wrote back in a similar vein, crying all the while. There were some jokes to lighten the mood. Her friend Fi suggested she might meet some hot boys at boarding school—assuming it was co-educational! The mention of boys made Raza feel gloomy, and brought back memories of blood. She quickly changed the subject. They vowed to be friends forever and to always keep in touch. Raza promised she'd text them and call them if she could. But would she be able to? Just where was this boarding school anyway? In all the confusion she'd forgotten to ask, and she didn't feel like talking to her parents again. It seemed like they'd both gone to sleep—or at least were pretending to have done so. Pretty soon her friends went to sleep too, texting her goodnight. Raza lay awake with her phone on her chest.

Her mind was still reeling. The sense of betrayal she felt towards her parents was staggering. How could they have lied all these years? How could they have let her go around, thinking she was normal, when all the time she was some sort of monster—the spawn of a demon? They'd let her go off like some kind of time-bomb. It was their fault those people had died!

She remembered the blood on those walls and felt rotten. She didn't want to think about how much of that awful responsibility might also be hers.

She lay there, soaking in self-pity, feeling like she hated her parents. What a couple of impostors they were! And her father, the demon? She felt like she hated him too. He'd abandoned her, after all. Because he was 'busy' with something. And yet, as much as his negligence made her feel betrayed, she couldn't help but wonder about him. His vision in the mirror had been terrible, but beautiful, so full of power. Was that to be her birthright as well? Did she want it? Did she maybe even want his approval, his love—whatever that might look like?

She didn't want to think about any of this shit. She took solace in her phone, scrolling through social media, looking at photos of herself and her friends, all of them smiling and laughing, looking so happy and normal. But as she saw herself she got a sense that she was looking at some sort of impostor. A freak. An outsider.

She scrolled through the photos faster and faster, trying not to meet her own eyes. When she saw photos of her parents she felt little spikes of anger and betrayal. Eventually she put down the phone and lay there. Thoughts swirled around in her head, getting more and more random, more and more meaningless. She fell into a fitful sleep. Her dreams were inchoate and bloody.

In the morning she awoke. The house seemed normal, with the smell of cooking toast and roasting coffee drifting up from the kitchen. Had it all been a dream?

She went downstairs and found her mother waiting.

"Here's your new uniform, dear," she said, handing her a bundle of clothing.

It looked like one of her regular uniforms, only black. The outfit consisted of a skirt, a shirt, a tie, two knee-high socks, and a blazer. On the blazer was a spooky-looking crest, blood-red, featuring skulls and scythes. Her mother must've embroidered it by hand. She was very good at crafts. But she couldn't have embroidered it overnight. She must've done it months ago, weeks ago, maybe even years ago.

Raza's sense of betrayal deepened. She sullenly got dressed, ate breakfast, then packed her bags. Her mother gave her two more uniforms, just like the first one, all of them embroidered with the symbol of the school she was now to attend.

*Our Lady of the Scythe,* the demon had said. What sort of school was it? Where was it? She still hadn't asked. She felt afraid to ask.

"Time to get going," said her mother, as Raza stood waiting in the hall with her bags.

She wondered what was to happen now. Would a school bus pull up with flaming wheels, driven by Satan himself? Or maybe an old-timey coach, with a headless horseman at the reins? Maybe a flock of winged monsters would descend and carry her off through the cracks in the sky.

She stood there and looked at her parents. The atmosphere was awkward. Her father had never been affectionate, physically or otherwise. He stood there shuffling his feet, looking as if he wanted to say or do something, but couldn't. Her mother smiled at her, trying to put her at ease, but it didn't work. The hug that they shared felt stilted and contrived.

At length they ushered her back into the kitchen and into a strange-looking triangle drawn on the linoleum. Candles and incense were burning; the grey light of dawn filtered in through the shutters.

In moments her mother was chanting again. Raza felt a rising sense of vertigo. Was that weed they were burning in the braziers, getting her high? No, it wasn't, but some other herb. Soon the familiar walls of her house began to dissolve into a spinning black infinity dotted with lights of purple and sapphire. A titan silhouette took shape in the shadows, spreading upwards and outwards, looking like a towering yew tree.

# CHAPTER 3:
## OUR LADY OF THE SCYTHE

**RAZA FOUND HERSELF** standing outside of her brand-new high school. It was a sight that took her breath away. The gigantic edifice sprawled into the sky like some fantastic version of a medieval castle, covered in minarets and merlons and other architectural features that she didn't know the names of. The bricks were the colour of blood; the mortar between them was the hue of bleached bone.

The towers rose up off the hub like branches sprawling from the trunk of a yew tree, coiling, twisting, spreading ever upwards and outwards in defiance of gravity. Some of them folded into one another or looped around recursively, like M.C. Escher staircases.

Raza's eyes followed the crazy curves of the towers. Looming above them was not the familiar sky of Earth, but a blazing, seething void, where alien nebulas flared with many colours, their technicolour light beating down upon the school like the coruscating glare of some cosmic, stellar dance party.

*Girl,* thought Raza to herself, *you are definitely not on Earth anymore!*

Behind her was an empty brick yard that stretched out for a few hundred feet and then dropped into darkness. She seemed to be standing on some kind of floating platform in the distant void of space—and yet somehow she could breathe.

She figured that out once she started hyperventilating.

At length she calmed herself down. She cursed her parents, both real and adopted, for tossing her into this madness. They hadn't even told her what to expect. And if there were any school in need of an orientation brochure, then it sure as shit was this one!

She pulled out her cell phone and held it up to the seething void above. No bars.

"Big surprise there," she grumbled.

She made a post on her offline Tumblr anyway. "FUCK YEAH NEW SCHOOL!" it read, combined with a photo of the building in front of her. The picture didn't turn out too well. It showed a haze of shapes that seemed to resent being captured on digital media.

She put away her phone and reluctantly made her way towards the massive iron fence that surrounded the school. The gates looked impassable, heavier than bulldozer blades. She looked around for a bell, or an intercom, finding nothing. She sighed and stepped closer, then drew back in surprise as the gates opened up with a groan.

She stepped through the narrow gap and into the courtyard that bordered the school's colossal building. Blood-red pathways coiled between overgrown thickets of trees. The boughs were the colour of bone, the leaves like solidified moonlight. They shone in the light of the nebulas. The pallor of the branches reminded her of James' dead flesh, and her thoughts took a dark-angled turn.

*I was the one who killed those people,* she thought once again. *Because I'm a monster. Conceived by the serpentine dicks of some absentee demon-dad!*

Then the gate closed behind her with an almighty CRASH!, shaking her loose from her morbid conceptions. She picked a twisting path through the thickets and began to make her way towards the school. The trail was very narrow; the branches above her began to converge, obscuring the light of the stars. Pale, sprawling thickets disrupted her view of the building ahead, sometimes obscuring it completely. Still she kept moving, sticking to a sense of the direction she'd chosen.

Suddenly she froze, catching movement from the corner of her eye. Something was creeping nearby, something as pale as the trees. She glimpsed it for a moment and then it was gone. But had it really been there, or had her mind been playing tricks on her?

She heard the rustle of undergrowth as something went brushing through the ranks of white weeds at her rear. Perhaps it was nothing. Just a broken branch, shaken loose by the strange stellar winds that went soughing through the courtyard and blowing through her hair. But no; somehow this sound seemed more deliberate, more furtive—more alive.

She started to hurry. The noises behind her started hurrying, too. Branches groaned; twigs cracked in quick succession.

She started running. Her pursuer emerged from the undergrowth and gave chase behind. A single glimpse told her it wouldn't be a good idea to stop. The thing wasn't like any single animal she'd ever seen before, although it had the features of many. The vague dimensions of a dog. The lanky legs of a newborn calf. A muzzle like a rat's, but hairless as the rest of its body. Hairless and covered in pale white lesions that blended with the trees like natural camouflage. It hissed and whooped as it gave chase behind her. She saw its open maw, filled not with teeth but with wriggling, worm-like things that extended from the gums, tipped with hollow pipettes, as if each were a squirming syringe ready to suck out her blood—or her soul.

Raza's mind became a steady chorus of *oh fuck oh fuck oh fuck oh fuck* as she ran along the footpaths that coiled between the thickets.

She glanced back and saw that two more pursuers had joined with the first, responding, perhaps, to its calls. Each of them looked more repulsive than the last.

Raza put on a burst of speed. She was fast, too, a star of track and field. Her coach had even urged her to train for the Olympics. Maybe it was her father's demon blood that gave her such gifts. Still, she doubted she'd be able to outpace the creatures behind her. They all had four legs, and moved as if spurred by some ravenous hunger. No, she needed something else, a burst of that unknown power that lurked deep inside of her, that gave her the strength to tear men limb-from-limb. She reached deep inside—

And nothing happened.

*Shit!* she thought. *What do I have to do, wait for one of these monsters to try and fuck me before I can Hulk-out?!*

As if in answer a larger creature tore through the undergrowth and out onto the wider path behind her. This one was as big as a pony, and seemed to be in heat. The prick that bobbed between its legs looked like a fleshy version of one of those trocars plastic surgeons use for performing liposuction.

*You've gotta be kidding me!* thought Raza.

She hurtled through the brushwood, abandoning the path. Pallid white branches scratched across her skin. Silvery petals stuck in her hair. She lost sight of the building completely and began rushing blindly through the thickets as the creatures drew closer and closer. She could hear their breathing behind her, so too their strange, ululating cries, rising up as if to signal the hunt's impending closure. They fanned out, converging on her flanks. Their toothless mouths opened up so ridiculously wide that each set of jaws became like a vertical plane, a platform for the proboscises that wriggled from the gums. They'd be on her any moment!

She was so busy glancing back at the creatures in horror that she very nearly slammed into the doors of the school.

She skidded to a halt and tried to pull the door open, only to find that it was locked.

"Help!" she cried as she hammered her fists against the timbers.

The creatures closed in behind her. For a moment they slowed their pace, as if in fear of the door. Then they rushed forward, pouncing high—

Just as the door opened inwards and brought Raza tumbling in through the gap.

She landed on a cold stone floor, while beams of burning light blasted out from the darkness above her, searing the things into oblivion. She saw them haloed by fire, like sculptures made of burning black matchsticks, withering, shrinking, then suddenly—gone.

She looked up and saw a pair of fiery eyes peering down at her.

# Chapter 4:
## Orientation

**SLOWLY RAZA'S EYES** grew accustomed to the gloom. Above her stood a creature with the body of a man and the head of a bulldog. Crimson scales covered most of his hide. His hands and feet were like the talons of a bird, demarcated from his trunk by a glittering epidermis of gold. Between his legs was the likeness of a face, complete with dozing eyes. His other eyes were staring down at her, filled with the fire that had blasted the creatures to nothingness. They looked like cigarette lighters from Raza's father's old car, a pair of glowing circles slowly dimming to black.

Raza huddled on the floor, staring fearfully up at the demon. He started barking in some weird-sounding language. It sounded a bit like the words that her mother had used, when she'd summoned up the vision of Raza's biological father.

For a moment the demon kept barking. She stared up at him, uncomprehending. At length he sighed, walked over to a desk, and started rummaging around through one of the drawers.

Meanwhile Raza picked herself up and glanced around. She was in a foyer of blood-red brick. There were notice boards on the walls, festooned with overlapping posters. Each of the posters was covered with some kind of gibberish—runes, sigils, strings of words in unknown alphabets.

Presently the demon returned, thrusting something down

towards her—a necklace with a pendant that was shaped like an egg. In the centre was an eye, flanked by an ear and a wide, grinning mouth.

*Creepy,* thought Raza.

The demon handed it to her, gesturing for her to slip it round her neck. The look of the thing sent a chill down her spine, but she put it on anyway. By the time it settled on her chest the demon was talking again. And this time, she could understand what he was saying!

If indeed this was a he. The timber of the voice suggested that to be the case. But the face between his legs? Raza hadn't encountered any junk that looked like that before.

"I said what were you doing, going through the courtyard all by yourself?" he asked.

Raza hesitated. "I, um . . . "

"Spit it out, kid!" he snapped.

"I just got here!" she said, the words spilling out in a rush. "My parents sent me, but they didn't tell me anything, just sent me through some triangle, and I don't really know where I am, where I was, I just found myself at these gates, which just opened up on their own, like the doors at a 7-Eleven, and then I was in this creepy garden, with creepy trees, and those *things* came out —"

"Okay, okay!" said the demon with a sigh. "What's your name?"

"Shahrazad," she said. "Shahrazad Suloev."

The demon walked over to a tome on the desk and started flipping through the pages till he found what he was looking for.

"I see what's happened here," he said, pressing a talon on the page. "Looks like there's been a clerical error. Says you were supposed to arrive at the next supernova of Carrion's Eye."

"What's that?"

"A sun that regularly explodes. It's one of the ways we keep time around here. But in your terms, it means you were supposed to arrive at noon, tomorrow."

"Oh," she said.

"That's why there was no-one at the gates to meet you."

He sighed, slammed the book, and walked back to Raza.

"You're lucky you made it," he said. "That courtyard's full of hazards. It's off-limits to the students. There's a hole in the void-roof, you see –" He paused for a moment, catching the look of incomprehension that dwelled in her eyes. "That's a sort of transparent ceiling that goes over the school," he explained. "But there're holes in it. And the holes above the courtyard are the worst. There's all kinds of void-trash that comes slipping through the cracks. Stellar vampires, moon-calves, you name it. You're lucky to still be alive. Those things out there've eaten dozens of students. They've even been known to take out a teacher, from time to time."

"Is that what you are?" she asked. "A teacher?"

"Where're my manners?" he said, flashing a smile full of gleaming black teeth. "I'm Belzoa. And I'm not a teacher, at least not *this* term. But I will be, come the next Staff Bludgeon."

Raza peered at him quizzically. "Staff bludgeon?" she repeated. "Don't you mean staff meeting?"

"Nah," he said. "See, the teaching positions here aren't handed out by some kind of stupid bureaucracy. Every term there's a new Staff Bludgeon. That's when the demons on staff get to fight each other in a free-for-all battle. Whoever comes first gets their pick of the jobs, followed by whoever comes second, and so forth, right on down to the loser. Last term, I got cold-cocked by that bastard Zenneff, right before the whistle blew. But no-one noticed the foul, so I came in last and got stuck with all the shit work, like manning the desk and managing enrolments."

"Oh," she said.

"But usually I get a good pick. I prefer to teach Chaos Theory."

"Oh," she said. "Is that, like, physics?"

"No," he said. "Not like physics. But don't worry, you'll soon find out."

"Okay," she said.

"So, young Shahrazad—you got any immediate questions?"

*Only about a million*, she thought.

She picked up the pendant that hung round her neck, cupping it curiously. A tiny pulse of electricity seemed to thrum through the stone. Otherwise it felt like smooth, sculptured marble.

"This thing," she said. "I'm guessing it's got some kind of magick, that lets me understand you?"

"Very astute," said Belzoa. "But it does a whole lot more than just translate speech. See, the only thing the students here have in common is that they're all demon-spawn, like you. Otherwise, they're drawn from dozens of different worlds and dimensions. So it's not just language that sets them apart. Some might come from worlds like yours, technological dominions with globalized economies. Others, not so much. Take the Swirling Asteroids of Zega, for example, a collection of revolving micro-worlds ruled over by sorcery. There, travel isn't achieved by the use of trains, planes and automobiles, but by teleportation circles that can zap people millions of miles through space at a time. Communication isn't carried out by smart phones and Skype, but by scrying mirrors and astral projection. Drugs aren't manufactured by pharmaceutical corporations, but by alchemists brewing the blood and tears of primordial titans."

"Whoa," said Raza, reeling from the weirdness of it all.

"I suppose that's pretty strange to you, huh? But the realms of Earth and Zega are actually pretty similar, with a lot of neat parallels. So now consider the Inverted World of Crezka, where warrior tribes use an economy based on 'kill points,' a fiduciary currency derived from transferable murders. There, social status is based on the accumulation of harvested skulls. It's a decapitocracy."

"A what?"

"A society ruled by the greatest of head-loppers. And then

there's the Dark Plain of Zelen, a flat, lifeless realm made from the frozen ichor of an aeons-dead god. Nothing grows there, so the people are completely reliant on magick for the summoning of fresh food and water. Their only energy source is living bodies and harvested souls, which they collect by carrying out raids on other dimensions."

"What the fuck!" said Raza.

"Indeed. And so you see, the cultural differences between many of the students here are immense. But that's not all. Other than being demon-spawn, the students here are also drawn from numerous different species, with wildly differing anatomies and dietary needs. Some might only eat fresh, red meat; others might drink in the pallid rays of Maudlin Blue, the misery star. Some have skin that's completely transparent. Others keep their organs *outside* of their bodies. Others consume food, not with a stomach, but with sentient sacs of symbiotic bacteria that follow them around on a leash."

Raza's eyes opened wide.

"And then there's the fact that you're all descended from demons. True demons are creatures of Chaos, completely unique. Ours is a birthright of transcendental mutation. And despite being only half-demon, that birthright is yours, as well. That makes you, and every other student here, truly unique. In fact, I doubt you've even begun to understand the uniqueness inside of you. But don't worry, that's why you're here, to learn about your heritage."

"Right," said Raza, still profoundly confused. "And this, um, this necklace thingy?"

"Think of the *talisman* as a sort of 'contextualizer.' It translates languages, but also creates a series of benevolent illusions, tailored to make the environment more familiar to you. Over time the illusions will gradually fade, giving you a truer picture of what your fellow students and this school of ours are really like. But it's important to take things slowly at first, and let the talisman do its work. Otherwise, the shock of this place might just make your head explode. And we wouldn't want that to happen, now would we? Especially since I've also been stuck with the duties of janitor."

The demon grinned. Raza grinned back. She couldn't tell if he was joking or not. Would the shock of all this naked weirdness really make her brains pop out her eyeballs?

"Hold on," she said, suddenly realizing something. "If this, um, this *talisman* is supposed to make things look less weird to me, then how come I can still see what you really look like? Because, um, no offense, but you do look pretty weird . . . "

Belzoa's bulldog muzzle twisted into a smile. "Nice pick up," he said. "You're clearly not as dumb as some of the meatheads who come through these doors. To answer your question, the reason you can still see me as, well, as *me,* is because I'm incarnate in my true demonic form. The magick of the talismans can't hide true demonic incarnations."

Raza squinted at him in confusion. She didn't want to seem dumb, but she still didn't get it.

"I . . . I don't understand," she said. "Isn't everyone always in a 'true incarnation' all the time?"

"Not exactly," said Belzoa. "Take your appearance at the moment, for example. You're wearing a facade of human flesh, with your true demonic power concealed underneath. It's only when you release that power that you'll be truly *incarnate*—a demon in the flesh. Then the talismans won't be able to hide the truth of your appearance, either."

Raza's pulse quickened as she thought of her "true demonic form," in which she had ripped two people to shreds. What would it look like? Did she even want to know?

"Okay," said Belzoa, with a hurried note in this voice. "I've got time for one more question. We've got a Buddy System here, so the rest of your orientation will be carried out by another student."

"Oh, okay . . . " Raza paused, wondering what her final question would be.

She could ask how the school came to be floating on a plane of rock in some interstellar void.

She could ask about her mysterious father.

She could ask a question about the nature of the cosmos. After all, if demons were real—and they obviously were—then what else was out there? Belzoa had already mentioned things like captured souls and the blood of an aeons-dead god. Were there angels, too? An afterlife? A supreme being? Unicorns? Dragons? Leprechauns hoarding gold at the end of the rainbow? Was Melek Taus really the lord of all matter, as her adopted parents' people believed? There were so many questions!

Instead Raza found herself staring at Belzoa's groin and the sleeping face that lay there.

"Your, um, your other face," she said, pointing between his legs. "Does it talk, too?"

The eyes on the groin-face popped open.

"You bet, baby," it said. "I speak the language of love!"

The groin-face licked its lips with a tongue that looked distinctly like a semi-hard cock.

"Shut up, you!" snapped Belzoa, glaring at his groin.

Then he looked back at Raza, and sighed.

"Typical teenager," he said. "I give you one question, to ask about anything, and you focus on my junk. I guess you'll fit right in here, with all these other horny little brats. Now come on, I've got a mountain of shit work to get on with. Why don't you go clean yourself up, and I'll fetch your brand-new student buddy. You can ask her all the demon-dick related questions you like."

"Um, sorry," said Raza, worried she'd offended the demon.

Belzoa just stared at her inscrutably. It was hard to read his emotions, given the fact he bore the face of a bulldog with dark crimson scales.

"Bathroom's over there," he said, pointing to a nearby doorway. "Once you're done, just take a seat in the hall and wait for me. And don't go wandering out into any more infested areas."

"Okay," she said with the smile.

The demon's mood did not seem to improve. He strode off, grumbling to himself as Raza walked to the bathroom. She got a look at the noticeboard on the way. The talisman seemed to be doing its work, as the myriad posters on the board were now readable. They seemed normal enough. There were advertisements for a school fete, said to take place during the Blood Moon of Balkatraz. There was a sign-up sheet for an interschool sports championship, taking place in just under two months. Apparently Our Lady of the Scythe was playing another school, called Divinity College. It sounded like the kind of stuck-up private institution one might find back on Earth. But what kind of students went there? It certainly didn't sound like a college for demon-spawn.

Raza sighed and shrugged. There were too many questions, and she was still so exhausted by her flight from the monsters in the courtyard. She pushed open the door of the bathroom. It was a unisex facility, filled with stalls and urinals both. The walls and fixtures were covered with graffiti. "THE AEON OF CHAOS IS COMING!" had been written in gigantic brush strokes on one of the doors. Other than that enigmatic statement, the messages seemed pretty prosaic, just like the stuff on the notice boards. "Zenneff Chugs Balls" said one piece of graffiti; another had an arrow pointing to a cubicle, with the words "JENKEM REFINERY" written in capitals; elsewhere someone had pointed out that "Divinity College Sucks."

"I guess some things never change," said Raza with a smile.

Then she paused. Just how much of this stuff was really so earthly and prosaic, as opposed to being an illusion generated by the talisman, to stop her brains from exploding from some kind of inter-dimensional culture-shock? For a moment she thought of taking off the amulet. Would the toilets transform into monsters with porcelain mouths, clamouring to be fed with the contents of her bowels? Would the tap handles transmute into claws? Would the urinal cakes metamorphose into marshmallows?

For a moment she grabbed the amulet, intent on removing it—then froze. *Probably best to follow the demon's advice,* she thought. She didn't want her brains to get splattered all over a bathroom. Especially not one as dirty as this was!

It seemed Belzoa wasn't a very good janitor at all. The room was rank, the mirrors dirty. Raza inspected herself, finding her hair in a mess, whipped around her head and dotted with leaves from her dash through the courtyard. She started plucking out the foliage and combing her hair. At the same time she inspected the cuts on her body from the thorns and the brushwood. They already seemed to be mending themselves. She'd always been a fast healer, but this was impressive. Had her demonic metabolism kicked into gear, somehow fed by the blood of the men that she'd slaughtered? She caught her eyes in the mirror and quickly looked away.

Looking down she saw her uniform was wrecked. She searched through her bag, finding another. She dressed and returned to the hallway.

The place was chilly, silent. Without Belzoa the foyer was empty. The hall she'd been bidden to wait in seemed a solid mile long, a gloomy tunnel of blood-red bricks and wooden pews all gouged with graffiti. A series of light fixtures dotted the walls, flickering.

Raza drifted off into thoughts of self-pity. She thought about her parents, the ultimate liars. A vague sense of anger flared up in her head. She thought about her real father, the demonic sperm-donor with his phoned-in parenting. Cat Stevens oughta write a song about the guy. Curiosity and resentment mingled in her mind as she thought of him. His image in the mirror had been a vision of power. How much of that power was in her? And was it a gift, or a curse? So many things seemed undecided. Like this place, for example. Was it a grand adventure, or an absolute nightmare?

As her thoughts kept on drifting she stared up at one of the lightbulbs. At first it looked like an ordinary globe. Then, ever so slowly, the source of the light began to wander inside, like an imprisoned firefly. She forgot her thoughts and peered at it intently. Suddenly it seemed as if the source of the light really was a firefly, or something else with wings and an incandescent body. She stood up on the pew to get a closer look. The thing looked like an insect, albeit seen through a thick, blurry lens. It seemed as if her mind were refusing to process the image in full. Either that, or the talisman she wore was interfering with her senses, and refusing to show her some hideous reality.

Once more she thought about taking it off. Then she looked closer, stared harder, focusing her mind on the thing in the globe. All at once she saw it in its naked reality, a tiny maiden with wings and a diaphanous dress, like the fairy in the *Peter Pan* animated movie, except that its clothes were ragged and its eyes were insane as it darted about around inside the globe, slamming its form into the glass again and again. It seemed to be trying to kill itself, but didn't have enough mass to get to terminal velocity, not in such a diminutive prison. So it just kept beating itself up in some suicidal frenzy.

Raza glanced around. The whole hallway was filled with such lights, glassy prisons for fairy-like beings, each of them spinning, whirling, slamming their bodies and heads against the sides of the enclosures. The talisman had blinded her to the truth at first, then steadily unveiled it, as if responding to her own curiosity.

*Creepy,* thought Raza.

The true nature of the lights was definitely disturbing. That, and the dreary cast of the corridor, combined to fill her head with an even greater sense of unease. As was often the case back on Earth, she took comfort in her phone, scrolling through photos of herself and her two best friends, Lilly and Fatima. In truth, they were her only friends at all.

It wasn't just the incident with Emiel that'd stopped Raza being popular. She'd always felt like an outsider. It was a feeling that went back to her earliest memories of childhood. She'd always felt different, as if she had some quality that set her apart from others. It was a source of secret pride, but also self-loathing. Her guidance counsellor at school, who was perhaps too brusque for such a profession, had characterized such feelings as "your basic teenage combo of depression and narcissism." But Raza wasn't so sure about that.

She was even less sure about it now. Maybe those feelings of isolation had come from some awareness of her own demonic blood. Something subconscious, biological, maybe even mystical. More likely it was the way her parents had treated her that had clued her in to her outsider status. She'd seen the way her friends' parents behaved. Open, loving, offering passionate support. They were so involved in the lives of their children. Hers, on the other hand, were more like bureaucrats in charge of some impersonal project. They'd always held her at arm's length. She'd thought for a while that they were merely aloof, taciturn, perhaps even emotionally crippled by their formative years in Iraq. Some immigrant parents could be like that, after all.

But now she knew the truth—or thought that she did. They were nothing but babysitters, pressed into service by a demon. Their remoteness wasn't due to some inability to express their true emotions. Their true emotions had been fear and alienation. She was, after all, not even their child, but some adopted monster. She must've picked up on that truth from the very beginning. Was it all those negative vibes, spilled out across the years, that had made her feel like a freak? They might've lied to her about her heritage, but they'd certainly broadcast the clues.

And now they'd uprooted her life and shunted her off to

another dimension, where she was even more lonely than before. She looked at the photo of her two best friends and felt a tear well up in her eye. How the hell was she supposed to make friends here, in a place full of weirdos from worlds full of wizards and head-lopping murder-crats? Self-pity sank through her soul like a stone, until it hit rock bottom. She stared at the screen, then took a sorrowful selfie and posted it to her offline Tumblr account. "FUCK YEAH ORIENTATION!" she wrote, with ironic enthusiasm.

Then someone crept up and snatched the phone right out of her hands.

# CHAPTER 5:
## BUDDY SYSTEM

"**W**HATCHA LOOKIN' AT, new girl?"

Raza looked up to find a girl about her own age standing in front of her, dressed in an identical uniform. She was fair-skinned and pretty, with fluorescent blue hair. Around her neck hung a similar talisman. She stood there inspecting Raza's phone, apparently with no real clue how to use it.

"Give that back!" snapped Raza, leaping up and snatching it.

"Whoa, relax!" said the girl. "I was only kidding around. I'm Vel, your buddy! That's short for Velazelza, by the way. Bit of a mouthful, so I go by Vel. Belzoa sent me to show you the ropes. What's your name?"

"Shahrazad," she said, still a bit peeved about the transitory theft of her phone. "But friends call me Raza."

"Cool name!" said Vel. "I'll call you Raza, then, since we're gonna be great friends. Where you from?"

"Glenroy," said Raza.

"Where the fuck is that?"

"It's sort of near Essendon . . . "

Vel sighed, then grinned. "I didn't mean what kingdom are you from, dude, I meant what world! What planet! What asteroid!"

"Oh," said Raza. "Sorry. Force of habit, I guess. I'm from Earth."

Vel's eyes lit up. "Earth? No way! Earth is the coolest!"

"You think?"

"No kidding!" said Vel, still grinning. "Earth's got the best fucking music in the whole fucking cosmos! A bunch of Earth alumni left a whole heap of records in the music room. We listen to them all the time, awesome bands like Pink Floyd, Motorhead, Iggy and the Stooges! They're fuckin' killer! You like those bands?"

Raza paused. She was only vaguely aware of any of those. They sounded like something someone her dad's age might listen to. Or a punk, or a metal head. Raza wasn't any of those things.

"I, um, I don't really know those," she said.

"No biggie," said Vel. "There's probably so many awesome bands on Earth that it's impossible to keep track of them all. Who do you like?"

"Um, Taylor Swift?"

"Never heard of 'em," said Vel. "But they're called 'Swift,' right? So they're probably some sort of speed metal outfit, like Judas Priest, yeah?"

Vel flung up the sign of the horns and started head-banging, singing in a high-pitched voice.

*"He—is—the PAINKILLER!*
*This—is—the PAINKILLER!*
*Pain—pain—killah—killah*
*EY-AAAAHHH!!!"*

She stopped just as suddenly. "You know that one?" she asked.

"Not really," said Raza.

"Never mind, we can talk about music later." She paused, grinning at Raza. "But Earth people are so cool. And hot! And you're super-hot. You're making me go all lesbo!"

Raza glanced at her awkwardly. Vel punched her in the shoulder.

"I'm just kidding, man!" she said. "I like boys. What about you? Do you like boys?"

"Yeah," said Raza.

"Then come on! I'll show you all the hottest boys in the school!"

Vel grinned and held out her hand. Raza took it, smiling back. She could feel her spirits lifting already. Vel's optimistic aura was infectious. And the barrage of compliments didn't hurt either.

They walked hand-in-hand down the long, gloomy corridor, chatting as they went. Vel did most of the talking, offering a breathless monologue about who's-who and what's-what at the school. Raza tried to hold onto some of the information, but the pace was just too frenetic.

Halfway down the hallway Raza stopped to have a look at a weird statue that sat on a plinth against one of the walls. It depicted a beautiful but terrifying woman with a fang-filled smile and a nubile body. She was naked save for a skirt and a cape. At first Raza thought the skirt was a grass skirt, like one of those ones women wear in Hawaii. Looking closer she saw the skirt wasn't made of grass at all, but from tiny human figures whose bodies were stretched out like those of victims on the rack and bound end-to-end by hooks that punctured their ankles and palms. The woman's cape was made of the same material—human bodies, or perhaps human souls, all of them stretched out and hooked to each other, their collective blood pouring down to pool at her feet in a transparent puddle of sculpted red glass. The woman's eyes were made of the same material. They let out an eerie crimson glow, as though the statue were electric or filled with some numinous power. The statue itself had been smeared with ash, thick and white, like the ashes from cremated bones.

"Spooky," said Raza.

"That's the Lady of the Scythe," said Vel with a casual air. "Patron of the school. Some kind of bigshot. Made a huge donation some time, or something."

She allowed Raza to stare at the statue for a few seconds more, then grabbed her arm and dragged her away.

"Come on!" she said. "I wanna show you around before recess is over!"

They hurried on together down the hall. Soon they arrived at the schoolyard, a vast expanse of blood-red paving stones dotted with copses of trees. These plants looked healthier than the ones in the courtyard, with leaves of brilliant blue. The school's lunatic architecture sprawled overhead, defying gravity. Towers intertwined like serpents, the spaces between giving way to the void. They formed a steepled sort of dome above the schoolyard. At the height of the dome was a miniature sun, shedding golden light across the red bricks below.

The yard itself was filled with chatter and movement. There were dozens of students milling about everywhere, sitting at tables, lounging on lawns, crouching on steps. They all looked more or less like normal human teenagers, dressed in black-and-red uniforms embroidered with the symbol of Our Lady. The girls wore skirts, the boys wore slacks. Many looked over at Raza and Vel as they emerged. A few waved at Vel. Others glanced at the new girl with curious eyes or affected indifference.

"Wow," said Raza, staring up at the miniature sun.

"Pretty mind-blowing stuff, huh?" said Vel. "When I first got here I almost lost my shit!"

"Where are you from?" asked Raza.

"The Chasm of Kirrible," she said.

"Oh," said Raza. She had no idea what that was. Was it a planet? A black hole? A city in the mouth of a monster?

"Don't worry if you've never heard of it," said Vel. "It's sort of a backwater. This place is way more cosmopolitan! We've got people here from all over."

"Is there anyone else from Earth?" asked Raza.

"Nah, 'fraid not. But that just makes you even more special! Here, let me point out some of the cool people before we go and get you introduced. That's Karanora, from the Oblique of Zarathrax. She's one of my besties. That's

Zibbilique, from Hester's Hollow. She's a bit of a bitch sometimes, but she's mostly super-fun. There's Puragaglia, from planet Dio-Beetus. She'd got body-issues, but she's a total sweetie . . . "

Raza's eyes glazed over as she tried to keep up with the flow of information. Vel quickly noticed she was losing the new girl's attention.

"Oh, what am I thinking!" she said. "I said I was gonna show you the hottest boys, right? Let's forget all these fish tacos and get straight to the sausage. So, there's a lot of hunks around, sure, but if you ask me, there's only one that's really worth salivating over. And I mean, like, salivating buckets! There he is. He's from Rubex, and his name's Star Geddon. As in 'Geddon' his dong, is what you wanna be doing! Am I right, or am I right? Just get a look at him. He's a total dreamboat!"

Raza followed Vel's pointing finger across the schoolyard. There stood a tall, handsome boy. Tall might be an understatement. He towered almost seven feet high, with a slender yet muscular physique. Raza stood entranced by his broad shoulders, narrow hips and casual aura of cool as he lounged against a blood-red wall, smoking a black cigarette. His face was smooth and bold, with lush red lips, dark hair and a magnificent quiff.

"Wow," said Raza.

"I know, right?" said Vel, flashing a lascivious grin. "He's a real panty-soaker. And he's not all thunder and no lightning, either. He's got the skills to match his looks, and some genuine equipment under the hood. I should know, me and him party all the time."

"You mean . . . you mean you've done it with him?"

"Sure!" said Vel. "What else do you think goes on in this place? They oughta call it 'Our Lady of the Fuck-School!' Or whatever. But it's a total free-for-all. I mean, some people still like to be exclusive. And that's cool, if that's your thing. But where's the fun in that? We're demon-spawn, after all. Our blood runs hot!"

Raza smiled, then looked away, growing suddenly unsettled.

"I've never done it," she said, surprising herself with her honesty. "I tried a couple times, back on Earth, but there were some . . . problems . . . "

Vel looked her dead in the eye. "What, you mean you turned into a monster and tore some dude's dick off?"

Raza's jaw dropped. "How . . . how do you know that? Who told you?"

Vel laughed. "Relax!" she said. "I didn't read your permanent record, or anything. I was just guessing. Besides, you're not the only one. That sort of thing happens to demon-spawned girls all the time."

"It does?"

"Of course it does! You get all hot and bothered, then POW! Instinct takes over, and you've disembowelled your date."

"So it's like some kind of primitive mating instinct?"

"Some people think so. Because in pretty much every species, sexual selection is done by us girls, right? The men come to us and put on some sort of display—wearing tight jeans, preening their feathers, whatever—and then *we* pick the winners. It's instinctive. That's what it's like for my people, and that's what it's like for humans, too. But *you're* not just human, you're demon, as well. So when it came time for you to select a mate, instinct took over. You turned into your demon form, and gave those prospective partners a test. And being squishy little mortals, it was a test they totally failed. Some demons think it's a biological imperative. Real animal-type shit, to ensure stronger offspring."

Raza frowned. "That sounds sort of . . . racist."

"Yeah," said Vel. "Plus, it sort of goes against the whole demonic philosophy of fucking anything that moves. I mean, how else do you think *we* ended up here? Which is why most demons think it's just sort of random. Sexual arousal can trigger demonic transformation, simple as that. And when you transform, you tend to get pretty aggressive. The difference between killing and fucking something can get a little bit . . . blurry. A kiss can turn into a bite, a grope can become a sudden urge to rip someone's leg off. It happens with ordinary people and animals, too. Difference is, they're not usually powerful enough to accidentally tear their fuck-buddies a brand-new butthole."

"So I just . . . I just got all horned up and crazy, like a beast?"

"Pretty much. You went into full-bore demon fuck-mode, and those puny little mortals couldn't survive it. *But,* if you did it with a powerful demon-spawn, like, say, Star Geddon over there, then you wouldn't be able to kill him. You'd just have wild, crazy sex together. That's what happens when students here hook up. Demon sex! It's the hottest thing ever! Just wait till you try it," she added with a grin.

Raza smiled, and looked shyly away. Then something other than sex took hold of her imagination. Well, technically it *was* still about sex, but it definitely wasn't erotic—at least not to her.

"But hold on," she said. "There's one thing I don't get. I mean, my dad's some kind of powerful demon, with horns and everything. But my mother, she was just a regular person. How come he didn't just tear her to pieces?"

"Because he knew how to control himself," said Vel. "And that's what we're here to learn, as well. To unlock our inner power, and master it. That strength you used to dismember that ding-dong? Soon you'll be able to harness it at will. How cool is that?"

"I guess that is pretty cool."

"No kidding," said Vel. "Meanwhile, you can feel free to unleash your lusts without accidentally killing anyone. Just take your pick!"

Raza bit her lip and glanced around. There were a lot of handsome boys in the yard, but she found her eyes drifting back to Star Geddon as he lounged against the wall, exhaling a plume of cigarette smoke. It was a sort of yucky habit, she thought. But it was also kind of sexy! And who knew? Maybe demon lungs couldn't get cancer.

"Still looking at Star, huh?" said Vel with a smile.

"Yeah," she said. "He is pretty cute. And he looks kinda human, too. Come to mention it, so does everyone else . . . "

Raza trailed off, remembering the influence of the talisman. How much of what she was seeing was an illusion, and how much reality? Was Star Geddon really a handsome boy, or a three-hundred pound monster, with screaming dick-nipples flaring from his chest? Vel seemed to sense the direction her thoughts were taking.

"You're still new here, so I'm betting your talisman is making everything look like something from Earth, yeah?"

Raza nodded. "Yeah."

"I bet you wanna see what Star really looks like, huh?"

Raza nodded again.

"Then just take the talisman off!" said Vel, talking in a whisper.

"Are you . . . are you sure?"

"Of course! We all do it, sometimes. I've done it a bunch. In fact, my buddy got me to do it the first day I got here. It's a sort of like a rite of passage. And it'll totally blow your mind! But not literally, of course. All that stuff about your brain exploding is just something the teachers say to freak us all out."

"I don't know," said Raza, still tormented by visions of her brains bubbling out through her ear-holes.

"Come on!" whispered Vel, wheedling her.

Raza paused, then gave into peer pressure. "Okay!" she said, feeling a surge of excitement.

"Cool!" whispered Vel. "Just let me cover you, alright? You can get in big trouble for taking that thing off. It's an automatic detention! And believe me, you do *not* wanna get sent to the Time-Out Zone."

Vel shielded Raza as she carefully took off the amulet and

clutched it in her hands. She kept her eyes closed, took a deep breath, then glanced around.

The first thing she saw was Vel. The girl still had blue hair. She was still pretty. But she was totally naked. Not just naked, either, but transparent. Her skin was a neon shade of purple, solid but diaphanous, like the flesh of some well-toned jellyfish. Beneath the surface was a host of candy-coloured organs, none of which looked even remotely recognisable. Some of them were moving, swimming inside of her. They looked like demonic eels, with beady eyes and horn-like proboscises jutting from their heads.

Raza glanced around the schoolyard. Her eyes peeled back in astonishment.

She saw a girl whose head was severed and her torso ripped open. The wounds looked bloodless and neat, and not really like wounds at all, more like the edges of un-zippered clothing. The girl's head and organs were floating above her, held fast on a string of intestine. She looked like a child with a bundle of helium balloons, save that each balloon was a glistening organ—a lung, a kidney, a palpitating heart. At the top of the bundle her severed head was smiling and chatting to a friend.

Her friend had a face full of teeth. In fact, her entire head was one giant maw. It looked like some overzealous Halloween enthusiast had carved a Jack-O-Lantern with a massive set of zigzagging fangs, forgetting to leave room for the nostrils and the eyes. Except that this Jack-O-Lantern was flesh, with teeth like knitting needles.

One of the students was little more than a floating eyeball. Optic nerves hung down from the orb, forming a rudimentary body.

Another was colossal, like some kind of *oni* or troll. His skin was brilliant blue. His clothes were made from primitive pelts, with a trio of human faces mixed in.

He was making out with a girl with three heads. The central one was almost human, its slender tongue caressing his. The other two were like the heads of black-furred foxes. Both were joining in with the make-out session, slathering spittle on his neck as they gave him canine hickies.

Raza felt her senses swirling with vertigo. The spectacle was just too much. A riot of neon flesh, glowing eyes, fur, fangs, tentacles, slavering mouths, a myriad of hybrid, demonic shapes. She searched the scene quickly, looking for Star Geddon. Would she even be able to find him amongst all the madness? Or would he blend in with the others, disguised in a sea of inhuman faces?

A moment later her question was answered. There was Star Geddon, looking almost the same as he had before, save that he wasn't wearing an Earth-style uniform. His clothes were crimson and gold, with burnished buttons and epaulettes, like the uniform of some imperial aristocrat.

Raza felt a surge of relief, but the scene was still overwhelming. It wasn't just the sights, but the sounds. The yard was a cacophony. A hundred different languages spoken at once, in cadences distinctly inhuman. Growling, rasping, buzzing like bees. Raza felt her heart start to hammer, her body getting hot. And not in a horny way. Perhaps all the excitement was about to trigger another transformation!

Vel seemed to sense the danger. She started whispering something, but her voice was like sweet, unknowable singing. Raza just stood there, paralysed, gripping the talisman. She wanted to put it back on, but her brain was melting, dissolving fast into bestial urges of fighting and killing.

Then Vel pried apart Raza's hands, pulled out the amulet, and slipped it over her neck.

At once the scene took on the semblance of an ordinary human schoolyard. Raza let out a deep breath, feeling the heat in her body begin to simmer down.

"You all right there?" asked Vel. "You looked for a moment like your brain really was gonna explode!"

Raza laughed, feeling a surge of relief.

"Yeah, I'm okay," she said. "It was just so crazy. But I guess it was pretty cool, as well."

And it *was* pretty cool. Certainly a lot more exciting than the boring suburbs that Raza was raised in!

"And what about Star?" asked Vel. "You get a good look at him? Bet you still found him pretty hot, huh?"

Raza nodded, and smiled.

The smile fell off her face as people started booing and hissing and shouting abuse. She turned towards the commotion, worried the students might've started picking on her for some unknown reason. But she wasn't the target of the bullying. A group of figures had emerged from a nearby building and were making their way across the schoolyard, attracting the anger of the demon-spawn.

Whoever the strangers were, they sure didn't look like students from Our Lady. For a start, they were all dressed up in luxurious uniforms of white trimmed with gold. The outfits had a fascist aesthetic, complete with jackboots, jodhpurs, and buttoned-down jackets. On the left breast of each was a curious symbol—a winged eye surrounded by a blazing ring of fire.

And then there were the strangers themselves. They all had statuesque physiques and aquiline faces. Their skin was of bronze, their hair of gold, their eyes of gleaming silver. The males wore their hair down over their shoulders. The girls wore it tied back into ponytails. They might've been beautiful, if it wasn't for their unbelievably haughty expressions. They walked through the crowd, smiling smugly as the students of Our Lady rained down their abuse.

"Oh look," said Vel, her voice crawling with contempt. "If it isn't those stuck-up demigods from Divinity College!"

"Demigods?" asked Raza.

"That's right," said Vel. "They're half-mortal, half-god. The natural enemies of the demon-spawn!"

"How come?" asked Raza.

"How come?" repeated Vel, taken aback. "Get with the

program, girl! Gods and demons've been fighting for eternity. It's a total vendetta! A blood feud! They're our ancestral foes! There's a cease-fire right now, of course. No-one's allowed to break the peace. So the only way we get to attack these snooty jerks is by thrashing their arses at interschool sports!"

Vel paused for a moment, then joined in the shouting.

"Bastards think their SHIT DOESN'T STINK!" she said, raising her voice to megaphone volume. "Maybe that's why they like RIMMING EACH OTHER SO MUCH!"

The demigods ignored her, as they did the rest of the abuse, strolling smugly through the sea of angry demon-spawn. Vel kept going, undeterred.

"Hey, I wonder why they wear those rings of fire? It's cause they're all a raging bunch of HAEMORRHOIDS!"

That seemed to draw their attention. One of the male demigods glanced over, scowling at Raza and Vel. Through his imperious facade came a hint of humiliation.

"Quick!" said Vel, throwing up both middle fingers. "Flip 'em the bird!"

Riding the wave of peer pressure again, Raza did likewise. The demigod's glare turned into a dismissive, arrogant smile.

"That's right, laugh it up, you sack of deity-jizz!" shouted Vel. "But you'll be laughing on the other side of your face when I knock your teeth out at the next hockey meet, you vainglorious FUCK-WAD!"

The demigods kept walking, striding towards the self-same corridor that Raza and Vel had used to enter the schoolyard. They seemed to be in the process of leaving the campus.

"What're they doing here?" asked Raza.

"Beats me," said Vel. "Probably organising the roster for the Interschool Championship. Still, they're lucky someone doesn't TEAR THEM NEW ASSHOLES! Not that they'd notice, of course. They've already got a bunch of auxiliary shitholes, right under their NOSES!"

Raza was impressed by her new friend's command of insulting language. She tried to join in.

"Yeah!" she said. "Go suck a fuck, you bunch of . . . DOUCHE CANOES!"

"Nice one!" said Vel, tossing her a high five. "Did you just come up with that?"

Evidently Vel wasn't up-to-date with 21st century Earth-slang. Raza made a guilty decision to claim credit for the insult.

"Um, yeah!" she said.

Suddenly the outpouring of hatred grew physical. Demon-spawn started throwing garbage at the demigods, soiling their perfect white uniforms with handfuls of pasta and half-drained cartons of milk. Then someone raced up and started vomiting all over them. Raza felt sure she was witnessing the action of some demonic superpower, albeit a disgusting one. The stream of bile and half-digested sandwiches had the force of a firehose. One moment the demigods were walking proudly along, their starched white uniforms only lightly besmirched. The next they were being forced back across the yard by the blasting stream of vomitus.

"Gross!" said Raza, cupping her hand over her mouth.

"Yeah!" shouted Vel. "Let 'em have it!"

Someone threw a blood-coloured brick, hitting one of the demigods right in the head. Their silver eyes began to glow with the promise of terrible power.

"Shit," said Vel. "Looks like it's gonna be a brawl!"

Raza felt a surge of fear and excitement. Would she She-Hulk-out and tear the demigods apart? Or would they roast her with their deific radiance? And what about this truce that was supposed to be happening? Would they start a cosmic war between demons and gods, re-igniting an ancient vendetta? Shit was about to go down!

Another brick flew through the air, launched from the demon side. It was about to hit one of the demigods smack in the mouth, when a field of energy sprang up around them, shielding them from harm. The clamour died down as a shimmering figure appeared out of nowhere, hovering in the sky above the prefects from Divinity.

Raza gasped. The figure was a genuine angel! It wasn't as beautiful as Christian iconography had led her to believe, but inhuman and terrible. Every single petal on its fourfold wings was furnished with a glaring, sapphire eye. Its naked body was likewise covered with eyes, arranged in symmetrical patterns that ran from the soles of its feet to its shoulders and clavicle. Its body looked sexless, with eyeballs in place of nipples and genitals. Or were those eyeballs some kind of ocular junk? Did it try and fuck you with its gaze, like some pervert on the train?

Who could tell! Raza was in any case frozen by the angel's androgynous face. It was perfectly symmetrical in every single detail. Many people think symmetry equals beauty, but that's only partially true. True beauty needs a measure of disorder to work. Raza had learned that in art class, when their teacher had demonstrated the principle. He'd taken photos of attractive people's faces—actors, models, and so on—and cut them in half, discarding the right side of each. Then he'd duplicated the left side, inverted the lateral axis, and combined the two pieces, creating a series of perfectly symmetrical faces. The results were freakish, even ugly. Raza would never have believed that her darling Chris Hemsworth could be made to look so awful. He almost got withdrawn from her rub hub!

And the angel? The angel was even worse. A vision of total symmetry and order. What's more, its face was eerily familiar. The bald head and beady eyes reminded her of Mr. Willis, the most reviled of her teachers back on Earth. He'd started working at the school the same year she'd got there. He was always staring at her during class, as if he had some kind of creepy obsession. At first she'd thought he was just a perv, but there wasn't any lust in his gaze, just a cold hostility, like a scientist studying a microbe. Over the years he'd gone well out of his way to torment her, always singling her out and hassling her about homework. He'd turned her off science forever. Her grades in his subject had plummeted.

Once she'd even had a panic attack when she'd realised it was time to go to his class.

But this wasn't Mr. Willis. It couldn't be. Yes, the beady eyes in the face and the general cast of the features were a little bit similar, but this was an angel, a sexless, androgynous being with skin like alabaster and a thousand sapphire eyeballs covering its body. Raza doubted such a creature would be moonlighting as a high school science teacher!

"Great," sneered Vel. "Looks like these Little Lord *Felchleroys* have got themselves a chaperone."

The students of Our Lady backed away immediately, wary of the angel. The sexless thing blinked its myriad eyes. Light flared out, cleansing the schoolyard of vomit and filth. Once again the prefects of Divinity College looked pristine in their shining white uniforms. Their hair, now free from globs of chunder, was lustrous and radiant. Without a word the angel flew onwards, leading them out of the schoolyard. The demon-spawn whispered to each other, their torrent of abuse reduced to a murmur.

"Now there's something you don't see every day," said Vel. "Looks like you picked an exciting time to enrol!"

"But I don't understand," said Raza, still beleaguered by infinite questions. "Why're the gods and demons against each other? And why didn't that angel have any junk?"

"The gods stopped giving the angels reproductive organs after the whole Nephilim incident," said Vel. "And as for the blood feud? You'll have plenty of time to learn about that during history class. Right now, it's time for you to meet some new friends!"

Vel grinned and held out her hand. Once more Raza smiled back and accepted it. She was giddy with excitement. Back on Earth she'd been a loner, alienated. Maybe here she'd fit in? Maybe she'd finally found her niche. Maybe she'd get to have sex without eviscerating someone! Her spirits soared as she followed Vel through the yard, preparing to meet her new schoolmates.

# Chapter 6:
## The In Crowd

**R**AZA'S FIRST WEEK at Our Lady passed by in a whirl of excitement. She found herself catapulted immediately into Velazelza's friendship circle. It turned out they were some of the most popular girls in school, and at Vel's own insistence, they accepted Raza's presence pretty much immediately. There were almost a dozen of them, and by the end of the week Raza was still struggling to remember all their names. Still, a few of them stuck out, the core of the group that revolved around Vel's magnetic presence, like demonic planetoids around an incandescent sun.

There was Karanora, or Kara, for short. Slender and pale, she seemed to be the 'cool' counterpart to Velazelza's burning excitement. Not that she was a bore, or anything. Despite her generally quiet demeanour, she was always ready with a carefully-considered quip that'd have the other girls in stitches. She seemed to accept Raza's presence in their ranks almost as immediately as Vel did.

Then there was Zibbilique, or Zibb. A skinny girl with bright purple hair and luxurious accessories. Every object in her possession, from her pencil case to her hairbrush, seemed to be festooned with jewels—rubies, amethysts, and gleaming black diamonds. And they weren't fake, either. Raza thought she must be wearing the GDP of a small island nation. What's more, Zibbilique had the pedigree to match her accessories. She was literally a princess, from a family of aristocratic sorcerers who carried out a very specialized form of exogamy, summoning demons to impregnate the maidens of their family, so as to engender demonic offspring. The maidens that survived gave birth to children like Zibbilique— pampered, rich, and exceedingly powerful. She'd given Raza a hard time at first, acting like a cliquey, stuck-up bitch. But the arrogant façade had faded pretty quick, revealing a warmth underneath. She even let Raza borrow from her extensive collection of jewellery!

Then there was Puragaglia. There was no ignoring her. Puragaglia, or Pura, was definitely a plus-size girl. Raza knew it was wrong to size-shame people, but she couldn't help but laugh at some of the jokes the other girls made at the big girl's expense, at least when Pura wasn't there. Still, if anyone could pull off such a look, it was Pura. She had a cherubic face and luscious lips. Her magnum boobs made Raza jealous. She could've been a model in a plus-sixteen catalogue. She was sweet, too, if a little bit aloof. Her passion seemed reserved almost wholly for eating. She'd unleash her hunger in the cafeteria every day at lunchtime, eating her own considerable bodyweight in donuts, hamburgers, milkshakes and deep-fried Mars bars. Raza thought she must have an eating disorder, until she found out that Pura's appetites would've been considered quite dainty on her planet of origin.

One of the things the girls talked about most was the places they'd come from. Raza regaled them with synopses of popular movies, tales of rapper feuds, and the lurid sexual exploits of movie stars. The other girls found such stories exciting, but Raza couldn't help but feel boring in comparison to them. The places they came from were pretty weird.

Take Karanora, for example. She came from the Oblique of Zarathrax. It wasn't really a planet, as such, but a giant, oblique disc that hung there in space, surrounded by a peculiar field of gravity that made the whole place diagonal, like a ramp. No-one knew where it'd come from, but theories abounded. Some said it was the abandoned experiment of some interstellar wizard, others the broken facet of a cosmic machine. In any case, Karanora's spacefaring ancestors had colonized the disc, carving out a massive series of staircases, balconies and platforms on its surface. Thus they lived on the tilted face of the oblique, like characters in some Doctor Seuss storybook. The result was that Karanora seemed to be most comfortable while walking up stairs or standing on balconies. The vast, open spaces of the school made her uncomfortable, like a land-lubber at sea, or a seadog in port.

Zibbilique's home—Hester's Hollow—was even weirder. The place was a colonised black hole. Raza hadn't thought such a thing could be possible, but with the powers of sorcery, apparently it was. The Hollow's legends told of a wizard named Hester. On the run from his enemies, Hester took refuge in a place he thought no-one would be able to follow—the devouring mouth of an inverted star. He built a single dwelling at first, an artificial planetoid. When his enemies came, he used the power of the Hollow to grind them to oblivion. The terrible gravitational forces that dwelled in the hole became the keystone to his magick. He was able to harness those forces and direct them at a distance, crushing moons, consuming suns, and obliterating fleets of spacefaring vessels.

Over time he became feared, admired, and unstoppable. Others flocked to his newfound dominion, seeking a place as one of his apprentices. Thus his disciples grew more and more numerous. Additional planetoids were built, then combined at last into an artificial chain that circled around the black hole's interior. The descendants of Hester and his sorcerous cabal became wealthy aristocrats. They started breeding with demons, adding yet more might to their magical arsenal. It was from such luminaries that Zibbilique traced her descent.

Pura was from a planet called Dio-Beetus, throne-world of the Imperium of Zloorg. They were a conquering race that sought out other planets, other cultures, other species—and ate them.

Raza thought the whole thing was pretty horrible, but then again, it wasn't really Pura's fault who her parents were, now was it? Just like it wasn't really Raza's fault that her father was a demon. Just like it wasn't her fault that her demonic libido had made her Hulk-out and tear two people apart. Being in the company of monsters certainly made Raza feel better about what'd happened back on Earth. Still, compared to Pura's people, Raza's destructive transformations seemed positively benign.

The Beetus-Zoids were a species consumed by ungovernable hunger. They had long ago evolved into the dominant species on their home-world. Over time they ate everything—animal, vegetable, mineral. They were on the verge of eating each other when they discovered the secrets of interstellar travel. Armed with this technology they launched the Great Beetus-Zoid Culinary Expeditionary Fleet, which set about colonizing other worlds and farming the inhabitants, sentient or otherwise. This time they learned from their original mistake. Instead of eating everything in sight, they turned the conquered worlds into giant abattoirs and game preserves to feed their ever-expanding population. Of course it wasn't just their numbers that were ever-expanding, but the Beetus-Zoids themselves. The Beetus-Zoids were immortal, just so long as they had enough to eat. Instead of getting older, they got bigger. Pura was only seventeen, a year younger than Raza and Vel, but she was already well over two hundred pounds.

Raza thought it was a bit unfair that Pura's world was called Dio-Beetus, which sounded a lot like the English word diabetes. Almost as if the universe itself were making fun of the girl's weight. But then again, it was probably just a linguistic coincidence. Like how there was a Thebes in Egypt, but also one in Greece. Or how Dikshit was a common name in India. Or how there was a Roman emperor called Pupienus, which sounded a lot like poopy anus.

The only one who didn't like to talk about her home world

was Vel. The Chasm of Kirrible was a hole in the tooth of a monster, a monster of such unbelievable size that it drifted through space, feasting on planets and asteroids. By some freakish chance its back molar had cracked long ago, creating a cavity the size of a planetoid. The soup of bacteria inside became a primordial ooze that brought forth increasingly complex organisms, including Vel's own ancestors. These natives were soon joined by various strangers who ended up getting stranded in the Chasm. Some were spacefarers who got swallowed up. Others fell into the festering cavity as the monster ate its way through the worlds. Trapped there together, the natives and the newcomers struggled to eke out a living in the harsh environment. Based on the few details Vel was willing to share, it was definitely a hard-scrabble lifestyle. The constant gnashing of the monster's teeth created gravitational disturbances and terrible toothquakes. Chunks of sundered worlds came crashing down into the Chasm whenever Kirrible fed. Skyscrapers, cities, reduced to a torrent of hail.

Such desperate circumstances led to constant warfare over resources. The influx of space junk and alien lifeforms meant a steady supply of brand-new diseases. Every few years the Chasm would be inundated with plague, challenging the natives' own hefty immune systems. Perhaps because of the dangers, a lot of demons liked to vacation in the Chasm, which led in turn to the birthing of numerous demon-spawn. Still, even a good dose of demonic blood didn't guarantee survival there. Raza got the sense that a lot of Vel's friends and family had died. The girl got moody whenever the subject came up. Then the topic would change, and she'd revert to her usual bubbly, excitable self.

Raza was surprised that such a mean-sounding upbringing hadn't ruined Vel's outlook on life. In fact, it seemed like she'd somehow thrived on all the adversity. In contrast, Raza felt like her suburban background, with its low expectations, lack of challenges, and adult condescension had only made her weak and uncertain in comparison. Still, maybe she might thrive here, in the environment of Our Lady? It certainly wasn't suburbia!

In addition to learning all her new friends' names and origins, Raza also had to try and absorb the content of Our Lady's curriculum. The subjects on offer were a bit like those back on Earth, but with a distinctly demonic dimension.

```
     Lesson 1: Cosmic History.
 Silback's Room, from the ebbing
of the Crone Sun to the fleeting
    of the comet of Vallista.
```

Like it said on the tin, Cosmic History class taught about the history of the cosmos, from the founding of the universe all the way up to the present.

The teacher was Sketh. Her body was made from a shifting coalescence of rainbow-coloured snakes. The serpents reminded Raza of those Killer Python candies from the 7-Eleven, being covered in variegated patterns of neon blue, green, orange, and yellow. Most of the time the serpents held together in the likeness of a petite, attractive young woman with mottled neon skin. Other times the teacher seemed to lose control of the snakes that made up her body, so that individual serpents came loose, emerging from her head, back, or shoulders, even from the space between her legs. Sometimes, when she hurried across the classroom, her feet and calves would split into a flurry of snakes, allowing her to glide with incredible speed on a host of slithering bodies.

Despite her often freakish and terrifying appearance, Sketh was really chilled-out and friendly. Raza was excited to find out that Sketh was a former student who'd decided to return as a teacher. Gossip held that Sketh's father was a demon called the Serpent of Light, a very popular and famous individual. It seemed like a lot of the demons went by similar epithets and pseudonyms, hiding their true names from others.

Having arrived so late in the term, Raza was literally millions of years behind the rest of the class, at least in terms of her familiarity with cosmic history. So, on Raza's first day, Sketh had given her a seat at the back and handed her a book. It looked like an ancient, medieval-style manuscript, with pages made from skin. Exquisite illustrations bordered the text, inked by a wild, demonic hand.

"This is a very special book," said Sketh. "It'll help you catch up in no time!"

The teacher returned to the front of the class, continuing her ongoing lesson plan. Raza found herself distracted by the classroom. Belzoa was indeed a very poor janitor, and the bins were overflowing with rubbish. The flip-top desks were covered with graffiti, most of it gouged into the wood by knives or demonic claws. Some of the benches even had bite marks on them.

And then there were the students themselves. They were a rowdy bunch, constantly chatting, laughing or interrupting the lecture. Sketh seemed noticeably lax in the department of discipline. Some of the students weren't even pretending to pay attention.

The biggest slackers were with Raza at the back of the class. Apparently some things never change, not even at demon school.

On Raza's right side was a skinny girl with green hair, who'd made punk-style alterations to her uniform. Her tie was cut in half. Her sleeves were ripped off at the shoulders, and a ragged leather jacket was slung over the top. Her skirt was cut criminally short. Her legs and arms were covered with absent-minded ink doodles. Of course, Raza realised that most of the aesthetics of the girl's rebellion had been translated by the magick of the talisman into something she could recognise. It made her wonder what the girl really looked like. Was she covered in scars and mutilations, like that Pinhead monster from the *Hellraiser* movies?

But it wasn't just her wardrobe that screamed out rebellion. Most of the time the girl looked stoned out of her mind! Raza had experimented with weed, like most of her peers back on Earth. But what sort of drugs could be found at a place like Our Lady?

The other delinquent was on Raza's left side. He looked like a roughneck, with bulging muscles and wild black hair. His tie was nowhere to be seen. His shirt was untucked and open, revealing a T-shirt with a horrible image: a bestial foetus punching its way out of a screaming woman's belly.

*Totally gross!* thought Raza.

The boy spent all his time carving graffiti on the top of his desk. He took a break now and then to throw crumpled-up papers at the back of people's heads, or to perve on the girls. Raza caught him staring at her a few times and shot him a glare. He definitely wasn't her type!

Still, she couldn't quite help but be a little bit intrigued by both him and the stoner girl. They had that enigmatic aura of cool that bad kids always seemed to possess, a by-product of just not giving a solitary fuck. Later on she asked Velazelza about both of them.

"Those kids are trouble," said Vel. "Stay away from them!"

Raza laughed. She found it ironic that someone as reckless as Vel, who'd rejoiced at the prospect of brawling with the prefects from Divinity College, would call someone else "trouble." Vel sensed her dismissiveness and got suddenly serious.

"I'm not kidding, Raza," she said. "Those two are no good. They'll end up in the Time-Out Zone any day now, and so will anyone else who hangs out with them. And trust me, you do not want to go there!"

Raza promised not to associate with them. Still, their presence made the class just that much more distracting. Of course, the biggest distraction of all was Star Geddon. Seated in a ray of sunlight from the window he looked even more appealing than usual. Raza found herself mooning over him at length, studying the back of his neck, the side of his face, the glimpse of his backside through the back of his chair. Situated as she was at the rear of the class, she could ogle him all day without fear of discovery.

Nevertheless, she eventually peeled her eyes off Geddon and turned to the tome Sketh had given her. At first she thought it might be hard for her to concentrate, given all the background noise, not to mention the visual distraction offered by Star's magnificent man-candy. And yet she found herself effortlessly drawn into the content of the book.

Because it wasn't an ordinary book at all. Written by demons, it recorded their very own version of history, starting with the dawn of the universe.

In the beginning there was nothing but 'Celestial Fire,' the quintessence of Chaos at the heart of an infinite void. Raza was reminded of the story of the Big Bang, in which there was a sort of nothingness, followed by an expanding explosion. The Big Bang theory was pretty much the only thing she'd retained from Mr. Willis' dreaded science class. She'd learned about it while he was off on sick leave, and a friendly substitute teacher had taken his place, showing them a series of Stephen Hawking documentaries. She wondered if yet more parallels would follow.

But they didn't. The Celestial Fire wasn't an explosion. More like a bubbling, boiling soup. Being purely chaotic, it was both infinitely creative and infinitely destructive as well. So it would sometimes expand, like an explosion, but then suddenly contract. It would give birth to almost infinite forms of energy and matter, then quickly melt them down again to create something else. It was like some lunatic artist who just couldn't make up their mind and kept painting over and over again on the same mixed-up canvas.

Being so utterly random, the purity of Chaos created a kind of paradoxical inertia. After all, if everything is constantly changing, then it's almost like nothing is changing at all. Every time the Celestial Fire made something new, it would eat it up and spit it out as something else. Then it would eat *that* up, change it, spit it out, eat it up, and change it again, and so on and so on. The process went on for aeons undreamed of.

But eventually something happened that changed all of that. A consciousness developed inside the Fire. But it didn't get eaten up. It *emerged* from the flames, creating a body for itself. It was the first differentiated, individual being, and it came to be known as the Demiurge.

The Demiurge harnessed the Celestial Fire, creating more persistent forms of matter from the ever-changing energy. He made rules that held all the new things in place, sort of like the rules that get studied by physicists on Earth. Laws of gravity, time, space, distance, and velocity. He mapped out the void and filled it with planets and stars.

And that point Raza had to pause. The Demiurge was starting to sound a lot like Melek Taus, the entity worshipped by the Yezidis. Not an all-powerful deity, but a universal architect. Perhaps her human ancestors had been onto something after all?

Eventually the Demiurge got lonely. He sat in the void, wanking himself raw. Out popped a daughter, fully-formed. Perhaps because she was the only other being in the universe, the Demiurge's amorous attentions quickly turned to her.

*Gross!* thought Raza.

They had children, a whole inbred race of gods. But then again, most gods from human mythologies were pretty inbred, too. So it wasn't that different from the stories Raza already knew about Zeus and Hera, brother and sister, parents of the Olympian pantheon who'd been worshipped by the ancient Greeks and Romans. Maybe the whole incest-heavy vibe of human mythology was based on reality?

The other gods were less powerful than the Demiurge, so he lorded it over them. Eventually he got tired of that and started making other life forms. Not by wanking this time, but by transforming the Celestial Fire into biological matter.

At this point the story got even more terrifying. If Raza hadn't already been upset at the Demiurge for raping his daughter and his other female offspring, the next part would've clinched things for sure. Because, like some supervillain scientist conducting a series of evil experiments, the Demiurge started creating race after race of mortal creatures, destroying them all whenever he decided he didn't like the results. Some he killed with fire, flood, or plague. Others he slaughtered with his own bare hands.

Eventually he stopped all the killing and let a bunch of lifeforms develop. Maybe he felt like he'd achieved his aims; maybe he just hit the point of diminishing returns. He was, after all, an imperfect being.

For a while the Demiurge was King Shit of the universe. He ruled over his children and all manner of mortals. He contained the Celestial Fire in some sort of giant, cosmic forge, harnessing its power whenever he wanted to make something new. He had everything measured out, the whole universe aligned in a neat little package.

But the universe was still *made* from the energies of Chaos. Little by little it started to skew his designs. Organisms started evolving, mutating. Suns started exploding. Black holes started opening up in space, sucking in everything. Even the Demiurge's laws couldn't keep it all in check. He made angelic slaves to help with the upkeep, but even then it was still too much to handle.

Then came the demons. The Demiurge didn't create them at all. Or at least, not deliberately, though his actions certainly led to the conditions that allowed their existence. They started popping up all over the place, without his deliberate design, born from the Chaotic energies that dwelled in the cosmos. Some emerged from the burning hearts of suns. Others popped out of rocks, like Sun Wukong, the magical monkey that Raza had learned about in Cultural Studies. Pretty soon they were everywhere, messing up the Demiurge's neat, ordered universe.

They started hanging out with mortals, giving them all sorts of ideas. They started fucking like rabbits, breeding not just amongst themselves but with pretty much anything they could get their horny hands on. Due to their chaotic nature, they seemed able to produce offspring with just about anything—humans, horses, beehives, wild flowers—you name it!

So it wasn't long until the gods and demons came into conflict. At first the Demiurge tried to control them, just like he tried to control everything else. Some he bought off, giving them cushy jobs as collectors of souls and wardens of the afterlife. But most were too free-spirited to settle for an office job. So he made magick to enslave them, creating a whole slew of sigils, seals, and special words of power that would bind them to his will. One thing he used most of all was their names—their true, secret names, the ones that made them weak to his magick.

They didn't like that, of course. It led to a terrible war. At first the demons got creamed. They were numerous, but the gods were more powerful. Demons started dropping like flies. Things were going very badly for the demonic resistance, at least until some badass managed to kill one of the gods.

At that point the gods sued for peace. They might've still had the upper hand in the war, but the shock of the deicide filled them with terror. Neither the Demiurge, nor any of his inbred kin, had ever imagined they could possibly die. So they backed off and negotiated the uneasy peace that was now still in place all over the cosmos. The magick that had shackled the demons was banned. In return, the demons agreed not to totally trample all over the universe.

Raza reeled from the knowledge she'd acquired. And it wasn't just because the book contained a stirring, well-written narrative. It was a magickal tome. As she read the words, images exploded before her mind's eye, like some kind of potent, preordained acid-trip.

She saw the Celestial Fire roiling and burning in the heart of the void, a clash of rainbow forms and mutating colours.

She saw the Demiurge emerge from the Fire, naked, terrible—and close to being perfect.

She saw him measure the void, put a girdle round the earth.

Saw him hammer out planets and moons on his celestial forge.

She even saw the gross part where he molested his daughter!

She saw countless races perish in fire and flood and by the god's red hand.

She saw his host of angels in their terrible symmetry. She saw the two that sat beside his throne. One was a disembodied mouth with wings, the other a floating sapphire eye.

She saw the demons born from wombs of rainbow fire and rents in the face of reality. Beautiful, terrible, no two of them alike.

She saw them lie with men and women. Now that part was much sexier than the scenes of divine incest!

She saw them rut with animals, which wasn't so sexy at all.

She saw the terrible war between demons and gods. Demon bodies falling, burning, struck down by deific fire. Angel bodies butchered, dismembered, their sexless bodies punctured to make way for stabbing demon cocks. Talk about war crimes!

And then the primordial deicide. A giant axe falling, heavy as a moon and as bright as the sun. A shadow of horns across an ocean of blood that poured from the deity's truncated neck.

Then the truce. A treaty signed, uneasy meetings of demonic generals and heavenly hosts.

The images finally faded and Raza took a breath. She felt like she must've looked even more stoned than the girl to her right. When she finally left the classroom she was weak at the knees. And it wasn't just from staring at Star Geddon for the first fifteen minutes of the lesson. No, that Cosmic History was powerful stuff. But her next class would prove to be even more visceral.

# CHAPTER 7:
## THE DEMONIC DOJO

Lesson 2: Demonic Martial Arts.
The Halls of Hazzard. From the
waxing of the Crone Sun to the
fall of Lucaressa, the Yo-Yo
Moon.

**T**HE NEXT CLASS took place in a vast and sinister hall of red stone. The walls were covered with life-like statues of terrified adolescents.

"Creepy," said Raza as she filed into the room on that very first day.

"You don't know the half of it," whispered Vel, walking beside her. "Every one of those statues is made from the calcified corpse of a student who died during class."

Raza froze, staring at the walls with a newfound sense of horror.

Vel just grinned.

"Don't freak out too much," she said. "It doesn't happen very often. It certainly hasn't happened while I've been here. Besides, they won't make a newbie like you dive straight into the rough stuff. Unless you volunteer, of course . . . "

Raza didn't feel like volunteering for anything that might lead to her being transformed into a piece of creepy decor. She sat down with the others, cross-legged on the floor. Straightaway she noticed a definite change in the attitude of the student body as they waited for the teacher's arrival. They weren't nearly as rambunctious as usual. Their constant chatter died down to a murmur. Some were completely silent, sitting up straight and alert as they waited for the lesson to begin.

Even the delinquents seemed more attentive. The rough-looking boy who'd sat to her left in cosmic history class wasn't even vandalising anything. He looked like he was actually ready to learn! The stoner girl looked a lot less stoned. She sat there silently, her short-cut dress riding up high, giving a full-on view of her camel toe. Surprisingly, few of the boys were sneaking a peek, being much too focused on the lesson to come.

*I guess the possibility of dying tends to make people behave with a little more self-discipline!* thought Raza.

But that was only part of the answer. The rest was supplied by the teacher. Raza heard his footsteps long before he entered the room. They made a heavy, thudding sound in the adjoining corridor that shook the room as they approached. The students sat bolt-upright, a tremor of fear collectively running through their frames. Raza realised she was sitting bolt-upright, too. What's more, she hadn't even tried to sneak a peek at Star Geddon the whole time she'd been waiting.

A moment later the teacher entered the room. He was twelve feet tall and built like a rhinoceros on steroids. Most of his body was covered by a suit of armour that resembled that of Henry the Eighth, save that the codpiece was much larger, extending over eighteen inches from his groin.

*Much bigger than King Henry's!* thought Raza.

That wasn't the only difference. The armour was fused to his frame by a series of thick, bone-like protuberances that had grown through the gaps between the metal. The armour looked sealed, impregnable, and utterly terrifying. But worse still was the teacher's face, the only part of him not covered by the armour. Huge, hairless, and covered with scars, it bore the likeness of an old wooden chopping board. The skin had been burned, slashed, hacked, beaten, and mashed. Raza wasn't even sure where the teacher's scars ended and his facial features began. His nose was a scarified nub. His ears—or what remained of them—made the cauliflower earlobes of UFC champions look smooth by comparison.

Raza knew that demons had incredible powers of healing. She'd even begun to experience those powers herself, when the cuts she'd received in the courtyard had vanished within minutes. It made her wonder what terrible injuries this man could've possibly endured.

The teacher glanced across the room with glowing yellow eyes. It reminded Raza of the gaze of some big, predatory cat. The stare was a palpable thing, a searchlight of fear-inducing gravity. She heard some of the students whisper his name.

"Zenneff looks angry today," one said.

"Are you kidding?" said another. "He always looks angry!"

So this was Zenneff. Raza remembered Belzoa complaining about him. That "bastard Zenneff," he'd said, had unfairly knocked him unconscious during the last Staff Bludgeon. Then there'd been that piece of graffiti in the bathroom, boldly proclaiming that "Zenneff chugs balls."

*Well, that's certainly his prerogative*, thought Raza.

Still, she doubted the graffiti was accurate, more likely a manifestation of the fear and loathing that was felt by the students. She could feel those emotions around her now, tremors of terror and hostility, mixed with a grudging respect.

Zenneff stood silent for a moment, staring at the students. Raza felt his eyes upon her, met his gaze, and quickly looked away. No way she was game for a stare-off with this guy! Still she felt him looking at her longer than he did at the others. Perhaps because she was the new girl?

Another figure entered the room, dressed in a hooded purple robe. The figure was under three-feet tall, and carried an old, wooden clipboard. Standing next to Zenneff he looked ridiculously small. The teacher had to kneel to take the clipboard from his hands.

"Looks like we've got a noob in our midst," he said as he glanced at some papers on the clipboard, then back at Raza.

Raza dared to smile up at him. He said nothing, then casually opened his mouth and *ate* the clipboard, papers and all, as though it were a cracker with cheese. His stare remained unbroken as he chewed on the splinters.

*Is he trying to intimidate me?* wondered Raza. *Or does he just like eating clipboards?!*

"Right then," he said. "Let's start with meditation, as usual."

*Meditation?* thought Raza. *What the fuck?*

Zenneff didn't look like a Buddhist or a hippy, the only sort of people she knew of who practised meditation back on Earth. Maybe his looks really were a deception? But then the meditation began, and she realised her mistake. It wasn't placid meditation, like that practised by the lamas of Tibet. It was demonic meditation.

"Close your eyes," said Zenneff. "Focus on the motes of Celestial Fire that burn in your blood. That's the source of your power. Find the fire and stoke it to a frenzy. Draw out the heat, and assume the killing shape."

Raza did as instructed, closing her eyes and trying to focus. She had an inkling of what Zenneff was talking about. As esoteric as his words might've been, she knew he was referring to that self-same sensation she'd experienced before, when she'd blacked out and killed those two men. A build-up of heat she'd assumed had been simple, sexual desire, but which had really been much more than that. Maybe she could harness it by thinking about sex? She started imagining Star Geddon's arms around her, both of them naked, their bodies wound tight and rubbing each other. Her cunt became wet. She felt a heat, but it wasn't the Celestial Fire.

*Enough!* she thought to herself. *If all you had to do was get horny, you would've Hulked-out in your bed at night a hundred times already. Not to mention in the shower, on the bus, or that time you went horse riding. It's time to take this seriously. Stop getting distracted and follow the instructions!*

Raza was surprised she could be so stern with herself. Zenneff's imposing presence must've been having an impact on her! She cut off the erotic thoughts, as hard as it was to do so, and tried instead to do as he'd told her. To find that fire, burning within, and ignite it. To let the heat encompass and fill her, let it burn its way out from the centre of her veins and overflow her body, bringing the change.

Presently she felt something. A twitch, a twinge, a flicker of heat. It was elusive, but definitely there. She tried to clasp it with her mind but it teased her, like something wild that didn't want to be captured. Like a dancing flame darting aside from the fuel she'd pour on it, if only she could grasp it and hold it in place.

She felt close to the source of the heat when something distracted her. A medley of sounds rose up all around. Skin ripping, bones creaking, the tell-tale noises of transforming flesh. Other students were commanding the change!

She felt their altered presences around her immediately. The room filled up with sweltering body heat, the pungent scent of demon sweat. She sat in the shadow of huge and terrible bodies. She heard their breathing, heavy and bestial. Raza began to feel very vulnerable and small. She wanted to look, to see the monsters that had taken shape around her. After all, the talisman couldn't hide any true demonic incarnations. She'd get to see the real shapes of her classmates. And yet she was too afraid. Afraid that Zenneff might catch her peeking, when his instructions had told her to keep her eyes closed. Afraid too that she might flip out from the shock of the sight, start crying and screaming and making a fool of herself.

The heat started filling her body again, but this time from

fear. Just like when she'd taken off the talisman out in the schoolyard. But this wasn't her doing. She wasn't stoking the fire, making it swollen. It was swelling up all by itself, threatening to stir itself out of control. Once again her thoughts began to fragment into slivers of rage. The heat blossomed outwards—

"All right!" said Zenneff. "That's enough of that for today."

Raza felt a surge of relief as she sensed the transformations reversing around her. She heard the sound of bodies shrinking, bones clicking back into place. Much of the heat drained out of the chamber immediately. At length Raza opened her eyes, finding the rest of the students had reverted to their ordinary shapes.

Zenneff launched into a series of spitfire critiques.

"Nice work, Sorrex. Excellent control. You did a good job, too, Star Geddon. Crisiux, that was pathetic. I've seen better demonic transformations floating in the toilet after breakfast. Get your act together. At least the new girl's got an excuse for not showing me anything. Vel, solid as always."

Raza turned to Vel, finding her beaming. Raza couldn't help but feel like a failure. She'd come close to transforming, but not as a result of her own will or volition. Vel seemed to catch the dejection in her eyes. She smiled, patting Raza's thigh.

"Don't worry," she said. "It takes aaaaages to learn how to transform. You'll get the hang of it!"

Raza smiled back. Vel was always so positive!

"All right," barked Zenneff. "Time for something a little more hands-on. Let me see some volunteers!"

Raza kept her hand down. So did the stoner girl, and quite a few others. Star Geddon had his arm up. Vel grinned and waved, trying to attract the teacher's attention. The rough-looking kid from history class was pretty eager too, raising half his arse off the floor to hold his hand high.

He looked surly when Zenneff ignored him and called

instead on Star, Velazelza and a couple of students Raza didn't know. The volunteers took their places at the front of the class.

"Right then," said Zenneff. "Let me see those transformations. Show the others how it's done!"

Vel's transformation began almost immediately. Raza saw her friend's true form as it took shape before her, blasting through the amulet's illusion. The girl's skin turned transparent. Her uniform faded like the garments of a ghost. Her candy-coloured organs started blazing with light, like a cartoon rendition of radioactive slime. The demon eels that dwelled inside her body swam upwards, erupted from her shoulders, and flanked her face like a pair of extra heads. That last part looked painful. Raza winced as she saw the hurt on Vel's face.

Then the girl's grimace turned to a grin. Her teeth grew down into bestial fangs. Her hair rose up into a shapely arrangement of neon-blue horns. Her body grew taller, harder, more muscular. Her transparent skin became plates of purple chitin, like an insect's exoskeleton. The light from her organs could no longer be seen, hidden by the armour. She let out a roar that set Raza's ears ringing.

*Whoa!* she thought.

Then she turned to watch Star Geddon. His transformation was a little bit slower, but even more impressive—at least in Raza's eyes. Once again the persistent illusion provided by her amulet started to fade, taking his uniform with it. She might just get to see him naked!

Lamentably, she saw, he still had clothes of his own. The garments transformed as he did. He grew another three feet tall, towering almost as high as Zenneff himself. Crimson scales grew over his skin, soft and shimmering, like those of a serpent. He kept most of his good looks, adding a feral cast to his grin as his teeth became fangs. His glorious quiff transformed into a single, curving horn.

*So hot!* thought Raza.

The other students had transformed as well. One was a terrifying rabbit-boy, with a vicious-looking muzzle that bubbled with venom. The other bore the likeness of a terrible flower, her chest adorned with boobs that stretched open like a pair of Venus flytraps.

"Bring out the fodder!" shouted Zenneff.

The teacher's diminutive assistant nodded, then started chanting in a weird-sounding language. A series of runes started glowing in the chamber's far corner. Raza hadn't seen them before. Painted in blood upon the red brick paving, they'd barely been visible. Now they were unmistakeable, pulsing with a neon-red glare.

Lightning cracked around the centre of the runic arrangement. The fabric of space tore open like a curtain at a magic show. Smoke oozed out around the spatial distortion, filled with inchoate shapes, glimpses of faces and forms from some other reality. Raza rose up instinctively, backing away. Others did the same.

"That's right, kids," said Zenneff. "Stay well clear!"

Raza looked on in horror as a host of figures emerged from the portal. They bore the commingled features of humans and swine, with porcine noses and fat, mottled frames. Atop their heads were coronets of bone strung together with sinew. They carried a host of filthy-looking weapons encrusted with dried blood and rust. Maces, flails, and murderous straight swords. Their squeals rose in pitch to a cacophonous cry. There must've been at least fifty of the things!

*Oh shit,* thought Raza. *We're all gonna die!*

But she wasn't just concerned for herself. Her new best friend was facing off against the monsters, along with the handsome Star Geddon and two other students. Surely they'd be overwhelmed by the army of pig-men!

"To those about to die we salute you!" came Zenneff's ominous remarks.

But was he talking about the swine-things, or the

students? Would Star and Velazelza's bodies end up petrified on that horrible wall? Raza could scarcely bear to watch. But like a spectator at a train derailment, she stared at the pig-things as they charged across the room.

Vel turned towards her and winked a glowing eye. Then she rushed at the pig-men, slicing one of them open from neck to groin. Her claws passed through its dirty metal hauberk like a hot knife through head cheese. The stench of cleft entrails was added to the barnyard reek of the creatures that filled up the room like steam in a sauna.

*Whoa!* thought Raza, shocked by her friend's killing power. It was only the second time she'd seen a demon in action, after Belzoa had saved her. Maybe the students would really prevail?

She had second thoughts as the pig-things closed around Vel, swinging their weapons. There was no way the girl could evade!

It turned out she didn't have to. Their blades bounced off her sleek, purple carapace. Some of them even looked blunted by the contact. Vel lashed out, decapitating two of the creatures. It wasn't a clean set of cuts from her claws, but a duo of punches that tore their heads clean off their shoulders.

From Vel's own shoulders the demon eels whipped out, biting into bodies and hurling them skywards. They flew through the air, plummeting down towards the spectating students. One of them headed straight towards Raza, but the crowd was too thick to permit any movement.

"Oh shit!" she said as she struggled to flee.

A bolt of yellow fire shot out of Zenneff's right eye and lit up the creatures. Bodies turned to ash and rained down upon the students. The air filled up with the smell of roast pork and the crematory stench of incinerated bone. Raza breathed a sigh of relief and wiped the sweat from her forehead.

Meanwhile the other volunteers joined in with the carnage. Star Geddon's tongue took the form of a serpent, delivering doses of venom with each hissing strike. Despite the present situation, Raza couldn't help but think about the possibilities that lingered on the tip of that tongue, and all along the length and girth of its six-foot extension. It could tie her, entwine her, delve deep within her. Even in the midst of such slaughter, Star Geddon had managed to get her crank turning.

Beside him the demonic rabbit was delivering his own dose of venom. His thick front teeth, bubbling with fearsome bacteria, bit down into pig-hide. His victim started melting like a time-lapse photo of acid consuming a carcass. Smoke bubbled up from the dripping flesh overflow.

The plant-girl thrashed like a punk in a mosh pit. Glistening thorns shot out from her body, puncturing swine flesh. The pig-men fell down in a paralytic stupor. Their lips curled backward, framing grimacing death-grins. All three students, it seemed, had poison in their bodies.

Soon Raza lost sight of Vel and the others as the pig-men started surging around them, oinking and squealing. She caught glimpses of gory explosions from the centre of the melee. Then a dozen swine-folk rushed towards Zenneff and the spectating students, swinging their weapons.

Caught in the front ranks, Raza tried to move back, but the crowd was too thick. She glanced around, seeking a way to retreat as the things rushed towards her. Once again she'd ended up sandwiched between the roughneck and the stoner girl. The latter seemed to have been pushed by the flow of the crowd, just like Raza. The former? He was making his way to the front ranks deliberately, spoiling for a fight with the pig-men! Raza watched as he began to transform, his rough-looking face distending into a muzzle that looked like a cross between that of a wolf and a crocodile. Maybe he wasn't such a bad kid to have on your side in a brawl?

Raza felt her blood heating up as the pig-men drew closer. The rough kid started laughing excitedly. She let him squeeze past to the front. Not that she had much of a choice. He raised up a claw of black-and-red scales, preparing to rip the monsters a new one.

Then Zenneff himself stepped in front of him. His eyes flashed yellow lightning and the swine-folk evaporated.

"Nice try, Vogg," he said, turning to the roughneck, his deep voice booming above the sound of the carnage. "But you weren't chosen this time, remember? Maybe this'll teach you to stop all that brawling outside of the dojo!"

Vogg let out a disappointed sigh and shrank down into the semblance of a human. It was as if he'd just breathed out all of that raw demonic power. Raza wondered if she'd ever have that much control. Would she be able to assume her true shape and inspect it in the mirror? And if so, would she even like what she'd see staring back at her? Would she be able to look that killing thing in the eye?

The numbers of pig-men were dwindling. There were hardly any left now. Raza watched Geddon pull one of them apart like a freshly roasted chicken. Velazelza picked up another by the ankle and started swinging the beast like a weapon, using its body to batter its comrades.

Something strange caught Raza's eye. At the back of the chamber a pig-man was lurking, alone. He hadn't charged forth with the others, but had hidden there waiting, partly obscured by the fog that swept in from the portal. He wore an elaborate headdress of bones twined with sinew that spiralled up three feet above him. His pink-skinned body was scarified with runes.

Could he be a chieftain, or some kind of wizard? It seemed like he might be the latter. He started waving a staff and oinking in some esoteric language. At the same time something weird started happening. The corpses of the pig-men collectively wriggled. The guts that remained in their bodies started slithering outwards like serpents. The organs that lay on the floor started moving to the sorcerer. Raza saw hearts bouncing like tennis balls, beating their way across the chamber. Lungs and livers squirming like slugs through the gore. Soon they started to coalesce, rising up to form some kind of Frankenstein's monster made out of offal. A whirlwind of bones whipped up from the battlefield and spun around the creature, encasing its myriad organs like an ivory scaffold. Last but not least, the collective skins of the pig-men slithered up over the creature like a dripping, pink shroud, as did the dozens of disembodied heads, affixing themselves to the wizard's creation.

Raza thought the result looked a little bit like Voltron, if Voltron had been made out of pigs by a maniac butcher-cum-taxidermist. Thirty feet tall, it loomed into the heights of the chamber. Its fingers were arms with even more fingers at the end of them. Its face was a bundle of faces affixed to its shoulders by mutated flesh. Its scream was that of three-score hogs getting ready for the slaughter. Riding on its shoulder was the rune-covered wizard, glaring down vengefully.

Zenneff shot his assistant an irritated look.

"You let a porkromancer in here?" he asked.

The assistant just shrugged, as though it were an honest mistake.

Raza watched in horror as the titan reached down, snatching up Star and Velazelza. Finger-arms enclosed them, tipped with the hands of the dead. Vel screamed as the strength of the monster started cracking her carapace. The other two students stepped back in fear. It seemed such a beast could scare even a demon!

Raza's blood turned hot. She felt utterly helpless. Even if she managed to transform, she knew she'd have no control. Could she do anything to save her brand-new best friend, not to mention her crush, the handsome Star Geddon?

Beams of yellow light shot out from Zenneff's eyeballs. He struck at the shoulder of the titan, evaporating the porkromancer, then cut his way down through the torso, slicing the creature down the middle. It split into two oinking halves, dropping its captives. Zenneff didn't stop there. The beams kept scything, burning the thing until nothing remained but a layer of charcoal and fat. The floor looked like an oven pan, fresh from a ham roast. Smoke and the smell of cooking pork loins filled up the room, making Raza both hungry and nauseous. It was hard to reconcile such horrible sights with the rumbling of her tummy as the odour of the pork crept into her nostrils.

She startled herself by running out into the smoke almost immediately, searching for her friend. She found Vel lying on the ground, turned back into the semblance of a mortal. Her uniform—or at least, the one supplied by Raza's talisman—looked filthy and torn. She groaned and coughed. A dribble of blood ran down her chin. Raza knelt beside her, tears in her eyes.

"Vel?" she whispered, grasping her hand and cradling her head.

Vel groaned again, eyes fluttering back to the whites.

Raza started weeping.

"Vel!" she said.

This time Vel opened her eyes, and grinned.

"Gotcha!" she said.

"You're . . . you're okay?"

"Of course I'm okay!" said Vel, getting up and dusting herself off. "Takes a lot more than that to take out a demon girl!"

Raza just stood there, stunned, and a little bit hurt by the deception.

"Sorry," said Vel with a cheeky smile. "But I couldn't resist."

Raza smiled back, the tears still wet on her face. Vel reached out and hugged her.

"You're a real sweetie, you know that?" she said. "But you'd better dry those eyes. You don't wanna let Zenneff see you crying, believe me."

Raza hurried to dry her eyes before the smoke cleared. Soon she was standing back with the others while Zenneff addressed the class.

"So, looks like we had a little mishap today," he said, glaring at his assistant. "Nevertheless, I want you to treat this as yet another learning experience. Because in a real-life battle, nothing's ever certain. There's always some chance that the enemy might have some sort of weapon you don't even know about. Like that pork golem, for instance. In a situation like that, you need to know when to flee, and when to fight to the death. Sometimes you won't get that much of a choice. The important thing is to always keep your head. I think our volunteers today acquitted themselves well, and they deserve a round of applause."

Vel beamed as her classmates clapped and cheered. Star Geddon smiled softly, taking the whole thing in stride.

*He's so cool!* thought Raza.

Any other guy might've annoyed her by being so affectedly nonchalant, but somehow Star Geddon made arrogance look sexy. Probably because he was just so freakin' hot he could make anything look sexy—a trash bag, a Hawaiian shirt, maybe even cornrows or a mullet!

"I think that's that for the day, then," said Zenneff. "Class dismissed!"

Raza filed out of the hall with the others. She felt exhausted, and she hadn't even really done anything.

"Wow that was intense!" she whispered to Vel.

Vel flashed another cheeky smile.

"If you think that was intense," she said, "then just wait for the next class. It's the hardest one of all!"

# CHAPTER 8:
## CHAOS THEORY

Lesson 3: Chaos Theory. Hezekel's Theatre. For the full incandescence of the Stuttering Nebula.

**R**AZA ENTERED THE theatre with a prickling sense of dread. What could possibly be harder than a class in which the teacher's assistant summons a horde of murderous pig-men to set upon the students?

The room in which she stood looked innocuous enough, a standard auditorium with a circle of chairs arranged in the centre. Raza sat down with the others and waited for the teacher. Once again the students were quieter than usual, and yet they didn't seem muted by dread, just tired and drained after their lesson in the dojo.

This time Raza found herself sitting across from the stoner girl, who once again looked high as a kite. She must've managed to snort, smoke, or even inject some kind of substance during the brief intermission between classes. Once again her short-cut skirt was riding up her thighs, exposing her underwear. Boys were openly gawking, but the girl seemed too stoned to notice. Or maybe she was playing it cool while secretly wallowing in all the attention. Either way Raza felt embarrassed for her. Embarrassed, and a little bit jealous. She'd obviously mastered the art of not giving a fuck. Raza wished *she* could be so immune to shyness and awkwardness. Then again, maybe she *would* be immune to such things, if she got herself so thoroughly wasted as the girl was right then.

The rough kid—whose name was apparently "Vogg"—was sitting across from her as well. He seemed to have resumed his previous sullen temperament, dividing his time between scratching graffiti on the chairs and kicking the backs of people's seats.

*What is this guy's damage?* wondered Raza.

At length the teacher arrived, a demoness called Kellikassey. Raza's eyes opened wide as she saw her. The woman was uncannily beautiful, with a curvaceous figure and big amber eyes. White hair tumbled down past her shoulders, a striking contrast with her neon-red skin. Atop her head was a tiara made from black hellebore. Amidst the petals were a collection of still-living eyes. Her short-cut dress seemed to be made of tailored white smoke. It clung to her sumptuous body, rippling and coiling, almost diaphanous. Otherwise she seemed to be naked.

If Raza was awed by the woman's appearance, then the boys were another matter entirely. She saw them staring at the woman with gazes of lust they could scarcely conceal. Soon they were crossing their legs or balancing books on their laps to hide their erections. Talk about hot for teacher! The room became a veritable sauna of adolescent boy-lust. Raza felt a tingle of jealousy, then turned towards Star Geddon. Was he enamoured with the sultry demoness as well?

She was relieved to see him sitting casually, apparently unfazed. *Clearly he's not such a horny pig as the rest of them*, she thought. Then she took a moment to study him again, luxuriating in the sight of his full red lips. She decided just to look at those for now. Make a feast of it, unpack him like a lunch box. As her eyes roved her pussy got wet. It wasn't entirely unexpected, but she'd been ogling him all day without such a powerful, physical response. Then she thought of all the boners that were springing up around the room. Perhaps the teacher was exuding some kind of aura of lust. Could Miss Kellikassey be a succubus, or something of that ilk?

The woman turned to her with a smile.

"Hi," she said. "You must be Shahrazad, right?"

Raza nodded, smiling back. At the same time she felt herself getting wetter, as if the teacher's proximity and gaze were turning up the dial of her libido. They definitely wouldn't let this person in a classroom on Earth!

*But maybe that's what she's here for,* thought Raza. *Maybe this is really some sort of sex education class! And who knows how demons would run a sex ed course? Maybe they make the students get naked, and give live demonstrations! Is that why Vel said the class was the hardest of all? It's certainly getting the boys pretty hard!*

Raza started getting nervous. She didn't fancy getting sexually educated by a demonic orgy. At least not until she'd gathered more experience! In any case, she'd definitely prefer something intimate and romantic, preferably just involving herself and Star Geddon.

Meanwhile Kellikassey was still smiling down at her.

"Well, it's very good to meet you, Shahrazad," said the teacher. "Now, this class is all about applied philosophy."

*Applied philosophy?* thought Raza. *That doesn't sound very daunting at all. Vel must've been teasing me, getting me all upset for no reason!*

She glanced over at Vel, expecting to find the girl grinning back at her with a "ha, ha, I fooled you" look on her face. Instead she found Vel looking nervous. Maybe the girl really was freaked out by the rigors of philosophy?

"Since you've started so late in the term," continued Kellikassey, "I'm afraid you'll be pretty far behind. You might find it difficult to join the discussion. So I've decided to give you some one-on-one tutoring time with my assistant, Mr. Jellen, to get you up to speed. He's a student teacher."

Kellikassey motioned to the side of the room, where the student teacher stood. For a moment Raza's heart thudded. Maybe he'd be an incubus, with an irresistible body and an infectious aura of lust. Maybe their "one-on-one time" would consist of her immediate deflowering. Maybe that wouldn't even be a bad thing. But she wanted her first time to be with Star Geddon!

She needn't have worried. Mr. Jellen, as it turned out, looked like a bit of a dork. In fact, he didn't even look like a demon at all, but like an ordinary twenty-something human, with dowdy black clothes and a pair of black spectacles. He waved to her, flashing a smile that was somehow both awkward and smug all at once.

*He's a demonic academic!* she realised.

She stood up and strode over to meet him. Soon they were sitting together in the corner of the hall. The rest of the class engaged in debate, occasionally erupting with uproarious laughter.

It seemed to be a lot more fun than Raza's one-on-one time with Jellen. For the first few minutes he barely said anything, just coughed and glanced at his notes. At length he removed his glasses and polished them with a cloth, thus revealing what seemed to be his only demonic feature. For without the glasses, his eyes transformed into orbs of cascading, iridescent light, like a psychedelic screensaver. Raza stared into them until he put his specs back on.

"So, Raza, why don't we begin by exploring your own understanding of cosmic history. First of all, why don't you tell me what you think about the Demiurge?"

Raza paused, glancing down into her lap. All of a sudden the situation felt a little intimidating. Surely this was the sort of thing that should wait until she started University? Maybe Velazelza had been right to be fearful of philosophy! At length she put an answer together.

"Well, he raped his own daughter, which is pretty gross. I mean, there's not much you can do that's more awful than that. Plus, he tried to enslave the demons, who're my ancestors. So I guess I don't think that much of him at all. In fact, I think he's a total dick-hole!"

Raza felt embarrassed about her swearing as soon as the words left her mouth, but Mr. Jellen just nodded and smiled, as if pleased with her answer.

"Good," he said. "And how would you characterise his actions, overall?"

"Huh?"

"What would you say was the biggest thing he did?"

"Oh," she said. "You mean creating the universe?"

Mr. Jellen sighed. That hadn't been the answer he was looking for.

"Okay," he said. "But did the Demiurge really 'create' the universe? After all, he just drew out the energies of the Celestial Fire, like a babe from a womb. Sort of like a doctor, or a midwife. Now, would you say that a midwife 'creates' a baby, just because she helps one to be born?"

"I guess not," said Raza.

"Indeed. So in a way, it would be true to say that the Demiurge didn't really 'create' anything at all, yes? And that the true creative force in the universe is in fact the Celestial Fire, the pure essence of Chaos at the heart of the void?"

"Um, I guess so. I mean, I see how that makes sense . . . "

It sort of did make sense. Nevertheless, Raza couldn't help but feel that there was something a little bit off about the argument, as if Jellen were tricking her into giving him the answer he wanted. And yet she couldn't quite put her finger on what was wrong with his rhetoric. She didn't have time to, either.

"Good," he said with a smile, once again happy with her answer. "And why do you think he decided to bring forth the Celestial Fire the way that he did?"

Raza shrugged. "Well, I guess maybe he just wanted there to be something. I mean, something's better than nothing, right? It would be pretty boring just floating around in a void all day long. I mean, the universe, existing the way it is, is better than just a blob of pure madness, right?"

Jellen pursed his lips, as if considering her answer. But the posture was patently false. The rest of his body language told her it wasn't what he'd wanted to hear.

"Perhaps," he said. "But why does someone create something at all?"

Raza shrugged. "I don't know. For fun? From inspiration?"

"But why? What's the ultimate, primordial motive?"

Raza shrugged again.

"*Desire*," said Jellen. "And what does desire proceed from?"

Raza gave yet another shrug. She felt like her shoulders would be tired by the end of the lesson.

"Why do you desire food, or water, or a seat by the fire? When you're lonely, why do you seek out companionship?"

"Um . . . because I need it?"

"But why do you need it?"

Raza just stared at him, increasingly perplexed.

"Because you don't have it," said Jellen. "All desire proceeds from lack. A perfect being lacks nothing. The Demiurge *lacked*, and was therefore imperfect. He was so imperfect, and so lacking, in fact, that he had to build an entire cosmos to address his unbearable need."

"I suppose," said Raza. "But what if he just liked creating things?"

"But we've already determined that he didn't really 'create' anything, remember?"

"Oh, right," said Raza. This stuff was getting complicated!

"Okay," said Jellen, apparently deciding to move on. "Why don't we talk about the Demiurge's need to be worshipped. He's appeared in countless guises over the ages, demanding obeisance from mortals. But let's think about this behaviour for a moment. The Demiurge has acted as a midwife to the universe, and now he expects unswerving obedience from everyone in it. But if you helped bring a child into the world—even if you gave birth to it yourself—would you ever insist that it bow down before you?"

"No way!" said Raza.

"Indeed," said Jellen with a smile. "And what sort of person do you think would do that?"

"A jerk," said Raza. "A dictator, like Hitler, or Saddam, or that Italian guy who always wore those stupid little hats with the tassels on top."

"Indeed," said Jellen, smiling again. "The type of person with a dictatorial personality. What people on Earth might call a 'malignant narcissist.' Do you know what that is?"

"I think so. It's someone who's really stuck-up, yeah?"

"Sort of," said Jellen, a little condescendingly. "But what it really refers to is a person who thinks—without any legitimate evidence—that they're better than everyone else. Such a person wants to be treated as if they're perfect. But we've already determined that the Demiurge *isn't* perfect. Which means his desire to be treated as such is completely unacceptable. Wouldn't you say?"

"Yeah," said Raza. "Yeah, definitely."

Jellen smiled again.

"Great," he said. "Now, let's leave the Demiurge for a bit and turn to something else. Let's talk about the universe. What's the one constant force in the cosmos?"

Raza thought back to her cosmic history lesson, and immediately figured out the answer.

"Chaos!" she said.

"Good. And what's the original, primary cause of the universe?"

"Um, Chaos again?"

"Indeed. And where did the demons come from?"

"Chaos," she said a third time. This was starting to get repetitive!

"Okay," said Jellen. "So why do you think the demons were created?"

She shrugged, then considered the question. Her shoulders indeed were getting a workout.

"Well, they came from Chaos, right?" she said eventually. "So it was just sort of random. I guess?"

It was Jellen's turn to shrug, but it seemed insincere. "Maybe," he said. "Or maybe they were created for a reason. After all, Chaos flows through all things, like the blood of the universe. So maybe it's making some antibodies?"

Raza furrowed her brow. Now *this* line of argument was definitely suspect.

"I dunno," she said. "I mean, isn't Chaos just random, like it doesn't really want or need anything? And didn't the Demiurge come out of Chaos as well? So wouldn't that make him, like, an antibody, too?"

Jellen sighed. "It's true that the Demiurge came out of Chaos originally, like all things. But he differentiated himself and became a creature of Order. Now he's the *opposite* of Chaos. The archenemy, if you will."

Raza's brow stayed furrowed. This seemed pretty dubious as well, especially in light of what she'd already learned in cosmic history class.

"But isn't Chaos a force of infinite possibility?" she said. "So how could any one thing be its opposite? Unless it was some kind of nothingness? But wait, hold on. Chaos is infinitely destructive, too, right? So it's sort of like Chaos is everything and nothing all at once. So how could any one thing be the opposite of everything and nothing?"

Jellen took off his glasses and rubbed the bridge of his nose, as though he were getting a headache. She got another glimpse of his psychedelic eyes, burning a hostile shade of crimson and purple.

"Chaos is the principle of genesis and destruction," he said. "Order is the principle of individuation and refinement . . . "

Previously Jellen had been poking and prodding, leading her towards the answers he'd wanted to hear. Now he gave up all pretence of conversation and just started lecturing. He said that Order—although necessary for the existence of the universe—was a dangerous force that was spreading like a virus, causing stagnation. It manifested on Earth as fascism and slavery. The Demiurge wasn't really a creator, but a rapist and a thief who'd arrogated the forces of creation to placate his uncontrollable ego. His actions were oppressing the universe and threatening to overwhelm Chaos with endless stagnation, engendering a system of total inertia. It was the job of the demons, as children of Chaos, to prevent this by any means necessary.

By the time the bell rang, signalling recess, Raza's head was throbbing. It was a lot like that time she'd been cornered by a socialist activist in the city. A lot of their ideas had sounded good, but then again, a lot of them just didn't make much sense to her. Now as then it was as if someone had tried to hammer ideas directly into her brain, except that the ideas were square pegs, and the hollows were round. The resulting cognitive dissonance gave her a migraine. She tried talking to Vel about it as they walked down the corridor, running through some of Mr. Jellen's arguments.

"Ugh," said Vel. "Don't even mention all that junk outside of class. All this blah-blah-blah and thinking in circles. Makes me wanna tear my hair out!"

*Okay, so Vel's definitely not a fan of philosophy,* thought Raza as Karanora sidled up beside her.

"Sounds like Mr. Jellen's a real Chaosian," said Karanora.

"What's that?" asked Raza.

"They're a sort of radical faction in the demon community. Sounds like Jellen was trying to brainwash you into joining their ranks! But Chaos Theory class is supposed to be all about the free exchange of ideas. So you should tell Miss Kellikassey that he tried to indoctrinate you. She'll tell him off and give him a bad grade for his teaching assessment."

"I don't know if I wanna go that far," said Raza. "But who are these Chaosians, anyway?"

"Like I said before," said Kara, "they're a radical faction. A lot of their beliefs are pretty crazy. Like how they think us demons are 'antibodies' or something, spawned by Chaos to help save the universe from Order. But Chaos is supposed to be random. So how could it possibly come up with a plan like that one? There's a whole bunch of other paradoxes in their thinking. For starters, they claim that Chaos is supreme and invincible, the ultimate force in the cosmos. Then they say it needs a helping hand from them. Which doesn't make a whole lotta sense, now does it?"

Raza thought about all the religious extremists back on Earth. Terrorists who murdered people because they claimed to be serving the interests of an omnipotent being. But if their god was omnipotent, then why the fuck would he need their help at all? The Chaosians were starting to sound like a similar bunch of extremists.

"There's another problem, too," said Kara. "The Chaosians claim to serve the interests of Chaos, but their view of the universe is in fact very ordered. They see everything through the lens of some black-and-white conflict between Chaos and Order. It's really very ironic."

"Huh," said Raza. "I guess that *is* pretty ironic. But how *can* a person serve Chaos? I mean, since we're demons, and we come from Chaos, and all . . . "

Karanora laughed. "You can't 'serve' Chaos, silly! It doesn't want or need anything. All you can really do is be free and follow your heart. 'Do What Thou Wilt Shall Be The Whole of the Law.' *That's* the only rule that most demons follow. Some call it the anti-rule, or the Credo of Chaos. Of course the Chaosians claim to follow it as well, but they've used it as the basis for a far more complex ideology than it seems to imply. That's pretty much the major philosophical split within the demonic community right now. Old-school demons think their allegiance to Chaos means they should just do whatever. Chaosians think they've got some kind of duty to uphold."

Raza froze as she heard the words "Do What Thou Wilt Shall Be The Whole of the Law." It was the same phrase her parents had said to her over and over again, a mantra of guidance passed on from her absentee father. She couldn't help but think that the whole thing sounded pretty selfish, not to mention downright irresponsible. After all, what if the Chaosians were right about a few things? Like what if the Demiurge really was a tyrannical dictator, like Hitler or Saddam? It certainly sounded like that was the case. Surely it would be correct to oppose him, rather than just go gallivanting around, doing whatever you felt like? Karanora seemed to sense her confusion.

"Of course," she said, "there's a sort of a paradox with the old-school demon code, as well. Because it's a rule that can't really be broken. After all, if you're free to do whatever you want, then you're also free to believe in some sense of personal responsibility, just like the Chaosians do!"

Vel groaned as she eavesdropped on their conversation. Raza knew how she felt. Total personal freedom was starting to sound a lot more complicated than she'd initially believed. Maybe Chaos Theory really was the hardest class in school? But as much as the content made her head hurt, it was still a lot more exciting than the moral messages she'd been taught back on Earth, most of which seemed to revolve around getting a job, paying taxes, and following rules.

The rest of Raza's subjects were electives and sports.

Electives included—among other things—Demonic Literature, Alchemy, Angelic Studies ("know your enemy," the sign-up sheet read), and Art class.

Raza picked art. She'd always been fond of drawing. Of course, she'd found that a lot of the students weren't using traditional media. Or at least, not any media that she was familiar with.

One of the students was making sculptures from their own incandescent bile. It wasn't as gross as Raza would've imagined. For starters, the bile smelled sweet, like rosewater. Secondly, the substance was actually quite beautiful, a gleaming rainbow slime that was steadily being formed into the image of the student's demon ancestor, a being with the head of a lion and a crown made of scorpion tails.

Another student was burning a scene into a panel of wood with focused, demon eyebeams.

Another was making vignettes from plumes of posable fire. The flames had different colours, delineating the figures in a medieval carnival scene. Raza watched in amazement as the bodies flickered and danced—jesters, jugglers, kings and haughty queens.

Raza got charcoal and paper and settled down drawing. She spent most of the class sketching out images of Star Geddon. Naked, of course. Many of the details she acquired from her own imagination. When the teacher—a huge, hairy demoness with a mellifluous voice, called Bambexa—came to check on her progress, she shyly hid the drawings away.

After art class came time for her to sign up for her pick of the sports. Vel tried to talk her into playing hockey with her.

"Come on!" she said. "You can help me kick the crap out of those demi-turds from Dick-vinity College!"

Raza settled on running instead, her previous area of athletic interest. She wasn't sure she was cut out for the violence of demonic hockey.

"Okay," said Vel. "You do what makes you feel happy. Just make sure you win! The interschool championship's coming up in seven weeks. We've gotta make sure we cream those Divinity jerks and keep hold of the trophy!"

"That shouldn't be too hard," said Kara. "We've kept the Cup for almost five hundred years."

"Don't get complacent," said Vel. "It's the mother of all cock-ups!"

Raza was surprised to find that the demons of Our Lady

had been winning at interschool sports for almost half a millennium. She'd assumed they'd be the underdogs against the Divinity demigods. She stared at the trophy in its rune-covered case, a diminutive cup carved from humble old wood. Something red was inside, like a remnant of wine—or of old, dried-up blood.

She took to her running with a passion. The track was a ring of red dirt around a copse of black trees. The beautiful nebulas glittered above between the school's sprawling towers. As dramatic as it was, she let the scene slip away and focused on running, feeling the burning in her lungs and the stellar winds racing through her hair. It was cathartic to do something so simple again, amidst all the madness of her first day at Our Lady.

The rest of the week passed by in a veritable flash. She read through the interactive tome of Cosmic History, getting as far as the Velezex Mutiny. She meditated again and again in Zenneff's dojo, trying to draw out the fire inside. It felt like she was getting closer and closer to that elusive transformation. Meanwhile she watched Vel and the others as they slaughtered summoned legions of enemies. Not just pig-men but cyclopes and serpents. Skinless gargoyles. Giant lizards with neck frills decorated with carcasses. She joined in with the debates in Chaos Theory class, trying to ignore the aura of lust that poured from Ms. Kellikassey. It wasn't easy.

All the while she grew closer and closer to Vel and the others. Her feelings for Star Geddon grew stronger, though the two of them had scarcely even spoken. Hers was the infatuation of a voyeur. Would it ever amount to anything reciprocal?

Such were her thoughts when Vel came and found her sitting on a bench beside the race track, still covered with sweat, seeing Star Geddon's face in the flash of a nebula.

"Hey sweet-cakes!" shouted Vel as she snuck up behind her. "Whatcha doin? I've been looking for you all over."

"I was just running," said Raza with a smile. "You know, training. So I can help smash those demi-dicks from Divinity, just like you keep telling me!"

"Forget about that now," said Vel. "It's the end of the week. Which means it's time for a big, blowout party. It's gonna be awesome! And guess what?"

"What?" asked Raza.

"Star Geddon's gonna be there! So you wanna go, or you wanna do some more running?"

Raza smiled eagerly, and followed her friend.

# CHAPTER 9:
## CHERRY RED

**RAZA STARED AT** herself in the mirror, appraising her outfit. She wore a sleeveless dress of crushed black velvet that hugged her figure from neck to mid-thigh. Her hair was tied up at Velazelza's insistence, baring the fullness of her face.

"It'll look so hot!" said Vel.

In spite of her occasional shyness, Raza had to admit that she *did* look pretty hot.

She wore velvet gloves and a pair of sheer black stockings that made her long dark legs look even longer and darker. She wore a platinum tiara from Zibbilique's collection, dotted with gems that flickered with images of revelry. The gems had served as sorcerous cameras at some ancient Bacchanal, imprinting the scenes on their facets forever.

Behind her was the messy space of Velazelza's dorm room, reflected likewise in the mirror. It was much like Raza's own, save for the piles of clothing and magazines and sundry items that lay sprawled across the carpet, making it look like it'd recently been ransacked. Raza wondered why Vel had so many clothes lying around. After all, on the two occasions when she'd seen her friend's true form, the girl had been totally naked!

Vel, Kara and Zibb dashed to-and-fro behind her, their bodies reflected in the mirror as they tried on different items of clothing, helped to apply each other's makeup, and gave each other feedback on various outfits.

Vel seemed to have settled on a neon-blue dress that aligned with her hair colour.

Karanora was wearing blood red. Combined with her pale skin and black hair the ensemble looked both sexy and sinister. Raza thought of snow, blood, and the plumage of ravens as she looked at her friend in the mirror's reflection.

Zibb was wearing a dress sewn from diamonds. Their facets swam with shadows, like storm clouds careening at dusk. Not to be outdone even whilst being generous, her tiara was festooned with gemstones imprinted with images of eyeballs that followed the viewer, occasionally blinking. Her fingers were fitted with rings, her bare legs with jewel-covered anklets.

Raza knew that her friends' true appearances were still hidden from her gaze by the power of the talisman. Likewise the truth of the clothes they were wearing. Everything was still being mediated by the amulet's illusions, translated into something earthly and familiar.

Still, she'd been delighted to find that the strength of the illusions was already diminishing, at least in some cases. It all seemed to be based on the time she spent interacting with someone. She'd spent the most time talking with Vel, and thus the illusion that surrounded her new best friend was coming undone pretty quickly. She could see Velazelza's natural skin tone of bubble gum purple. She could even see some of the transparent quality her dermis possessed.

She was starting to see truer aspects of the others, as well. Some of those aspects were disturbing, like the maggots that crawled beneath Karanora's skin. Others were awe-inspiring, like the incandescent power that dwelled in Zibbilique, shining like the gemstones she wore. She was starting to see Pura's slimy, slate-grey skin as well.

"Where is Pura, anyway?" asked Raza, noticing the big girl's absence.

"She's gone to find a dress," said Vel.

"Good luck with that," said Kara. "I doubt there's one that'll fit."

"Maybe she's gone to tear down the curtain from the theatre," said Zibb. "That oughta provide enough fabric!"

The two girls started chuckling.

"You bitches!" said Vel, before she broke down laughing as well.

Raza covered her mouth and chuckled in turn. A moment later Pura squeezed herself through the doorway, wearing a bright yellow dress. Again Raza was amazed at how well the girl managed to pull off her weight. Her lips appeared luscious. She looked not so much fat as profoundly buxom and ultra-curvaceous. Then again, she was a Beetus-Zoid. She was *supposed* to be that big. Maybe the talisman was translating her natural size into something that looked fitting on a human?

"You look great, Pura," said Raza with a smile.

Pura smiled back. Then Vel clapped her hands.

"Right, everyone gather round!" she shouted. "It's time for a pep-talk."

Raza and the others gathered in a circle.

"How do we look?" asked Vel, sounding like a sports coach inspiring her players before a big game.

"Sexy," said Karanora.

"How sexy?" asked Vel.

"Really sexy!" shouted Zibb.

Vel sighed. "I'm just not that sure you *believe* it," she said.

"We look HOT!" bellowed Pura.

"Now that's what I wanna hear!" said Vel. "We look super-hot. The dance floor's gonna be sticky tonight!"

"How come?" asked Raza.

"How *cum*? Because when we walk in there, all the dudes are gonna pop boners and start spontaneously jizzing all over the place, because of how freakin' hot we look. It'll be like dance floor bukkake!"

"Don't be so gross!" said Zibb.

"Okay," said Vel. "So maybe that was a little too much. But you get the idea. We look great. It's time to make this party ours! Let's go!"

They traded high-fives and headed out the door. A moment later Vel rushed back in.

"Shit," she said. "Almost forgot the minibar!"

She hefted up a massive backpack that resounded with the tell-tale CLINK-CLINK of numerous liquor bottles. Then she rushed out and joined the others as they made their way down the corridor.

"Where is this place again?" asked Kara.

"Boltskin's Hall," said Vel.

"Aww man," said Pura. "That's really far."

"S'not that far," said Zibb.

"Is too!"

"Who cares if it's far?" said Vel. "We're still going!"

Raza followed the others down the corridor. She was still only vaguely familiar with the layout of the school. The place seemed almost impossibly vast. She doubted if even the staff were familiar with all of its alcoves and rooms.

They left the female dorms and entered a disused wing of the building, where the corridors had a baroque, antique feel, with crimson carpets and patterned wallpaper that showed an older rendition of Our Lady's sinister crest. As they progressed the halls grew more ramshackle. Much of the wallpaper was faded and buckling. Whole sheets were peeling and covered with graffiti. The carpet was misshapen and mildewy. Some of the boards creaked as though they might give way. Strange smells wafted from the nooks and the crawlspaces, where unknown animals had made their nests or engaged in territorial pissing. Sometimes the musty odours became almost overpowering.

"You sure we're allowed in this part of the school?" asked Raza.

"There's no rule against it," said Vel. "Besides, the old dorm's much nicer than this. We party there all the time!"

They kept going, ascending through some of the hallways and towers that snaked through the sky.

The process was disorienting, to say the least. The towers

contained their own internal gravity. No matter their orientation as it appeared from the outside—whether vertical, horizontal, or spiralling through the air like a corkscrew—you could still move through them as though the floor was parallel to earth. It led to some pretty shocking moments, especially when gazing out the windows. Raza would find herself standing at some bizarre angle, relative to the courtyards below, so that she seemed to be standing on a wall or hanging obliquely from a ceiling like a crooked chandelier. She'd feel a sudden onslaught of vertigo, as though she were about to tumble out through the gap and be splattered on the ground many hundred feet below, but each time the school's uncanny gravity would hold her in place.

Still Raza flinched every time she passed a window. The others seemed used to it.

At length they heard the sounds of revelry drawing nearer and nearer. First came the music, a careening tune backed by demonic vocals, a mixture of wailing and ethereal singing that struck Raza as both beautiful and terrible at once. Then came the sounds of the students themselves, a hubbub of chatter and laughter shot through with screams and shouts of exuberance. They made their way through the disused dormitory corridors and into the hall itself, where the sounds got louder and louder, rising to an almost deafening volume.

The party was in full swing. It looked like some of the warehouse parties Raza had attended back on Earth. The massive hall was mostly dark, save for the roving beams of light that shot down from a disco ball above. Looking up, Raza saw that the ball was covered not with mirror shards, as she might have expected, but with blinking, stuttering eyes. Every bat of the eyelids brought forth a new beam of light in a series of alternating colours, turning the floor into a rainbow kaleidoscope.

Students danced wildly in the centre of the room. Others were sitting on couches in small, chattering groups, straining their voices above the commotion. Uniforms had been eschewed for a riot of clothing.

"Wow," said Raza as she glanced around the room.

"Pretty cool, huh?" said Vel, catching the look of amazement on her face.

Raza nodded as they made their way deeper inside. Students were drinking, passing around bottles of potent demon liquor. Much of it was brewed from the dust of Deliritus, the inebriate's moon. It glimmered in the shadows like liquefied light. Other students were smoking joints rolled from the buds of celestial flowers. Coils of heady smoke hung like vines across the room. Raza waved them aside and tried to hold her breath. She didn't wanna get hot-boxed by demonic drugs. At least not until she knew what they might actually do to her!

Other students were into even harder stuff. She saw them racking up lines of luminous powder on a table in the corner. Nearby sat the stoner girl, along with a couple of others. That group looked especially secretive. They passed around an object that looked like a bong, filled not with smoke but with tiny, ghostly figures. If Raza had to guess, she'd say they were inhaling human souls!

Still, she wasn't conducting a survey on demonic drug use. Her purpose in scanning the hall was to look for Star Geddon. She searched through the shadows and the flash of the dance floor, trying to find his familiar handsome features. Her search turned up nothing. She whispered to Vel, sounding a little bit anxious.

"Where's Star?" she asked. "I thought you said he'd be here?"

"Chill out," said Vel. "He's always fashionably late. Come on, let's hit the dance floor. But first, a drink!"

Vel set her bag down and pulled out a bottle of neon-blue liquid. It looked disturbingly like some kind of industrial detergent. Raza took a sip of it gingerly, finding it surprisingly sweet—and strong. Her head was swimming a little when they left the minibar behind and rushed out onto the dance floor, careening to the sounds of the music.

The demon song seemed to have no beginning nor end. It reminded Raza of some of that psychedelic rock or stoner metal she'd heard back on Earth, the kind of stuff the weird kids had listened to, an endless sprawl of screaming riffs and crescendos of drum beats that built up and scattered, cascading, before climbing back together into newfound escalations.

Still, it could only vaguely be compared to any human music. Some of the sounds were made by instruments that Raza had no name for, and the vocal range was beyond any mortal biology. Most of all it reminded her of the images she'd seen in the tome of cosmic history—images of Celestial Fire, the quintessence of Chaos that bubbled and roiled at the heart of infinity.

She danced for a while until she felt giddy, then stumbled off the dance floor with the others.

"Hey, get out of there, dickweed!" shouted Vel, chasing off a student who was trying to poach their collection of liquor.

They passed the bottle around again and started mingling with the revellers, moving through a series of shouted conversations. Names and faces mingled with the shadows and explosions of light. Raza was only half involved in any given conversation, spending most of her time on the lookout for Geddon. She was just about to give up hope when she saw him enter the room.

He came with an entourage, but Raza ignored them. They looked like mundane planets orbiting his light. The real attraction was Star Geddon himself. His quiff was even more magnificent than usual, dusted with cherry-red glitter that sparkled like paint spots on a vintage El Dorado. He wore an elegant outfit that looked like the uniform of some 1800s admiral, though infinitely cooler and a great deal more louche. Maybe it was Star's casual air that made the outfit work. Anyone else might've look overdressed in such an ensemble.

Still, Raza couldn't help but think he *was* overdressed. She wanted to see more of him, all of him, and without the interference of the talisman. She whispered to Vel.

"Star's here!"

"Hold your horses," said Vel. "He's only just arrived. Just wait a bit longer and I'll get him, okay? Then you two can get acquainted. Cool?"

Raza nodded, trying to keep a lid on her growing excitement.

Star Geddon strode into the party, feeling like he already owned it. He sucked on an ebony cigarette, surveying the room. Of the good-looking girls in attendance, he figured he'd slept with most of them already. He knew he could probably have any one of them again, if that's what he wanted. Still, he preferred not to settle for a rerun. Not if some other, more novel experience should come to be on offer, which it probably would. Truly the night was pregnant with possibility, but he wasn't overly excited. It wouldn't fit with his demeanour of cool.

He chatted for a while with his friends, sliding into the partying atmosphere. Soon he saw Velazelza hurrying towards him. He wondered if she'd try and get him into bed again. If so, he'd have to take a hard pass on the offer. She was attractive and sexually adventurous, to be sure. But she was also headstrong and bossy. Satisfying her demands in the past had proved to be exhausting. And to top it all off, she just never stopped talking!

"Hey Star!" said Vel, bubbling with typical excitement.

"Hey," he said.

"There's someone I want you to meet. The new girl, Raza. And I'll let you in on a little secret, too," she added, whispering closely. "She's totally got the hots for you!"

*Well, that's only natural,* thought Star.

He glanced across the room, searching for the new girl. For a moment his view was blocked by the massive form of Puragaglia. Then Raza stepped out from the shadow of the big girl.

He was already aware of her existence, of course. He'd seen her watching him in class, and had pretended not to notice. Her gaze had been rapacious. Now it was time for him to study her. She had a runner's body, slender and athletic, with just the right amount of curves. Her skin was tawny and smooth. She had prominent cheek bones, lush red lips and a cute button nose. Her dark eyes looked fulsome and deep.

*Not bad,* he thought. *Not bad at all.*

She was undoubtedly attractive. What's more, she seemed to possess that combination of traits that Geddon prized in women more than any other—shyness and beauty. He doubted this girl would be as bossy as Vel. More likely she'd be pliable, acquiescent, gushing and awed by his mildest affections.

A girl like that might even be a virgin. Geddon felt a surge of rare excitement. The flower of the evening, it seemed, was growing even fuller. He'd plucked more cherries than any other student he knew of, probably more so than any of Our Lady's alumni, dating back through all the untold centuries of the academy's existence. If Raza was indeed a virgin, it would only add to the excitement of the evening's festivities, not to mention his own growing legend amongst the school's student body.

He hid his excitement from Velazelza, of course. Feigning reluctance, he gestured to his friends.

"Well, I was supposed to be hanging out with Zicky and Greebo tonight," he said. "But I suppose I can come and meet her. As a favour to you, of course," he added with a smile.

Vel grinned back. "Thanks, Star," she said. "I really appreciate it. She's been dying to meet you all week. And she's a real sweetie, too. I'm sure you'll like her!"

He smiled as Velazelza turned her back, then followed her across the dance floor.

Raza felt giddy as she caught sight of Star Geddon approaching. She took another gulp from the bottle, hoping for some liquid courage. A moment later Star was standing in front of her. Raza was tall for a girl, but at almost seven feet he towered above her. His quiff added another six inches of height. Raza found herself craning her neck to look up at him. His casual smile filled up her vision.

"Hi," he said. "I'm Star."

"Raza," she said.

He took her hand and kissed it. The move might've seemed cheesy and sleazy coming from anyone else, but somehow from Star it felt okay. Maybe because he was just so gorgeous. A tingle of excitement shot up her spine.

"So, Vel says you've become pretty great friends," he said.

"Yeah!" said Raza, a little too excitedly. "She's really cool."

After that titbit Raza fell speechless. She stood in nervous silence until Star started talking.

"So, where are you from?" he asked with a smile.

"Earth," she said.

"Oh." It sounded like he either wasn't very impressed, or he'd never heard of Earth at all. "So, who's your great demonic ancestor?"

"Oh," said Raza. "I don't really know his name. It was in some, like, really weird language. But it sounded sort of like 'Axe-Kill-Gore,' or something."

"Huh," said Star. "Never heard of him. He must be some kind of minor demon." He paused for a moment, then smiled. "Sorry," he said. "I'm not trying to belittle you. I can't stand all that status stuff. I get enough of all that back home . . . "

For a while he regaled her with tales of his home world, Rubex, an industrialized planet ruled by feuding monarchies. It reminded Raza of the old Europe she was familiar with from history classes back on Earth, especially the period of

111

time surrounding World War I, when monarchic states had plunged the world into untold bloodshed and industrialized slaughter, using soldiers like pawns in some horrible chess game.

Except that on Rubex the war had been going for centuries. There'd been no rise of democracy, no October Revolution, no storming of the Bastille, no surcease to the bloodshed of any kind, just kings and queens feeding their subjects through a never-ending meat grinder as they fought for scraps of territory. Over time the wars had grown more and more desperate, until, like the aristocrats on Zibbilique's world, the rulers of Rubex had turned to sorcery to gain an edge over their opponents, summoning demons to mate with. Thus was born a new demonic aristocracy, an officer class charged with leading armies into battle. The first side to take such a step had won some immediate gains, until the other nations cottoned on and started copying the process, luring demons with promises of pleasure and wealth. Soon there were demon-spawned kings and princes everywhere, manifesting terrible powers. The bloodshed multiplied as the war took on an even more savage dimension.

Star was a result of that process, the child of a prince and a demoness, born into the military elite. Once he was finished honing his skills at Our Lady, he was destined to go back home and take to the battlefield, leading armies of fodder through a maze of barbed-wire trenches. He'd be on the front lines, and yet most of the danger would be felt by the mortals. Machine guns couldn't do much to a demon, after all, nor could missiles or mustard gas. Thus the aristocrats of Rubex remained impervious to the bloodshed that was wrought in their names, just as they had been before the advent of the demon-spawn, when they'd stayed in their command posts, far behind the bloody front lines.

The whole thing sounded pretty awful to Raza. Still, she couldn't fault Star for where he'd come from, any more than she could fault Puragaglia for coming from a race of devouring slugs. Besides, there was something undeniably romantic about his aristocratic lineage. It conjured up a whole host of girlish, Disney-movie fantasies she maybe should've ditched long ago.

*My very own prince charming!* she thought, with stars in her eyes.

Eventually he ran out of things to say about his home world. He'd been carrying the conversation for ages, while Raza just stared at him, shyly infatuated. At length he leaned closer.

"So," he said. "Would you like to go someplace more private?"

Raza smiled. She nodded so hard she thought her neck might dislocate.

"Follow me," he said with a grin, taking her hand and leading her away.

Raza glanced back at Vel, finding the other girl grinning, flashing her a thumbs-up sign.

She followed Star from the hall and into the maze of corridors that traversed the old dormitory. It seemed as if many of the rooms had been converted into suites in some free-for-all love hotel. Cartoon hearts had been painted on the timbers; the sounds of coupling came from within. Star started opening doors, searching for an unoccupied room. Raza shielded her eyes as he interrupted a series of lovers in various states of copulation. Indignant students cursed and shooed them away. One hurled a pair of wet panties through a gap in the doorway, narrowly missing them both.

*They oughta have "Do Not Disturb" signs on these doors!* thought Raza.

She wondered what the staff thought about all the unchecked fornication. She hadn't seen hide nor hair of any chaperones, like one might expect at any normal school dance. Maybe that was one of Belzoa's many duties, and he'd decided to shirk it, just like he had with the cleaning? Or maybe the teachers just didn't care. She certainly hadn't heard them espousing any advice on sexual morality. Perhaps this sort of behaviour was perfectly in line with their free-living philosophy. Then again, of all the things she'd encountered at the party thus far, none of them had been that much different from what teenagers got up to back on Earth anyway. The only difference, it seemed, was there weren't any adults making futile attempts to stop it all from happening.

At length they encountered an unoccupied room and stepped inside. It wasn't as filthy as Raza had expected. It was in fact quite clean, and furnished with a queen-sized bed.

She felt a surge of excitement as he closed the door behind them.

*It's finally happening!* she thought, feeling echoes of that night back on Earth.

Still, things would be different now. Velazelza had assured her of that. Whatever madness might be unleashed by her inhuman libido, she needn't have to fear. Being a demon-spawn himself, Star would be able to withstand any violence her body might throw at him. It might be wild, even vicious. But it would be a meeting of equals, the passion of demons conjoined.

They sat down on the bed, beside one another. Neither said a word. Raza didn't care. She'd felt awkward talking to him anyway. But now, in the relative intimacy of the room, her excitement was finally outweighing her shyness.

She took the first move and started kissing him. They made out on the bed, groping each other with a growing intensity. His arms were strong, his body warm and supple. She felt the wet begin to bloom between her legs.

Wordlessly they started undressing each other. First came the talismans. The room around her changed, but Raza hardly noticed. Her eyes were glued to Star Geddon. He looked even more beautiful without the illusion, his features imbued with a demonic majesty. His nakedness was better than expected, his body tanned and toned. Her eyes popped open wide as his stiffening cock hove into view.

For his part Star was a little disappointed when he took off the talisman. She looked like an ordinary human, without much sign of her demonic heritage. Maybe she was thin-blooded, after all, from a watered-down lineage, the product of a feeble demon father. Still, there was no denying her beauty. Her breasts were firm, with small, pointed nipples that stood out stark against the shade of her skin. Her legs were long and sleek. He ran his hands up both of them, then slipped one between. She was wet to overflowing, her juices seeping out to moisten her thighs. He felt the heat flowing from her cunt like warmth from a radiator. The smell of it perfumed the air, metallic and intoxicating.

Raza watched his body start changing, responding to hers. Sleek crimson scales grew over his skin. She reached out and touched them, finding them smooth, like soft oiled leather. A tingle of electricity ran through her fingers, as though his body were a livewire thrumming with current.

She could feel the heat inside of her responding to his. It mingled with the lust, but was not indistinguishable. It was the same sensation she'd felt before she'd blacked out on Earth. The same sensation she'd tried to tease out during all those hours of demonic meditation. Zenneff's classes had made it more distinct, more familiar. She didn't fear it so much now, but almost embraced it.

Star picked her up by the ankles and spread her body out on the bed. The movement was sudden, almost violent. It sent another surge of excitement through her limbs. She grew hotter, wetter, feeling the flare of demon fire start to mingle with her need.

Then he was down between her legs with his serpentine tongue. It slithered from his mouth, tipped with a tapering head like that of a viper, from which yet another, smaller tongue emerged, flickering, following the trail of juices up her thigh to the lips of her pussy. He licked around her clit with a growing intensity. The speed and deftness of his movements made James' short-lived efforts look distinctly pedestrian. She writhed with pleasure and thrust her hips towards him, aching to get some part of him inside of her.

He obliged, sliding in the head of his viperous tongue. She winced as it penetrated. Her hymen was a tight ring of flesh that spread open and ruptured with blood as the tongue slid in and out. The pain seemed to trigger more heat. Her thoughts started spinning in a fiery delirium. The fire was flaring up now, hotter and hotter, bursting from the blood in her veins.

Star tasted blood on his tongue and his prick grew even harder. There were few things he liked better than deflowering a virgin. Naked in the shape that his demon blood gave him, his excitement flared up even wilder. He had good control, perhaps more so than most other students. Still, the demon form brought with it a haze of lust and violence that was hard to control. There were few thoughts in his head when he withdrew his tongue and pushed his cock inside of her.

Raza moaned and bucked from the shock of it. Almost fully transformed now, Star's prick was nearly too big to fit. Still he gripped her sides and started rutting, lifting her body up off the mattress. He was almost ten feet tall and still growing, holding her in his arms like a lion with its paws around a rabbit. Pain and pleasure swirled around the entry. The fire flared up, bringing the change.

Star was only vaguely aware of Raza's transformation. Caught in a cycle of lust, he thought only about the sensation of his prick stabbing into her, forcing her flesh to accommodate it. His vision was a blur of lust as Raza started growing, changing in front of him as he pierced her and held her aloft.

Her skin assumed a hue of red neon. A second pair of arms grew out from her sides, extending forth from an expanding apparatus of muscle and bone. A second pair of breasts bulged up below the first. Then all four opened wide, revealing beds of gnashing teeth and foaming saliva. It seemed she was a proper demon after all.

Her body grew in size to rival his. Her teeth turned to steel with canines like a wolf's. Her hair became a wild black mane that rippled like shadows of firelight. She grabbed him with all four arms, puncturing his flesh with her claws as she pulled herself close to his chest. Cherry-red blood dribbled down from the wounds, glittering.

Star healed almost immediately. The lashings of pain mingled with his lust, swelling him thicker inside of her. This was becoming a true demon coupling!

The change had come suddenly as usual, but this time Raza's consciousness hadn't fully dissolved. Still, she wasn't quite in the pilot's seat, either. More like in the backseat as her body was driven by flashes of instinct. There was pain between her legs, but pleasure as well. Her altered body seemed to thrive on them both, responding aggressively. She gripped him with her claws, biting him and pushing him backwards. He tried to fight her, but Raza was evidently stronger. Much, much stronger.

She threw him on his back and impaled herself on top of him. She barely even noticed that the bed was now a flattened-out ruin beneath them, or that part of the floorboards had cracked and given way. Nor did she notice the blood on the walls, splattered by her breast-mouths as they savaged his skin. Nor did she consider the sound of her grunting and roaring as she mounted him, which was loud enough to be heard from the dance hall.

Star's cries were almost as loud as hers, but they were not cries of pleasure. Her pussy was deeper now that she'd assumed her true demonic shape, but it was also tighter—terribly tighter. He could feel it crushing him, grinding him, and not in a good way. He tried to fight her off but she was far too heavy to move, having grown larger than he was.

Sitting trapped in the back of her mind like some

delirious passenger, Raza was vaguely aware of his suffering. Still, it didn't seem like there was much she could do about it. Some greater drive had taken over, a mixture of lust and hunger and violence. It drove her body like a blazing commandment. Her own conscious thoughts, such as they were, were soft and dim by comparison.

She bounced on him faster and faster, feeling a climax approaching. Blood welled up from his arms as she pinned them to the bed and punctured his flesh with her claws. More blood was pooling round his crotch, and not just from her stretched-out hymen. His prick was constricted and abraded by the pressure and friction of her pussy, almost flayed raw. He was screaming now, a terrible sound that spread through the halls and started drawing the attention of the students at the party.

The nub of Raza's consciousness grew increasingly appalled. She saw the pain in his eyes as he thrashed underneath her. He came inside of her, despite all the agony, but the moment of pleasure seemed lost amidst the fear in his eyes. His serpentine tongue was thrashing, biting her, desperately injecting her with venom.

Raza's nub of consciousness looked on in horror as one of her arms reached out and ripped off his tongue. A simple reflex, as though she were swatting a fly. Her demonic instincts didn't want anything to get in the way of her pleasure, to stop the climax that was so soon approaching. Not his agony, not even the fact that he'd already ejaculated. The pressure and friction of her pussy kept him hard as she kept bouncing on top of him, surging her hips. The conscious part of her mind tried to stop herself, but it was like the hand of a child trying to reach out and tackle a giant. The rest of her mind—the part of her that was really in control—just wanted to CUM!!!

Was that instinct separate from her? Was she like Jekyll and Hyde, with two distinct personalities? Had the transformation brought about the emergence of some other persona? The answer, she knew, was a definite no. The desire was Raza's own, however wild and ungovernable it was. Even a part of her consciousness rejoiced as she came, riding the ragged remains of his prick to a shuddering orgasm. At the same time she leaned down—and bit off his head.

# CHAPTER 18:
## DEICIDE'S DAUGHTER

**B**ELZOA WASN'T HAPPY. He'd been dragged away from a perfectly good, late-night, solitary drinking session by a bunch of panicking students who'd told him something terrible was happening in one of the disused dormitories. He'd grumbled and followed after them, collecting Sketh on the way, who also worked as the resident councillor. If something had gone down—a brawl, a murder, a rape—then he'd need her assistance to get things under control and find out the answers.

Together they followed the students to the old dormitory wing, the one that housed Boltskin's Hall. Belzoa knew it was a favourite haunt of the pupils, who must've been using it for one of their end-of-week parties. But when he got there the music was off, and the hallway was jammed with drunken students, all shouting and muttering as they crowded round one of the rooms.

"Outta the way!" shouted Belzoa as he and Sketh pushed through the crowd.

"What's going on?" asked Sketh.

"There were horrible noises coming out of there," said one of the students, a girl called Velazelza. "All kinds of screaming and growling!"

"So what's new?" asked Belzoa. "There's always horrible noises around here!"

"I know," said Vel. "But these ones were *really* horrible!"

The rest of the students muttered their assent. Belzoa sighed, stepped up to the door, and rapped on it loudly.

"Hello?" he called. "Is everything okay in there?"

No reply, though he thought he could hear a faint sound of whimpering or whispering within.

"What's going on?" he asked again. "This better not be a prank!"

Still no answer. He checked the door, finding it locked from the inside. He turned to Sketh, and the two of them nodded to each other.

"Right," he said. "Time to get to the bottom of this!"

Belzoa smashed through the door, and froze. Huddled on the floor was the new girl, Shahrazad. She was butt-naked and covered in blood. She kept rocking back and forth with her arms around her knees, whispering "it happened again, it happened again," over and over to herself.

On what remained of the bed lay what remained of one of the boys. He was still in his demon form, his bleeding prick sticking up from some kind of morbid tumescence. It took Belzoa a moment to realise who it was, as his head was totally missing.

"Geddon," he whispered.

Raza glanced up to see Belzoa and Sketh standing in the doorway. Dozens of students were crowding behind them, gasping and muttering as they stared at the carnage. Without her talisman they looked like a myriad of monsters. Still she could recognise Vel, Karanora, Zibbilique and Pura, all gathered together and gawking. She huddled into herself, hiding her head. Belzoa stood there frozen for a moment, then reacted.

"Stop rubbernecking!" he shouted at the students. "I want all of you back in your rooms, immediately, except for those of you who might know something about what's been going on here. Anyone who *does* know anything, I expect to see you gathered outside my office within the hour. Understood? And

don't even think about not coming forward if you know
something, because I'll find out about it eventually. And if I
catch you lying, you'll be sent to the Time-Out Zone! Are we
clear?"

The students muttered in the affirmative and started
departing. They peered into the room as they went. Raza felt
a procession of eyes passing over her, staring at her body and
the horror on the bed. She huddled into herself even further.
She heard their excited whispers as they made their way
down the hall, though she couldn't understand what they
were saying at first, not until Sketh hurried forth into the
room and placed Raza's talisman back around her neck.

"Fuck me!" said one of them. "Did you see Star's head?"

"What head?"

"You think she tore it off with her teeth?"

"Maybe her pussy bit it off," said a smart-arse.

"No way! It must've been some kind of monster from
outside of the dome. A moon-calf, or a stellar vampire!"

Meanwhile Sketh put a blanket round Raza's shoulders,
covering her up.

"Are you okay?" whispered the teacher. "What
happened?"

Raza stayed mute, daring to glance up. She saw Vel and
the others loitering anxiously. She'd never forget the looks
she saw on their faces as they stood staring down at her. Total
fear and alienation. It was just like all those looks her parents
had given her in the past, only worse. Raza hid her head as
Belzoa yelled at Vel and the others to hurry up and get going.
She heard their footsteps retreating down the hall as the
myriad voices yielded to silence.

Raza sat in Sketh's office for almost an hour before she said
anything. The teacher didn't ask her any questions at first,
just towelled the blood off her face, wrapped her up in a

snuggly white dressing gown, and gave her a cup of hot cocoa. Then she knelt down beside her, speaking softly, urging her gently to tell what had happened.

Eventually Raza burst into tears and blurted out the whole thing. How she and Star had been having sex when she'd transformed and killed him. She held back a few details, of course—like how great the orgasm had felt, or the visceral thrill she'd experienced when she'd bitten his head off. She minimized as well her own conscious involvement, saying the whole thing had been blurry, and more like a dream. That she'd had no control at all. Which seemed partially true. The urges had been her own, unmistakeably, tethered to her consciousness like the limbs of her body were connected to her nerves. And yet she'd felt powerless to stop them. Had she been governed by irresistible instinct? Or had she just been too weak to fight off her desires as they sprang up like fire from inside?

She thought about it all as the tears rolled down. Sketh wiped them away with a tissue and placed a comforting hand on her shoulder.

"Try not to be too hard on yourself, okay?" she said, smiling kindly. "What happened tonight wasn't really your fault. These things just happen, I'm afraid. Now just wait here, and me and the rest of the faculty will get all this sorted. All right?"

Raza nodded, still softly weeping.

Sketh left the room and hurried into an adjoining chamber. The rest of the staff were there waiting. Zenneff was the first to speak. He stood there with his armoured arms folded, towering over the others.

"Did you find out what happened?" he asked.

Sketh nodded. "I'm afraid it's a clear-cut case of fuckicide," she said.

"Fuckicide" was the somewhat irreverent term that demons used to describe what happened when one of their kind went berserk during intercourse and slaughtered their mate. It most commonly occurred when young, inexperienced demons had sex with squishy mortals, though it was also known to happen between two mating demons, especially when one of the parties involved was a great deal more robust than the other.

And yet for various reasons, the case of Raza and Star seemed highly unusual. Our Lady was a school for 'first-generation' demon-spawn, meaning the direct offspring of a full-blooded demon and an ordinary mortal. Theoretically, most of the students were evenly matched in terms of power and resilience. They could claw each other, bite each other, even rip each other's limbs off, without ever incurring the least risk of dying. At most they might end up staying overnight in the sick bay, while their miraculous powers of healing restored them to health. But that one should be killed in an outburst of fuckicide? Such an event was almost unthinkable. Even an act of deliberate murder was hard to achieve between creatures so powerful and evenly matched, and would normally involve a knock-down, drag-out melee that could go on for hours before one party yielded.

Thus a lot of the teachers were very surprised. Especially Zenneff.

"You've got to be kidding me!" he said. "Geddon was one of my very best students. You expect me to believe that this rookie tore his head off?"

"What's so hard to believe about it?" asked Belzoa. "She is the spawn of the big horned bastard."

The room went silent. Everyone knew to whom he referred. Raza's father was the demon called Azkilgor, otherwise known as the God-Killer. He'd slaughtered more angels during the war than anyone else. He'd also carried out an act that few had thought possible: the primordial deicide.

"I served as one of his captains during the war," said Zenneff. "And sure, he was tough. Still, there's no way his daughter could be that strong already . . . "

"It's the only explanation that fits all the facts," said Belzoa.

"The room was sealed from within when we got there. No sign of any intruders. Plus, it corroborates the reports from the students I interviewed. They all said Shahrazad and Geddon went off together for some adolescent rutting. Soon after the sounds were heard, coming from the dorm room. A good deal of grunting, thumping and moaning, apparently, followed by a scream. It's fuckicide, Zenneff, pure and simple."

Zenneff shrugged. "Well I guess it must be, then," he said. "If it fits all the facts."

He paused for a moment, considering, then grinned. His smile, so rarely seen on his scarified face, looked like a gash in a side of aged beef.

"What're you grinning about?" asked Sketh.

"Well, here I was getting all upset that I'd lost a good pupil," said Zenneff. "But if this girl Shahrazad really did kill Geddon, then she's worth a dozen fresh recruits. With that much raw potential, I could mould her into the very best killer this school's ever seen!"

"Trust you to see the bright side of a decapitation," said Sketh.

Zenneff scoffed. "Gimme a break. Decapitation's nothing. I've been decapitated seventeen times, and you don't see me going around whingeing about it! Kids these days are too soft. This Raza girl might be just the sort of monster we need at this academy."

Kellikassey sighed. "I think we're getting a little bit side-tracked here," she said. "The question is, what're we gonna do about all this? Geddon's family are powerful patrons of the school. They'll no doubt be very upset."

"Fuck 'em," said Belzoa. "We've been churning out war brats for those arseholes for centuries. They've been happy to reap the rewards, but they've always known the risks. Not every student survives this academy, and that's a fact. It's on all the application forms! Let's just say their little darling died in training, instead of with his dick hanging out. That oughta satisfy their military ethos."

"Did anyone ever tell you you're a mean old bastard?" asked Kellikassey.

"You did," said Belzoa. "Right before you blew me at the last staff party."

A few teachers chuckled. Kellikassey raised a red middle finger.

"Okay," said Sketh. "So we'll tell Star's parents that he died during training. That should let them save some face, and maybe even stop them pulling their support from the school. But there's no way we can stop this information getting leaked amongst the students. There were dozens of kids in that hallway, not to mention at the party. By tomorrow the rumours will be everywhere."

"So?" asked Zenneff.

"So Shahrazad is new here," said Sketh. "And Geddon was very well-liked. At worst she'll be targeted for some kind of reprisal. At best she'll be feared and avoided. She might have a very tough time of things from now on."

"Well, she *did* kill the guy," said Vorovox, the alchemy instructor. The statement came from the seven toothsome mouths that made up his circular face, like rents on a basketball.

"Don't be an asshole," said Sketh. "What kind of demon hasn't gotten a bit overzealous in the bedroom at one point or another? And at her age? The girl was just following her nature."

Vorovox fell silent, thoroughly chastised.

"So she'll be feared," said Zenneff. "So what. What's wrong with being feared? Best way to be, as far as I'm concerned."

"Not everyone's the same as you," said Sketh.

"That's true," he replied. "Many are weaker."

"Let's have an assembly," said Belzoa. "Tell the students the truth, since they're gonna find it out anyway. After all, fuckicide is a risk for all demons. It'll teach them not to get complacent about practising safe sex. And we can hammer home the point that it wasn't her fault."

"Good idea," said Sketh.

"Agreed," said Kellikassey.

"Touchy-feely bullshit, if you ask me," said Zenneff. "But go for it, I don't care."

The demons nodded. Their meeting adjourned by mutual consent, they made their way from the room to begin preparations.

Unbeknownst to the teachers their meeting had been watched by a single, sapphire eye that lurked in the shadows of the room's ventilation duct. Presently it crawled away on a dripping bundle of nerves, to see what else it could see in the halls of Our Lady.

# CHAPTER 11:
## PARIAH

**THEY KEPT RAZA** in the sick bay over the weekend, in a private room with a bed and a window. Sketh said she wasn't a prisoner, and she wasn't to be punished for what had happened to Star. Still, they wanted her to be safe and looked out for while everything got "sorted."

Raza didn't mind being secluded in the sick bay. She didn't feel ready to confront the other students.

The first night she lay there awake for a very long time, trying not to think about the killing. But the memories came rushing back, lurid and blazing. The frenzy of lust as he'd licked her. The pain of him plunging inside. The fires of her own transformation. The feel of his flesh as it tore beneath her claws, the taste of his blood in her five feasting mouths, the towering pinnacle of pleasure before she had—

She forced herself not to think about that last part. Instead she wondered if Belzoa would be on nurse duty. Perhaps that was one of the myriad pieces of "shit work" he'd been stuck with? She imagined him dressed in a pretty nurse uniform, with a white skirt and cap. It made her laugh until she cried.

*I must be cracking up,* she thought.

At length she fell into a fitful sleep. It brought no release from the memories. She relived the fuckicide over and over in her dreams, waking up as her fangs shot down to devour Star's head. She'd taste the phantom blood in her mouth, feel herself wet between the legs, find her body covered with sweat and her bedclothes torn apart as if she'd grown out her claws in the midst of the dreaming.

Finally she fell into a sort of dreamless oblivion. She woke up with a start to find a nurse standing over her. The nurse was indeed dressed in a pretty uniform, with a white dress and cap. But her skin was like translucent head cheese around a coal-black skeleton.

The demoness took her vitals and gave her breakfast. She gave her a pregnancy test too. Raza looked at it in horror. With all of the awfulness she hadn't even thought about the possibility of pregnancy. Her mind began to whirl. What if it came back positive? What would she do? She didn't want to be a teen mum. Would she abort it? Could she abort it? Maybe demon babies were immune to abortion! And what if she couldn't bring herself to snuff out its tiny little life? She'd end up a teenage mother to a child whose father she'd slaughtered at the very same moment of said child's conception. Could things even *get* any more fucked up than that?

Her hand trembled as she peed on the testing strip and held it up.

It was negative.

*Thank fuck,* she thought.

The nurse looked at the test and nodded.

"You should take another one in a few weeks," she said. "Just as a precaution. But I wouldn't worry if I were you. Demonic pregnancies generally progress very quickly. If there's no result now, then it's extremely unlikely that conception occurred."

Raza nodded, and the nurse left. Later that day, some of the staff came by to look in on her.

First came Zenneff. He said nothing, just stood over her bed staring down at her. She wondered if he'd come to kill her in revenge. A tiny part of her wanted him to do it. The rest felt terrified. He filled up the room, stooping to fit his head beneath the rafters. At length he nodded curtly, then left.

*Well that was fucking weird,* she thought.

Next came Belzoa. He gave her a pep talk, told her she shouldn't feel too bad about what'd happened. She lied and told him she was feeling okay.

Sketh came by and hugged her. She didn't talk about the incident, just gave Raza some history books to keep herself occupied. She also said her friends had been made welcome to drop in and see her on the morrow. Raza felt anxious when she thought about facing them.

She dived into the hallucinogenic history books almost immediately, trying to distract herself from her thoughts. She read about the war between demons and gods. Along the way she came across a demon with myriad horns, the head of a bull, the teeth of a wolf, the body of a man, and a cock made from a pair of intertwining serpents. It was pretty close to what she'd seen in the mirror that night back on Earth, when she'd first met her father.

His name was Azkilgor. Which really did sound a lot like "Axe-Kill-Gore." He'd been born from the molten core of Zenelb, the Murder Planet. His explosive nativity had blown up that star system. He'd killed his first angel by the time he was five. Later on he'd killed a god, though the details were sketchy. He drank a third of the god's blood straight from the neck stump, then formed the rest into a flat plane in space that measured over six hundred million square miles. There the demonic armies had gathered to challenge the Demiurge to a final great battle. A battle that was never fought, because the ceasefire was sought and the peace treaty signed.

Her father was a deicidal beast.

*No wonder I'm such a freak!* thought Raza.

Her second night of sleep in the sickbay was almost as fitful as the first. The images from the textbooks mingled with the killing, creating nightmares of terrible potency. But were they nightmares, or sex dreams? In truth they were both. She was fucking Star Geddon on the Dark Plain of

Zelen, an endless expanse of dried crimson ichor. The climax came. Her teeth shot down—

She woke up wet. The nurse was above her, opening the window to let in the light from the school's tiny sun. She spent the day waiting in apprehension, hoping and fearing that her friends might come visit her.

No-one came. What did it mean? That her friends had forsaken her? She cried under the covers in a cocoon of white linen.

Later that day alarms started blaring. Smoke drifted in through the windows and hallways. She was about to get up and leave when the nurse came in and told her not to worry. One of the towers was burning, but the fire was being fought.

Raza craned her neck to see the tower from the window. It curled high above the campus, a serpentine silhouette haloed by fire. Ashes rained down with the falling debris.

*The sky is falling,* thought Raza. *The world is coming undone.*

After more spooky dreams she was discharged on Monday. Or, at least, Our Lady's equivalent to a Monday, which ran from the first flare of the Toad Star to the eclipse of Orlum, the fifth star of Rubex.

Rubex. Star Geddon's planet, close enough to be visible. She fancied she could hear his princely father's cries of grief travel out through the space ways, straight from his throne to Our Lady, as if a strand of that sorrow ran through the void like a quivering string on a tin-can radio.

Such were the maudlin nature of her thoughts as she travelled back to her room to gather materials for class. She had her uniform already, which Sketh had been kind enough to bring to her, but she still needed her schoolbag and its sundry supplies.

A cold sweat passed over her as she entered the halls. Students were already bustling about, getting ready for their classes. She tried to avoid eye contact, heading straight for her room. Still she couldn't help but catch their stares. Some seemed filled with alarm. One boy dropped his books as he saw her, then scooped them up and hurried away, as if afraid for his life. Others glared at her frostily or gawked with expressions of morbid excitement. She could hear their whispers as she passed through the hall.

"It's her!"

"I heard she bit his head clean off. Talk about a man-eater!"

"I heard that wasn't the only part of his anatomy she took a bite out of. She ate his cock and balls, too, right down to the chode. Now that's a blowjob you'll never forget!"

Raza thought about taking her talisman off, so as not to hear their whispering. But she thought the sight of all those strange, inhuman faces staring at her might be even more disturbing. So she kept the amulet on and hurried to her room, feeling a growing sense of panic. By the time she reached her dorm she was almost running. Sweating, too, but the perspiration was fearful and cold.

She froze as she arrived at the door to her room. Someone had written "psycho bitch" across the front in giant, red cursive. The rest of the door was likewise covered with graffiti, stuff like "fuckicidal maniac" and "CAUTION: VAGINA DENTATA. WEAR AN IRON CONDOM."

Raza's shoulders slumped. She put her key in the door, but found it unlocked. Stepping inside she saw that the place had been trashed, her meagre possessions strewn out and stomped on. Her smart phone, perhaps her most prized possession, was smashed into pieces. A few of her things were missing, including a bunch of her panties. Other items had been added to the room. They lay on the bed, bulging and bleeding through the covers. Gingerly she pulled back the sheets, finding a pig's head and a pair of goat's testicles sitting in a puddle of blood and effluvium. The meat was already rank. Someone had left a note next to the pieces of anatomy:

*Here's a treat, just in case you get hungry. Eat up, psycho.*

Raza covered up the organs and slumped down against the wall. She thought she might cry again, but instead just felt numb. She sat there in a daze until she heard the clamour of the school bells calling her to class. Robotically she gathered up what remained of her stationery, piled it into her backpack, and hurried from the room. The smell of dead pig seemed to follow her.

The halls were crowded now. The stares of the students steadily multiplied, as did the whispers. She hurried through the crowds with deliberate tunnel vision. Most people got out of her way, but she could still feel them staring as she passed, muttering behind her.

She was headings straight towards Sketh's classroom when something made her freeze in her tracks. There in the hallway were Vel, Pura, Kara, and Zibb, all walking together to class. Raza felt a bolt of fear shoot straight up her spine as they noticed her. Then they froze too, staring at her.

Raza tried to swallow, but it felt like the muscles of her throat were made from rusted iron. The fear of rejection was very nearly paralysing. But she also felt hope that her friends would take her back, that things would revert to the way they'd once been.

She took a faltering step towards them. Vel stepped out from the others to meet her in the middle. They stood for a moment in silence in the centre of the corridor as other students gathered to whisper and gawk. Raza couldn't bear to meet Vel's eyes at first. She stared at her shoes and started muttering.

"I'm sorry about what I did," she said. "But I really didn't mean it. I know you all liked Star a lot, and everything, and he was here before I was, but I hope we can still be friends . . . "

She managed to smile and glance up at Vel. Vel was trembling, tears in her eyes. Was this the start of a tender, sobbing reunion? Maybe there was light at the end of the tunnel. Maybe everything really would go back to normal?

Vel slapped her hard across the face and pushed her away.

"Get away from me, freak!" she snapped. "You fucking *killed* Star!"

"But . . . but it wasn't my fault!" said Raza. "I couldn't control it!"

"That just makes it even worse," said Vel. "You're like a mad dog, Raza. Just stay the fuck away from us, all right?"

"Better back off, Vel," said Zibb coldly. "She might freak out and bite your tits off."

Vel glared at Raza. Then she and the others strode off into the classroom.

Raza ran to the bathroom and locked herself in one of the stalls. There was no numbness this time, just sorrow. She started weeping as she sat on the porcelain throne. Soon she heard the secondary bell, telling her the class was about to begin.

It took her a few minutes to stop crying and pull herself together. She dried her eyes and shuffled off to class. Sketh greeted her warmly, smiling as she entered. At the same time serpents popped out from the side of her head and turned towards the classroom, hissing, warning the rest of the students to behave.

"Good morning, Raza," she said. "I hope you're feeling better."

"Thanks, Ms. Sketh," said Raza.

She shuffled off to her seat at the back, avoiding eye contact with Vel and the others. On her desk was another volume of cosmic history, supplied by Sketh. Raza sat down, but didn't open it at first. Instead she glanced around. The stoner girl was to her right, once more looking high as a kite. She glanced at Raza with a casual expression. She was either too stoned to realise what Raza had done, or she just didn't care.

Vogg, the rough kid, was sitting to her left. He smiled at her widely. It wasn't a mocking look, either, but one of admiration, even camaraderie. He'd clearly come to see her as something of a fellow delinquent, a ne'er-do-well in very good standing.

She sighed and turned away. She took out the shattered remains of her phone. The thing was so broken she couldn't even take solace in the photos of her friends back on Earth. She'd been lonely there too, but at least she'd had Fatima and Lilly. How quickly she'd forgotten about them in the whirlwind first week at Our Lady. Swept up in Vel's friendship circle, she'd been certain her awkward days were over, that she'd finally found some place to fit in, to be popular, maybe even have a boyfriend as handsome as Star. But it'd all been a delusion. She was an outcast even here, a freak among the freaks, a monster to the monsters. Dreaded, alienated, just like she'd been back at home with her ostensible parents.

*So this is what it's come to, then,* thought Raza. *Maybe I really do belong with these weirdos at the back of the class. I could start doing drugs and beating people up. It doesn't seem like I've got that many other options in life.*

She escaped from her self-pity deluge into the tome of cosmic history. It told of the treaty that had ended the war between demons and gods, in which the demons had pledged to keep their influence on certain worlds to a minimum, allowing the Demiurge and his children to continue their project of governing the universe. For their part the gods had agreed to more or less leave the demons alone. Specifically, they'd vowed to no longer make use of their magicks of demonic binding.

Raza felt a chill run down her spine every time she read about those binding spells. Via the use of certain sigils, signs, and words of power, coupled with the true names of the demons themselves, the gods and their servants reduced many demons to slavery. The demons thus enslaved remained conscious and aware, but had no control over their own actions. The very thought of it filled Raza with horror. To be a passenger within your own mind, and yet subject to the will of another. What could be more horrible than that? It reminded her of how she'd felt during the incident—a passenger, her conscious mind at the mercy of instinct. Except that those ungovernable instincts had somehow been her own. Maybe someday she'd learn to control them, absorb them. But did she even want to integrate such desires, impulses that told her to feast on blood and bite off heads and fuck her lovers until they were dead? Where did the conscious mind end and instinct begin?

She concentrated again on the book. Even though the gods had promised not to use the spells, they still had them in their possession as a kind of deterrent, like the atomic bomb after World War II. Naturally the demons had wanted a nuke of their own. And they'd got one. After a series of talks, the Demiurge had agreed to give up a cup of his very own blood. For any demon that tasted the blood of a god could gain an insight into his weaknesses. And not just his weaknesses, either, but those of all his creations. And since the Demiurge was the universal architect, a sip of his blood would confer the knowledge to unmake the cosmos, atom by atom.

The demons had promised not to drink from the cup, so long as the gods abided by the terms of the agreement. But had they followed the directive? They were demons, after all. Maybe they'd just thrown a blow-out party and imbibed all the blood, like wine from a cask? Would the Demiurge know if they had, through some deific, sensory power? And just what would it mean to taste such terrible knowledge, to gain the means to bring ruin to all things?

Raza tried to imagine it. Would such a person be able to blow apart worlds at a glance? To unmake stars? To tear matter apart, like Lego? To undo time, gravity and space, plunging the universe back into a cauldron of Celestial Fire?

Then again, maybe the powers weren't so extreme. Maybe they'd just make you better at killing and breaking things. Who could say? The cup had been hidden away by the demonic generals, one of whom had been Raza's own father. Its present location was a close-guarded secret.

The bell rang finally and the class was dismissed. Sketh smiled at Raza as she stepped out into the hall, but it was small comfort. Raza felt herself plunged back into a storm of anxiety. The class had been like a warm cocoon in winter, the solace of the book like a blanket. Now she was out in the cold, being buffeted and whipped by the glances of the students. She shuffled reluctantly on towards the dojo.

The silence of the hall was welcome. Once again she felt the dread that filled the air as the students sat waiting for Zenneff to arrive. But perhaps he wasn't the only one they were afraid of today. How much of that dread was directed at her?

The sound of Zenneff's footsteps presaged his arrival, metallic and booming. He strode into the room and towered over the students. He spent some time staring down at them, lingering on Raza. His gaze was hard and inscrutable, like it had been in the sick bay. She glanced away, unable to meet his eyes. At length he spoke.

"Circumstances dictate that today's lesson be a little bit different," he said. "After all, last week we lost one of this academy's very best students."

*Oh no,* thought Raza. *He's gonna start talking about Star!*

"You all know who I'm talking about," he said. "Star Geddon. That boy had more control over his powers than many of you lot put together. But he was slaughtered like a lamb. I'm guessing you've all heard the story, so I won't mince words. The new girl, Shahrazad, bit his head off."

Raza's eyes popped open wide. She could feel the students staring. What was Zenneff playing at? Was he trying to shame her, attack her with guilt? She was miserable enough to begin with.

"Clearly the girl has a lot of raw potential," said Zenneff. "She is, after all, a child of the God-Slayer."

Excited whispers filled the room. Most of the students had had no idea who Raza's father was, which wasn't surprising, given that Raza herself had only found out the truth a couple of days ago.

"Still," said Zenneff, "raw power and pedigree don't mean shit without technique and discipline. So today I'm gonna put Raza through her paces. Let's see what she can do with a little bit of focus!"

He turned towards her. "Raza, stand up and come over here!"

Gingerly Raza stood up and stepped into the middle of the hall, standing opposite Zenneff. His massive body towered over her. The room was utterly silent as the students stared at them with captive attention.

"Right," said Zenneff. "I want you to show me what you've got. Bring out that power you used to slay Geddon. You don't have to worry about the consequences here. Anything you dish out, I can take. Now, start meditating."

Raza nodded and closed her eyes. She tried to block out the distraction of all the staring eyes. She reached deep inside herself and sought out the fire. Quickly she found it there, flickering. She felt a rush of savagery as her searching consciousness connected with the flames. It was like touching a livewire, filled not with electricity, but with currents of instinct. Sensations and images filled her mind immediately. Star's body beneath her, his unravelling manhood inside of her, his screaming face as her jaws snapped down towards it—

She recoiled from the flames, wincing.

"Come on," said Zenneff. "This is no time to be getting all squeamish. Don't get sooky, get angry. Find the power and use it!"

Raza tried again, digging deep as Zenneff circled around her, offering encouragement.

"The power is yours," he said. "It's a part of you. You control *it*, not the other way around. Find those instincts and bring them to heel. Show the others what you're made of. Show them you're more than just an animal!"

Raza gritted her teeth, balled her hands into fists, and tried to summon all the anger she could think of. The hurt of being rejected by her parents and abandoned by her father. Of being bungled off to boarding school, then rejected again. She thought about the leering eyes of the students, the whispers that took place behind her back, the graffiti on her door, the filth that they'd put in her bed. Most of all she thought about Vel's stinging hand as it slammed across her face, followed by Zibbilique's cold and mocking words. She connected with the fire—

And recoiled. As bright as her rage was, it couldn't equal the violence that burned there. The fire of her anger met the fire of her blood and shrank back, like a beast overawed by superior savagery.

Her fists went slack at her sides. Her anger evaporated, replaced by a feeling of weakness. Sadness and shame, guilt and rejection, smothering the flames like a dose of cold water.

Zenneff snickered. "Pathetic!" he said. "This is the spawn of the God-Slayer? The killer of Star Geddon? She looks like she's about to cry!"

Some of the students started laughing and jeering, egged on by the teacher. Raza felt lower and lower. A ball of gravity gathered in her throat, about to bring tears. Zenneff leaned in closer.

"Is this what you want?" he whispered. "For all those brats to treat you like a laughingstock? Make them fear you, instead. Show me what you can do!"

Raza tried to find the fire again, but her mind was a mess of conflicting emotions. She could barely even sense the presence of the flames. She was floundering, unravelling, coming apart.

"Show me what you've got!" shouted Zenneff again.

"I can't!" she yelled, opening her eyes. "I don't know how!"

A single tear fell down her cheek. Zenneff looked

offended by its presence, as though it were the most abominable thing that he'd ever laid eyes on.

"I said SHOW ME!" he yelled, slapping her across the face.

The motion was slight, little more than a casual backhand. Still it knocked her flying. She crashed to the ground and skidded on her side till she hit the far wall, her face a blazing mess of agony. Her nose was broken. Blood and teeth were swimming in the back of her mouth like some horrible stew. Her jaw was hanging off her face like a strap from a helmet. She put a hand to the mess and started screaming, gargling blood, wagging her tongue from the mangled red void of her mouth.

Her blood became hot. She could feel the fire blazing, bidden by the pain. Her face came back together like a video on rewind, reforming as if nothing had happened. She spat out teeth as new ones grew in, then picked herself up off the ground.

All across the room the students were staring with wide-open eyes. Excited whispers filled the hall as Zenneff strode towards her. Raza caught sight of a couple of students—the stoner girl, watching hazily; Vogg, his eyes a rapture of excitement; Vel, watching the spectacle with something like sadness.

"Impressive," said Zenneff. "You clearly have powers of healing. But I don't want to be wowed by your autonomic nervous system. I want to see volition! Aggression! Show me what you've got!"

He slapped her again, knocking out the teeth she'd just regrown. The pain flushed all thoughts from her head. The fire grew even hotter.

"Do something!" he shouted.

Another slap caved in the side of her face. She looked for a moment like the victim of some terrible car crash. WHOOSH! went the flames.

"I can do this all day!" shouted Zenneff.

He ducked low and rose, catching her guts with an uppercut. A geyser of blood erupted from her mouth as the force of the blow turned her organs to mush. She flew through the air and crashed down to the ground. Her blood turned to napalm and nuclear fire.

Zenneff charged across the room as she rushed up to meet him, her eyes blazing red as the flames overflowed.

# CHAPTER 12:
## BEATDOWN

**GAIN, WHEN THE** change came, it happened fast. One moment she was lying on her back, paralysed below the waist. The next she was standing on her feet, coming toe-to-toe with Zenneff. Not just toe-to-toe, but face-to-face, as well. Her body swelled up to a full thirteen feet, making her even taller than the teacher.

Her four arms whipped out and grabbed Zenneff's own. Her four breasts were snarling on her chest, eager to bite him. Black hair whirled around her steely fangs and blazing red eyes. Her consciousness was in those eyes, too, less of a backseat passenger now and more like a willing participant, joined with her instincts. She didn't want to stop the violence this time. She wanted to let it run rampant!

Zenneff peered at her with something like pride. He tried to pull free, then realised he couldn't. Pride gave way to increasing exertion as he struggled in her grip. Her claws dug in deeper, scrunching his armour and piercing the skin. She was going to crush him like a lobster in its shell!

The students were shouting and clamouring, standing up to watch the brawl. Raza was barely aware of their existence as her slitted eyes focused on the teacher.

"Impressive," he said, breathing hard. "You're strong, that's for sure. But this is about technique, remember?"

Yellow fire shot out from his eyes and hit her in the shoulder. She roared and let go of him, backing away from the sudden flash of agony. Glittering blood dripped down upon her breasts.

Zenneff might've been twelve feet tall and built like a rhino on steroids, but he moved as fast as a bantam weight boxer. He was on her immediately, landing a flurry of jabs, one to her stomach, one to her face, one to her snarling, upper-right tit. She stumbled backwards, then lunged forth and grabbed him again, trying to pull off his arms like the wings of a butterfly.

"This is why I'm trying to teach you technique," he said, gritting his teeth as the sinews in his shoulders started tearing. "You've already tried that move before!"

Beams shot out from his eyes once again. Raza didn't panic. She knew her instincts had the answer. And they did. Crimson fire exploded from her eyes in two searing beams, clashing with Zenneff's. For a moment the energies clashed in the air, yellow and red, vying for dominance. Then Raza's red beams devoured the yellow, chasing them back into Zenneff's own sockets. He roared as his eyeballs cracked and exploded.

Raza roared too as she ripped his right arm off and drew it back like a baseball bat, ready to swing. Blinded, he tried to ward off the blows as she battered his face. The students went wild, shouting and screaming. Some began to flee from the room. Raza paid them no heed. Her thoughts were a wordless blaze of violence. She tossed his right arm away and ripped off the left one. Armless and eyeless he stumbled away from her, bleeding golden blood that bubbled like champagne.

She grabbed him by the heels and whipped both his legs out from under him. He fell to the ground with an almighty CRASH, shattering the paving. She put a clawed, hairy foot atop his chest and used it for leverage as she ripped off his legs and cast them aside, first one, then the other.

Zenneff passed out. Raza turned towards the students, but they were already fleeing the dojo. Alone and victorious she stood atop his body, threw back her head, and roared until chips fell down from the ceiling.

Once again Raza found herself in Sketh's office, wrapped in a snuggly dressing gown and sipping a cup of hot cocoa. She cast her mind back to events in the dojo.

She'd stood atop Zenneff's body and howled herself hoarse. It wasn't just a cry of primordial, predatory victory, but one of catharsis. She poured out all her horrible feelings until the change subsided and she shrank back down to the size of a human.

She knelt down beside Zenneff, listening to his breathing. It was laboured and bloody. She felt sure he would die. She put a hand to his scarified face, and stroked it.

"Is that you, Shahrazad?" he asked, with a voice like cement in a mixer.

"Yeah," she said.

"That was . . . very good work you did, back there," he said. "I'm gonna give you an . . . A+ for your assessment."

Raza was taken aback. She'd just burned out his eyes and torn all his limbs off, and he was going to give her top marks?!

Soon the other teachers arrived. Raza followed meekly as they led her away, feeling exhausted and numb. Naked and blood-soaked, she followed Sketh through the halls as the nursing staff bundled Zenneff's body on top of a stretcher. She was taken to Sketh's office, where she presently sat.

The serpentine demoness was standing before her. She looked concerned, as before. Concerned, and more than a little dismayed.

"What happened this time, Raza?" she asked.

"He attacked me," said Raza. "Told me to fight back. So I did."

Sketh sighed. "Zenneff's always had some very . . . hands-on teaching methods. I suppose what happened today was the inevitable result of that. So I wouldn't worry too much, if I were you. I'm sure this will all turn out okay. Just sit tight here, all right?"

Raza nodded. Sketh left the office and went to the sick bay, where the rest of the staff were gathered round Zenneff. His arms and legs had already begun to regrow, but they were tiny and pink, like the limbs of a toddler, making him look utterly ridiculous. The staff would've laughed, if it wasn't for the fact that his eyes had already grown back, allowing him to stare them all down.

"What the fuck, Zenneff?!" shouted Sketh as she strode into the room. "The girl goes through a traumatic fuckicide incident, and you decide to call her out in front of the class and start physically attacking her?!"

"I was just trying to help her find her true potential," said Zenneff. "Excuse me for doing my job."

"I'd say she found her true potential, alright," said Belzoa. "You look like an overturned tortoise."

The rest of the teachers glanced down at Zenneff as he lay on the gurney in the remains of his armour. He did in fact look like a tortoise trapped on its back, his stumpy little limbs wriggling out from the corners of his vast, steely shell. This time they couldn't stop themselves from laughing.

"Very funny," said Zenneff. "Just remember I've still got my eyebeams. I can blast you all to smithereens, even stuck on my back."

The laughter subsided. Only one of the teachers hadn't laughed at all—Kellikassey, the red-skinned demoness of lust.

"What's to be done about all this?" she snapped.

"Nothing," said Zenneff. "I've already decided to give Raza an A+, and some private lessons, as well. She's got incredible talent."

"You can't be serious," said Kellikassey.

"Why not?" said Zenneff. "It's my class. And it's my arms

and legs that got ripped off. I'd say I can handle it however I want."

"Think about the bigger picture!" said Kellikassey. "Students can't just go around attacking the teachers and tearing them apart, not even in the dojo. Letting her go unpunished would set a terrible precedent. We'd lose face in the eyes of the students."

"So what do you suggest?" asked Sketh.

"Send her to the Time-Out Zone," said Kellikassey. "That'll teach her some discipline, and stop our authority from crumbling."

"I'm against it," snapped Zenneff. "She beat me fair and square. To punish her now would be an act of cowardly revenge. I won't have a part of it."

"It's not up to you," said Kellikassey. "Belzoa's in charge of discipline, remember? Let's see what he has to say."

Belzoa sighed. "It seems like this girl is indeed very powerful. She's also unable to control herself. That's a dangerous combination. First she kills Star Geddon in an outburst of fuckicide. And now she's almost killed Zenneff, in a simple training exercise."

Zenneff scoffed. "I'm fine!" he said.

"You're not fine," said the nurse. "You almost died."

"Bullshit," he said. "This is barely a scratch. I once got eaten by a manticore giant. Chewed up, swallowed, the whole bit. I had to regenerate myself inside his intestines, and punch my way out through his asshole!"

Kellikassey looked queasy. "I wish you'd stop telling that story," she said.

"The point is that this is no big deal," said Zenneff. "I've been through far worse before."

"You were younger back then," said the nurse. "But your body's sustained a great deal of accumulated punishment over the centuries. Your powers of healing aren't nearly as strong as they once were. I'm telling you now that that girl almost killed you."

Zenneff shrugged. "No matter. It was still a fair fight, and I don't think she should be punished for it."

"Luckily it's not up to you," said Kellikassey. "But I say this girl, right now, is a menace. Not just to discipline and morale, but to the students and faculty, too. She needs to be made an example of."

"A menace?" said Sketh, incredulous. "She's just a kid! A scared kid who can't quite control herself yet. She needs to be guided, nurtured, not cast to the wolves! I can't believe I'm hearing you say this shit!"

"You're too soft," said Kellikassey. "You can't take on every student like a surrogate child. She's not your daughter, she's the spawn of the God-Killer. And who knows how many others she'll murder or maim before she finally learns some self-discipline." She turned to Belzoa. "Belzoa, the decision is yours," she said.

Belzoa paused, stroking his muzzle in thought. At length he sighed.

"I agree with Kellikassey," he said.

Zenneff growled. Sketh started shouting.

"You've gotta be fucking kidding me!" she said. "The girl needs our help, not punishment!"

"And I want to help her!" snapped Belzoa. "But just think about it, Sketh. The girl *is* dangerous. If Zenneff can't handle her, then who the fuck can? Until Raza learns how to harness her power, she's a serious threat to the safety of the school. As much as I hate to say it, the Time-Out Zone is probably the only place where a girl like Raza can learn to control herself without putting everyone else around her in danger."

"But what about the danger *she'd* be in?" asked Sketh. "Have you thought about that? You know what the Time-Out Zone is like. What if she doesn't come back alive?"

Belzoa looked away. "That's a risk we'll have to take," he said. "I'm sorry, Sketh, but it's the only way. One month detention, starting today. Come to think of it, I've got a few other candidates who can join her in there. That way at least she won't be alone."

"Fine," said Sketh. "I guess I'll go tell Raza the bad news. She deserves to hear it from someone who actually gives a shit about her."

Sketh stormed out of the room and made her way down the corridor. She found herself blinking back tears as she went. She felt a lot of compassion for Raza, perhaps more than she felt for most other students. There was something about the girl that reminded Sketh of herself, all those years ago, when she'd been enrolled at Our Lady as a scared, overwhelmed teenager. She didn't like to think about the girl having to face the terrible dangers of the Time-Out Zone. She steeled herself as she stepped into her office, preparing to deliver the news.

"Hi, Raza," she said. "How're you feeling?"

"Okay, I guess." Raza peered up at Sketh. There was something unsettling in the teacher's manner. She looked shaken up. Could Mr. Zenneff have died? "Is he okay?" asked Raza. "Zenneff, I mean?"

"He's fine," said Sketh. "That old war horse has been through a lot worse, trust me. But I'm afraid I've got some other bad news."

"Oh?" asked Raza.

"I'm afraid a decision's been reached to punish you for what's happened today. It wasn't a decision I agreed with, myself. Nor did Zenneff. In fact he was quite pleased with your performance, and even wants to offer you private lessons. But I'm afraid we were both overruled."

"So what's . . . what's going to happen?" asked Raza.

Sketh's voice was grave. "You're to be given one month's detention in the Time-Out Zone," she said, "starting this very afternoon."

# CHAPTER 13:
## DETENTION

**RAZA DIDN'T KNOW** what the Time-Out Zone was, nor was Sketh forthcoming on the details. Apparently the secretive nature of the Zone was part of the punishment. All she knew was the look of dread she'd seen in people's eyes whenever the topic came up. Thus it was with a sense of trepidation that she stepped through the door with a "Detention" sign thumb-tacked to the front of it.

Inside was a standard-looking classroom, albeit mostly empty. There were only three other students in attendance. She recognised Vogg and the stoner girl immediately. In the corner was a boy she'd never seen before. He had a skinny body and a big head, with giant eyes that were unusually close together. He glanced at her nervously as she entered the room. Vogg's reaction was far more overt. He stood up excitedly, flashing a grin.

"Check it out!" he said to the others. "It's the ultimate badass!"

"Who?" said stoner girl.

"How fucking stoned are you?" said Vogg. "It's the girl that killed Star Geddon. She tore Zenneff's arms and legs off, earlier this morning. You were standing right beside me!"

Stoner girl shot Raza a sideways glance. A flash of recognition passed through her eyes.

"Oh yeah," she said. "I didn't recognise her without that stupid uniform she's always wearing."

Indeed Raza was no longer wearing her uniform. Sketh

had told her to dress for rough conditions, as though she were going on some kind of excursion, so she was presently outfitted in a pair of black jeans, hiking boots, a T-shirt, a sweater and a thick denim jacket. The other students were likewise in streetwear. Vogg wore another ghastly T-shirt, showing an image of a man being force-fed his own intestines.

*Gross!* thought Raza. *That's almost as awful as the one with the foetus monster!*

Otherwise he was dressed like a metal head, his black jacket covered in band patches. Even with the power of the talisman, the names of the bands looked esoteric and unreadable. Raza wondered what he'd look like with the talisman off. Probably like a troll, wearing flayed human faces. Or maybe he really was a metalhead, from some metalhead planet, where the people worshipped riffs and bestial vocals.

Stoner girl was wearing her rugged leather jacket as usual. Otherwise she didn't look dressed for rough conditions at all. Her torso was wrapped with a neon-pink boob tube, though her chest was quite flat.

*Not much boob to tube,* thought Raza.

The girl's skinny stomach was bare. Her jeans had been slashed open so many times they scarcely qualified as pants anymore. Huge rents in the inner thighs left her panties exposed.

*Come on!* thought Raza. *Does this chick ever cover up?*

The big-headed kid in the corner was attired more conservatively, with an argyle sweater and a pair of pleated slacks. She wondered what a clean-cut kid like him was doing in detention. Vogg beat her to the punch.

"Bet you're wondering what we're all doing here, huh?" he said, resting his arse on the side of a desk. "Like, what're we all in for, and shit?"

"I guess," said Raza.

Vogg pointed a thumb at himself. "I'm here for doing

some unauthorized training, outside of the dojo. Trying to hone my ass-kicking skills, you know? Which means I was basically just doing homework! I mean, what kinda bullshit is that, punishing someone for trying to better themselves?"

"Huh," said Raza. "I guess that does sort of sound like bullshit."

"Don't listen to him," said stoner girl. "What he calls 'unauthorized training' means teleporting to other worlds and slaughtering people for fun."

"It's not just for fun!" snapped Vogg. "It's also for learning. Besides, I only attack people who're armed with deadly weapons. Or people who have it coming. Or people who look at me funny. Or annoying people, you know? Like ones who whistle out of tune, or ride their bikes on the footpath . . . "

"You're a maniac!" said stoner girl, laughing.

"Oh, and I suppose you think you're better than me, huh, Zester?" he said. He turned to Raza. "Have a guess what she's in for," he added, pointing his thumb at the stoner girl.

"Um, getting high?" said Raza. It seemed like the obvious conclusion.

"Fuck yeah getting high!" said Zester with a grin.

Raza turned to Vogg and shrugged. "Sorry," she said, "but I don't really see how getting high's on a par with killing people."

"That's because you didn't ask what she's getting high *on*," he said. "Sick bitch likes to get high on human fucking souls, man!"

Raza stared at Zester in shock. Then she remembered the party, where Zester and a bunch of other secretive students had been passing around a pipe filled with ethereal, human-like figures.

"That's . . . that's really fucked up!" said Raza.

"Give me a break!" said Zester. "This whole place is full of hypocrisy, man! The teachers say 'do whatever you want is gonna be the whole of the rules,' or some shit. Then they try and tell you what drugs not to take! And now I'm getting lectured at by a couple of murderers? It's not like I killed those people whose souls I got high on. They were already outside of their bodies when I found 'em! Just floating around, like ghosts. They weren't going up to heaven, or down to hell, or any place in between. They'd slipped through the cracks in the afterlife bureaucracy, man! They'd been forgotten by the gods. You ask me, I was doin' 'em a favour. Who'd wanna float around like that for all eternity?"

Raza remained unconvinced. So, it seemed, did Vogg and the other boy. Zester seemed to sense the disapproval in the room, and changed tack.

"It's not like I *want* to suck on souls," she said. "I'm an addict! My whole family are addicts. My mum, my sister, my stupid inbred cousins. All of 'em! I was raised in a cycle of addiction. A substance-abusing environment! Ms. Sketh says I deserve compassion, not condemnation. Besides, you should see the shithole I was raised on. There's nothing to do on Zelen except suck on souls all day long!"

Raza narrowed her eyes as she heard the name Zelen. Was this the same Zelen she'd learned about already, a flat plane in space that measured six hundred million square miles, made from the blood of an aeons-dead god, the one who'd been slain by her father? The place had no natural resources at all, not even any real features. No hills, no oceans, no mountains, just an endless stretch of dried-up ichor. The people who'd settled there were forced to carry out raids into other worlds and dimensions to steal what they needed to survive, including the souls they used to power their magick. If Zester really was from such a messed-up place, it would surely help to explain her unseemly habit of soul-sucking. Raza decided to find out.

"You're from the Dark Plain of Zelen?" she asked.

"Yeah," said Zester. "So what?"

"So her father *made* Zelen," said the kid in the corner, breaking his silence.

"Oh," said Zester. "Well, you can thank your dad for making a total crap-hole, then."

"He didn't expect anyone to actually live on it," said the big-headed kid. "It was supposed to be a battleground, where the demons could fight with the Demiurge. It's not his fault your stupid ancestors decided to settle in a place with no real food, water or natural resources!"

"Shut up, dork!" said Zester.

The kid fell silent, but smiled, content he'd won the argument. He certainly seemed to know his cosmic history. Once again Raza wondered what such a studious boy was doing in detention.

"What about you?" she asked him. "Why're you here?"

"Well, I'm really into alchemy," he said. "And I wanted to do this experiment, see. But Mr. Vorovox wouldn't let me, said it was way too advanced. So I borrowed some equipment . . . "

"Stole," said Vogg. "He means he *stole* some equipment."

"Right," said the kid. "I stole some equipment and went to do the experiment by myself, in one of the empty old towers." His over-sized eyes filled up with excitement. "It was gonna be really, really cool! I was gonna make this brand-new alloy, a type of metal that could cut through other metals. But I made a few miscalculations, and the experiment went bad. I ended up burning down a part of the school."

"That was *you*?" asked Raza, remembering all the fire alarms that'd gone off while she'd been in the sick bay, not to mention all the smoke that'd gusted through the corridors.

"Yeah, that was me," he said, smiling sheepishly. "I'm Skiddix, by the way. Nice to meet you. It's Raza, right?"

Raza smiled and nodded. The kid seemed to have a keen awareness of his surroundings. She hadn't noticed him, but he'd noticed her. Then again, she was pretty infamous ever since the incident. Still, she felt like things might be finally looking up. These were the first other kids who'd actually been nice to her, after the fuckicide. Vogg had even paid her a compliment, and the others had treated her respectfully. Maybe she'd find a home among the outcasts?

She sat down and smiled again. The measure of camaraderie she'd experienced since she'd entered the room had done a lot to lighten her mood from its burden of misery. It was amazing what a few simple smiles could achieve!

"I guess this is all pretty cool, in a way," she said. "Sort of like *Breakfast Club!*"

"But it's not breakfast time," said Skiddix. "In fact, it's more like afternoon tea."

"She's talking about a movie, dumbass," said Zester. "You know, those things from Earth?"

"A human movie, huh?" said Vogg. "Some of them are actually pretty good, like *Cannibal Holocaust* and *Texas Chainsaw Massacre*. What happens in this one? Wait, don't tell me, let me guess. I bet someone gets killed by a club, right? Like, they're sitting, eating breakfast, then WHAM! Some guy comes in with a hockey mask and bashes their brains in. Blood swirls into their corn flakes, and the title sequence rolls—*Breakfast Club!*"

Vogg made a square with his fingers, as if watching the movie in his mind's eye. Raza laughed. She didn't tell him what the movie was actually about, just let him enjoy his fantasy.

"Earth sounds pretty cool," said Vogg. "I should go there for my next off-the-books training mission!"

*This guy's incorrigible!* thought Raza.

She dreaded to see what would happen if a teenage, demonic metal head went down to Earth and started cracking skulls. Then again, maybe it wouldn't be such a bad thing. There were a lot of people on Earth who could do with their skulls being cracked, after all. Warmongers, terrorists, dictators, human traffickers. The list seemed endless.

Suddenly Vogg let out a burp and put his feet up on the desk. Zester did likewise.

Raza laughed. She couldn't quite muster up a burp, but

she did put her feet up. She was starting to feel pretty relaxed in her new, detention environment.

"I suppose this isn't so bad," she said. "Just having to come here every day for a month. And here I was thinking the Time-Out Zone was gonna be some horrid ordeal!"

The other students stared at her, wide-eyed. Vogg and Zester took their feet down immediately.

"You mean you don't *know*?" asked Zester.

"Know what?" asked Raza.

"The Time-Out Zone isn't this room," said Skiddix. "It's another dimension. A place of incredible danger. We'll be sent there any minute now!"

Raza's eyes popped open wide. At the very same moment someone locked the door from outside. The tumblers CLICKED. The lights began to dim. Strange-looking runes began to blaze all over the room, as if they'd been written in glow-in-the-dark ink. On the floor was a gigantic, mystic triangle, just like the one that had teleported Raza from her parents' house to the steps of Our Lady.

"Buckle up," said Vogg. "It's happening!"

Raza felt a sense of vertigo as the room began to vanish. The walls shrank down and decayed into darkness, like bits of burning paper in a fireplace. Soon there was nothing but the students themselves and a massive, swirling blackness. They gathered together instinctively, huddling in a void without end, an interstice between the dimensions.

Then came light—searing, blinding light. Raza blinked and looked around. The four of them stood in a clearing, surrounded by the foliage of some primeval forest. It reminded Raza of the documentaries she'd seen about dinosaurs, in which CGI graphics had offered a glimpse of the prehistoric past.

Except that this was much weirder. The trees were a myriad of colours—peach, violet, and sunburnt orange. On the trunks were fleshy-looking boles that heaved like wombs in the middle of childbirth. There were bubbling puddles of slime that glistened like iridescent oil spills. From all around came the sounds of untold creatures squawking, chirping and screaming.

One living creature stood before them. A giant, polka-dot caterpillar, sitting on a rock. The thing was as big as a hippo. It had a human face. Raza couldn't help but be reminded of the caterpillar from *Alice in Wonderland*, save that this one didn't have a hookah. It glanced down at them with friendly-looking eyes. It looked like some kindly old grandfather.

"How cute," said Raza, stepping towards it.

"Don't!" snapped Skiddix.

The thing rose up, revealing the vertical mouth that ran down its stomach. The mouth split open wide and roared. Strings of saliva rippled in the gust of charnel breath that blasted from within. The thing slithered down off the rock and reared up before her, ready to swallow her whole.

Then something swooped down and ate it. The flying thing looked like a moth, albeit many times larger, large enough to scoop up the caterpillar with its unfurling tongue and carry it skywards.

No sooner had the moth-thing devoured the caterpillar than a pack of hopping lizards leapt up from the jungle and sank their jagged teeth into its wings, tearing them apart. The moth-thing screamed and fell down from the sky, its colossal tongue unfurling in panic. It crashed to the ground at the edge of the clearing. The reptiles were upon it immediately, dozens of them, feasting like rats on a carcass. Indeed they looked like rats compared to the creature, though each of them was really the size of a horse. They ate the stems of its wings and punctured its thorax, spilling blood that bore the hue of fluorescent honey.

"What the fuck!" shouted Raza.

"It's a Demonic Demesne," said Skiddix, "steeped in the energies of Chaos. One of the many realms that was granted to the demons, after the war. The creatures here mutate super-fast, absorbing the traits of whatever they feed upon.

It's a sort of evolutionary vampirism. That's why that thing had a person's face. It probably ate a human."

"Or a student from Our Lady," said Zester.

"Right," said Skiddix. "Powerful demons throw things in here, just to see what'll happen. Demonic exiles, different species from all different planets, you name it. The alpha predators that live here devour the exiles, then adopt their abilities, becoming even deadlier. All they ever do is eat, evolve, then eat even more. This whole place is one non-stop, murderous free-for-all!"

A terrible screaming sound echoed from the forest. Something was charging towards them from the darkness under the canopy.

"So is this like what happens in *Breakfast Club?*" asked Vogg, as the things charged out into the sunlight.

# Chapter 14:
## Time Out

**T**HE CREATURES CAME out squawking. They looked like giant, murderous turkeys, with sickle-shaped beaks and wattles caked with gore. Their talons were of platinum, their feathers of onyx, like the blades of Aztec warriors. Their numbers grew and grew as they surged from the shadows on their fast-running legs—a dozen, two-dozen, thirty, forty, fifty!

"Fuck!" shouted Vogg.

"Looks like you're gonna get plenty of training in here, tough guy!" said Zester.

Vogg just grinned. Raza watched as he and the others assumed their demon shapes.

Vogg rose up to a full ten feet, a hulking, slouching thing with red and black scales. His muzzled face was a distinctive, demonic fusion of jackal and alligator, with terrible fangs and glowing white eyes.

Zester rose up almost as tall. She stayed just as pale as before. Her neon-green hair became tresses of snakes that slithered and hissed. Her two eyes became four. Her pussy transformed into a chomping, tooth-filled maw.

*Whoa!* thought Raza.

Skiddix's close-set eyes became a single orb that grew and grew until he was little more than a giant, floating eyeball. Dozens of irises spun in different speeds and directions, like the workings of some ocular centrifuge, powering a build-up of light in the centre of his pupil that unleashed into the creatures like a laser beam, scything them down. Raza watched as dozens of murder-turkeys exploded into ashes and lumps of oozing charcoal. The place started smelling like a Christmas-time cook-off.

But it wasn't nearly enough. Dozens more of the things came charging into the clearing. Vogg met them eagerly, picking them up and snapping their necks, like a farmer preparing for some giant chicken dinner.

Zester leapt atop one of the murder-turkeys, impaling her pussy on its head. But this wasn't just some perverted sex act. It was also an act of violence! Her pussy-mouth snapped, beheading the bird. Zester gave a lascivious laugh as the severed neck spurted blood across her snarling vagina. It looked like a mutant cock shooting streams of crimson cum.

*And people said I was a fuckicidal maniac!* thought Raza as she watched in wild-eyed amazement.

Meanwhile Skiddix's eye-beams scythed through the creatures and into the forest, toppling trees and setting flora on fire. Bits of the jungle started burning. Creatures howled as their homes were destroyed.

Still the murder-birds kept coming, crowding the students. Alone at the vanguard, Vogg caught the worst of it. A horde of claws tore his hide into ribbons. Onyx beaks descended like pickaxes. His flesh was healing, but not nearly fast enough. Every time a wound closed over, another two were created. He struck out desperately, biting off heads and cutting down bodies.

"Little help?!" he shouted.

Zester and Skiddix came to the rescue. Zester's serpentine locks envenomed the turkeys, turning them shrivelled and black with necrosis. Too close to use his eye-beams, Skiddix struck out with his electric optic nerves, zapping the murder-birds dead.

All the while Raza was trying to commune with the fire that dwelled inside of her. She could feel it flickering in her veins, bidden into readiness by the proximity of danger. Still it was elusive, like a wild thing that resented being called forth by her consciousness. She managed to catch it, connect with it, feeling a surge of transformative power—but then it was lost. It was as if she were trying to kindle a fire on a windswept beach. She needed more fuel, more heat, more shelter!

But there was no shelter. More of the things kept coming. Soon they'd be overwhelmed.

"New girl!" shouted Zester as a bird bit her hand off. "Hurry up and do something!"

Raza felt a surge of desperation. She didn't want to cower behind the others while they held off the things. Maybe she should leap into the fray, let the murder-birds puncture her body and savage her flesh, until the fire responded from within with murderous violence? But it was one thing to think about leaping into a gaggle of monsters, and another thing to actually do it. Her instincts recoiled from the act. She hung back as the others fought bravely, their bodies covered with more and more wounds. Would she just end up standing there, helpless, watching them die?

Then another set of sounds rose up from nearby. Not squawking this time but terrible roaring. The jumping reptiles had finished with the moth-creature and were now being drawn by the fresh smell of blood. Their bodies were bloated by the banquet, yet they still wanted more. They began to bound across the clearing like mutant kangaroos, covering dozens of feet at a time.

Soon Raza would be completely surrounded. Trapped in her human body, the things would knock her down and start feasting on her flesh. Then surely the change would begin. But would it come in time? Zenneff had been toying with her, back in the dojo, dishing out punishment in manageable doses. But these things ate like piranhas. Would she even be able to react before they'd stripped the very flesh from her bones? She could hardly transform if her skin and organs were already inside of their hungering bellies!

Raza dug deep. This time she took an aggressive stance towards the fire. She didn't try to coax it or catch it, to hold its elusive plumes in her hands. Instead she blew on it, adding fuel to the embers. It flared and grew, spilling out from her veins.

All the while the lizard-things kept leaping towards her, getting closer and closer.

The first one came down—and came apart. Raza swiped out with her claws and tore it to pieces. Once more the change had come in an instant, shredding her clothes and causing her body to grow. At thirteen feet tall she towered over the lizards. Was that shock in their inhuman eyes as they came hurtling towards her, unable to reverse their trajectory? She cut them apart like balloons filled with offal. Weird-looking guts and clots of blue blood shot out hundreds of feet through the forest. Her eye-beams shot out likewise, roasting a dozen before they even hit the ground.

Raza moved like a whirlwind of death. This time her conscious mind was even closer to the fire, as if each successive change brought with it a new phase of intimacy. She didn't have time to think about what that might mean for the future. She just fought on, with a mixture of instinct and intellect, ducking, weaving, slashing, biting, burning with the beams of her glowing red eyes. Soon the reptile horde was no more. She glanced around, feeling a surge of anger as she saw her fellow students buried deep beneath a pile of feasting murder-birds.

She leapt into the fray, giving no heed to her safety. Her claws lashed out, hurling the birds overhead like clods of red earth. Snapping them, rending them, pulling them apart. Blood filled the air in a hot red mist. She lapped it with her mouths as she continued the massacre. The world became a haze of gore and flying black feathers. She could just make out the bodies of the others underneath the scramble, camouflaged by blood and their own ragged wounds. They were moving, squirming, struggling, striving.

She unearthed them like the victims of some avian avalanche, clearing off a mountain of murderous poultry. Onyx feathers snapped between her fangs. Platinum talons reached out to rend her, but she barely even noticed. Her blood was too hot, her attention too focused. Not just on the plight of her comrades, but on the frenzy of the moment. The slaughter was FUN! Not to mention sexy. Juices from her cunt began to mingle with the blood on her thighs. A part of her wanted to kill and fuck and devour all at once in a frenzy of carnal and charnel oblivion. Even when the slaughter was over these urges persisted, making her see even the mangled bodies of her fellows as nothing but pieces of meat to be jammed up her pussy or crammed into her slavering mouths. But her conscious mind was now in tune with her instincts—in tune, and in control. When she saw the state of the others she pulled back from the violence. The fire shrank down before her conscious commands.

"Vogg!" she shouted. "Zester! Skiddix!"

They'd turned back into the likeness of mangled human bodies. Was it too late? She could barely even figure out the state of them, they were so covered in gore from the murder-birds. She picked them up in her claws and shook them one-by-one, trying to rouse them.

Vogg muttered and coughed, spitting out a piece of dead bird. Zester rose up and grasped at her head, as if she'd just awoken with a hangover. Her severed right hand had already grown back. Finally Skiddix picked himself up, warily glancing around.

It seemed like the danger had passed. The clearing looked like a third world slaughterhouse, filled with bodies both dismembered and burning. Sensing they were safe, Raza shifted back down into human form. She was naked but for the talisman.

Vogg looked at the scene of devastation with awe. Half the carnage had been caused by Raza alone.

"Nice work!" he said, giving her a fist-bump.

Raza smiled as her knuckles met his.

"Took her long enough," said Zester. "She spent half the time just standing there!"

"Who cares?" said Vogg. "She still saved our butts."

"I suppose," she said, putting on a show of reluctance. Then she smiled at Raza and gave her a high-five. "Good work, new girl!" she shouted.

Raza grinned again. She was waiting to hear something from Skiddix, but he was too busy staring at her nakedness. She crossed her arms over her nipples and looked at him reprovingly. He stopped perving and blushed so brightly she could see it through the gore on his face.

"Sorry," he said. "I just . . . "

"It's okay," said Raza with a smile. "No biggie."

And she meant it. She was butt-naked, after all. And boys will be boys. Plus, Skiddix was just too sweet to give her the creeps. She already regarded him as something of a friend.

"Where are your clothes, anyway?" asked Zester.

Suddenly Raza realised she was the only one naked. The others, through covered in gore and fresh from the change, were dressed exactly as they had been back in the classroom. Her eyes popped open in surprise.

"Whatta you mean where are my clothes?" she asked. "I should be asking you how come you've still got yours!"

"Duh, because they're magick," said the stoner girl. "Most demons wear clothing that changes when they do. Otherwise you'd have to buy a brand-new set of threads every time you transform!"

"She's right," said Skiddix. "How come you don't have any magickal clothes? Didn't your parents give you any?"

Raza shook her head.

"Wow," said Zester. "Talk about parental neglect. Even my loser junkie mom got me magickal clothing!"

"They didn't mean it as a sign of neglect," said Raza, surprised to find herself sticking up for her parents. "At least

I don't think they did. Magickal clothing just isn't a thing back on Earth."

"Wow," said Zester. "And here I thought Zelen was a backwater! Looks like you'll have to spend the whole time here naked."

Vogg smiled, sleazily. "Hey, I'm not complaining," he said, appraising Raza's figure. "Neither's Skiddix here. Are ya, buddy?"

Vogg elbowed Skiddix in the ribs. He started blushing even brighter. Raza started blushing as well. She couldn't believe she'd be stuck naked for the whole duration of detention! It was like an anxiety dream come to life.

Meanwhile Vogg was still ogling her. It wasn't creepy, more a comical exaggeration. He fluttered his eyebrows like Pepe Le Pew or some cheap-ass gigolo.

"Lay off, pig!" said Zester, slapping him.

"Ouch!" he said. "Give it a rest, will ya? She knows I'm just kidding around. Besides, I'd never mess with Raza. She's murder incarnate!" He gestured to the field of dead bodies. "Still, you've got one thing right. It *is* unfair that Raza has to go naked by herself. Especially after she saved all our butts. So I say it's time for a gesture of solidarity."

Raza watched in surprise as Vogg tore off his jacket and T-shirt with one mighty rip, then started unbuckling his belt. He was both muscular and chubby round the middle, like a Rugby player.

"You, um, you don't have to do that . . . " said Raza.

"It's no problem!" he said. "Besides, it'll make you feel more comfortable."

He kicked off his boots and whipped off his pants. He wasn't wearing any underwear. Raza tried to avoid the sight of his meaty white thighs and dangling member, but the presence of the latter was pretty distracting.

"Come on, you two," said Vogg, addressing Zester and Skiddix. "Get naked!"

"No way!" said Zester.

"Oh, come on," said Vogg. "You go around with your pussy hanging out all over the school anyway. Now's not the time to get modest!"

"You just wanna see my boobs!" she snapped.

"Gimme a break," said Vogg. "You don't have any boobs!"

Zester scoffed, then took off her clothes anyway. She was skinny and pale, like 90s heroin chic. Her bush and unshaved armpits were as green as her hair.

"Happy now?" she said, handing Vogg her clothing.

"Almost," he said, turning to Skiddix. "Come on buddy, your turn."

"I . . . um . . . " Skiddix froze. If his blushing was conspicuous before, it was ridiculous now. He looked like a cheap iron kettle coming to the boil.

"Come on!" said Vogg. "This is Team Naked Badass now. You've gotta be nude to include. Everyone else has done it already. Don't you wanna show solidarity? Besides, this is the forest primeval, man. It's only natural to go in the buff!"

Skiddix hesitated in spite of the pep talk, glancing down awkwardly.

"He's just worried he's gonna pop a boner over Raza," said Zester.

"Am not!" snapped Skiddix.

"It's okay, buddy," said Vogg. "If you get a hard-on, you can just use it to chop your way through the forest, like a machete. That's what I'm gonna do. And I could use someone else to help me clear all the brushwood!"

"Gimme a break," said Zester. "As if your dick could chop through those branches."

Vogg smiled at her. "Babe, just yell 'timber,' and I'll have this whole fucking *forest* coming down."

Zester scoffed, then took a sneaky glance at his groin, as if checking his claims with a visual inspection. Her eyes lingered.

"All right, all right!" said Skiddix suddenly. "I'll do it, okay? Just give it a rest with the peer pressure."

He shyly removed his clothes and handed them to Vogg. His body was skinny and small, making his head look even bigger.

"Okay," said Vogg. "No turning back now!"

He heaved the pile of clothing into a bubbling pit of slime. The garments melted immediately. For a moment the four of them just stood there. Then they started laughing and smiling at each other, like skinny dippers at some isolated swimming hole. There was something thrilling about being naked in that forest. Something terrifying, too. But Raza felt the fear only vaguely. It was as if some part of the fire had crept into her mind and stayed there. She felt like she could face any danger they might come across, brave any horror— even the sight of Vogg's ogrish body.

At length Skiddix spoke, breaking the silence.

"Huh," he said, staring at the melting remains of the clothing. "You know, I just realised something. We could've all just given Raza an item of clothing. Then none've us would've had to go naked."

Vogg paused, pursing his lips. "Oh," he said. "Right."

"Dumbass!" shouted Zester, punching him on the shoulder.

"Hey!" he said. "It's not my fault. You guys went along with it!"

Raza laughed. "Well it looks like we're all naked now," she said. "Except for the talismans."

"Right," said Skiddix. "And they're the only hope we've got of ever getting out of here. Once our time is up, the teachers will use them to bring us back. Which means we need to keep them safe, guard them with our lives."

Raza picked up the talisman that dangled from her neck. It looked pretty precarious, hanging on its string. Still, she figured it must be deceptively robust in some magickal way. After all, it had survived their gruelling battle with the creatures, not to mention the radical changes that her form had undergone.

"If you're so worried about yours, little buddy," said Vogg, "then try sticking it where the sun don't shine. You wouldn't want some critter running off with it. Zester, you could stick yours up your pussy. It'll definitely fit, after all the dicks you've had up in there. Not to mention all those turkey heads!"

Raza was shocked by his frankness, but Zester seemed to take it as a joke. The two of them clearly shared a rapport. Who knew how much time they'd spent together on the fringes of the school? Still, it didn't stop Zester chasing him off across the clearing, her hand raised high to deliver a slap.

"Why you!" she yelled. "Get over here!"

They both started laughing as she chased him hither and thither, leaving Raza and Skiddix alone.

"So, what now?" asked Raza as she stared out across the primordial forest.

"What now?" repeated Skiddix. "Now we do our best to survive!"

Velazelza stood with the others, watching the new students arrive. There were just over a dozen of them. Thanks to the magick of the talisman they all looked like natives of the Chasm of Kirrible, naked and transparent. The new teacher, on the other hand, had the appearance of an incarnate demon. She was short and hairless, with cold blue skin and beady black eyes. Her ornate gown was covered with sapphires. Many students had turned out to watch both her and the newbies arrive, drawn by the unusual promise of so many new faces. Looking for prospective friends, lovers, even targets for bullying.

"This is pretty weird," said Kara, eyeing the arrivals. "We've never had this many new students starting so late in the term. Not to mention a new teacher. It's like they're just coming out of nowhere!"

"Stop being so negative," said Vel. "Some of them might just be decent hockey players. They might even help us cream those demi-jerks from Douche-vinity College!"

"Yeah," said Zibb, eyeing the boys. "Plus, some of them are pretty cute. We need a few new hotties in residence, especially after what happened to Star."

Velazelza's eyes turned dark.

"I told you not to mention him!" she said. "Not him, and not what's-her-name, either."

Vel had taken to referring to Raza by a series of epithets. She got upset whenever anyone mentioned the fuckicide. She'd had feelings for Star, even though she knew he'd seen her only as a once-a-month fuck-doll. And she'd cared about Raza, too. So much, in fact, that she'd decided to share Star with her. And just look what'd happened! She'd lost a lover, and a friend. Sometimes she thought she should just forgive Raza, but the very idea brought up such a maelstrom of conflicting emotions that she couldn't bear to deal with the issue. So she'd settled for banning the topic completely. Only Zibbilique, it seemed, was game to bring it up, indulging in her intermittent bitchiness.

Suddenly Pura's stomach rumbled, very audibly.

"Come on," she said. "Lunchtime's already started!"

They followed the Beetus-Zoid to the cafeteria, passing the procession of arrivals as they went. Vel felt the new teacher's beady eyes upon her. Cold and clinical, like a scientist studying a microbe.

*Creepy!* she thought.

She would've found it even creepier if she saw what the teacher was carrying in her pocket—a slimy, glowing, sapphire eye.

# CHAPTER 15:
## TEAR ASS

**R**AZA AWOKE TO a roar that shook the earth. Other sounds followed, a medley of chirping and screaming that echoed from every single corner of the forest. She sat up, yawned, and stretched her arms above her head.

*Just another day in the Time-Out Zone!* she thought.

She used the term "day" pretty liberally. True to its nature as a realm steeped in Chaos, the Zone possessed cycles of darkness and light that seemed more or less random. Sometimes the triple suns that lit the place would rise up for less than an hour before yielding to periods of long and deep darkness. Other times the light beat down for dozens of hours before finally fading. With no clocks or watches at their disposal, Raza and the others had simply given up trying to accurately reckon the passage of time. Still, it seemed like they'd been in the Zone for quite a while now.

Presently there was sunlight. It shot through the gaps in the roof of their shelter, a makeshift thing made from branches and leaves. In the dappled darkness beside her lay Skiddix and Vogg, both snoring softly. The terrible dangers of the Zone had ensured that Zester was not sleeping with them.

Instead, she was outside on guard duty.

"Good morning!" said Raza as she stepped out to greet her.

"Hey!" said Zester.

She was sitting by the fire, roasting a lizard leg. At first

Raza had wondered how they'd get a campfire going. Then she'd face-palmed! After all, her own demonic eyebeams could kindle one easily. Not to mention the far more powerful beams that could be summoned by Skiddix.

She sat down beside Zester on a carpet of leaves. Once again Raza was amazed by the change that had come over the stoner girl. Not that she could really call her a 'stoner' any longer. The girl hadn't sucked any souls in the whole time they'd been there. She hadn't been able to. Without specialized equipment, Zester couldn't even capture the spirits of the mutating monsters that filled up the Zone.

For the first few days she'd gone through terrible withdrawals. The others had been forced to literally carry her as they fought their way through the jungle. Eventually she'd sweated out the final remains of her physical addiction and been able to assist with the business of survival. Sobriety had changed her noticeably. She was a lot more alert than the bleary-eyed girl Raza had encountered back at Our Lady. Her skin had acquired a healthy-looking tan. She'd even started putting on some weight! To Zester's own delight, most of it had gone straight to her boobs.

It was a change that all of them had been able to notice, being completely butt-naked. For a brief while Raza had tried to cover herself with a leaf, like biblical Eve. But the act was both futile and ludicrous. She'd thought about using the skins of the creatures they'd killed, as well, but without the means of curing them, the pelts remained stinky and gory. No way was Raza gonna put something that gross so close to her pussy! She wondered where Tarzan and Shanna the She-Devil got all those leopard-print loincloths they were all the time wearing. Garments like that would certainly be handy. Still, she'd gotten used to the nakedness after a while. It seemed like they all had, though she'd still catch Vogg and Skiddix perving on her occasionally, when they thought she wasn't looking. She'd even caught Zester sneaking a peek, and more than a few times. She was starting to think the girl was bisexual.

Not that it bothered her. Raza wasn't judgemental about people's sexuality. And even if she was, she'd probably make an exception in this case. Because Zester was her friend now, and so were the others. More than friends, in fact. They'd been living in the Zone for who knew how long. Fighting together, eating together, sharing fire and shelter. They even slept beside each other, cuddling up when the nights got too cold. Not in a sexual way, of course, though Vogg and Zester had started boning pretty quickly, after the latter had finished going through her withdrawals.

Sometimes it was a little bit awkward when they went off to fuck in the forest. Due to the dangers of the Zone, they never went far. Thus Raza and Skiddix were left alone, forced to listen to Vogg's manly grunts and Zester's screaming orgasms. They were louder than most of the creatures that lived in the forest!

Those times were indeed a little bit awkward. Mostly because Raza knew that Skiddix had a crush on her. He'd never made a move, of course. He was too shy—or too considerate—to try it. Raza was grateful for that. She cherished his friendship, but he wasn't her type. After all, his natural form was a floating eyeball with a body made from dangling optic nerves. He looked like a piece of rogue anatomy from a demonic giant. In fact, that's sort of what he was. Skiddix's race had been born from the dismembered body of a titanic monster. Some of the organs had survived independently, including the eyeballs, becoming sentient and mating with each other. Skiddix's planet—Gorlum— was peopled by the evolutionary offshoots of those original organs.

Some of those races didn't seem to get along very well. In fact, Skiddix came off as prejudiced whenever he talked about them. The hearts were stuck-up, he said. The kidneys were dirty. And the less said about the intestine tribe, or the Democratic Republic of Phalloi, the better. Still, she forgave him his bigotry, because he was her friend now, just like the others.

She'd never felt so close to any group of people in her whole life, not even to her parents or her friends back on Earth. She thought it must be somewhat like the bond that soldiers come to feel, when they've been stuck together in some terrible wilderness, or behind enemy lines, forced to rely on each other for everything.

And if nothing else, the Zone was a battlefield. Every other day brought a brand-new conflict with some horrific inhabitant. Creatures who took on the traits of the things they devoured, mutating through some form of evolutionary vampirism. Some, like the giant caterpillar, or the leaping lizards, or the murder-turkeys they'd fought on the first day, looked vaguely like creatures from Earth.

Others were things for which Raza had scarcely any frame of reference at all. Scuttling, undulating monsters that looked like they'd escaped from under a scientist's microscope, like gigantic head lice or titanic germs. Things that didn't even seem to make any sense. Things that bled light, or sound, or heat. Things that vomited sadness or radiated agony. For some reason the talisman had chosen not to shield her from such horrors. Perhaps it was a part of the punishment. Perhaps the magick simply wasn't strong enough to deal with all that madness at once. In any case, the sight of them had given her enough fuel for a lifetime of nightmares.

The good news was that Raza and the others had beaten them all. Vogg was a consummate killer. Zester was no slouch in that department, either. Skiddix's eye was like a cannon of napalm and demonic lightning.

But deadliest of all was Raza. Over time her transformations had gotten easier and easier, as if the fire, like some savage animal adopted and nurtured, had since become her fiercest companion. She only had to reach down now and pour out some fuel. A single impulse was like a tanker of petrol, igniting the flames and bringing the change in an instant. And when she wore the blood-red form of her birthright, she was never again just a passenger. Her conscious thoughts mingled with her demonic instincts, like a pair of electrical storms that had taken to mating. Scintillating, bright, indivisible. The uncontrollable frenzy that had triggered her fuckicidal rampages seemed light years away.

And yet the impulses were there. The urge to eat, fuck and kill all at once. She'd kept a lid on that particular complex of instincts throughout her time in the Zone, but in the throes of an orgasm, would she lose control again? Would she end up chomping off the head of another Star Geddon?

Her guilt about the killing was something she'd discussed with the others, opening up during one of the many long nights they'd spent together in the Zone. They'd been sitting around the campfire. She'd started talking about Star, and all the regret she felt about the fuckicide.

Suddenly Vogg interjected.

"Are you kidding me?" he said. "Why the fuck do you feel bad about killing that guy?"

Raza was shocked. Zester flashed Vogg a look that said *don't go there.*

"What?" he snapped. "She deserves to know."

"Know what?" said Raza.

"That guy was a total jerk!" said Vogg. "All he ever did was ponce around the school, bragging about how he got more ass than a toilet seat. Fucking dandified dickhead. Used to call himself 'the cherry harvester,' or some shit, said he'd bagged more virgins than anyone else in the academy's history. And maybe he had, too, with that whole Prince Charming act of his. Every time a new girl showed up he'd be on her ass within the week, kissing her hand and combing up his stupid fucking hairdo." He glanced at Zester. "I bet he even made a run at you, when you first started out at the academy!"

Zester nodded.

"And I bet you fucked him as well!" said Vogg.

Zester shrugged. "Sure I did. He was hot!"

"Right," said Vogg. "So he was. But afterwards, I bet he dropped you like a flaming hot turd. Am I right?"

Zester shrugged again. "So what if he did?" she said. "It was just a casual thing. It's not like we were married, or dating, or anything . . . "

Zester had a point, but she still looked pretty hurt by the memories.

Vogg turned back to Raza. "And he would've dumped you, too," he said, clicking his fingers. "Just like that."

"So the guy liked to sleep around," said Zester. "And yeah, he probably would've dumped Raza straightaway. But that doesn't mean he deserved to get killed!" She paused, glancing at Raza. "Sorry," she said. "Didn't mean to rub your nose in it."

"It's okay," said Raza sadly.

"The fuck it is!" said Vogg. "That guy was a dick. I'd been wanting to clean his clock for years, but he was always surrounded by his posse of ass-clowns. I say Raza did the school a valuable service. They should've given her a shiny gold sticker. Guy had 'kill me I'm an asshole' tattooed on his forehead. And it's not just because he was a pussy magnet, either. Shit, I'm a pussy magnet, and I don't deserve to die."

Zester snickered. "Yeah, right," she said.

"Well I sure got your pussy magnetized, didn't I? But the fact is the guy was a jerk. He deserved to die on general principle."

"What general principle?" asked Zester.

"On the general principle that I didn't fucking like him!" said Vogg. "And be honest, neither did you. You can't tell me you weren't happy to see him go, not after the way he dumped your skinny ass."

Zester paused, looked into the fire, and shrugged. "Maybe a little," she said. Then she smiled and laughed. "Okay, maybe a lot!"

"Exactly!" said Vogg. "Skiddix hated him, too."

Skiddix wasn't especially keen on being dragged into the

conversation. He didn't seem comfortable talking about sex, especially when it involved Raza. He muttered, his voice trailing off.

"I, um, maybe I . . . "

"Just admit it!" said Vogg. "When Star Geddon died you gave me a high-five in the hallway. Remember?"

Raza was shocked. Had Skiddix also rejoiced over Star Geddon's death? He smiled at her sheepishly, then nodded. Vogg grinned, feeling vindicated.

"See, Raza?" he said. "You were just taking out the trash. I know garbage woman isn't the most glamorous job in the cosmos, but it's still a pretty honest occupation. Certainly nothing worth beating yourself up over!"

Raza fell silent. Her head was whirling. Clearly a lot of Vogg's hatred of Geddon came from jealousy. Probably Skiddix's, as well. Zester's dislike of him came from having been jilted. None of their feelings on the matter were pure. But did they still have a point? Had Star Geddon in fact been a total, raging dickhead?

She'd known Star Geddon was a lady-killer, but she'd had no idea he was so crass and fetishistic about his conquests. She'd even imagined them being in a long-term relationship together. Clearly that had all been an illusion. The more she thought about things in hindsight, and in light of fresh revelations, the more she started to see his actions as . . . what was that word Karanora had used? That's right—disingenuous! He'd been disingenuous. Even through the haze of her infatuation she'd noticed his insincerity. The way he'd played at talking to her, feigning interest just to get her into bed.

Then again, she'd *wanted* to go to bed with him. Even though the way he'd taken her virginity had been sudden and rough, and not at all the way she'd imagined it, she'd still wanted it to happen. But she'd also wanted more, a real love that he'd clearly not been willing to give to her. Maybe her demonic self had sensed his intentions better than she had, and decided to rip him apart before he could do the same to her emotions?

Or maybe it'd been even simpler than that. She thought more and more about the violence of it all. The way he'd torn her open with his tongue, then picked her up and plunged himself into her, with nary a word but a grunt. Maybe her demonic self had simply been responding in kind?

Or maybe she was trying to rationalize it all, think up excuses to let herself off the hook?

Her thoughts remained conflicted. Still, the fact her new best friends all hated the guy made her feel a little bit better. Was it okay to kill someone, just for being a tool? What would her adoptive parents say on the matter, or her deicidal dad? They'd probably just tell her "Do What Thou Wilt Shall Be The Whole of the Law!"

Raza was mulling the whole thing over again as she sat by the campfire that morning, while Zester gnawed hungrily on the lizard leg. Presently Vogg emerged from the shelter, stretching and yawning.

"Good morning, ladies!" he said.

"Morning!" they said.

Vogg walked over to Zester as she sat by the fire. He stood behind her, his penis level with the back of her head.

"You look drowsy from staying up on watch," he said. "Here, let me help wake you up!"

He swung his hips, giving her a turkey-slap across the back of the skull.

"You shit!" she shouted.

He took off laughing as she sprang to her feet and give chase.

*That'll probably end in sex,* thought Raza, chuckling to herself.

Skiddix emerged from the shelter and sat down beside her.

"What's with all the racket?" he said, glancing around. "Are they going at it again?"

"Not yet," said Raza. "But the day is young. And they did just run off into those bushes over there . . . "

Skiddix groaned. "Man, I should've brought earmuffs!"

She glanced at him and laughed, staring into his solitary eye. The illusion provided by the amulet with regards to his features had started to fade by degrees, so that his close-set eyes had merged into one big cyclopean orb. Perhaps soon he'd be all eye, with a body of glistening, electrified nerves.

He smiled back at her. For a moment it looked like he was about to say something. Then he froze and stared down at her chest.

"Skiddix!" she snapped.

She always used his full name, because it had poor nickname potential, and could only really be shortened into some variation of "Skid" or "Dix," neither of which sounded very flattering. Not that it stopped Vogg from using both nicknames liberally.

A few moments later he was still staring at her chest.

"I thought we'd agreed to knock off the perving," she said.

"It's not your boobs I'm staring at," he said. "Look!"

She glanced down. Her talisman was pulsing with a neon-red glow. Suddenly his started flashing as well.

"What does it mean?" she asked.

"It means our stay here is over," he said. "It's time to go back!"

"But how?" said Raza. "Are we just gonna get magicked out of here?"

He shook his head. "No, there has to be some kind of teleportation triangle. I thought maybe the teachers would come in and get us. But it looks like we'll have to find the extraction point ourselves!"

Raza looked up as Zester and Vogg rushed back into camp.

"The talismans are glowing!" shouted Zester.

"We know!" said Raza, leaping to her feet.

"That's funny," said Vogg, holding up his amulet. "The light on mine seems to have faded a bit."

"Mine too," said Zester.

"That's it!" shouted Skiddix. "They're working like homing devices. The brighter they are, the closer we are to the extraction point. We've just gotta go find it. But we'd better move fast. If we don't get there in time, the magick will fade, and we might end up getting stuck here!"

The four of them nodded to each other and took off running through the forest, following the pulse of the amulets. This time the creatures in the Zone seemed to give them a wide berth. Maybe they'd gotten wise to all the carnage being caused by the students, and had finally given up trying to eat them.

Onwards they went, crashing and sprinting through the jungle. The thick canopy cast down a blanket of darkness in which the light of the amulets burned brighter and brighter. Up ahead lay a clearing, in which the foliage gave way to what looked like the side of a mountain.

Except that it wasn't a mountain.

Raza and the others froze as they saw what lay in front of them. In the centre of the clearing sat a monster the size of an apartment building, looming a hundred feet high. One of the apex predators that dwelled in the Zone, it must've been devouring other creatures for untold ages, growing vaster and vaster and more and more mutated as time went by. Its mottled hide was covered with almost every facet of anatomy conceivable, from leathery scales to iridescent sealskin. Banks of limbs and orifices teemed on its pelt—claw-racks, eye-walls, and suppurating masses of varied genitalia.

"Oh fuck!" shouted Vogg as he and the others prepared themselves for battle, adopting their true demonic shapes.

And yet the creature was asleep, a fact they quickly discovered by virtue of its many shuttered eyes and its slow, relaxed breathing. The students froze, standing there as quietly as possible.

Raza glanced down at the talisman that now hung between her four snarling breasts. It was no longer pulsing, but blazing with a solid expression of light. It seemed like they'd reached their destination.

She stared up at the creature. Its face was a gigantic free-for-all of anatomical difference, from the centre of which hung an elephantine trunk with an aperture as wide as a sewer tunnel. The inside was filled with mucus and spiralling rows of dagger-sized teeth.

"Oh shit," she whispered. "We don't have to go in *there*, do we?"

"I sure fucking hope not!" said Zester.

"The teleportation triangle should be inscribed on the ground," said Skiddix. "We just have to sneak past this thing and keep looking for it."

"And if that thing's sitting on top of it?" asked Zester.

"Then we carve our way through it!" said Vogg.

Despite the bravado of his statement, even he seemed unconvinced. The creature was mammoth! And many of its features were distinctly demonic. Who knew how many students of Our Lady it had previously devoured?

"Come on," said Raza, seizing the initiative. "Let's skirt the clearing around it!"

They did as she suggested, following the tree line, searching for the site of the teleportation triangle. And yet every time they drew away from the creature, the light of the talismans faded and started anxiously flashing. Soon they'd described a half-circle around the creature, arriving at its backside.

"It's the moment of truth," said Skiddix. "Either the triangle's somewhere further afield, or it's right under that thing's giant arse!"

"You don't know how right you are, buddy," said Vogg. "Look!"

They glanced into the clearing. The creature was sitting almost cross-legged, so that its giant backside was plonked on the ground just a few feet in front of them. Its butt cheeks rose up like a pair of giant, dimpled rock faces, covered with blubber, scales, and plates of gleaming exoskeleton. Jutting outwards just below its left butt-cheek was the very edge of the teleportation triangle. The rest was covered by its titanic arse.

They watched as the runes on the edge of the triangle started to glow. The magick was activating, preparing to take them back home. All they had to do was step into the triangle whilst wearing their amulets. But that was easier said than done.

"Fuck!" said Zester. "It's sitting right on top of it!"

"Well we have to do something," said Skiddix. "The magick's already active. It won't stay that way forever. We've gotta get inside the triangle, now, before the power fades! But how?"

"Isn't it obvious?" said Vogg. "We've gotta tear that ass up! And not in a sexy way. You think you're up for it, Raza?"

Raza glared at the monster's giant backside, and grinned like a wolf.

"Let's do it!" she said.

They crept into the clearing, trying to keep the element of surprise. It wouldn't last long. On a silent count of three they rushed at the monster, performing a synchronised attack on its butt-cheek.

Raza tore into the flesh with her claws.

Vogg bit a chunk of it out. "Tastes like ass!" he yelled.

Zester lashed out with her serpentine hair, injecting the arse-cheek with necrotic venom. Slabs of variegated tissue started dissolving immediately.

Skiddix unleashed his eye beam, burning through the dermis and fat. The cheek was particularly full of the latter. It crackled and boiled and poured onto the ground, soaking the soil with a sudden, loud HISS!

Smoke whipped up as they continued their attack. When it cleared they felt their hearts begin to sink. The cheek was only lightly chipped away. Enough of it remained to cover the bulk of the triangle. They'd never fit between the lines and sigils of power that would send them back home to Our Lady—not unless they managed to tear up more of that arse!

But it sure was one powerful badonkadonk. So tough, in fact, that the creature had so far remained oblivious to their assault and was still sleeping soundly.

Their talismans started flickering feverishly.

"Oh fuck," said Skiddix. "That must be a warning. The magick's starting to fade!"

"Give it all you've got!" shouted Raza, once again taking charge.

She opened up with her eyebeams on the backside. So too did Vogg, Zester, and Skiddix. A rainbow of destruction blasted the arse like some kind of psychedelic death ray. Molten fat poured out, burning their feet, but they kept their heels dug in firmly, giving it everything they had.

At length the beams faded. They blinked their eyes, exhausted, having poured out so much of their demonic energy. Like a sprinting athlete or a champion boxer, even a demon could only perform for so long before being overwhelmed with exhaustion.

They'd given it their all. They edged closer, waiting for the smoke to clear. It did, revealing a blasted crater in the cheek that looked almost big enough for them to fit in, if they'd only shift back to their smaller mortal bodies.

"Hurry," said Zester. "We have to change back!"

"And if the creature attacks us?" said Skiddix. "We won't have the strength to shift again. We'll be defenceless!"

The talismans were flickering faster and faster, a desperate crescendo. It was now or never.

"We'll have to take that chance!" said Raza, shifting down to human form. "Come on!"

The others followed suit, shifting back and huddling up inside the cratered left butt-cheek. They just managed to fit inside the edge of the triangle. Their talismans started to pulse in tune with the runes on the ground, synchronizing themselves to the magick. It was working. They were about to get sent back home to Our Lady!

A terrible roar split the air. Whether finally roused by the pain of its wounds or the scent of its own burning backside, the beast had awoken.

Raza huddled down and covered her ears, but it was already too late. The sound had blown out both of her feeble human eardrums. Blood pooled on her palms as she vainly tried to shelter her ears from even more damage.

The earth quaked as the monster started to rise. Its backside lifted up like a levitating mountain and hung in the air for a moment above them.

It was a horrible moment. Above them the cratered cheek loomed, smoking and gaping. Underneath was a bevy of anal architecture Raza wished she'd never had to gaze upon. The creature seemed to have absorbed the sphincters of every being in creation, adding them to its posterior like stickers to a scrapbook.

*So gross!* she thought.

Fear replaced revulsion as the creature lost its balance and its gigantic backside fell back down toward them like a misshapen meteor. None of them dared leave the circle and get stuck in the Zone, but could they escape before that posterior turned them to paste?

The triangle flared.

The cheeks slammed down.

The world was plunged into darkness.

# CHAPTER 16:
## HOMECOMING

**R**AZA SAW A familiar landscape cohere from the blackness between the dimensions—the interior of the detention room, the same one they'd left so long ago. The triangle had worked its magick just in time, preventing them from being butt-slammed into oblivion.

"Talk about a tear-ass journey!" said Vogg.

Raza's eardrums grew back just in time for her to hear the joke—and groan at it.

"I guess we're finally back," said Skiddix. "You think the place'll be the same as before?"

"Are you kidding me?" said Vogg. "This joint never changes. It'll be just as crazy as it was when we left it!"

*Like the Celestial Fire at the heart of the void,* thought Raza. *Roiling and boiling in a state of mutation so extreme that it stays ironically consistent over the long term.*

It did indeed feel good to be back. After the terrible dangers of the Zone, Our Lady's interior seemed like a sheltering womb. Even if it *was* filled with students who looked down on her with a mixture of fear and derision, who vandalized her dorm room and put goat's balls in her bed. Somehow all that stuff no longer seemed to bother her so much. She'd faced an army of monsters and survived. She'd mastered the arts of demonic transformation. And perhaps, most importantly of all, she'd found a new group of friends who'd stick by her side through anything—fire, flood, even cosmic invasions of cannibal clowns and flesh-eating centipedes. She'd probably still be an outcast in the halls of Our Lady, but she was no longer alone, and that difference meant everything.

Suddenly the door clicked open and a demon walked in. Raza had been expecting Belzoa, Sketh, or another familiar member of staff. She was surprised to see a demoness with cold blue skin and a shiny bald head. Her black dress was dotted with sapphires. Her beady eyes regarded them with casual disdain, like a scientist studying a microbe. Raza felt a sense of creeping dread. The woman reminded her of Mr. Willis, the loathsome teacher from Earth.

In certain ways the resemblance was uncanny, mostly in the cast of the eyes. For a moment she got the eerie sense that Willis and this demoness were one and the same being! But surely that was just her imagination talking. After all, Mr. Willis had a been a middle-aged human with wattles and a paunch. This demoness was ethereal, majestic, a vision of eternal youth with an aura of inestimable age. Just because they had similar eyes and the same creepy stare surely didn't mean anything. Right?

*Wow,* thought Raza. *I must've been really traumatized by Mr. Willis' class!*

After all, this was the second time she'd been reminded of him since she'd arrived at Our Lady. She'd seen an echo of his features in the symmetrical face of the angel on her very first day at the school. Both sightings had sent chills up her spine. But surely it was all a coincidence, a phantom of fear summoned forth by her loathing of Willis. What was next? Would she see his face in the dregs of her breakfast cereal, in the glittering nebulas that hung in the void above campus? She had to get this morbid fear out of her head. After all, she was a demon. She could tear Mr. Willis apart with her bare hands if she wanted to. Maybe one day she'd take a trip back to Earth, and do just that!

For a while the mysterious demoness just stood there, staring disdainfully at their naked, gore-covered bodies.

Then she tossed each of them a towel embroidered with the logo of Our Lady.

"Congratulations on surviving the Zone," said the demoness. Her voice was cold, her breath even colder, misting like dry ice and sending a chill through the room.

Raza got goosepimples all over. She shivered and wrapped the towel around herself, suddenly feeling acutely aware of her state of undress.

"I'm Noviscula," said the demoness. "The new school principal."

"But Our Lady doesn't have a principal," said Skiddix. "All appointments are decided by the Staff Bludgeon . . . "

"I'm afraid that's a thing of the past," said Noviscula. "There've been some changes around here. After Mr. Zenneff's brutal dismemberment, the schoolboard decided it was time to carry out some reforms, starting with the introduction of a proper staff hierarchy. I was sent to get things in order. In a way, I suppose I should thank young Shahrazad here for my appointment." Noviscula paused, staring coldly at Raza. "But that would be an unfair reward for bad behaviour," she added. "Which brings me to some of the other changes that have been implemented here, namely in the area of discipline. In the past it was thought sufficient that troublesome students should merely be sent to the Zone. Those who survived would be pardoned for their actions. It is my feeling that this system lacks a sufficiently punitive dimension . . . "

"Are you serious?" asked Skiddix. "The Zone is a horrible place. We had to fight to survive every day!"

"Indeed," said Noviscula. "And yet punishment should not merely be a test of one's capacity for survival. After all, should we just have all the murderers murder each other in some free-for-all, and set the most successful ones free? Such a practice would constitute a mockery of justice, and would only create more consummate killers. And yet that's exactly what's been going on at Our Lady. The Zone rewards brutality, and eschews all aspects of rehabilitation, allowing troublesome students to become even more turbulent. True punishment, on the other hand, requires a form of deprivation that cannot be overcome by the application of violence. How else are the guilty supposed to learn from their mistakes, and achieve positive growth? Therefore you are all to be subjected to additional penalties. Skiddix, you are to lose your laboratory access. All of your alchemical research will be purely theoretical. Any experiments you wish to carry out will be conducted by a lab partner, and only then after you've acquired written permission."

Skiddix looked crushed. The principal moved on.

"Vogg, it seems like you're only interested in physical brutality. You need to expand your horizons. Thus you are banned from all martial arts competitions in the upcoming Interschool Championship against Divinity College. If you want to compete, you may apply to join the netball or badminton teams, instead."

"But those're the girliest sports in the whole fucking universe!" said Vogg.

Noviscula ignored him and turned to Raza.

"Shahrazad. Since your infractions are the worst of all, you are to be banned from the Championship completely. You may continue to run, but you may not compete. Is that clear?"

Raza nodded. She didn't really care that much about competing against Divinity College anyway. Next to the others, she felt like she was getting off lightly. Finally the principal turned towards Zester.

"Zester. Since you don't seem to partake in any extracurricular activities, other than the use of narcotics, your punishment will be to develop a work ethic. You are to report to the cafeteria for dishwashing duty, starting today, and continuing every day until the very end of the term. Understood?"

Zester let out a moan, then nodded.

"And now," said the principal, "may I all suggest you all go clean yourselves up and get ready for class? The day is about to begin."

With that she turned and strode away.

"Man, what a see-you-next-Tuesday!" said Zester as the principal's footsteps receded down the hall.

"I can't believe I'm banned from the lab!" said Skiddix. His giant eyeball quivered, as though he were going to cry.

"Chin up, buddy," said Vogg, placing a comforting hand on his shoulder. "It's only till the end of term. That's only two weeks away."

"I'm sorry, guys," said Raza. "It feels like this is all my fault."

"Don't be ridiculous," said Vogg. "Students've done way worse stuff than dismember a teacher, and the schoolboard's never reacted like this before. I say something fishy's going on around here!"

"Like what?" asked Zester.

"I don't know," said Vogg. "But did you hear the shit that bitch was coming out with? All that stuff about justice, morality, and rehabilitation? She didn't sound like any demon I've ever met before!"

"And just what is a demon supposed to sound like?" asked Zester. "We're all free to believe whatever we want. So I guess she's free to be a total cow!" Zester paused, sighing. "Fucking dishwashing, man. I can't believe it!"

"Right," said Vogg. "And here I was, saying everything would be just the same as before. Serves me right for shooting my mouth off!"

"Come on guys," said Skiddix dejectedly. "Let's go get ready for class."

Dressed in their towels, the four of them shuffled out into the hallway.

"At least the rest of the place won't've changed too much," said Zester.

But she was wrong. The corridors were eerily quiet. It was

early morning, which might've explained a great deal of the silence. After all, few of the students were early risers. And yet the place still should've been resounding with noises, if not from the early birds, then at least from the pupils who'd stayed up partying all night and into the morning. Instead the place was as quiet as a tomb. They could hear the soughing of the astral winds through the trees of the courtyard, and the sound of their feet on the tiles echoed down the hall.

"This is creepy, man!" said Zester.

The place was cleaner too. A lot of the ever-present graffiti had been scrubbed off or painted over. Soon enough they found out why. Belzoa was kneeling in the hallway, dressed in a filthy boilersuit, cleaning one of the walls with a sponge and a bucket of water.

Raza's eyes popped open with shock. Was the cantankerous old demon finally getting to grips with all the "shit work" he'd been stuck with? He glanced up at the four of them.

"Oh, hey, kids," he said. "Good to see you all survived the Zone."

"Yeah," said Vogg. "But I'm starting to feel like this place is even scarier. What're you doing cleaning the place up? You're getting rid of all its charm. Besides, how am I supposed to find my seat in class if my name isn't written there anymore?"

"Principal's orders," said Belzoa as he went back to scrubbing the wall. "And if you ask me, it's about time this place got sorted out. Now get to class and get out of my hair!" he snapped.

The students saw his eyes flare up with fire, and they shuffled along.

"Man," said Zester. "That principal's really got Belzoa's balls in a vice. I never thought I'd see him taking orders from anyone!"

"This whole place is going to the dogs," said Vogg. "I can't believe it's changed so much in the month we've all been gone. I might have to try and get myself transferred!"

"Don't say that!" said Raza. "I thought we were in this together?"

"I'm just kidding," said Vogg. "I'd never leave you guys. This place might be turning to shit, but Team Naked Badass is still going strong. As long as we stick together, everything will be cool!"

The four of them smiled at each other. Then the morning bell rang, telling the students that classes would begin in thirty minutes.

"Shit, we'd better hurry," said Skiddix. "We still have to shower and get dressed. Who knows what kind of punishments that bitch is dishing out for being late? Pretty soon we'll have to have hall passes!"

"Don't let her intimidate you," said Vogg. "We conquered the Zone. Ain't no stupid new rules gonna slow us down. Besides, if she tries anything else, you can just burn half the place down, like you did before."

Skiddix gave a reluctant smile.

Raza's eyes popped open wide.

"Shit!" she said. "I just realised I've run out of uniforms. They've all gotten wrecked since I started here! I don't think I've got any clothes left at all . . . "

"That's what happens when your ghetto parents don't give you any magickal threads," said Zester, jokingly. "Guess you'll have to go naked here, as well!"

"Maybe we can all go naked," said Vogg. "Start a brand new fashion trend."

"No way!" said Zester.

"You're just worried I'll get swamped with chicks once they see my package, and you'll have to go back to diddling yourself every night, all alone in your room," said Vogg.

"Get fucked!" she retorted.

"That's exactly what I'm predicting would happen," he said.

Zester slapped him. Then they started kissing, bumping up against a nearby wall. Vogg's towel fell loose, exposing his big, hairy arse.

"Come on guys," said Raza. "We're back at school now. You can save that stuff for behind closed doors!"

"Preferably sound-proofed ones," said Skiddix.

"Ha, ha," said Zester as she and Vogg broke loose from their embrace.

"Besides," said Skiddix, "have you guys forgotten about the problem at hand? Raza doesn't have any clothes. She can't go to class in a towel!"

"Is there a school shop?" asked Raza.

"Yeah," said Vogg. "But the clothes there are lame. They might be magickal, but you'll come out looking like a total dork."

"But I bought my clothes at the school store . . . " said Skiddix.

Vogg just grinned, as if to say *I know*.

"I know what to do!" said Zester. "Raza, you just relax. Go have a shower, then head to your room and wait for us there. We'll be there in fifteen minutes!"

# Chapter 17:
## Team Naked Badass

**R**AZA STOOD IN front of the mirror, modelling her new outfit. The others had raided their wardrobes to supply her with clothes. On her feet were a pair of Vogg's heavy boots. She was surprised how well they fit. Despite his brutish size, the guy had some dainty little feet. Nevertheless, there was no way his pants would fit her skinny legs, so she wore a pair of Zester's torn-up jeans. The absence of fabric around the arse and inner thighs made her too exposed, so underneath she'd donned a set of stockings with red-and-black stripes to cover up the skin. It gave her a Nineties punk look.

On her chest she wore one of Vogg's metal T-shirts. It'd shrunk in the wash, making it cling tightly to her figure. Zester didn't have any bras to give her, so Raza's free-floating boobs were outlined clearly by the fabric. She didn't mind so much. She'd grown used to going braless in the Zone, and was starting to enjoy the lack of restriction. And bras always gave her a strip of pimples on her back, where the straps clung tightly to the skin and caused the hairs to grow in, providing her with yet another reason not to wear one. Still she wondered whether she'd have to worry about sagging, or if her demonic birthright would keep her breasts perky forever. Only time would tell!

She inspected the T-shirt. It bore the same gruesome image she'd seen Vogg sporting before, that of a monstrous foetus punching its way from a woman's pregnant womb. The image still disgusted her, but wearing it made her feel rebellious and cool. Besides, it was mostly other people who'd have to put up with looking at it anyway. Like all those boys who'd no doubt try and get an eyeful of her braless chest. This way they'd get a dose of horror at the very same time! The idea of juxtaposing her nipples and curves with that image of gore felt fun and mischievous. She supposed at some point she'd actually have to listen to the band whose name was emblazoned above the image in barely-readable writing. Otherwise she might feel like a bit of a poser!

Last but not least she wore one of Zester's leather jackets. It fit Raza perfectly, like an old glove. Clearly Zester had been wearing it for years.

"Thank you!" said Raza, giving her a hug. She felt honoured to have been given such a prized piece of clothing. She almost felt like she could cry.

The only person who hadn't contributed to her outfit was Skiddix. Vogg and Zester had insisted that his clothes were too lame. In fact, they'd made him go through a wardrobe change, as well. He stood there beside her, looking sheepish in his new ensemble of black jeans, sneakers, and cowboy shirt embroidered with pistols and skulls. His single eyeball was covered by a monocle that looked like a pair of classic aviator shades, albeit with only one lens.

"I'm not sure it's me," he said, staring doubtfully at his reflection.

"I think you look great," said Raza.

"Really?" he said. He blushed, then preened before the mirror. Suddenly it seemed like he appreciated the outfit very, very much.

"You both look cool," said Zester.

"Shit yeah," said Vogg. "But most importantly, Team Naked Badass now has a definite aesthetic. It's just a shame we didn't bring any trophies from the Zone to tie things together more. Like, we could've all worn a set of dried-up lizard balls, or something!"

"That makes me glad we *didn't* bring anything back," said Raza.

"Well maybe we could make some patches," said Zester. "Then we'd be like a real gang. We just need to come up with an image! What's right for Team Naked Badass?"

"A bare ass, obviously," said Vogg. "A bare ass with an angry face on each cheek, and a fist coming out of it, WHAM!"

The others laughed.

"That's the worst idea I've ever heard," said Zester. "A bare arse shitting a hand?"

"It's not *shitting* the hand," said Vogg. "The hand's just coming out from between the cheeks. Because it's a Bad Ass. Get it?"

"Sounds like people would think we're into fisting, or something."

"Don't be stupid. You can't fist in reverse!"

"I could fist you in reverse. I'd just have to shove my hand all the way down your throat!"

"Kinky!" said Vogg.

They started wrestling on the bed.

"Well," said Raza, "if we do come up with a design, I could maybe get my mother to make the patches. She was always great at embroidery . . . "

Raza paused. That was the second time she'd said something nice about one of her parents in recent weeks. Was her anger toward them beginning to soften?

Vogg and Zester rose up off the bed, joining the others in front of the mirror. They did indeed look a bit like a gang. Raza felt a surge of excitement. No way any other students would mess with her now! And if they did, they'd have to tangle with Team Naked Badass.

"Hold on," said Vogg. "I've got the perfect song to play!"

He took some kind of mobile music device from his pocket. It looked to Raza like an iPod with a small dock of speakers. But that was just due to the magick of the talisman.

What did it really look like? A severed, singing human head? A ball of flesh with a mouth on one side? A tiny, singing figure, trapped in a rune-covered jar, forced to belt out tunes or be zapped by bolts of lightning?

The music started blaring. Raza had been expecting the Cookie Monster vocals and super-fast drumbeats of a death metal track. Instead she heard Patti Smith singing the opening lines of "Rock N Roll Nigger."

Raza had never heard the song before. The tune was wild and exuberant. She started dancing with the others, then stopped when the chorus kicked in. To her ears it sounded pretty racist!

"Um, isn't this a bit offensive?" she said.

Vogg groaned. "She's not making fun of black people, Raza," he said. "When she says 'nigger,' it's not used like a racial slur. It's referring to outsiders in general, people who aren't a part of the mainstream. Artists, rebels, individualists, people like that. And she's not saying it's bad to be a 'nigger,' or an outsider, either. She's saying she is one, and that's all she wants to be!"

"Huh," said Raza. "When you talk about it like that, it doesn't seem racist at all . . . " She was shocked that Vogg could show such a subtle appreciation of Earth culture, maybe even more subtle than her own. "But hold on a second," she said. "This is an Earth song. So how come you know so much about it?"

"We studied it in the 'Cultures of the Cosmos' elective. That's when I got to watch *The Hills Have Eyes, Natural Born Killers,* and a bunch of other masterpieces of human cinema. But I especially liked this song. And it's perfect for Team Naked Badass. Because we're a bunch of niggers, too!"

Raza felt a flush of discomfort when he said the N-word.

"Okay," she said. "I see your point. But maybe we could still not say that word?"

Vogg ignored her and started singing along with the track.

"Nigga nigga nigga nigga nigga nigga NIGGA!"

Raza shrugged and went back to dancing with the others. She was sweaty and flushed by the time the song finished. A moment later the bell rang, giving them a five-minute warning. They let out a collective groan.

"Guess it's time to go to class," said Zester.

They strode out into the hall, where other students were bustling about. Raza felt a tremor of anxiety. Then she paused, and smiled. The unease she'd felt before she left for the Zone was still there, but only at the back of her mind, shrivelled and feeble, her confidence soaring above it. With her friends by her side, she felt invincible. She walked with a swagger in her step. They all did.

Students paused to gawk at them as they strode down the hall. There was fear in their stares, even more so than before. Raza sensed it with the keenness of a wolf, courtesy of the demonic instincts that had fused with her consciousness during her time in the Zone. What's more, the sight of those terrified eyes no longer made her feel self-conscious, but exultant.

Maybe it was her demonic instincts that made her revel in the atmosphere of dread. Then again, she felt like she'd earned the right to be feared, having faced the horrors of the Zone.

She wondered if her newfound status as a detention survivor would make people think twice before they messed with her again. *If not*, she thought, *then they'll have to face the consequences.* Raza still felt bad about what'd happened to Star, but she wasn't about to take any shit for it. Not any longer, and not from any other source than from her very own conscience.

Suddenly a pair of boys started whispering, as if responding to her own inner monologue.

"Check it out," said one. "They survived!"

"Guess that means Raza didn't have sex with them!" quipped the other.

*Guess that gives me my answer,* thought Raza.

She and the others might've been objects of dread, but they were still outsiders, a tiny group at odds with the majority. Perhaps sheer weight of numbers made the others feel safe enough to keep engaging in ridicule? It wasn't a feeling they'd get to hold onto much longer. Vogg broke away from the group and walked over to the whispering pair.

"What'd you just say, shithead?" he snapped, addressing the one who'd made the joke.

The other boy slunk off. The joker stayed face-to-face with Vogg. Unfortunately for him, he had his back to a steep flight of stairs. Vogg reached out and pushed him, hard, sending him hurtling down to the landing below. He broke his neck with an audible CRACK!

*Holy fuck!* thought Raza. *Guess we're going back to the Time-Out Zone!*

Then the boy sat up, his wound already healed. Raza felt a surge of relief. Even after all this time, she still found herself forgetting just how tough demons were. Any human would've been crippled or killed by such blow, but the boy seemed more or less fine. Physically, at least. Otherwise he seemed terrified, shrinking into himself as Vogg took a step down the stairs.

"Spread the word, dick-breath," he snapped. "From now on, anyone who messes with Raza is gonna be on a one-way train to Mutilation Station, Dismemberment City. It'll make what happened to Zenneff look like a minor shaving accident. You got me?"

The boy nodded frantically. Vogg sneered down at him, then smiled as he strode back to the others. A small part of Raza felt appalled by the casual violence. But the rest of her felt great. She grinned back at Vogg, and the four of them strode on down the corridor.

On the way, Raza heard Patti Smith's "Rock N Roll Nigger" start to play in her head. She imagined herself and the others in their own private movie, walking in slow-motion to the sound of the track. She felt so cool!

The student body parted before them like the waves of the Red Sea as they strode off to class. Eventually Skiddix peeled off from the group, waving goodbye. Raza still couldn't believe he was two years below them. He was probably the smartest member of Team Naked Badass.

Soon they arrived outside Sketh's cosmic history class. Raza froze as she saw Vel and the others striding down the hallway from the opposite direction.

She felt another tremor of anxiety. But most of all she felt anger. These girls had claimed to have been her friends, but when she'd needed them most, they'd tossed her away like a soiled tampon. She oughta knock their fucking teeth in!

Instead she just strode past them, cutting them off as they walked towards the classroom. It was an epic snub. Raza felt a surge of triumph as she entered the class, leaving them standing in the hallway behind her, dumbfounded. She took her place with Zester and Vogg at the back of the room.

She was expecting to find another volume of cosmic history waiting on her desk, another hallucinogenic tome that would help her catch up with the rest of the class. She thought there'd be a pair of tomes waiting for Zester and Vogg as well, since they'd all been gone for so long in the Zone, but there was nothing on any of the desks save graffiti.

"Miss Sketh?" she said, raising her hand. "Could we get some catch-up volumes, please?"

For a moment Sketh stared at her. Gone was her warm, friendly smile. Instead she looked both sad and exhausted, like one of those overworked, underpaid teachers on Earth.

"I'm sorry, Raza," said Sketh. "But I'm afraid students will no longer be given any specialized, individual treatment. It's the principal's orders. You'll just have to join in with the rest of the class as best as you're able."

Raza tried to follow Sketh's instructions, but it wasn't easy. The lesson dealt with events, people and places she'd never even heard of. Eventually she just gave up trying to engage with the material, and spent her time glancing around the classroom. A new boy was sitting in Geddon's old seat, bathing in the sun that came streaming through the window. He was almost as handsome as Star, with tanned features and long blond hair. Come to think of it, it seemed like there were a lot of other new students in the class, too. Had she just forgotten people's faces during her time in the Zone, or had there been an influx of pupils during her absence?

She ignored the other newcomers and focused on the boy, feeling a tingle between her legs as she studied him. Maybe he'd provide her with a chance to test her sexual limits, to see if she'd truly attained control over her demonic instincts? The idea was both scary and exciting.

*Of course, maybe he'll be scared off by my fuckicidal reputation*, she thought. *Maybe all the boys will be. Maybe I'll get desperate enough to hook up with Skiddix!*

Immediately she felt bad about the impulse. Skiddix was her friend, and it wouldn't be right to exploit his feelings like that, not when she didn't feel the same way. That would make her just as bad as Star Geddon had been.

Suddenly she felt another tingle, but not between her legs. It was the chilly feeling of her hackles rising from some instinctive sense of dread. She glanced across the room and found the reason why. The principal was standing in the doorway, auditing the class. The woman's beady eyes were staring right at her, scrutinizing her, as though she were an insect about to be dissected. It reminded Raza of the way Mr. Willis had stared back on Earth. And those beady black eyes were so similar. It gave her the creeps!

At length the principal strode off down the hall. Soon after the lesson was complete. Raza and the others headed to the dojo, where Zenneff arrived in a more punctual manner than usual. His arms and legs had grown back, and were sheathed in brand-new pieces of armour. Bone-like scabs had grown out through the gaps in the plates, fusing them to his flesh. He looked as good as new.

And yet his manner was different. He seemed even more

curt than usual, and made no particular mention of Raza or the others, nor the fact that they'd returned from the Time-Out Zone. Instead he just guided the class straight into demonic meditation. Sitting with the others, Raza was able to transform immediately. Despite the demonic bloodlust that went shooting through her brain, she sat there meditating in her monstrous murder-form, as still as a statue. She felt sure that Zenneff would remark on her incredible progress.

Instead he said nothing. She wondered if he was somehow angry with her, but that wouldn't make any sense. After all, he'd congratulated her after she'd torn off his limbs, even pledged to give her an A+ for her efforts. So why was he ignoring her now? It turned out he wasn't giving individual feedback to anyone. Just what was up with him, anyway?

Soon it came time for a combat exercise. Raza put her hand up immediately. She wanted to make Zenneff proud. He might've knocked her around, but he'd just been trying to help her, albeit in his own unique and very violent way. To tease out her true potential. She also knew he'd tried to stop her from being sent to the Zone, even after the injuries she'd given him. Along with Sketh, it seemed like he was the only teacher who truly believed in her.

But Zenneff didn't choose her. He didn't choose anyone—not specifically, anyway. Instead the students were called up to fight in alphabetical order. Raza would have to wait days, maybe even weeks, until the alphabet revolved and her own name was called out. She sat there disappointedly, watching the kids with the "B" surnames fight against a horde of summoned monsters. The creatures looked like zebras whose stripes were zigzagging mouths filled with gnashing black teeth.

At some point during the melee, Raza felt her hackles rise again. She glanced around, finding the principal standing in the doorway, auditing the class. The woman was staring at her again.

*What is this creepy bitch's problem?* wondered Raza.

At length the class ended. Raza rushed up to Zenneff as the others filed out of the hall.

"Hi, Mr. Zenneff," she said with a smile. "I'm glad you're all better. I'm so sorry about what happened. But I wanted you to know I learned a lot about controlling my powers while I was stuck in the Zone. So maybe, if you still want to, we could do some of those private lessons you told Sketh about?"

Zenneff's face was hard and inscrutable.

"Students are no longer allowed to receive any forms of special treatment," he said. "Principal's orders. Now run along, Raza. The class is dismissed."

Raza left the hall, feeling both puzzled and saddened. She didn't understand how anyone, even a demonic principal with breath like dry ice, could make a teacher like Zenneff change his tried and true methods.

*Whoever this bitch Noviscula is,* thought Raza, *she must have some serious mojo at her disposal! I wonder how many other weird-arse changes she's implemented?*

There were many. The free-flowing debate that had previously characterized Chaos Theory class had been banished entirely, replaced with a series of multiple-choice questionnaires. Ms. Kellikassey handed them out with an almost robotic air. The demoness seemed withdrawn, deflated. Even her aura of lust was noticeably dampened. Instead of raging hard-ons, the boys in the class only got semi-erect. Raza could tell—she was watching very closely! For her part Raza's pussy barely even got moist as she sat there filling out the questionnaire. It dealt not with philosophical questions, but with ostensible facts about the universe. The questions had a leading, condescending quality, and weren't very challenging at all. Raza felt like the whole thing was an insult to her intelligence. Eventually she gave up in disgust, and just answered "C" to every single question.

Art class was almost as weird. Instead of working on their own individual pieces, the students were forced to make collages using clippings from magazines. Raza felt insulted yet again. It wasn't that she thought collage was an inherently shit form of art, or anything, although her feelings on the matter did lean rather strongly in that direction. It was just that she wanted to draw! As a sign of protest she made a brown collage, with as many pictures of shit in it as possible. But the teacher just smiled, nodded, and accepted her work. She looked just as beaten down as Kellikassey had.

Track and Field was the only class that hadn't really changed. And even though Raza had been banned from competing in the Interschool Championship, she didn't really care. She just enjoyed running. Not for others, but for herself. To feel the burn in her lungs, the rush of exertion, even the tiredness that followed. It was a pleasurable constant in an ever-changing universe.

Which was good, because the changes that governed life outside of class were even more extreme. A curfew had been set for the first flash of Bedderken's Sun, which corresponded roughly to 7pm, Earth-time. It ran until the first detonation of Carrion's Eye—5am.

The principal had added dozens of hall monitors to enforce the new rule. Not recruited from the student body, as they might have been on Earth, but fashioned from corpses like Frankenstein's monster, save that these particular golems were not ragged and stitched, but moulded like pale white clay into identical automatons with hairless bodies and beady black eyes.

Raza wondered where the principal had gotten so many corpses from. Had she raided the killing fields of some otherworldly battlefield, searching for parts? Had she harvested the flesh from her very own victims? There wasn't any explanation that didn't make Raza's skin crawl. And yet even more disturbing than the cadaverous origin of the golems was their sculpted appearance. Every single one of them looked disturbingly like the principal herself, and was dressed in black uniforms dotted with sapphires. Raza's hackles rose every time she felt their eyes upon her. It was as if Noviscula was staring at her, even when the bitch wasn't there. Not just Noviscula, either, but Mr. Willis, whom the golems likewise resembled, at least with regards to their beady black eyes.

The only way to get past them after the hour of curfew was with a hall pass, and those were only handed out under very strict circumstances. For emergencies, of course, and for students who were studying for a test, and therefore needed access to the library. Raza applied for a library pass, only to be informed that she'd been put on a waiting list.

She spent the evening in her dorm room, bored out of her skull. She longed for a mobile phone or some other device with which to contact her friends. A scrying mirror, a short-wave radio, even an antique telegraph. But there didn't seem to be anything like that available at Our Lady. Raza marvelled that the demons, a race who could teleport themselves untold light years across the cosmos, and who could supposedly even traverse the gaps in time itself, hadn't bothered to invest in a simple Wi-Fi network.

For the first five days after her return from the Zone, the only time she saw the other members of Team Naked Badass was in class, in the halls between curfew, and at lunchtime. They hung out with Zester while she scrubbed dishes in the kitchen, reminiscing about the Zone, complaining about the principal, and trading gossip about recent events.

Apparently many of the students had been punished for infractions, especially curfew-breaking. None of them had been sent to the Time-Out Zone, at least not yet. Most had just been banned from competing in the Interschool Championship. A lot of the school's best athletes had been barred in this fashion, and there was a growing fear that Our Lady would lose the Championship Cup for the first time in almost five hundred years.

"Who gives a shit about sports?" said Raza suddenly.

It was Friday, almost a full a week of classes since they'd returned from the Zone. Vogg had been complaining about their declining odds of winning the championship for over ten minutes.

"A lot of people care about sports," he said.

"I don't," said Raza.

"Neither do I," said Skiddix. And he wasn't just agreeing with Raza, either. It would've been hard to find anyone less interested in athletics.

Vogg sighed. "You didn't let me finish," he said. "I was going to say that not everyone cares about sports, but *everyone* ought to care about thrashing those deific jizz-stains from Divinity College. I mean just look at how stuck-up they are now. They already think they fart rainbows and piss out champagne. If they beat us this year, they'll be smugger than ever. It'll be, like, a holocaust of smugness. I'll need to start carrying a barf bag whenever they show up on campus!"

Raza sighed. "Forget about the rivalry with Divinity for a second," she said. "We've gotta talk about Our Lady. The place is turning to crap. It's like a prison. It's starting to suck more than school back on Earth!"

"Tell me about it," said Zester, turning away from her giant mound of dishes. "Just look at my fingers! I'm starting to get dishpan hands. Plus I'm getting a kink in my back from bending over this sink. Soon I'll end up like some kind of twisted old washerwoman!"

"I didn't wanna hurt your feelings, babe," said Vogg, "but you are kinda right about the hands. I've been noticing how rough they're getting every time you jerk me off between classes. I think maybe you should start to use some moisturiser or something, next time you give me a handy. Of maybe some soft leather gloves."

"I'll use a cheese grater next time, ya jerk!" she snapped, tossing a dish cloth at his head.

"I'm serious, guys," whispered Raza. "This place is our home, and the new principal is ruining it!"

She glanced around, half-expecting to see a pair of beady eyes staring back at her. That bitch Noviscula had sure made her paranoid.

"You're not the only one who feels that way," said Skiddix. "Word is a bunch of kids've vanished in the weeks since she started. They must've used illicit teleportation triangles to run off back home."

"Well I'm not saying we should run away, or anything," said Raza. "But we've gotta do something to make this place fun again."

"Way ahead of you on that score," said Vogg. "I hear there's a blow-out party happening at Boltskin's Hall tonight, just like in the old days, and Team Naked Badass is gonna be in attendance."

"But how're we supposed to get there?" asked Raza. "Those fucking hall monitor creeps are everywhere!"

"We could kill 'em," said Zester. "Tear 'em apart. I mean it's not like they're really alive, or anything."

For a moment Raza thought Zester was joking, but she didn't seem to be.

"We don't have to kill 'em," said Vogg. "Though that *would* be pretty fun."

"So what are we gonna do?" asked Skiddix.

Vogg just grinned as he reached into his pocket and pulled out four crisp hall passes. He handed one to Raza, another to Skiddix, then paused, withholding the third one from Zester.

"Better dry your hands first, babe," he said. "These things cost me a pretty penny."

Zester dried her hands on a rag and eagerly snatched up the pass. "Where'd you get these?" she asked, scrutinizing the text. "They look real!"

"Forgeries," said Vogg. "Courtesy of that dork who works on the newspaper. And you wouldn't believe what he wanted in trade. I had to give up all those naked photos you took for me!"

Zester raised a fist.

"I'm just kidding!" he said. "But I did have to trade him a bunch of vintage albums. So we'd better not waste these, okay? They're all passes to the sick bay, dated for this evening. And the sick bay is right near the stairs that lead up to Boltskin's. All we have to do is use the passes to get past the monitors, then sneak off to the party. It's a foolproof plan!"

"Maybe," said Skiddix. "But what if we get caught? I mean, what if they notice these are all fake?"

Vogg sighed. "So what if we get caught?" he asked. "What're they gonna do, make us wash some dishes? Ban us from the volleyball team? Who gives a shit! Besides, Raza's right. We've gotta do something to make this place fun again!"

The four of them glanced at each other, then eagerly nodded. The plan was agreed upon. Raza felt a surge of excitement at the prospect of partying with her new best friends. It was gonna be a night to remember!

Six hours later they were creeping through the hall that led past sick bay. They'd each departed their  dorm rooms and met up together. So far so good. The cadaverous golems had found their passes convincing. Now all they had to do was bypass the sick bay and head up the darkened stairwell that led into the maze of old dormitories, and ultimately, to the party taking place in Boltskin's Hall.

They nodded to each other and tiptoed past the sick bay's open doors, stepping through the column of light that shot out from within. Once back in the darkness they rushed for the staircase. The old steps creaked as they ascended, painfully loud in the tomb-like silence that now attended the halls of Our Lady.

A figure stepped out from the shadows that screened the upper landing. They could just make out its bloodless, corpse-white flesh in the starlight that poured through the windows. Its beady black eyes looked like inkblots on parchment.

"Halt," said the hall monitor. "This is a restricted area."

"We, um, we just took a wrong turn at the sick bay," said Skiddix, somewhat unconvincingly.

Then Raza's red eyebeams shot out and roasted the golem to ashes.

# CHAPTER 18:
## PARTY TIME

"**H**OLY SHIT, RAZA!**" said Zester. "That was awesome!" Raza just stood there, staring at the ashes of the being she'd just blasted. She'd acted on impulse, and was a little bit shocked by it. But there was something about those beady black eyes that had triggered her anger. Probably the resemblance they bore to the haunting dark orbs of Mr. Willis.

"Fuck it," she said. "There's no way we're gonna miss this party!"

The four of them grinned at each other, feeling a pulse of demonic adrenaline. They raced past the remains of the golem and on towards the party.

Principal Noviscula sat in her private chamber, on a chair that was not a chair, but the writhing remains of a figure trapped in utmost agony. She took a break from her thoughts as one of the sapphires on her dress started flashing like a distant, dying star. She ripped it off the garment and stared into its facets, seeing what the golem had seen in its final few moments of existence: the four students halting on the stairway, one of them flagrantly lying, then a bolt of obliterating energy shooting out from Shahrazad's eyes, engulfing the golem in burning red light.

Noviscula laughed darkly to herself.

"The spawn of the Deicide," she said. "How predictably vicious she is."

She gestured to a figure in the darkness of her chamber. He came forth into the sapphire light. It was the handsome new student from Raza's cosmic history class, the one who'd come to occupy Star Geddon's vacant seat. His true name was Adagar, but the staff and students knew him as Gogorizel.

"Yes, mistress?" he said.

"A number of students seem to be absconding somewhere," said Noviscula. "I've seen dozens of them creeping off already. And one of them just destroyed a golem."

"It must be that party I told you about," said Adagar. "It's probably nothing, just a typical demonic bout of drunken fornication. I doubt it's a threat to our plans."

"Even so, I want you to go there and spy for me. Take one of these."

She reached into her mouth, regurgitating a glowing blue eyeball. It shrank down between her fingers into the form of a sapphire. Adagar reached out and took it, albeit reluctantly.

"Do I really have to go and mix with these scum, mistress?" he asked. "It's bad enough I have to endure their presence all day long, and wear this repulsive, false form . . . "

"No complaints!" snapped Noviscula. "We've got a job to do here. Need I remind you that you were chosen from a list of volunteers? It's time to make your school proud. And not just your school, but your father, as well."

"Yes, mistress," he said.

He strode from the chamber and headed off towards Boltskin's, the sapphire eye clutched tightly in his fist.

Team Naked Badass stood exhausted by the dance floor, trading sips from a bottle of moon wine. The party wasn't as packed, nor the music as deafeningly loud as it had been in the past, but it was a party nonetheless.

At first the other students had given them a wide berth. Raza had mentally prepared herself for a night of defiant isolation in the company of her friends. But as the evening wore on, and the guests got more and more inebriated, other students started steadily approaching them. It seemed like their zero-fucks attitude had earned them a lot of social currency.

*Guess that's the currency of cool,* thought Raza. *Looks like we might not be total outcasts, after all!*

Even more students approached, now that they were done with the dancing. Raza had fun meeting new faces, regaling them with tales of her exiting ordeals in the Zone.

Then Vel turned up with the rest of her clique and Raza's mood turned sour. She and Vel became engaged in a tense, evasive staring match across the landscape of the party. Raza would look up to find Vel staring at her sullenly. Then Vel would look away, and it would be Raza's turn to stare. This continued for what seemed like ages, their gazes meeting fleetingly across the vista of whirling, drunken bodies.

Raza was furious. A part of her wanted to go up to Vel and start slapping her silly. She still felt hurt and betrayed by how the other girl had treated her. But a part of her still really liked Vel, and wanted to reconcile. The conflicting emotions made her brooding and cranky. She stopped paying attention to the joys of the party, and drifted off into a private world of confusion and resentment. She only returned to the present when the new boy appeared. What was his name again, she wondered?

*That's right,* she thought. *Gogorizel. And he definitely is cute . . .*

Maybe a new romance was just what she needed to take her mind off Vel and their strange, bitchy staring contest. She excused herself from the others and hurried to meet him, then stopped dead in her tracks as Vel cut her off, reaching him first. Raza fumed as she saw her old best friend start overtly flirting with the new boy.

*That cow!* Thought Raza. *I bet she saw me looking at him, and she's just doing this to spite me!*

She returned to the others in a huff.

"This party blows," she said.

"Are you sure?" asked Skiddix. "I was just thinking maybe the two of us should have a dance together . . . "

A note of high-pitched laughter pierced Raza's ear like a nail. She looked across the room to see Vel smiling widely at Gogorizel, brushing back her hair, staring up dreamily into his eyes.

*Makes me wanna puke!* thought Raza as she turned back to the others.

"Well I'm done with dancing," she snapped. "Let's split this crap fest, and just hang out together. There's too many turds in the punch bowl here, anyway."

"Okay," said Skiddix excitedly. "Let's hang out just the four of us!"

"Hold up," said Vogg. "I've got something way more fun for us to do than just sit around drinking all night. See, I had a feeling this party might suck, so I made some contingency plans. Follow me!"

The others shrugged and followed him out of the hall. Raza shot a final, lingering glance at Vel and the boy. Vel turned towards her. Was that a gleam of smugness in her eyes? Raza made an ostentatious show of turning her nose in the air, and ended up raising her head so high she almost smashed into the doorframe on her way from the hall.

Her mood began to lighten as they made their way through the corridors.

*No more Vel,* she thought. *Good. She can have that new guy all to herself. If he falls for her he's got no taste, anyway!*

They passed the room in which Raza had killed Star Geddon. The door was still smashed off its hinges. The blood had been scrubbed off the walls, but the faint smell of death still seemed to linger in the air. Raza surprised herself by not caring that much about it. Maybe her demonic instincts were making her callous. Maybe she was just too tipsy and angry to get sucked into a guilt fest.

Vogg stopped in his tracks and gestured to a door nearby. "In here," he said.

Zester sighed. "You're not trying to get us into an orgy, are you?" she asked.

"Of course not!" he said, then paused, glancing cheekily at Raza. "Not unless you girls are up for it, that is . . . "

Zester slapped him immediately.

"Ow!" he said. "Give it a rest, will ya? I'm just joking. I've got my hands full satisfying your needs, without adding someone else to the mix! Besides, I don't think Skiddix would be into it. The size of my dong might traumatize him!"

Skiddix sighed. "I've seen it before, dude. Remember?"

"You've seen it floppy," said Vogg. "But never at maximum elevation! The sight of it would strain even your giant eyeball."

"Just tell us what the plan is, smart arse," said Zester with a sigh.

Vogg pulled out a key and unlocked the door. For a moment Raza wondered what it would be like if they really *did* have an orgy together. She had a feeling Zester was bisexual. And Vogg was definitely adventurous enough to do it. Skiddix might be too shy, but he was obviously so into Raza that he'd probably overcome his bashfulness. She felt a tingle between her legs as she imagined all those limbs sprawling together, licking and sucking and pumping in a frenzy of erotic abandon.

Then she checked herself. It would probably be gross. Not to mention awkward afterwards. It might even spell the end for Team Naked Badass! How could she have countenanced doing such a thing, even for a moment?

*Must be the liquor,* she thought.

Vogg pushed the door open, revealing an unfurnished room with a familiar-looking triangle chalked out on the floorboards.

"What's this?" she asked.

"Whatta you think?" said Vogg. "It's our ticket out of here."

# CHAPTER 19:
## STAR-CROSSED

**A**DAGAR STOOD TALKING to the girl with the transparent skin. Of course she referred to him by his false name, Gogorizel. For a while he remained indifferent to her and her blatant attempts at flirtation.

Then he recognised her. His wounded pride seethed. He remembered the day clearly. He'd been walking across the yard at Our Lady, wearing his natural shape. Students had started pelting him with offal. One had even vomited all over him, soiling his perfect white uniform. And this girl Velazelza had been there, mocking him, displaying obscene gestures. The other girl had been there too, the God-Slayer's spawn, the one with the long dark hair. They'd caught him in a moment of weakness, seen a chink in his pride. It was an unprecedented failure on his part, one that had haunted him ever since.

And now she was here, in front of him, trying to get him into bed, totally unaware that he was, in truth, the very quintessence of all that she despised.

His mind reeled at the possibilities. To take her up on her offer. To penetrate her, all the while wallowing in the sweet, secret knowledge that he was her uttermost enemy. Such complete humiliation would surely avenge his wounded pride. And yet it was against all the sacred commandments of his Father and the Host. The product of such a union, should it occur, could only be the most vile of all abominations. Did he dare to commit such a blasphemy, in the name of revenge?

Her hand was on him now, lightly, skirting his arm, his shoulder, the curve of his waist.

*The wanton hussy!* he thought.

She was pressing him harder. And he was getting hard. Was his arousal triggered only by his blasphemous thoughts of revenge? Or was he actually attracted to this—this thing? This spawn of ungovernable Chaos? This senseless vomit from the uncreated sludge of the universe? She was quite attractive, in a way. His loathing of her became loathing for himself as he experienced the urgings of physical lust.

*She's degrading me again,* he thought. *Making me falter from the path . . .*

Perhaps he *had* to punish her. Not just for her previous abuse, but for this newfound insult to his nature. He took a deep breath. If he was to do this, there would be no going back. Nor could there be any witnesses. Making a snap decision, he reached into his pocket and shattered the sapphire gem that functioned as his mistress' disembodied eye.

*The die is cast,* he thought, growing more and more excited by the second.

Velazelza stood talking with the boy. He seemed like a bit of a cold fish. Standoffish, aloof. For a moment she wondered why she'd even bothered to approach him in the first place.

But she knew exactly why. She'd seen Raza ogling him across the dance floor. When Raza had approached, she'd dashed in and cut her off, monopolizing his attentions before Raza could get there. It was a petty act of rivalry.

Vel started remonstrating with herself. This whole thing with Raza was getting ridiculous. And the most ridiculous aspect of it all was that Vel had already forgiven Raza for what happened to Star. She'd had time to think about it all while Raza had been trapped in the Zone. She'd made a resolution to bury the hatchet between them. She'd waited anxiously for Raza's return, hoping the girl would survive. And she had. Vel was all set to apologise, when Raza had snubbed her in the hallway. What's more, she'd taken to hanging out with those bad kids from detention, pretending Vel and the others didn't even exist. Suddenly Vel's resolution had crumbled to ashes, replaced with stubborn, prideful anger. If Raza didn't want to be friends again, then neither did she. Raza could be happy with her new clique of freaks. She didn't care . . .

But she did. Which was why she felt bad for poaching the object of Raza's desire. She was just about to break off the conversation with Gogorizel when he suddenly became more responsive. She noticed a bulge in his trousers. His breath grew heavy; his eyes attained a newfound erotic intensity.

*Maybe he's not such a cold fish after all!* she thought.

Then she paused. What about Raza? Surely this would only intensify the rivalry between them. But then again, the boy was undeniably hot. Surely she could have some fun first, then reconcile with Raza later? She smiled at Gogorizel, took his hand, and led him off down the corridor.

The girl was leading him down the hall.

*She really is a slut,* thought Adagar.

But she was also very beautiful. Her naked body shone. Light flared out from her candy-coloured organs. She looked like some luminous creature in the depths of the ocean, her lucent flesh an irresistible lure. It was a strange feeling to have, so much loathing mingled with so much desire. It made it hard for him to think.

Soon they were alone in one of the rooms. The sound of demonic rutting came through the walls, adding yet more layers to his frenzy of desire and disgust.

"Why don't we lose these first?" she said, discarding her talisman.

He took off his. Not that it made much of a difference. His talisman was a fake anyway, his deific senses more than capable of dealing with the myriad sights and sounds that Our Lady had to offer.

For a moment they stood there, staring at each other. In spite of his frenzy, Adagar felt suddenly paralysed. Would he even be able to go through with this?

She registered his nervousness and started acting for the both of them. He moved like a mannequin as she stripped him down, led him to the bed, and sat him on the edge of it. She knelt before him, smiling up eagerly.

"A bit nervy, huh?" she said. "Don't worry. I'll take care of that . . . "

She started stroking him with one hand, caressing his balls with the other. Her hands were warm and soft. His prick sprang up. She leaned in close and took it in her mouth, bathing it in wetness and warmth. His eyes popped open as he looked down and watched her. He could see himself through the transparent layer of her skin. His prick between the gap of her teeth, slipping past her tongue to the back of her throat. Her smiling eyes looked up at him. He started to melt. All those emotions were like a whirlpool of sludge, subsumed by sensation.

Suddenly she stopped sucking.

"Looks like you're ready for action," she said. "How about we make this more of a team effort?"

She stood up and pushed him back on the bed. He expected her to get on his lap, but instead she mounted his face in a sixty-nine position, sucking on his prick as her pussy sat above him. He lay there, paralysed by the sight of those glossy pink lips. To penetrate her was one thing. But to put his mouth on that gushing, demonic organ? Could he stand to take part in this? His blood became feverish as she worked her mouth and tongue. The heady sensation was making him reckless. Maybe he could take the plunge?

"Hurruh upfff," she said, talking with her mouth full.

She wagged her pussy in his face. He could see her glowing organs shining out from the skin. See, too, the demonic-looking eels that swam around inside of her. Would one of them pop out from betwixt the wet lips, like some kind of devouring, ambushing cock, and bite him in the face?

*These creatures are indeed an affront against intelligent design,* he mused.

Then he took the plunge, seizing her arse in both hands as he thrust up his face and licked into her. The demonic juices slathered his jaw and dripped down his tongue. The taste of her was sweet and tingling, like sherbet. To a part of his mind the sensation was terrible. To his physical senses it was delicious, addictive. He licked harder, faster, tonguing her clit.

*I'm letting this demoness degrade me again,* he thought. But he no longer cared so much.

Vel's own efforts grew a lot less precise as his tongue went to work. It got harder and harder for her to concentrate on giving a good blowjob as the waves of pleasure rolled out from her clit and made her whole body shake. She shuddered on top of him. The eels inside of her were dancing, swirling as if in a frenzy of hunger. The waves of pleasure made her mouth quiver on his cock, so that their bodies became a sort of fleshy feedback loop, a Mobius Strip of reciprocal lust. The mounting sense of bliss spurred her on to more intense, if not more coordinated, efforts. She bobbed her head fast, impaling her throat on his cock and letting out a muffled moan of pleasure as she came.

Juices poured down as she shuddered on top of him. Adagar swallowed as they inundated his mouth. He felt her stroking him fast; her parted lips were poised above his prick.

"Come on," she whispered, her voice husky from the orgasm. "I wanna taste it . . . "

But he didn't want to come yet. Once his seed was released, then it would all be over. He needed this to last for as long as it could.

"No," he whispered, trying hard to restrain himself. "Inside of you."

Vel looked back at him through the gap in her legs, and smiled. The expression itself was almost enough to make him lose control right then. Then she crawled forwards, hoisting her arse in the air. He hurried up onto his knees, staring down at the gushing pink lips of her pussy, the neon-pink knot of her arsehole. The eels were circling her insides in a frenzy. He no longer cared whether they'd bite him or not. He slid himself between her well-moistened lips.

She bucked and moaned. Her incandescent organs started glowing even brighter. Her body grew larger. The demonic eels erupted from her neck, panting and growling as they writhed beside her sweat-covered face.

"Transform," she muttered as he filled her from behind. "Let's bring down the house!"

Adagar paused for a moment. He didn't want to assume that terrible shape. But she was commanding him. And in his current, transfigured state, the urge to change came easily.

His body grew massive and covered with fur. Ram's horns shot up from his head, which now resembled that of an ox. His prick, too, grew larger, filling her wider and deeper. She howled with excitement.

Now he was wearing this demonic form. Now he was inside of a demoness, rutting like a beast. Was this really revenge, or just a cryptic plot, secretly arranged by his very own psyche? To cross the fence, to join them in their terrible, beautiful, amoral dance? What would the mistress say? What would Father say?

He put the thoughts from his head and threw himself instead into the fucking. Velazelza moaned and thrust back against him, matching his speed. Her scintillating organs cast up a kaleidoscope of light. The harder he fucked the less he had to think. But it was all rocketing towards an inevitable conclusion. An obliterating end that would bring but a single moment of conscious negation. The harder he fought to loose himself, the sooner he'd be dragged back to his senses. He rutted as long as he could, as hard as he could, until he climaxed with a roar and watched his cum shoot forth into her transparent pussy, gushing and swimming inside of her.

Velazelza slid off his prick and shrank down into human form. A froth of juices covered his cock. She glanced back at him, languid and smiling in the afterglow.

"That was really something!" she said.

He shrank down and smiled at her. His frenzy of lust tumbled down like the walls of old Jericho. He felt coldness come over him as he watched his seed start to stir up inside of her.

*Abomination,* he thought. *Abomination is the name of this union . . .*

# CHAPTER 20:
## THE IDOLATERS

**Z**ESTER STARED AT the teleportation triangle, and sighed.

"This was all just a setup, wasn't it?" she asked, addressing Vogg. "To get the rest of us to go along with one of your off-campus training sessions!"

"No!" said Vogg. "Well, maybe a little. But it's not just for me! I set this up for all of us. I figure it'll be just like old times, when we were in the Zone together, fighting side-by-side against a bunch of creeps and monsters. And I've picked out the perfect bunch of assholes for us to go kill. Idolaters, they are. A real bunch of god-worshipping scum."

"But wouldn't that be breaking the truce?" asked Raza. "You know, the one between demons and gods?"

Vogg scoffed. "Are you kidding me?" he said. "Get a clue, Raza. The war might be technically over, but demons and gods have never stopped fighting, not even for a second. They've just gotten a whole lot sneakier in the ways they go about it."

"So it's a cold war?" asked Raza. "Just like Russia and America?"

"Sure," said Vogg. "Just like those guys. And as long as we don't get caught, then it'll all turn out fine. Think of it like a covert operation."

"This is pretty dangerous, guys," said Skiddix. "I'm not sure if we should go . . . "

A part of Raza agreed with him. But the rest of her felt

excited by the prospect of guerrilla warfare against the lackeys of the Demiurge. Her demonic instincts were champing at the bit.

"Let's do it!" she said. "I'm in."

"I guess I'll go if you go," said Skiddix, changing his tune.

"Awesome!" said Vogg. "What about you, Zester?"

"What do you think?" she asked. "This is Team Naked Badass, isn't it? All for one, and one for all!"

The four of them stepped into the triangle.

"Hold on a sec," said Skiddix. "If this is a covert mission, shouldn't we wear disguises, or something?"

"Forget about it," said Vogg. "Once we're done, there won't be any witnesses left to tell the tale. Let's go!"

He muttered some mystic words under his breath. Raza thought they sounded a bit like the words her parents had spoken when she'd first been sent to Our Lady. Then the runes started glowing and the room disappeared, yielding to the blackness of the interstice. Mottled shapes roiled in the darkness around them, like shadowed waves in the depths of the sea.

Raza wondered what kind of threat they'd be dealing with. Murderous angels? Two-headed giants? Inhuman monsters leading their victims to altars of sacrifice?

Sprawling silhouettes took shape high above them, like the giant bodies of undulating worms. Huge statues loomed from the darkness, totemic, cyclopean. The air was home to shouts and high-pitched screams. Amidst the terrified voices came the sound of whirling motors and cacophonous music.

Raza felt a rush of excitement and fear. Just what sort of hell had he taken them to? It sounded like an abattoir, where the slaughtermen laboured to the dissonant strains of overlapping music.

Glaring light displaced the shadows. Raza's eyes opened wide. They were standing in the middle of a sprawling amusement park! The screams were those of children and adults enjoying the rides. The cacophony of noises came from dance halls and arcades. The giant, worm-like shapes were nothing more than roller-coasters. The cyclopean statues were images of cartoon characters that Raza didn't recognise. They looked like animals from some alternate world, though one of them resembled a rodent. He was bloated and hairy, with a mass of bristling whiskers. Sort of like Ratfink, or Mickey Mouse gone to seed. Raza and the others materialized beneath one of his statues, their miraculous arrival going seemingly unnoticed amongst all the commotion.

"Isn't it horrifying?" said Vogg, without the least trace of irony.

"I'll say," said Zester as she gawked at the rides. "Who's making these poor people submit to these tortures?"

Raza sighed. Just when she was starting to think Vogg had a nuanced view of other cultures, he goes and pulls a stunt like this. How could he know so much about the complex themes of "Rock N Roll Nigger," yet be so utterly clueless about a simple funfair? Clearly Our Lady had a spotty curriculum!

"It's just an amusement park!" she said as the others glanced about in horror. "Like Disneyland, or Luna Park. People come here to have fun, that's all."

"You call this fun?" said Zester. "Look up there. There's people screaming, trapped in spinning metal cages. They're obviously terrified!"

"She's right," said Vogg. "These people are being compelled against their will. It's a feast of fear, designed to appease their hideous god!"

He pointed dramatically at the giant statue of the cartoon rodent that stood looming above them.

"We have to stop this idolatry!" he continued. "We just have to find the high priest, and kill him."

Raza sighed again. "There is no high priest," she said. "And that giant rat, or whatever it is, is just a cartoon character! Besides, just look around at all the people having fun. I mean look at that kid, for example. Does he look like he's being tortured to you?"

She pointed to a child eating fairy floss. Skiddix stared at the kid with his ultra-sharp vision.

"I'm not sure you're right about this one, Raza," he said. "The stuff that kid's eating has no nutritional value at all. It's already rotting away at the fabric of his teeth. Soon he'll be in horrible pain!"

"That's just candy," said Raza. "It's not supposed to have any nutritional value. It's only meant to taste good! The fact that it rots your teeth is just an unfortunate side-effect."

"But look there," said Vogg. "There's a bunch of monsters. They must be servants of the rat god, collecting children to be sacrificed. We should slay them immediately!" He pointed to a bunch of amusement park employees in animal costumes entertaining a group of small children.

"Those are just costumes," said Raza. "Look!"

She ran up to one of them and pulled off his mask, waving it to the others. The mascot snatched it back from her, grumbled, and restored his disguise.

"See?" said Raza. "They're just people in suits."

"What about them?" asked Zester, pointing to a patrol of armed guards. "They look like enforcers for the theocracy that runs this place. They must be the ones that're forcing these people to suffer."

"*They're just security guards*," hissed Raza, starting to lose her patience. "They're here to protect people, make them feel safe."

"That's ridiculous," said Zester. "If they're here to make people feel safe, then why do they have weapons on their belts?"

"I agree," said Vogg. "I say we take them down. They're clearly a threat!"

Raza groaned. "We're not killing anyone!" she yelled.

She regretted yelling that out immediately. But then she remembered that they weren't on Earth, but some kind of weird, earth-like planet or alternate dimension. No-one could even understand what they were saying. She lowered her voice and spoke patiently to the others. "Look, we're not killing anyone here, okay? There's no human sacrifice, no monsters, and no rat god, just people having fun."

Vogg sighed. "So you're saying this whole thing is a washout?" he said.

"Afraid so," said Raza.

Now it was Vogg's turn to sigh. The others looked dejected as well. Raza scrambled for a way to salvage the evening.

"Well, we can't kill anyone," she said. "But maybe we could stay here and have some fun? I mean, it is an *amusement* park, after all. We could play some video games, maybe take a ride on the Ferris Wheel . . . "

Vogg looked horrified. "Are you kidding me?" he asked. "If we're not gonna kill anything, then I don't wanna waste another second in this shithole."

"Me either," said Zester. "This place is awful!"

"I'm gonna have to agree with the others on this one, Raza," said Skiddix. "This place is noisy and annoying. Plus, it kinda smells like vomit and pee."

*Huh,* she thought. *I guess he's got a point!*

"Okay," said Vogg. "Let's go home."

The teleportation triangle had replicated itself the moment they'd arrived, searing itself into the ground beneath their feet. Crushed cans and bits of dirty bubble gum littered the blacktop, mingling with the shapes of the runes. Soon the latter started to glow, plunging them back through the interstice and into the dorm room. An air of disappointment came with their return.

"Well that sucked," said Vogg. "And here I thought I had the perfect location scouted out for us."

"I guess we should've stayed at the party," said Skiddix.

Suddenly Raza had another brainwave. She was sure it was better than the last one.

"Hold on a second!" she said. "I think I've got the perfect bunch of god-bothering arseholes for us to wipe out. Can you guys reprogram this triangle?"

"Sure," said Skiddix. "You know this eyeball of mine is a pretty powerful thing. I can look out across the cosmos with it, scan the planets and stars. All you have to do is show me where you want to go. As long as I can see it, I can get the co-ordinates for the triangle."

"Okay then," said Raza.

She guided him over to the window, placing a hand on his shoulder as she pointed out into the void.

"Now what you want to do," she said, "is look for a pretty blue marble called Earth . . . "

# CHAPTER 21:
## Demonic Intervention

**ABU HABIB IBRAHIM** looked out upon the darkened desert landscape, and smiled. It had been six months since he'd left his middle class abode in Notting Hill, London, and joined up with ISIS in Iraq. And what a time it had been! The fighting had been thick, right from the get-go. Not that it was really 'fighting' in the strictest sense of the term. Most of their efforts had revolved around the massacre of defenceless civilian populations, acts of ethnic cleansing aimed against the targets of their particular brand of faith. Shiite Muslims, mainly. But they'd also done a thorough job of wiping out those devil-worshipping Yezidis.

Not that it was an act of absolute genocide. They'd killed the men, of course, and the old hags. But the young, beautiful women had been kept, funnelled into their extensive human trafficking ring. Proceeds from the sales of all those young women had gone straight back into ISIS accounts, buying new weapons and munitions. And yet not all of the girls had been sold off to bidders in other locations. Others had been purchased by soldiers, for use in the camp. Abu and his comrades got massive staff discounts. It'd only taken three packs of Marlboros for Abu to fill his tent with concubines. And he still had plenty of cigarettes left over, having purchased a whole carton at Heathrow Airport, duty-free.

The girls had been disagreeable at first, but they'd soon learned that if they didn't take his prick inside of them, they'd take the barrel of his gun, or a steel bayonet. After a few salient lessons they'd become much more compliant. And yet, despite all the pleasure they'd given him, they were still just infidel whores. His real affection was reserved for his bride, Amatullah, an English girl who'd come to find a righteous husband amongst the ISIS ranks. Fancy his surprise when he'd found out she was also from London!

It really was a small world. The two of them delighted each other. Her faith was just as profound and all-consuming as his was. She'd been taken aback, at first, by the presence of his sex slaves. But he'd explained to her that, as a prospective martyr, he was just taking a down-payment on his forty-two virgins. After that she'd come around. She'd even lent him a hand like any good wife should, berating the girls and laughing at their degradation. The two of them had become like a regular Fred and Rosemary West—albeit far more righteous, of course.

Indeed it was a grand time to be a righteous man. All the infidel filth was being washed away, like flotsam in the flood. And not just the human filth, either, but the material. All the blasphemous remnants of the cultures of yore. Statues, temples, ziggurats of Assyria and Babylon, blasted away by bundles of dynamite and packets of plastic explosive.

It was important work they were doing here. Abu still found it hard to understand why his parents had been so against him joining up. Probably because they were decadent apostates, corrupted by the blight of Western culture. He lit up a Marlboro and prayed for their return to the faith.

At length he became aware of a presence behind him. It was probably one of the impoverished local fighters who'd been pressganged into ISIS. Their faith was generally weaker than that of volunteers like Abu, crusaders who'd journeyed all the way across the world to fight against the infidels. What's worse was that they never had any money, and were always bumming cigarettes. He turned around, expecting to see one of the grubby little peasants standing with their hands out, like Oliver Twist asking for "more."

Instead he saw a quartet of teenagers. They'd come out of nowhere, materialising from the desert like the children of Iblis. Beneath their feet was a set of blazing and blasphemous runes.

"Djinn!" shouted Abu.

Then Raza's eyebeams shot out, scything through his kneecaps and cutting off his legs. He crashed to the ground, screaming, too shocked by the pain to go for his revolver. Raza's beam flashed down again, hitting him square between the legs, blasting his cock and balls into a smoking black ruin.

"All right, guys," she said. "Feel free to kill anyone in camo!"

Zester reached into her pocket and pulled out a cylinder tipped with a pipette. It looked like a magickal syringe, albeit without any plunger.

"Can I suck their souls out?" she asked, smiling eagerly.

"Oh no, Zester!" said Raza, feeling a rush of disappointment. "You're not gonna start using again, are you?"

"Of course not," said Zester. "I'm just gonna sell 'em! Souls fetch a pretty penny on the demonic black market."

Raza breathed a sigh of relief. Selling souls was better than huffing them, she supposed. And if anyone deserved to get their souls sucked out, it was these ISIS arseholes. After all, what if the Demiurge—giant dick that he was—really decided to give them some kind of heavenly reward? Raza couldn't have that! Thus she grinned as Zester knelt down and sucked out Abu's soul. It shot up the pipette like a whiff of tobacco smoke and swirled its way up into the cylinder, where it hung all distorted and agonized, like a victim of torture reflected in a funhouse mirror.

Meanwhile the camp was bustling with sudden activity, responding to Abu's agonized scream.

"The prayer monkeys are mobilizing," said Skiddix.

"Good," said Vogg. "This'll be a lot more fun once they start fighting back!"

Team Naked Badass nodded to each other, and transformed into their natural, murderous shapes.

Amatullah sat in the tent, waiting for her husband to come back from his smoke break and resume the festivities. His four naked sex slaves sat huddled nearby, each a few years younger than Amatullah's eighteen. She held them at bay with a Desert Eagle pistol. She didn't like using a weapon manufactured by Zionists, but its deadliness was undeniable.

Suddenly there came a scream, followed by sounds of panic from all around the camp. Then gunfire, explosions, and more and more screams. There was roaring and bellowing, as if a pride of desert lions had descended on the outpost. Something splattered on the tent roof, heavier than rain, but softer than hail. She saw a clump of intestines in vague silhouette as they slithered down the canvas and dribbled to the earth.

"Abu!" she yelled, worried about her husband.

She got up to take a peek out the door, momentarily taking her eyes off the prisoners. They rushed her, knocking her over. She got off a shot before they disarmed her. They were smaller than she, and lean from underfeeding, but they were very, very angry. Their wrath and their numbers combined to overpower her. They didn't have any weapons, so they used their hands and teeth, clawing her arms and biting off chunks of her face. The last thing she saw before they gouged out her eyes was a blood-red demon striding naked past the tent.

Raza let her instincts lead the way. The raid on the camp became a dizzying slideshow of mayhem and gore. Gun muzzles flashed in the darkness. Bullets bounced off her hide as her claws severed heads and slashed through viscera. She plucked up body parts and fed them to her breast-mouths—hands, tongues, eyes, even clumps of severed genitalia. Soon she was covered in blood, strings of muscle and sinew hanging from her fangs.

She caught glimpses of the others through the carnage. The ISIS fighters had a habit of yelling out "God is great!" every time they fired off a round. It was distinctly irritating. Vogg had taken to mocking them, yelling out random phrases as he tore them apart.

"Mashed potatoes!" he cried as he grabbed a soldier's gun, turned it around, and rammed it barrel-first down the man's screaming throat.

"Lee Marvin!" he shouted as he punched another's head off.

"STOCKTAKE SALE!" he roared as he ripped off another man's jaw and tossed it like some kind of ill-fashioned boomerang. The sheer demonic force behind the throw sent it plunging through another fighter's eyeball.

Truly Vogg was having a whale of a time. He seemed less like a demonic martial artist on an unauthorised training mission than a terrifying child in a playground of bodies. He kicked one man into the air like a hackey sack and kept him aloft with a series of blows until his body fell apart.

Other times he seemed less like a child than some artist of gore. He ripped off limbs and jammed them through bodies, creating charnel sculptures. Victims flew hither and thither, severed arms and legs crammed through their cavities and jammed up their arseholes, their faces re-arranged like grisly iterations of Mr. Potato Head.

At one point his killings took on a particularly sordid dimension. And ISIS soldier tried to stab him in the groin with a bayonet. Vogg grew enraged.

"You want some of this, huh?" he yelled.

His huge demonic dick sprang erect. He rammed it through the man's terrified mouth and out through the back of his skull, so that the punctured head hung impaled on the shaft, like a grisly trophy on a spear made of meat.

The sexual dimension of Zester's attacks was even more pronounced. She grabbed ISIS soldiers by the scruffs of their necks and rammed them face-first into her gnawing vagina. The teeth gnashed as she gyrated her hips, tearing off noses and lips. She extracted their eyeballs, too, the way a sex-show performer might suck up a ping-pong ball. Zester's mighty Kegel muscles flexed, spitting the eyeballs back out as she laughed and moaned from the pleasure of it all.

When they fell she harvested their souls. Soon the barrel of her magickal syringe was crowded with writhing and terrified spirits. This wasn't the martyr's afterlife they'd all been expecting!

Of all the members of Team Naked Badass, Skiddix seemed the most focused and disciplined. His eyebeam shot out, scything through bodies and tents like some mythical death ray. The desert stank with the scent of burning flesh. Carrion birds began to circle the carnage, cawing and salivating.

Raza stood on an ISIS fighter's chest and ripped off his arm. Maybe it was the sight of Zester and Vogg's acts of sexual violence—maybe it was just all the gore and excitement—but Raza was getting aroused. Juices ran from her pussy, mingling with the blood on her legs. She thought about stripping the skin off the arm and using the appendage like a glistening dildo. But she still wasn't comfortable with that aspect of her demonic instincts, so she tossed it over her shoulder instead.

She looked down at the man. He was grizzled and bearded, maybe some kind of commander. He was yelling at her, too, spouting off about how she was a godless abomination. For a moment she thought about giving him some self-righteous speech about how *he* was the real monster here. But what was the point? There was only one language these arseholes understood. She stomped on his head until it looked like a cross between a pancake and a mosaic of bone.

It seemed like he was the last of them. Raza had lost track of how many she'd killed and how long they'd been killing, but the sun was rising redly in the east. She shifted back down into human form, her magickal clothing taking shape around her. Soon the others were there at her side, taking in the scene of devastation. One of the fallen tents rippled and stirred.

"Looks like we missed some of 'em," said Vogg.

Raza nodded. Her eyes turned to balls of crimson fire as she prepared to immolate another group of ISIS fighters. And yet it wasn't fighters that emerged, but young women, half-naked and filthy as they crawled from the wreckage. Raza had to fight back tears as she saw the looks on their traumatized faces. Whatever had happened to them here, it was clearly a million times worse than what she'd been through in the Zone. She addressed them in bits of broken Kurdish, hoping they'd understand. It was, after all, the language her parents had spoken at home.

"Grab some guns and get in those vehicles," she shouted, pointing to a bunch of armoured trucks. "Haul arse across the desert!"

She wondered which way to direct them. She was vaguely aware that the Kurdish resistance had their defensive line positioned somewhere nearby, but she didn't know where, or even which direction. When Raza and the others had been looking for a place to lay down the triangle, she'd just told Skiddix to search for a military camp that was flying the black flag, the more isolated the better. She'd only been thinking about violence, not about rescue. She'd had no idea that this might turn into a humanitarian mission!

Meanwhile the women started picking up guns and supplies and making their way to the trucks. They didn't say anything to Raza and the others, only looked at them with gazes of gratefulness mingled with dread. What did it feel like to be rescued by demons?

"Can we help them get to safety?" asked Raza.

"Afraid not," said Vogg, placing a hand on her shoulder. "This is a covert mission, remember? The longer we stay here, doing demonic stuff, the more likely it is that one of the Demiurge's agents might spot us messing around inside of his domain. If that happens, it could endanger the treaty, and tear the whole cosmos apart."

"He's right, Raza," said Skiddix. "I'm sorry."

He held out his hand. Raza took it, choking back tears. Suddenly the full weight of all the human suffering she'd witnessed came down upon her shoulders. Not the suffering of the ISIS soldiers, of course. *Fuck those guys*, she thought. *I'd kill them again any day of the week!* No, it was not them for whom she mourned, but for all of their victims. Any one of those girls could've been her, if her parents hadn't escaped from Iraq. And if she wasn't the spawn of the God-Killer, of course.

*How could the Demiurge let this shit happen?* she wondered. *He really must be a total douche!*

Soon the liberated captives had driven away. A kettle of vultures descended on the camp as the sun began to rise above the mountains in the distance.

"Come on," she said gloomily. "Let's get back to Our Lady."

They strode through the carnage to the triangle. For a moment they stood there, staring back across the camp. The black flag hung forlorn across a field of mangled bodies.

"Well, that was pretty fucking cool," said Vogg.

Zester elbowed him in the ribs. Raza stared at him, sadness in her eyes.

"Sorry, Raza," he said. "I mean, that last part was pretty heartbreaking, don't get me wrong. But the rest of it was awesome!"

Raza paused for a moment, then smiled, then started laughing. Her face and hair were still covered in blood.

"I guess it was pretty cool, huh?" she said, grinning.

And it *was* pretty cool. She'd fed her demon instincts with an all-you-can-eat buffet of ultra-violence, and come out feeling satisfied. The screams of her enemies lingered in her ears like strands of sweet music. The smiles of her friends made her feel even better. It was hard to stay gloomy with Team Naked Badass by her side!

"This was a great night, guys," she said. "Thanks."

Then the runes of the triangle flared, whisking them back to the halls of Our Lady.

# CHAPTER 22:
## GENESIS

ADAGAR SAT ON the bed, staring through the transparent tissue of Velazelza's stomach. Cold chills ran down his spine as he saw that conception had occurred and the foetus was already growing like a fleshy bladder filling up with air. For a moment Vel remained oblivious to the changes taking place inside of her. Eyes closed, she lay on the bed in post-coital languor. Steadily she started to moan.

"Ah, I'm getting a tummy ache," she said, trying to sit up.

But she couldn't sit up. Her belly was already swollen as if in the final trimester of pregnancy. She screamed as she looked down at the creature inside of her.

With a wave of his hand Adagar erected a cocoon of silence around the room. No-one must be allowed to hear her cries, nor those of the thing she was about to bring forth.

"What the fuck?!" she shouted. "AHHHH!"

"Hush, now," said Adagar. There were tears in his eyes. "It will all be over with soon."

Her eyes sprang wide with terror. She slapped herself, trying to awaken from the nightmare—but she was already awake.

"What have you done to me, you creep?!" she yelled. "AHHH!"

She screamed again as the thing began to kick. Adagar peered through her belly. The sight of it startled him. He'd been expecting something misshapen and hideous, as the offspring of demons and gods were reputed to be. And yet the infant seemed perfect. Its skin was radiant, its features symmetrical and soft. Perhaps the tales had been lies? Or perhaps they'd done what no other star-crossed pair of their ilk had managed before, and brought forth a healthy hybrid of deity and demon.

His hopes were dashed as the thing began to bubble, like the Celestial Fire at the heart of the void. Its form mutated wildly. Its growing body was locked in conflict with its two warring essences—the blood of Order, and the fiery sparks of Chaos. Soon the sight of it was enough to make Adagar's stomach churn, and yet he could not look away.

The foetus was mobile now, devouring the demonic eels that dwelled inside Velazelza's body. It looked like the infant Hercules, albeit still unborn. Adagar wondered if it was male or female, or both, or neither. Its freakish anatomy made such a deduction impossible.

Despite the agony, Vel managed to shift back into her demonic shape. Just in time, too, for the foetus was still expanding, threatening to tear her insides apart. She reached down and clawed at her stomach, making a desperate attempt to abort the burgeoning monster.

"No!" snapped Adagar, grasping her hands and holding them back. His deific strength was terrible, pinning her wrists like a vice. "The die is cast," he said. "We must not interfere, now that conception has begun. Such is Father's decree."

"Speak for yourself, arsehole!" she shouted. "AAHHH! Help!"

"Hush, now," he said. "No-one can hear you."

Pinned by the demigod and paralysed by pain, Vel lay there watching as the thing just kept growing and growing. She felt her insides getting torn apart and pushed aside to make way for its presence. Its sleepy eyes opened, gleaming with scintillating fire that seared through her flesh and out through her stomach, setting the ceiling alight.

Adagar gestured again, quelling the flames and creating a barrier of energy to shield the room from damage. The birth must remain undetected.

Vel's screams got louder. Her demonic biology was struggling to keep pace with the damage being done to it. Wounds were piling up faster than her body could heal them. It kicked against her belly, harder and harder.

"No, no, no, no, NO!" she shouted as it kicked itself loose and flew up in the air.

Her insides were splattered, her stomach torn open like a seed pod. The pain was too awful to process. She started shutting down, going into shock. Hovering above her was the misshapen thing, uttering its awful, infantile cries. The umbilicus hung from its belly like a glistening red rope.

Adagar stood up. The girl was done for. His eyes flashed with merciful fire and burned off her head, leaving a smoking black hole upon the mattress just above her shoulders.

"I'm sorry," he said. "But it couldn't have gone any other way. Such is Father's will. And now we must both pay for our sins. Your suffering is over. But mine? Mine is only just beginning."

He reached out towards the hovering infant, feeling the bile rise up in his throat at the thought of its touch. It was screaming, bawling, unleashing a torrent of tears that burned and smoked like some kind of acid. Its flesh was still mutating, bubbling with colours and forms that made his mind reel.

Still he reached out, closer and closer, letting it feel his deific radiance. At length its cries grew softer and softer, its tears less frequent. It flew into his arms and snuggled close to his breast. He winced as it burned him. Then it bit down and started sucking his blood.

Adagar grimaced, but didn't cry out. After all, the thing was his Fate, his penance incarnate. He tried to soothe it as it guzzled his ichor. The blood seemed to nourish it. It was already growing again.

# CHAPTER 23:
## The Last Week of Term

**F**OLLOWING HER ADVENTURE in Iraq, Raza was filled with a sense of catharsis. And after the massacre came a glorious weekend, during which the students were free from classes and curfews. She spent the whole time hanging out with Team Naked Badass, telling jokes and goofing off. They hung around in the schoolyard, selling the souls that Zester had stolen. Raza felt a sense of satisfaction every time they made a sale, imagining the souls of ISIS fighters being huffed down and devoured, providing the users with a powerful high. By the time Monday came around, she'd almost forgotten about the pall of strange oppression that encompassed Our Lady.

Almost. And if she really had forgotten, the resumption of classes would've quickly reminded her. The teachers and staff were acting weirder than ever.

Belzoa was scrubbing down the halls like some neurotic fifties housewife dosed up on Dexedrine diet pills.

Sketh was looking more anxious and downtrodden by the day. Her passionate teaching methods had given way to monotonous lectures that amounted to little more than a timeline of events. She no longer asked the students to engage with history, just to memorize it, like some kind of timetable.

Zenneff's class grew more and more routine. Students were called up in alphabetical order to battle with monsters from beyond. When Raza's name was finally announced, she seized upon the chance to show Zenneff her fighting skills, slaughtering a horde of centaurs almost single-handedly. The things had the lower bodies of ponies and the upper bodies of private school prefects, as if a bunch of polo players had been fused with their mounts. When the smoke settled and the blood started pooling, Raza felt sure that Zenneff would remark on her progress. But he just checked her name off the list and gave her a mark of "satisfactory." He wasn't even using a bell-curve grading system anymore! Just what had happened to his Darwinian teaching methods?

The other classes remained just as humdrum. Chaos Theory was filled with multiple-choice questionnaires, art class with collages. The only excitement was centred around the upcoming Interschool Championship, but even that was marred with apprehension. Most of Our Lady's best players had been barred from competition, making the outcome look bleak. Some of the newer students had stepped in to fill the spots on the roster, but despite their obvious prowess, Our Lady's sports fans were concerned that the Cup would be lost in a humiliating spectacle of utter defeat.

The grim prognosis only added to the sense of malaise that encompassed the school. Raza felt it almost physically. She wanted to hurl. She wasn't being challenged to develop her demonic potential, just babysat and condescended to. It was starting to feel like school back on Earth! And it was all this new principal's fault. The bitch's creepy eyes were everywhere, inspecting the classrooms, staring out from the faces of the cadaverous hall monitors. By Thursday Raza decided she'd had enough. She was going to march right into Sketh's office, and ask what the deal was with all these awful changes.

Adagar spent the weekend locked in a cocoon of self-loathing. Still, he had his duties as a single parent to perform. He destroyed the girl's body and hid away the infant, creating a nursery of sorts in the bowels of Our Lady. At first he was afraid the mistress might find out about it. But the Interschool Championship was approaching next weekend, and she was far too caught up in her own machinations to pay attention to him.

Which was good. Because by the time Monday came around, he was feeling the call again. That night with Velazelza had been the best of his life. For the first time he'd been able to lose himself in total abandon, just like the demons did. He realised now that he'd envied them always. It only added further to his sense of damnation. But if he was already damned, then why not fall even further?

It was a simple matter for him to sneak past the monitors. They had, after all, been designed only to keep watch over the school's demonic population. Thus he started playing Romeo, knocking on doors and professing his love.

He visited the big girl first. Pura was her name. He'd seen her with Val at the party. She was shocked and flattered by his sudden attentions. She asked where Vel was, of course. He simply told her Vel had run away, consumed by jealousy when he'd rejected her in favour of her far more curvaceous companion. After that Pura was like putty in his hands. Or lard. He lost himself in her mountainous breasts and ploughed her pillow-like body. Afterwards her belly got even bigger, until it exploded with monstrous new life.

*And then there were two,* he thought, as he secreted the monster away with its sibling.

He visited Zibb next, the princess. He told her he and Vel had decided to elope. She was off-campus, waiting for him. But he couldn't leave yet. He was too infatuated with Zibb to depart without professing his feelings. He'd promised himself to Vel, and such was now his fate. But could he dare to ask for just one night with Zibb, to sustain him throughout the rest of his days?

The story was a gamble. Nevertheless it seemed he'd

successfully managed to size the girl up. The operatic grandeur of the lie seemed to appeal to her. She also seemed to jump at the chance to carry out an affair with her best friend's ostensible beloved. What a bitch! They fucked on a blanket studded with diamonds. When the monster was born from her torn-open belly, its terrible face was reflected in thousands of glittering facets.

Only Kara rebuffed him, slamming the door in his face. No matter. He just visited another girl, one of the many he'd seen staring at him in class. His false form was beautiful, after all. By Thursday the nursery was crowded with four newborn monsters. It was getting hard to feed them all. Not even his deific ichor could sustain their growing bodies any longer. And growing they were, larger than he was. Soon they'd need a much bigger nursery.

He scoured the school for fresh meat. There were many sources. He hunted the moon-calves that haunted the courtyard, bringing their bodies back to his children. He even led a few unsuspecting students down into the depths. His offspring seemed to prefer the live meals. How they warbled with delight as they played with the victims like chew toys, squeezing them, making them tremor and squeak. Adagar's heart began to fill up with pride. Perhaps it would be *his* new progeny that would one day inherit the cosmos, displacing the brood of his Father and the spawn of Chaos both?

Only time would tell.

Raza burst into Sketh's office and slammed the door behind her.

"I'm sorry, Raza," said the teacher, barely looking up as she scribbled at her desk. "But I'm very busy right now. If you want some counselling, then you'll just have to make an appointment."

"The fuck I will!" said Raza, slamming her hands down on the desk.

The papers and paperweights jumped. Amongst them was a glittering sapphire.

"Just what the fuck is going on around here?" snapped Raza. "Everyone's acting weird, especially you. I want some answers!"

"It's all very simple, I'm afraid," said Sketh. "There's a new principal in residence. The school is undergoing a lot of reform. I'm sorry if you don't like it, but we can't always get what we want in life, now can we?"

Sketh's words were measured, but there was a glimmer of terror in her eyes. Raza stared at her, perplexed.

"I just don't understand," said Raza. "Why're you letting that bitch walk all over you? She's ruining the school. I thought you and the others were tough. You're supposed to be demons. But you're all acting like a bunch of cowards! Even Zenneff. It's like Noviscula's got his balls in her handbag!"

Sketh rose and placed her hands on the desk commandingly. "Now that's enough, young lady!" she snapped. "As it happens, the rest of the staff tend to agree with the changes going on around here. And I won't have you disrespecting the teachers like that, especially not the principal . . . "

The lecture went on for what felt like an hour. At length Raza left the room in a state of deep confusion. Sketh had really chewed her out. It'd been the tongue-lashing of the century! But the woman's eyes had been tremoring and fearful, like those of a rat in a cage. What did it all mean? Raza played hooky the rest of the day and sat in her room, mulling over the weirdness of it all. Just what kind of terrible hold did Noviscula have on the rest of the staff?

At length there came a knock on her door. She was expecting one of the other members of Team Naked Badass, or even Sketh herself, having reverted to her pleasant demeanour and come to apologise. Thus she was surprised to find Karanora standing in front of her, looking distinctly upset. She glanced at Raza uneasily. There was still a great distance between them.

"Can I come in?" asked Kara.

"Okay," said Raza. "Sure . . . "

Kara pushed past her and shut the door. She sat on the side of the bed, quivering, but her eyes were defiant.

"Vel is missing," she said.

Raza had noticed the other girl's absence, but hadn't really thought about it, probably because she'd been trying to ignore her. Vel's vanishing act had only made the task easier.

"Pura's missing, too," said Kara. "As of Monday night. And Zibb disappeared on Tuesday. They've all just vanished into thin air!"

"Could they have run off?" asked Raza. "I hear a lot of students are absconding from the school, now that the principal's arrived."

Kara shook her head, crying. "No way," she said. "There's just no way they'd leave without telling me. Something's wrong! The last time I saw Vel she was going off with that new boy, Gogorizel."

"Well did you ask him where she went?" asked Raza.

Kara nodded. "He came to my room last night, told me some bullshit story about how they'd all run away together. Said he'd take me to see them. Then he started coming on to me. I slammed the door in his face." Kara froze, then looked up, her eyes full of fear. "Raza, I think he's killed them all! The way you killed Star Geddon, only deliberately. I think he really is a fuckicidal maniac! Either that or he's holding them prisoner somewhere, doing . . . *things* to them."

Raza's hackles rose. Could such a thing truly be happening? And right in the midst of all these other awful changes going on at Our Lady? She felt the presence of terrible forces moving in the shadows, like sharks beneath black water. But she couldn't quite see their shapes—not yet, at least.

"I need your help, Raza," said Kara. "I don't know who

else to turn to. All my friends are gone. You're the only one I can think of who might be able to handle something like this. You survived the Zone, after all. You could deal with a monster like Gogorizel."

Raza thought about helping, but she was still so upset with Vel and the others.

"And why should I help you?" she snapped. "You guys treated me like dirt!"

"I'm sorry," said Kara. "I'm sorry about all of that. About freezing you out, putting that stuff in your bed . . . "

Raza's eyes snapped wide as she remembered the pig's head and goat's balls that'd been stuffed beneath her bedcovers, along with that insulting note. *Here's a treat,* it'd read, *just in case you get hungry.*

"You guys did that?!" she snapped.

Kara shot a guilty glance at the floor. "It was Zibbilique's idea. I tried to talk them out of it. But Vel was really worked up. You know how she gets. She really liked Star, and I guess she felt like you'd betrayed her, or something. But she felt bad about it later. She said she wanted to make things up to you, once you got back from the Zone. We were all supposed to apologise. But then you came back with your new friends, and this brand-new attitude of yours, and Vel got angry again. Especially when you snubbed her, that first day back in the hall . . . "

Raza paused to consider. Had this whole thing between her and Vel really been so utterly stupid? Had they stubbornly held onto resentment and treated each other like crap, whilst secretly wanting to be friends once again? The answer, she knew, was "yes."

And now Vel was missing. She felt a surge of anger, both at herself, and at whatever sinister force had snatched Vel away.

"Okay," said Raza. "I'll help."

"What're you gonna do?" asked Kara.

"I'm gonna go find this Gogorizel guy," she said, "and get to the bottom of this."

# CHAPTER 24:
## STAFF MEETING

**S**OON AFTER RAZA left her office, Sketh was forced to rise from her desk. The invisible strings that bound her body were compelling her to move like a marionette.

And the puppet master was angry. Sketh could feel the tremors of wrath moving through the strings as they forced her through the hallway and into the staff room. Most of the staff were already there—Zenneff, Belzoa, Kellikassey, Vorovox the alchemist, Bambexa the art teacher, and a half-dozen others.

The thing that called itself Noviscula was there, too. It sat on a throne made from Jellen's tortured flesh. Sketh could hardly bear to look at the fate that had befallen the young student teacher. His form had been turned inside-out, his soft, wet organs used as cushions for the principal's backside. His face was skinless and inverted. His mouth, such as it was, was not allowed to scream. Like the rest of them, he could only express himself through the framing of his eyes as they quivered with terror and pain.

The principal rose. It was not a woman, nor a demon. Sketh watched as it unzipped its false flesh like a jumpsuit and resumed its true form—that of an angel. Sketh's skin began to prickle and itch as its radiance filled up the room, blazing forth from the thousand sapphire eyes that covered its body from its neck to its toes. The beady black eyes in its face glared at the demons with utmost disdain.

"You're all a great disappointment to me," said the angel.

Its voice was both mellifluous and horrible, like a beautiful tune being hummed by serial killers. It began to stride about the room, staring at the staff and flexing its fingers, which were fitted with ornate golden rings, one for each of the demons. Upon each ring was a series of sigils surrounding the demon's true name. This was the source of the forbidden and terrible magick that held Sketh and the others in slavery.

The angel flicked its hand casually. Invisible tendrils reached out from its fingers and lashed them with agony. Sketh wanted to double over from the pain, but the angel held her upright in spite of herself. The rest of the staff were likewise motionless. The only sign of the agonies they endured was the quivering cast of their eyes.

Then the angel's fingers fell still, ending the pain—for now, at least.

"I see what you've been doing," it hissed. "I see it all. Did you forget that I'm *His* fucking eyes incarnate?"

Another flex of the fingers, another wave of agony. Why did Sketh get the sense there was worse yet to come?

"I *see*," said the angel again. "I see the way you've been gazing at the students with all those meaningful looks, trying to tip them off to what's happening. It's pathetic, you know? The only thing dumber than a teenager is a demonic one. These brats'll never figure out what's going on. They're far too busy fucking and drinking and flouting your authority. But you shall not flout mine, do you hear me? I think it's high time you all took a lesson in servitude."

Sketh glanced over at Jellen's ruined body. Would such a fate now fall upon the rest of them? She felt clammy and nauseous. Trapped, in the most absolute way possible. Even if she were buried alive she'd still have more freedom of movement than this. She waited, knowing she was powerless against whatever horror was coming. The angel could tear them inside-out, or pull their bodies through the eye of a needle, and yet still keep them alive. Such were the nature of its gifts from the Demiurge. What brand of cruelty would it choose to deliver?

Sketh's pussy started getting wet.

*Oh no*, she thought. *Not this. Anything but this . . .*

She climbed up on the edge of the desk, hiked up her skirts, and started fingering herself. She had no control over any of it, of course. The commands were coming straight from the angel, conveyed along the invisible strings that bound her in servitude. She looked on in horror as Belzoa stripped off his boilersuit and started walking towards her. His crotch-face awoke and opened its lips. Out came a tumescent tongue that was shaped like a cock and dripping with fluid.

In moments Belzoa was standing before her. His eyes looked just as appalled as hers at what the angel was forcing him to do, but he had no more control over his body than she did.

Sketh glanced around the room. Kellikassey was bending over the table and thrusting out her butt. Zenneff was behind her, his giant steel codpiece removed, revealing a prick like a meaty harpoon. Other teachers and staff were getting naked too, arranging themselves on the furniture.

Sketh glared across the room at the angel. The thing was smiling smugly. But why was it doing this? A sexless abomination, the angel had no libido at all. It was created that way. So why was it torturing them thus? Just for the sake of their sheer humiliation?

Belzoa plunged into her, puncturing her thoughts. The angel made her buck and moan like a porn star on set, but inside she was howling. So too was Belzoa. His eyes began brimming with tears. Sketh was doubly shocked. She'd never imagined the gloomy old bastard showing any such emotion.

She couldn't bear the sight of it, and glanced away. A poor choice. Zenneff was ramming Kellikassey from behind, straining the limits of her demonic pussy. But he wasn't the only one surrounding her. Vorovox was on the table in front of her, stuffing her mouth. Gragoul, the music teacher, was slipping his prehensile prick up her butthole. Were there no limits to the angel's drive for degradation?

"I noticed there were a few more males in here than females," said the angel. "So I thought Miss Kellikassey could oblige. She is a big slut, after all. She's probably used to getting triple-stuffed. Still, who knows where the rest of the lunch break will take us? We've all heard about musical chairs. How about musical receptacles of lust?"

Sketh tried to close her eyes, but couldn't. Belzoa hammered into her, gripping her thighs as she fingered her clit and fondled her breasts. Her body was wracked with a horrible orgasm she just couldn't stop. She turned her gaze to the angel, and glared. Its smile just got even more smug.

"That's right," it said. "Soak it all in. It's time you learned your place, like I said. And what are you all anyway, but beasts? And beasts shouldn't trifle with the lords of creation. You're better off rutting in the fields, right where you belong."

Sketh felt a surge of anger that overcame all sense of humiliation. She had to fight back. But how?

Suddenly she realised. The angel was trying to enslave them. And it had, at least physically, but in their minds they were free. They still had some power of choice, however limited.

So Sketh decided to consent. She imagined Belzoa as the lover she'd always dreamed of being fucked by. She imagined she wanted him more than anyone else in the world. With the amount of pleasure the angel was forcing her to feel, it wasn't even so hard to achieve. She gazed up at the grumpy old demon with eyes full of lust.

*I've always wanted you,* she thought, trying to speak through her eyes.

He seemed to get the message. His eyes filled with light that seemed to burn through the pain he was feeling. A moment later they were filled with desire.

*That's it,* thought Sketh. *Give it to me, you old dog!*

Her eyes roved the room, flashing lusty looks at the others. She glanced at Kellikassey first. Zenneff and Gragoul were behind her, their pricks pumping her holes like a pair of alternating pistons. In front of her was Vorovox, on whose cock she was sucking, bobbing her head like a circus seal. Her lips and tongue moved like supple red velvet, but her eyes were burning with anger.

Then Sketh caught her gaze. She seemed to catch on immediately. Her glowing eyes filled up with desire as she got filled from all angles.

Sketh continued to glance around the room. Soon all the demons were looking equally horny, even the ones without horns. The lust in their eyes matched the ardour of their bodies. Sketh felt herself on the verge of another orgasm. This one she didn't try to resist. The sensation was all the more powerful now, both from the added volition and her sense of defiance as she stuck it to the angel. The climax came so hard it almost felt as though she were slipping loose from the magickal strings that bound her. Her body shook apart into a pile of writhing serpents. Her pussy took the form of a snake with a vagina-like mouth, its jaws open wide to swallow a blast of Belzoa's semen.

Kellikassey moaned. For the first time in weeks it sounded like her very own voice. Semen arced through the air and spattered her lips; Zenneff and Gragoul filled her up from behind 'til rivulets of cum trickled down her red thighs.

The angel shouted with rage. "That's enough!" it snapped.

The orgy came to an immediate end; the marionette lovers stepped apart. Sketh glanced at Belzoa with a languid look of triumph. He gave her one back.

"I should've known you degenerates would take pleasure in this," growled the angel. "I bet you think you're all very clever, don't you? Well I've still got plenty of time to make you suffer. Classes don't start for another ten minutes!"

Sketh glanced up at the clock. The angel was indeed correct about the time. For a moment she felt glad the angel was so obsessed with punctuality and order. A demonic principal would probably just cancel the day's lessons and torment them all evening.

Her gratitude didn't last long. The angel wriggled its fingers and unleashed another wave of agony. Once gain Sketh tried to scream—and failed.

# CHAPTER 25:
## TERROR IN UTERO

"**A**RE YOU INSANE?!**" shouted Skiddix.

"Keep your voice down!" whispered Zester.

It was Friday, lunchtime, and Team Naked Badass was huddled in the kitchen near a sink of dirty dishes. Raza had just finished explaining her harebrained scheme to the others. Apparently she suspected this Gogorizel kid of killing or abducting a number of girls. Her plan was to approach him that afternoon during sports class, lure him away towards the shower block—which would have already been cleared out by Vogg and the others—then seduce him, have sex with him, and thereby find out if he was indeed a fuckicidal maniac.

Skiddix could hardly contain himself.

"That is the worst, stupidest, most contemptible plan I've ever heard of!" he said.

"But what other option is there?" said Raza. "We can't go ask the teachers for help, they're useless at the moment. That bitch Noviscula has them wrapped around her little finger. That means we have to figure this stuff out for ourselves. We all know there's something spooky going on around here, and I'm not just talking about this batch of disappearances, either. The teachers are all acting weird, and the principal gives me the creeps."

"Me too," said Zester.

"Me three," said Vogg. "And I'm not usually scared of anything!"

"Right," said Raza. "And whatever's going on, I've got a feeling this new guy Gogorizel is the key to it all. If I can confront him alone, and find out the truth, then maybe we can figure out what the fuck is going on around here."

"Right," said Skiddix. "But are you forgetting the part of the plan that says you have to have sex with a total stranger, one who just might be a fuckicidal maniac?!"

Raza took a deep breath. She knew Skiddix had a crush on her, and this would be hard for him to hear. Still, she had to speak the truth.

"I've thought about that part a lot," said Raza. "And the truth is that Gogorizel is a really cute guy. So I kinda wanna have sex with him anyway. So if it turns out he's not the fuckicidal maniac, then I'll probably just wind up having a good time. And if he is, then this is the only way I can think of to catch him in the act before anyone else disappears."

"Now that's what I call a win-win!" said Zester.

Skiddix wasn't convinced. "But what if he hurts you, too?" he asked. "What if he . . . " He froze. He couldn't bear to voice the words *what if he kills you?*

Vogg gave him a disbelieving look. "Come on, buddy," he said. "This is Raza we're talking about. Carnage incarnate, remember? Spawn of the God-Killer! She can handle anything."

"She's not invincible," said Skiddix.

Raza put a comforting hand on his forearm. "I know that," she said. "Which is why you guys would be waiting, just around the corner. If I need you, I'll call out, and you can come to the rescue. This isn't a solo mission. It's Team Naked Badass, all the way!"

Skiddix pulled his arm back. "I still don't buy it," he said. "I mean, why're we risking our necks just to help out those bitches? They treated you like a leper, Raza. They don't deserve this kind of sacrifice."

"Vel was my friend," said Raza. "Maybe not a true friend like you guys, but a friend all the same. And like I said before, there's something fishy going on around here, and we need to get to the bottom of it. This could be the clue we've all been waiting for."

Skiddix paused for a moment, as if weighing up her arguments. Then he stormed off.

"Fuck this," he said. "If you wanna commit suicide, I'm not helping!"

Vogg sighed. "I'll go after him," he said.

He got up and jogged after Skiddix, finding the boy sitting out in a desolate corner of the schoolyard. His single giant eye was wet with tears. He wiped them off as Vogg sat down beside him.

"It's time to have a talk, buddy," said Vogg.

"About what?" asked Skiddix. "You can say what you want, but I won't go along with this. It's nuts."

"Right," said Vogg. "But just hear me out for a minute, okay? I know the real reason why you're so against the plan."

"Oh yeah?" he asked, dismissively. "What's that?"

"It's because you're in love with Raza, and you can't stand the thought of her banging that guy."

Skiddix scoffed, but the words rang true. Vogg kept on talking.

"But the fact is eventually she is gonna bang someone. And you know what? It ain't gonna be you, man. I know that sucks, and it hurts, and everything, but that's the truth. She just isn't into you like that. And trust me, she's never, ever gonna be."

Skiddix sighed. "Is it that obvious?" he asked.

"Are you kidding me?" said Vogg. "It couldn't get more obvious if you wore a giant neon sign with 'I love Raza' written on it."

"Well what am I supposed to do about it?"

"Ask me, man, you've got three choices. The first option is you stop hanging out with her, because you just can't stand all the pain and frustration."

"Stop hanging out with her?" asked Skiddix, horrified. "I don't wanna do that!"

"Right," said Vogg. "So the second choice is you keep on pining away. Pretend to be her friend whilst secretly carrying a torch, pathetically hoping that she'll one day settle for you, even though you know she never will."

"That sounds awful," said Skiddix. "I don't wanna do that either!"

"Good," said Vogg. "Which is why I suggest you go for option three. Man up, move on, accept how she feels, and just be the friend that she wants you to be. Think you can handle that?"

Skiddix sighed and glanced up at the sky. He peered long and far, all across the glittering nebulas of the cosmos to a place of pure and seething starlight. And he also looked inwards, as well. At length he wiped his eye again, and smiled. He'd made his decision.

"Yeah," he said. "I think I can handle that."

Vogg smiled and slapped him on the back. "Good," he said. "Now how's about we help Raza with this crazy scheme of hers, huh? There's probably no better way to get over your crush, than to help her go screw another guy!"

Somehow Skiddix was able to laugh. Then he paused.

"Vogg?" he asked. "How come you know so much about all this stuff?"

Vogg scoffed. "You think I haven't been in your shoes before, man?" he said. "Shit, every guy has. Probably every girl, too. It's just the way of the universe. And you can either accept it, or act like a giant, raging dick-hole."

"Let me guess," said Skiddix. "When this same thing happened to you, back in the past, you chose the second option, huh?"

"Big time, man," said Vogg. "Big time. But I learned my lesson well, and now I'm passing on that hard-earned wisdom to you. Now come on, let's get going. Lunchtime's almost over!"

They hurried back across the schoolyard, towards the cafeteria.

"PSST! Hey!"

Adagar was sitting on the bleachers, towelling himself dry after football practice, when he heard the voice. He glanced down through the gaps in the seats. There in the darkness underneath the stands was the spawn of the God-Killer, beckoning to him.

"Down here!" she said.

He glanced around to see if anyone was watching. They weren't, so he slipped through the cracks between the seats and joined her in the shadows below. She wore a short skirt and knee-high socks that drew his eyes toward her thighs like the vectors of a beautiful painting.

"You're Raza, aren't you?" he asked as he dragged his gaze toward her face.

She nodded. "And you're Gogorizel. I hear you're quite the lady-killer. Thought I'd come by and try you out for myself."

She licked her lips and stepped towards him, crossing into a slender beam of light.

Adagar's mind started whirling. Was this some kind of trap? Could she know what he was up to? It seemed impossible. More likely she was just a horny young demoness, enticed by his physique.

Before he could think any more she was already clasping his shoulders and pressing against him, staring deep into his eyes. Motes of red light sparkled in her pupils like stars in the void, a sign of demon blood piercing the façade of human form.

"You wanna fool around?" she asked. "I know just the place. It's not far from here."

Adagar's mind was still whirling. He felt a good deal of blood race down from his head, making it harder and harder to think. Something else was growing harder, too, straining the limits of his gym shorts. And yet a part of his mind managed to flash up a red sign of warning. It was mid-afternoon, and there were a lot of witnesses about. What if he was the last one to be seen with her?

*Who cares?* he thought. *It'll all be over tomorrow anyway.*

It was true. Something big was about to go down; this would probably be his last opportunity to lose himself in the blissful oblivion of demonic sex. And there were other, deeper reasons to take advantage of her offer. Raza was the spawn of the god-killer, the most feared and despised of all demons. If Adagar could kill her, he'd be doing his Father a definite service, one that might even earn him some measure of forgiveness for his current transgressions. And, if his seed should take root in her womb—as he knew it almost certainly would—the result would be an offspring of terrible power and almost unlimited potential, the greatest of Adagar's growing brood, a monster to rival even the might of his Father. He could use such an infant to tear down the heavens and scorch all the worlds. Then he wouldn't even have to worry about his burden of sins, or about earning forgiveness. He could be free. Free with his children, in a howling black void.

Plus, she was hot.

"Sounds like it might be fun," he said, echoing her carefree attitude. "But maybe we could get together later in the evening? When it's dark. I could come to your room . . . "

Raza smiled. "I'm afraid it's now or never," she said. "I'm all revved up. And when I get like this, something just has to be done about it. Of course if you're not interested, then I'm sure I'll be able to go find myself some other source of fun. Who knows, maybe I'll get back to you in a couple of weeks?"

She stepped back, as if ready to leave.

"Wait!" he said. "Where did you have in mind?"

Raza's heart pounded. She never thought she'd be so good at playing the seductress! She led him to the shower block. True to their word, Vogg and the others had cleared the place out. She didn't see them on the way in, but she knew they were hiding there somewhere. Their job was to keep the place empty and respond to her signal should things go awry.

Soon she and the boy stood alone in the humid dampness of the shower room. Adagar looked around nervously.

"Are you sure we're alone?" he asked.

"Totally," she said. "I made sure of it. What's the matter, you getting cold feet? Don't tell me you're worried about people spying on us. A guy like you doesn't have anything to be shy about . . . "

She strode up and kissed him. She could hear her demonic instincts shouting in her head, getting hotter and hotter with the advent of lust. Her cunt began to drip like a salivating mouth as she pressed against his hard, athletic physique.

He kissed her back. They started blindly undressing each other. She felt his prick against her stomach before she even saw it unveiled. She stepped back, taking in the sight of it. It was even bigger than Star's! Just how big would it get once he'd transformed? She gripped it in one hand, stroking it gently as they kissed.

Adagar's hand drifted down to her wetness. He slipped his fingers past her lips and further inside. She was hot and tight, squeezing his digits as her juices overflowed.

She stretched a thigh up over his waist, then reached down around the curve of her backside and guided him in. Slowly, tentatively. But she wasn't teasing. It seemed to him like she didn't have that much experience at this. Had her claims to promiscuity been nothing but a pretence?

He slipped inside of her. She really was tight. Her eyes opened wide with pleasure and shock.

Raza felt out of her depth again. Memories of her deflowering were hazy at best, but this was vivid, this was

NOW. His entry, for all of its slowness, was still pretty jarring. Jarring, to be sure, but also unbelievably hot. The exquisite shock of entry almost knocked her off her feet. After that he was pushing inside of her, deeper and deeper, filling her up and stretching her out. She went all weak in the knees. Could she even maintain this demanding position? It seemed like a feat for sexual veterans. Maybe she'd have to lie down, like a dead fish, and let him plough her from on top, the way Star Geddon had.

But no. This had to be face-to-face, eye-to-eye. If he really was a fuckicidal maniac, then the playing field had to be level. She couldn't let him get on top of her, couldn't let him get that sort of advantage if things came to blows.

Easier said than done. She had one leg around his waist, another on the floor. *He* had one arm around *her* waist, another on her backside, supporting her weight. Even so the position felt precarious. Soon his thrusts got harder, deeper. Waves of pleasure rippled out from her pussy. Her whole body shook. Her single leg connected to the floor like an unstable pillar, ready to fall.

He tapped her cervix with the head of his cock. She almost jumped out of her skin! Surely she'd fall, dragging him down on top of her.

*Silly me!* she thought.

In all the mind-melting excitement, she'd somehow forgotten the presence of the fire. Perhaps because in the past it'd always overwhelmed her, unbidden, every time she'd tried to have sex. But now it was hers to command. And it was waiting there, hungry and impatient, champing at the bit. She stoked it up and felt the change begin.

They started rutting faster and faster. Soon she seemed less like an ingénue to Adagar and more like a beast.

Adagar watched her. The pinpricks of redness in her pupils expanded and combined until her eyes became orbs of solid light. She started panting and growling as her body transformed. Her breasts and arms multiplied, doubling up on her torso. Her skin became blood-red, as if stained by her father's act of deicide.

Adagar grinned. It was time to surrender!

His body grew and grew. So did his cock, spearing her burgeoning depths. She gave a howl of pleasure. She was fully transformed now. Her face was a muzzle filled with metal fangs. She grinned as he transformed.

His head became massive and blunt, like that of an ox, crowned by a pair of curling horns. Now they were truly naked. She in her natural shape, he in the shape he wished was truly his.

A mounting frenzy overcame both of them. Somehow he had the presence of mind to raise up a shield around the room as they crashed into the walls and tumbled to the ground.

The playing field was no longer level. Raza was on top of him, riding him wildly. Her tightness was very nearly painful, the friction almost enough to skin him alive. Her breast-mouths were snapping, biting his chest as she leaned down to kiss him.

The kiss was savage. She bit off a part of his face and roared. They started snapping at each other like horses or dogs. Wounds opened up and healed in an instant, spilling out blood to mix with their mingling saliva.

Raza felt as if she might lose herself again. A climax was coming, one that threatened to eclipse all consciousness and give free rein to the fire. She felt those bloody instincts stirring up. How much hotter it would be if she bit off his head as she came!

She was no longer worried about whether or not *he* was a fuckicidal maniac. This became a test of her own will. She bucked and bounced, feeling the crescendo of pleasure start to mount towards a shuddering meridian. The flame got brighter, hotter, her consciousness dimming, shrinking, straining through the eye of a needle. There were no thoughts now, only sensation. Her eyes filled up with overflowing fire. She was close, so close!

She howled with ecstasy as the orgasm filled her. Her jaws shot down—

Chomping the air above his head. She'd managed to pull back just in time, to keep just a little of her consciousness afloat. She kept on riding, shuddering now, throwing back her head as the aftermath filled her. He seemed to sense her satisfaction. His pent-up lust shot up and overflowed from her pussy. His eyes rolled back, his body turning rigid and finally limp. What a rush!

Her body shrank down as she slipped off his prick. Semen dripped from her pussy. There was so much inside of her. Conception was surely unavoidable, Adagar thought.

He shrank down and lay there, panting, trying to recover his breath and get ready to act, to deal with the horror he knew was approaching.

Raza sat with one leg raised, soaked in sweat and splattered with blood. She smiled, satisfied.

*Guess he's not a fuckicidal maniac, after all,* she thought. *As a matter of fact, neither am I!*

Suddenly Raza felt a pressure in her belly, coupled with a growing sense of nausea, as though she were going to hurl.

*Shit,* she thought. *All the excitement must've messed with my stomach!*

"Be right back," she said, rushing to her feet and heading off to the bathroom.

Adagar watched her leave with a growing sense of panic. Evidently she'd recovered from the exhaustion much quicker than he had. He stumbled to his feet, still week in the knees.

"Wait!" he said, still almost breathless. He had to follow her, to be there when the monster was born.

Raza raced to the adjacent block of toilets. Adagar followed, still flushed with exhaustion. She ran into one of the stalls, slammed the door, and threw up right away. Her abdomen roiled with ever-growing agony. Something was squirming, pushing, trying to get out. She shrank down into a crouch instinctively. Her muscles began to heave and contract. She groaned from the growing sensations of pressure and pain.

Adagar stumbled into the bathroom, searching for her. He heard her cries coming from one of the stalls. His deific vision pierced through the timbers, finding her squatting on the floor, her back against the side of the cubicle. Should he kick down the door, or just stay outside, waiting to deal with the inevitable aftermath?

Raza screamed again. The pressure was growing, growing—

Then something popped out of her pussy and fell on the floor in a torrent of juices and blood. A horrible, vestigial thing, like a bird or a reptile, or a cross between both. Its dainty flesh was all but transparent.

Raza suppressed a cry of revulsion. Her eyes went wide. Instinctively she picked up the thing, cast it down into the vomit-filled bowl, and flushed. She tried not to look as it circled the drain, but she couldn't pull away. Was there a tremor of life in its embryonic limbs, or was it merely being stirred into a semblance of movement by the spiralling forces of water and waste? Was it gurgling and gasping for breath, or was that just the sound of the drainage system burbling to life? At last she looked away, too shocked to process the events.

Adagar watched as she flushed away the miscarried monster. Now this he had not been expecting. Like Raza herself, he too had no time to process events. Panicked he hurried from the bathroom, wrapped himself up in a towel, and sprinted off across the campus.

Zester saw him leaving, half-naked and splattered with blood. Had something happened to Raza? But there hadn't been any signal! She rushed into the shower block, yelling for the others.

They found Raza sitting wide-eyed on a bench, her face filled with shock.

Skiddix put a hand on her shoulder.

"What happened?" he said. "Did he hurt you?"

Raza shook her head. "No," she said. "In fact, as far as demons go, he seemed like a perfect gentleman."

"Then what's wrong?"

Raza shot a wide-eyed glance in the direction of the bathroom.

"I think I might've just had a miscarriage!" she said.

# CHAPTER 26:
## THE DEPTHS

"**ARE YOU POSITIVE?**" asked Zester.

"Definitely," said Raza. "I saw that . . . that thing, coming right out of me!"

"Are you sure you're not just having your period?" asked Vogg. "Maybe it was just a big, gloopy bit of period blood that happened to look like a foetus?"

Zester sighed. "What do you know about periods, dumbass?" she snapped.

"I know there can be big, gloopy bits sometimes," he said. "I also know a real man doesn't shirk from the Red Sea of Love. Which is why I don't mind creaming your raspberry roll whenever you're on the rag!"

Zester slapped him.

"OW!" he said.

Skiddix sighed. "Can we get back to the topic at hand, please?" he said. "Raza, are you sure you saw what you think you saw?"

"Of course I am," she said. "I can't fucking un-see it! It was all see-through, like a baby bird. And its face, its body . . . it was freakish, abominable. I think it was some kind of mutant!"

"All babies look like mutants, if you ask me," said Zester. "And foetuses look even worse."

"Trust me," said Raza, "this one looked really, really awful."

"It must've been from when you slept with Star Geddon,"

said Zester. "Who knew he'd be capable of making ugly babies?"

Raza shook her head. "No, that's not possible," she said. "They gave me a pregnancy test when I was in sick bay. And I took another one when I got back from the Zone. They both came back negative!"

Zester's eyes went wide. "So you're saying you got pregnant now, this very afternoon? Raza, that's crazy! It's totally impossible! I mean, everyone knows demons breed like rabbits. Sometimes they can pop out a baby in under a month. But a fully-formed foetus in less than five minutes? No way!"

"But I'm sure that's what's happened!" said Raza, starting to sob.

"Maybe it was just some kinda hallucination?" suggested Vogg. "Some demons secrete hallucinogens from their bodies. I used to date a chick like that. Every time I ate her pussy I'd be tripping balls for hours!"

Zester shot him a jealous glare.

"Don't worry, babe," he said, fondling her rump. "She couldn't compare to you!"

For a moment they stood there in silence as Raza wiped her tears away. Then Skiddix's cyclopean eye popped open wide.

"Oh shit," he said. "I think I might know what just happened."

"What?!" asked the others, simultaneously.

"I don't wanna speculate yet," he said. "It's too awful to contemplate. But I can find out the truth, easily enough. I just need to run a simple alchemical test on the foetus. Raza, where did you put it?"

She shot a glance at the toilet through the stall's open door.

"I flushed it," she said, gloomily.

"Well that makes things harder," said Skiddix.

"But not impossible," said Vogg. "Looks like we're taking a trip to the sewers!"

The giant rat came rushing from the shadows and into the torchlight. Of course it wasn't really much of a rat any more, having been transformed by the myriad bacteria that dwelled in the bowels of Our Lady. It filled up the tunnel ahead of them, bloated with buboes and masses of tumorous eyes.

"Blast it!" shouted Vogg.

"I can't, remember?" said Skiddix. "There're too many gases in the air. A single flame could blow the whole place!"

He was right. The tunnel was filled with a stinking miasma that smelled worse than a death-eater's doggy bag. And it was highly flammable, to boot.

"I'll handle it," said Raza, as the rat ran towards them.

She shifted up into demon form and met the beast head-on. Its massive jaws opened wide, its front teeth as big as the blades of a guillotine. Luckily they weren't nearly as sharp. Raza grabbed hold of its incisors, one in each hand, and wrenched. Its mouth cracked open like a bear-trap being violently reset, until its jaws were a vertical plane held apart by Raza's arms.

A colony of parasites festooned its open throat, wriggling their mouths at the promise of meat. They must've been feeding on the rat's victims for years, eating its kills and shitting down its throat. Talk about adding insult to injury! Raza felt like she was delivering a mercy kill as she tore the creature's jaws in half and left it to bleed out and die in the river of muck that filled up the base of the pipeline.

She shifted back into human form.

"Well that's that taken care of," she said, glancing at the junction that lay beyond the corpse. "Which way now?"

Our Lady's sewer system was almost as labyrinthine as the campus. They'd already been down there for hours, trudging through a stinking maze of tunnels and pipelines that would've put Daedalus to shame. They had some blueprints, of course, stolen from the library, but even those weren't much help. The ancient infrastructure was decaying, many of the passages blocked by fallen debris or mountains of accumulated waste.

And then there were the creatures. Not since the Zone had they encountered such horrors. And to think all the time these things had been lurking right under their feet! It was little wonder. Our Lady was home to students from all over the cosmos. The talismans they wore might've protected them from interstellar viruses, but it didn't protect their environment. All that waste from all those different biologies had created a nightmare maelstrom of bacteria in the bowels of Our Lady. And that bacteria brought forth monsters more repulsive than Raza could've ever imagined. Forget about all those albino alligators that famously haunted the toilets of Florida. There were tapeworms here the size of anacondas. Mutated rodents built like city buses.

And then there were the Shitmen. A colony of troglodytes made out of sentient bacteria and man-sized clumps of flushed-away waste. Raza didn't wanna think about the details of the stuff that composed their lumpy bodies. And she didn't have to. The name said it all!

Raza felt like she'd need about five million showers once they finally resurfaced. Their battles in the sewers had been far from glamorous, to say the least. Still, surely now they must be approaching their final destination? Skiddix scrutinized the map.

"The outflow pipe from the shower block should be just up ahead," he said. "We just need to take a right turn at this junction . . . "

They followed his directions, wading through the sewer stream in knee-high gumboots. Soon they came to a cul-de-sac. High above hung a pipeline, dripping its contents down atop a tower of filth. Interestingly, it wasn't quite a faecal as Raza had feared. Most of it was made up of wet paper towels.

"Huh," said Vogg. "So that's where they all end up."

"Don't tell me," said Skiddix. "You're the one who's always flushing all those paper towels down the toilets and blocking the drains, huh?"

"Guilty as charged!" he said with a grin. "But hey, it's like they say—you've gotta make your own fun in this world!"

Raza just stared up at the giant, horrible pile, scanning for the foetus.

"Where do you think it'll be?" she asked.

"Probably somewhere near the top," said Skiddix.

"Come on," said Zester, glancing at Vogg. "Start climbing. You're the one who built this leaning tower of *pooper mache*, so it's only fair *you* get to climb it!"

Vogg sighed, then steeled himself. "Okay," he said. "But I'm gonna deserve a medal after this!"

"Does Team Naked Badass give out medals?" asked Skiddix.

"We do now!" said Vogg as he started climbing the pile. His boots made wet sucking sounds as they scrambled for purchase.

Raza caught a glimpse of movement in the shadows. She turned to Skiddix. The look on his face said he'd seen them already, a quartet of figures that moved with the silence of Iga clan ninja.

"Heads up, Vogg," said Raza. "We've got company."

The figures stepped out into the torchlight. Their bodies were so barnacled with filth that Raza at first mistook them for another band of Shitmen. Then she realised what they were—man-sized, mutated tortoises, their shells covered with parasites, their beaks encrusted with blood. They wore bandanas made from wet wipes and belts made from panty liners.

"Check out these bodacious babes," said one of them.

He stepped into the light, spinning a pair of nun-chucks that were nothing more than two giant tampons connected with string. Two giant, ossified tampons, manufactured for some inhuman vagina. They were thick as rolling pins.

*Talk about heavy flow!* thought Raza.

Another of the monsters stepped forth, wielding a toilet plunger as though it were a staff.

"Don't get carried away, Koons," he said. "Those 'bodacious babes,' as you called them, just killed our sensei!"

*Sensei?* thought Raza. *Could they mean that giant, horrible rat?*

"I can't help it, Duchamp," he said. "I'm a party dude. And I wanna party with these babes!"

"We'll I'm the leader, remember?" said another. "And I say we have to punish them for what they just did!"

He brandished a pair of katanas fashioned from dental floss. The strands had been woven and folded together so tightly that the final result almost resembled the layered quality of Japanese steel—albeit white, and covered with bits of old dental plaque.

Another of the monsters stepped forth from the shadows, glaring angrily.

"Warhol is right," he said. "These jerks deserve to pay. Let's skin em alive!" He spun a pair of toilet brushes sharpened like prison shanks.

"Now let's not get carried away, Emin," said Warhol. "We're the good guys, remember?"

"Speak for yourself, bro. I'm bad!"

The monsters started advancing, brandishing their weapons like extras from *Enter the Dragon* and shouting out bits of outdated slang.

"Radical!"

"Cowabunga!"

"Totally tubular!"

Raza stared at them in disbelief. Who were these freaks, and why were they named after the four modern artists she hated the most?

*Who cares?* she thought. *We don't have time for this shit!*

She shifted into demon form and rushed at the leader. He swung his dental-floss katana. The weapons snapped in half against her hide. She grabbed his shell and tore it from his body, leaving him to flounder unshelled in the filth.

"How tubular is that, shithead?" she growled.

Meanwhile Zester was charging at Koons. Her pussy was growling, but she didn't wanna get down and dirty with this hideous mutant, even if he was a party dude. She swung a right hook and punched off his head.

Meanwhile the other two mutants came rushing at Raza, crying the name of their fallen leader.

"Warhol, dude! What has she done to you?" shouted Duchamp.

"You're gonna pay, bitch!" growled Emin.

Raza just sighed. She ripped off Duchamp's arms and used them to beat Emin to death, ramming one down his throat and the other up his arse. He slumped down, bleeding from his ruptured orifices, while Raza shifted back into human form.

"Well now that that nonsense is over with, maybe we can get back to looking for my lost monster foetus?"

"Way ahead of you!" said Vogg as he came skidding down the mountain of filth, clutching something in hand.

The others gathered around as he opened his palm. Raza took a deep breath, then gingerly stared down, half expecting the thing to quiver and call out "mummy!"

But it was quite dead. Perhaps it always had been, even before she'd flushed it down the toilet. Vogg stared at its hideous body, then shot a sideways glance at Raza.

"Huh," he said. "I guess I can see the family resemblance!"

"Jerk!" said Zester, slapping him.

"Ow!" he said. "Sorry, but I couldn't resist!"

Raza barely registered the remark. Her eyes were glued to the foetus. The sight of the thing was enough to chill her to the bone. A tiny monster that'd been growing inside of her, faster than a weed springing up through a crack in the sidewalk.

She picked it up and cupped it in her hands. She felt sad and disgusted all at once. Sad because the thing had been a life, her very own child. Disgusted because she didn't know just what type of lifeform it was. Its mottled flesh was covered with features that ran the gamut of organisms—avian, reptile, invertebrate, demon. Iridescence danced on its semi see-through skin. Some scintilla of radiance seeped out from its tiny, shuttered eyes. They looked like a pair of embers slowly fading.

"Should we, like, have a funeral, or something?" asked Vogg.

Zester elbowed him in the ribs.

"A moment of silence, then," he said, rubbing the sore spot.

And so they did have a moment of silence. Several, in fact, as Raza stared down at the creature.

At length Skiddix cleared his throat. "Sorry, Raza," he said. "But I have to run the test now . . . "

Raza nodded and handed him the foetus. He held it out between thumb and forefinger, while his other hand retrieved a stoppered vial from his coat pocket. He popped off the cork with his thumb, then slowly, cautiously, let fall a single drop of glowing white liquid. It hit the foetus and exploded in a flash, devouring the corpse and singeing his fingers.

"I guess that takes care of the cremation," said Vogg, earning himself another elbow in the ribs from Zester.

Raza stared at the ashes as they fluttered to the ground.

"Was that good, or bad?" she asked.

Skiddix glanced at her fleetingly. His expression was grave.

"I'd rather not talk about it here," he said. "I'm afraid this is the sort of news you need to sit down for . . . "

# CHAPTER 27:
## REVELATIONS

**R**AZA WAS GOBSMACKED.
"A demigod?!" she repeated.

She sat with the rest of Team Naked Badass, huddled on the bed in her dorm room. They were fresh from the showers. Skiddix had insisted the news had to wait until all of them were comfortable and clean.

"It's the only explanation," he said. "There's just no other way the embryo could've matured so quickly. It also explains some of the . . . peculiarities we saw in the foetus. The blood of demons and gods doesn't mix very well. The gods are creatures of Order—they made themselves that way. And demons are children of Chaos. When those two forces come together, and in such aggressive, powerful quantities . . . well, let's just say the results aren't very pretty, as we've all seen today."

"But how?" asked Raza. "I mean, Gogorizel sure looked like a demon to me. I even saw him transform!"

"Demons aren't the only ones who can shape-shift," said Skiddix.

"He must've used his powers to infiltrate the school!" said Vogg.

Raza thought of all those myths of divine transformation. Zeus becoming a swan, to make love to Leda. Or a bull, to abduct fair Europa. Had she been deceived in such a way? It made her want to puke. Then another realization hit home.

"Oh shit," she said. "That must've been what happened to Vel and the others. They must've all given birth!"

271

"If that's the case," said Skiddix, "then I don't think you should hold out too much hope of finding them alive. If you hadn't miscarried, there's a good chance that baby would've torn you apart from inside. Maybe it was luck, or maybe your immune system, but you dodged a bullet today, Raza. Big time."

"That bastard Gogorizel!" she growled. "I'm gonna get him for this. He's gonna wish he never snuck into this school!"

"You think he's the only one?" asked Vogg.

"I sure hope so," said Zester.

"I heard he showed up around the same time as all the other new students," said Skiddix. "A couple of weeks back, while we were stuck in the Zone. Come to think of it, that's when the principal arrived, as well."

They glanced at each other, eyes wide with apprehension.

"Oh shit," said Vogg.

"You think they're all demigods?" asked Zester. "Even the principal?"

Raza swallowed, hard. Suddenly it seemed so obvious! She knew she'd seen those beady black eyes before. They'd been haunting her for years. First in the jowly face of Mr. Willis, her hated science teacher. Then in the symmetrical face of that terrible angel. And now in the cold blue dome of the principal, Noviscula, as well as all her undead minions. It hadn't just been her imagination. They really were all incarnations of the same dreadful being. And they'd been following her for years, keeping tabs on her.

"I don't think Noviscula's a demigod," she said. "I think she's an angel. That same angel that was here at Our Lady, when I started seven weeks ago. That angel was covered in *sapphire* eyes, all over its body. Noviscula wears sapphires all over her dress. Shit, I even saw a sapphire on Ms. Sketh's desk!"

The atmosphere in the room grew even more tense.

"So there's an angel here," said Vogg, "and a bunch of

demigods in disguise, carrying out some kinda covert operation."

"Not just any angel," said Skiddix. "Don't you guys know who that was?"

Zester and Vogg shrugged their shoulders.

"Man," he said, "you guys never pay attention in history class! That angel is the Vision. The eyes of the Demiurge!"

Suddenly Raza remembered. The knowledge had been burned into her brain during all those hours she'd spent perusing Sketh's volumes of demonic history, the magickal texts whose living words had taken her mind on a guided tour of the history of the universe, like a preordained acid trip. One of those images came forward now before her mind's eye: an image of the Demiurge enthroned, flanked by a winged mouth and a floating, sapphire eye. A pair of angels known as the Vision and the Voice. It wasn't hard to figure out which was which. They hung at his sides like Odin's ravens, Huginn and Muninn. Each had their own appointed task. The Voice was his mouthpiece, delivering his commandments. Seducing, indoctrinating, deceiving. The Vision was his spymaster, watching the universe with its countless sapphire eyes. They weren't necessarily the deadliest of angels, but they were his most intimate.

By the time Raza broke loose from her reverie, Skiddix had finished filling in the others on the very same information.

"So this angel is big time," said Vogg. "And if it's here, then the Demiurge is probably also involved."

"Exactly," said Skiddix. "Pretty scary, huh?"

"Speak for yourself," said Vogg, even as the tremor in his voice belied his own words.

"What I don't understand is why the staff didn't do anything," said Zester. "I mean, how could they just let an angel show up and start taking over the school?"

"Don't you get it?" said Skiddix. "The angel must be using its nefarious magick. The rites and rituals of demonic enslavement!"

"But that's totally illegal!" said Zester. "They wouldn't, would they?"

"Can you think of any other reason why Zenneff and the others would submit to an angel?" said Skiddix. "They've been enslaved. The angel must've gotten hold of their true names and bound them to its will. It's a flagrant violation of the Treaty of Zelen, but it's the only explanation that makes any sense."

Just when Raza thought the tension in the room couldn't rise any higher, it did. Team Naked Badass traded looks of naked terror. Raza felt chills as she thought of that horrible magick. Through signs and sigils and words of power, not to mention the use of the demons' true names, the Vision had turned all the staff into puppets. That's why they'd been acting so weird. That's why Sketh's eyes had been filled up with dread, even while she'd been delivering that tongue-lashing lecture. It hadn't been her will framing the words, but that of the angel.

"But what does it want?" asked Zester. "Why risk breaking the truce and starting a war, just to take over Our Lady?"

"Maybe they wanna knock everyone up with monster babies?" suggested Zester.

"I highly doubt it," said Skiddix. "No-one hates the hybrids more than the Demiurge. He even made it a Treaty violation to knowingly conceive one! No, I think this sick bastard Gogorizel—or whatever his name is—is acting alone."

"Then he'll die alone," said Vogg, starting to rise. "Let's go rip his dick off and stick it down his throat."

"He'll keep," said Skiddix. "Right now we have to figure out what the angel's plan is."

Vogg nodded and sat back down. The four of them paused for a moment.

"I think it might have something to do with me," said Raza. "Back on Earth, there was this creepy teacher called Mr. Willis. He used to stare at me with these cold, beady eyes.

They were the Vision's eyes, I'm sure of it. That angel's been following me for years. And now it's tracked me here!"

Zester stared at her in shock. "Now that you mention it," she said, "there was this creepy old soul-trader back on Zelen who used to follow me around all the time. And she had beady black eyes, too . . . "

"Fuck me sideways," said Vogg. "Sounds just like my social worker back home! Bastard was always hanging around, sticking his nose in where it didn't belong. Trying to say my parents were unfit to raise me. Even tried to make me go to school a few times! And you'll never guess what his eyes looked like."

"Let me take a wild stab in the dark," said Raza. "They were beady and black?"

Vogg nodded, looking spooked.

"You think the Vision's here for us?" asked Raza. "That we're all being targeted?"

The three of them glanced at one another, wide-eyed.

"Let's not give in to any delusions of persecution, okay?" said Skiddix. "After all, the Vision isn't a singular being. It may have a primary body, but its eyes are everywhere, spread across the universe like germs. And also like germs, any single one of those eyes is able to invade a mortal host and subvert its biology. Those people who spied on you weren't the Vision incarnate, merely victims of angelic possession. There must be millions of them, scattered all across the cosmos, funnelling information back to the Vision, and thenceforth to the Demiurge. Clearly one of their tasks is to keep an eye out for demonic activity. There's probably a spy assigned to every demon-spawn that shows up on their heavenly radar."

Raza felt a sense of relief, but only a slight one. They might not have been the targets of the angel's attack, but the idea of all that spying was still pretty creepy. Had the hated Mr. Willis really been an innocent victim of angelic possession? And just what sort of exorcist could you get to help out with that? Clearly not a Catholic one!

"Okay," said Zester, "so it's probably not after us. But what is it after?"

"Maybe it's trying to ruin the school?" suggested Raza. "After all, if we're stuck with a shitty education, then the future of demonkind starts to look pretty bleak, now doesn't it?"

"Sounds a bit far-fetched to me," said Vogg.

The others agreed.

"Let's think about what the angel's been doing so far," said Skiddix. "That might give us an insight into its plans for the future."

They paused for a moment, mulling it over.

"It's been making the place nice and clean," said Raza.

"You mean charmless and sterile," corrected Vogg.

"It's established a curfew," said Zester. "Maybe it's been trying to stop us all getting laid?"

"Hasn't stopped us, babe," said Vogg. "We've just been getting busy during the day. And you can't beat a bit of afternoon delight!"

"It's been making all the classes suck," said Raza. "Though I sort of mentioned that already . . . "

"It's been kicking people off the sports teams," said Vogg. "Bastard's gonna make us lose the Championship!"

Suddenly his eyes peeled back like a pair of big grapes.

"Fuck me!" he said. "That's it! It's trying to make us lose the Cup, for the first time in almost five hundred years!"

"Gimme a break," said Raza. "As if the angel would risk plunging the cosmos into war, just to get some overrated sports trophy. What's so great about a stupid old cup anyway?"

She froze as she suddenly realised the import of her own words. She and Skiddix glanced at one another in shock. It seemed like they'd both come to the exact same conclusion.

"What?" said Vogg. "Why're you looking at each other like that? Did you both just shit your pants or something? Cause I've dealt with enough faecal matter for one afternoon!"

This time it was Raza's turn to explain.

"The Championship Cup," she said. "If the Vision really wants it, then it must be important. And there's only one really important cup in the universe—the Grail!"

"The what?" asked Zester and Vogg.

"Man!" she said. "You guys really *don't* pay any attention in history class, do you? During the ceasefire that led up to the Treaty of Zelen, the demons negotiated to get a pint of the Demiurge's blood. That way they'd have their very own W.M.D. to counter the Demiurge's rituals of demonic enslavement. If the heavenly host broke the rules of the Treaty, then the demons could drink from the cup, thereby gaining the knowledge to unmake creation. It was Mutually Assured Destruction, just like the United States and Russia!"

"Right," said Skiddix. "And if we lose the Grail, there'll be no more M.A.D. The Demiurge would once again have the undisputed upper hand in the war. Now *that* would be a prize worth jeopardising the Treaty over."

"And you really think this Grail thing is the Championship Cup?" asked Vogg. "That's retarded. Why would we let something so powerful end up in a cabinet in Our Lady's hallway? Why would we risk losing it to Divinity College over a fucking game of table tennis?"

"That's the part that doesn't make that much sense," said Skiddix. "Unless the Grail got lost, mixed up with a bunch of other old cups, and finally found its way here . . . "

Raza glanced at the others. Could it really be possible? Could her father and the rest of the demonic high command who'd overseen the war effort truly have been reckless enough to lose their only nuke in this cosmic cold war? It seemed ridiculous. And yet, she had to admit, that from all she'd seen so far, the demons sure were a lackadaisical lot. Maybe they'd been chaotic enough to misplace the Grail?

"It still doesn't make sense, though," said Zester. "Because we've lost the trophy before, hundreds of years ago.

Our winning streak is almost five hundred years long, but Our Lady of the Scythe is much older than that."

Skiddix glanced at the clock. It was still a few hours before curfew.

"There's only one way to find out," he said. "To the library!"

They hustled through the halls. Raza thought it was probably the first time Zester and Vogg had ever been in a hurry to get to the library. Maybe the first time they'd ever been inside of one!

Soon they were searching through the archives of Our Lady's school newspaper. They looked for articles that dealt with the Championship Cup. Not all of them, of course. There were far too many for that. Instead they jumped back through the decades—ten years, then twenty, then fifty, then a hundred, perusing the photos of victorious students as they held up the trophy.

To Raza the archives looked like giant scrapbooks plastered with sepia broadsheets, newsprint with monochrome photographs. But the text and images, whatever their true form, were hallucinogenic. The photos sprang to life right before her mind's eye, as if she were standing in the past. She saw students from 2008, rocking emo haircuts. Students from 1998, their T-shirts emblazoned with Eminem, Sepultura, or Marilyn Manson. Then on and on, back and back, through Jheri Curls, leg-warmers, bell bottoms, and suspenders, a whole weird kaleidoscope of faces that were young yet whose fashions were old.

Raza felt that eerie sensation of staring at youth that was already gone. A paradox of kinship and alienation. Sweet, because she felt an affinity with all those young faces, those fellow students of Our Lady's halls. And bitter, too, because one day soon someone else would be staring at a photo of her, peering back though the tunnels of dim and distant time.

And yet the true object of their search was the Cup, a modest wooden goblet that remained the same in every single picture going back hundreds of years, right back to 1526 AD, the year that saw the signing of the Treaty of Madrid and the birth of the Mughal Empire.

Raza froze. The image was from four hundred and ninety-two years ago, the beginning of Our Lady's winning streak. The students were dressed in voluminous Renaissance clothing, at least to Raza's eyes. Still, her gaze wasn't focused on their fashions, but on the Cup in their hands, which was no longer made of wood but of silver. It must've been switched with the wooden one after the image was created, sometime before the end of 1527.

Raza and the others rushed to find follow-up articles that might explain why the silver cup was substituted for another. They quickly found what they were looking for, in the very next edition of the newspaper. The article told a typically demonic anecdote. The Cup had been won back by Our Lady after a five-year losing streak. It was promptly devoured by an excited young student, who vowed that the demigods would never again get their hands on it. The digested trophy was replaced with an old wooden goblet that someone had dug up from the offices of one Corlamen Ghule, Our Lady's former librarian. The substitute trophy was secured in the cabinet in Our Lady's main hallway, before which the students and staff—apparently inspired by the pupil who'd eaten the previous one —made a vow that *this* Cup, however humble in appearance, would never fall into the clutches of the demigods. And it never had.

"Corlamen Ghule," said Skiddix. "I know that name! He was a major player in the war. It makes sense that a guy like that would have access to the Grail. He must've hidden it away in his office, then left it there when he went away on leave."

"So the Championship Trophy really is a nuke?" asked Zester.

Skiddix nodded.

Soon they were standing in Our Lady's main hallway,

staring through the glass of the cabinet. Inside sat the Cup, plain and unassuming, filled with the dregs of something that looked like dried wine—or deific ichor. Raza shuddered. To think they were staring at the demonic WMD, the key to the knowledge to unmake creation. And if they didn't do something the angel would get it, unbalancing the state of Mutually Assured Destruction that guaranteed peace throughout the cosmos.

"Can we break inside?" asked Vogg.

"No chance," said Skiddix, pointing to the runes that surrounded the cabinet. "It's locked up by magick. The only time it opens is if Our Lady loses the Cup to Divinity. We could whale on that glass all night long and it wouldn't come down."

"Well we'd better think of something, and fast," said Raza. "The Championship is happening tomorrow!"

They hurried back toward Raza's room, fetching Karanora on the way. Raza figured they needed all the help they could get, and given what'd happened to Vel, Zibb, and Pura, she thought Karanora would want to be involved. She was right. As soon as Kara got over the shock of hearing the truth, she pledged to help in any way she could.

The five of them stayed up most of that night in Raza's room, ignoring the curfew, wracking their collective brains as they desperately struggled to come up with a plan. A whole series of far-fetched ideas and hare-brained schemes got tossed out the window. Flow charts and doodles got scrunched up and thrown in the bin. Over and over they returned to the drawing board. For a while they talked in circles. At times they gave in to frustration. They drank a whole bunch of demonic sports drinks to keep their tired brains active. Finally, at last, they came up with a plan to save the school. It was daring, it was bold—it was perhaps suicidal. There was a chance it might make things even worse, and lead to the onset of total Armageddon. And yet, it was the only plan they had.

"You think it'll work?" said Zester.

The others just shrugged. They were too tired to think anymore. They curled up in the various corners of Raza's room and fell asleep—or tried too. In spite of her exhaustion Raza found herself writhing restlessly beneath the covers. She couldn't relax. Fears and concerns kept spiralling around in her head like the whorls of a cyclone, repeating themselves over and over, till at length they collapsed into inchoate fragments that carried her off into dreaming.

She found herself walking down the hall of Our Lady, just as she'd done on that very first day. Except that Vel wasn't there. No-one was. The school was deserted, desolate. Pieces of paper blew down the halls like tumbleweeds in a ghost town. She walked on, pulled by some inexorable dream-urge towards the statue of the Lady of the Scythe.

The woman's lascivious grin was gone. Instead her mouth hung open slackly, like that of a corpse. As Raza watched the statue's glass eyes turned to jelly and oozed from the sockets, while from somewhere far away came the sound of someone screaming.

Raza woke to hear the school bell ringing. It was time for the Interschool Championship to begin.

# CHAPTER 28:
## THE GRAIL

**R**AZA STOOD IN the stands, close to the door that led to Our Lady's main hallway. It was late afternoon and the Interschool Championship was well on its way to being over. The stadium was packed with students from both schools. Opposite Raza's side of the stadium the demigods from Divinity College sat in ordered ranks. To Raza they looked almost identical, a sea of bronze-skinned bodies with golden hair and neat white uniforms. Even their movements were synchronised as they chanted in unison, rising and falling in Mexican Waves.

Our Lady's demons sat opposite. Raza could see them all the more clearly now. The illusion of the talisman had started to fade, revealing a motley crowd of races in a riot of fashions. Their cheering and chanting was far more disordered, and far more bitter.

Because the demons were losing. Not that Raza was surprised, of course. True to its nature as a creature of Order, the angel had left almost nothing to chance. Our Lady's best players had all been barred from competition, leaving only the weaker demonic athletes to perform on behalf of the school. And if that wasn't enough, many of Our Lady's competitors were demigods in disguise, playing against their very own colleagues from Divinity College. If by some chance the underdog demons started to win, then the plants from Divinity would snatch defeat from the jaws of victory through some kind of deliberate fumble. Raza had been watching it happen all day. Demigod imposters had literally dropped the ball on numerous occasions, allowing Divinity to win match after match. And yet that wasn't the whole of it. The demigods in disguise were also there to make the losses look convincing. When the demons were getting shellacked, they'd lift their game and even the scores, just enough to create a façade of fair play.

Raza could only marvel at the totality of the deception. Not even Arnold Rothstein, who'd fixed the 1919 World Series, could've created a better semblance of honest competition. The demons weren't even losing by that great a margin. The angel, cold and calculating creature that it was, had clearly left its ego at the door. It could've arranged a whitewash, a crushing defeat that would've destroyed Our Lady's morale *and* secured the Cup for Divinity. Instead it had settled for a narrow, credible victory, one that would secure its prize without setting off any alarms amongst Our Lady's student body.

Raza glanced down into the stadium. The final bout was a hockey match—Vel's sport of choice. She felt a surge of anger as she thought of her friend, almost certainly dead now, murdered by Gogorizel and his rampaging semen. Raza glanced down at him as he sat below her in the stands. He'd done a decent turn as spearhead for Our Lady's football team, the Cannibal Unicorns. In fact, his star athleticism had carried the game for the demonic side. And yet, he'd fumbled a few important plays, handing the victory over to his demigod peers. Still the demons had cheered him as he strode off the field. If only they knew what a monster they were celebrating.

*He'll get his,* thought Raza, baring her teeth. *They all will . . .*

Shouts and cheers echoed up as the hockey game continued. It was down to the last few seconds on the clock, and the scores were neck-and-neck. An attacker from Divinity made a run for the goal zone. The puck shot across the grass in a blur. The goalie looked set to make an easy save. Then one of Our Lady's defenders rushed in, slung their stick—and scored an own goal.

*Must be another plant,* thought Raza. *Throwing the game!*

Suddenly the clock ticked down to zero and the horn sounded off, calling an end to the match. The Demigods let out an uproarious cheer, then started singing one of their many school anthems. They sounded like a giant Christmas Choir. Raza had always hated Christmas music. Their harmonious voices made her wanna puke!

It seemed like the rest of Our Lady's students felt much the same way. They started grumbling and shouting, cursing their luck.

Raza didn't have time to worry about Our Lady's morale. Soon the final scores would be tallied and victory announced for Divinity College. Then the magickal cabinet would open, releasing the Cup. She and the others had only one chance!

She rushed into the hall, heart pounding as she prepared herself for the final Hail Mary play.

Sketh strode towards the cabinet that contained the Cup. With her went Zenneff, Belzoa, Kellikassey and the rest of the teachers. Behind them followed the angel, controlling their bodies with invisible strings. Behind the angel came a bunch of Our Lady's students, captains, and star players drawn from various teams. Half of them were imposters, demigods in false demon shapes. Both groups had a purpose. It was the teachers' job to remove the Cup from the case, then hand it to the students, who in turn would present it to the victorious prefects from Divinity.

Sketh had long ago figured out what the angel's plan was, and yet she was powerless to stop it. She knew she could only watch, puppeteered and paralysed, as the greatest weapon in demonkind's arsenal was surrendered to their enemies. She wanted to cry out and vomit at the very same time. How could they have failed their school, their species, so utterly?

Soon they drew up in front of the cabinet. The runes that surrounded it started to gleam. The doors unlocked and flew open gently. Belzoa, moved by the angel's agonizing strings, stepped forth to claim Divinity's prize.

And then all hell broke loose. Rays of burning light shot out through the corridor, hurling the teachers away from the cabinet. Belzoa flew off his feet, slamming into Zenneff. Sketh tried to scream as a bolt of red lightning tore through her flesh and blew her apart. She collapsed to the floor, reduced to a pile of rainbow serpents.

"NOW!" shouted Raza.

Team Naked Badass rushed out into the hall, unleashing a barrage of eyebeams. The teachers went down in flames or got blasted down the corridor, clearing the way for Raza to scoop up the Cup.

"Go!" she shouted as she snatched it from the display case.

Team Naked Badass turned and ran.

"Stop them!" screamed the angel.

The teachers picked their smoking bodies off the ground and gave chase. The angel followed after, refusing to abandon its demonic disguise.

Vogg, Zester and the others shifted up into demon form and ran. Raza ran ahead of them. She had the Cup in one hand and a bottle of cola in the other. The soda was shaking, fizzing up and spilling out. She'd never tried to mix drinks on the fly like this before! She splashed cola in the cup as she ran, mingling the drink with the dried flakes of god's blood. She had to slow down to stop herself from spilling it. The others slowed with her, and the teachers started gaining on them.

"Keep them back!" shouted Raza.

But Zester and Vogg were already on it. They turned toward the teachers and unleashed their searing eye-beams. Belzoa went down, shorn off at the knees. A moment later he was back up again, standing on a set of newly-grown feet. It was hard to keep a good demon down.

But the students kept trying. Skiddix let loose his gaze of destruction. It tore through tiers of lockers and hurled the teachers back down the corridor. Alarms began to scream as the classrooms caught alight. Zenneff alone made it through the assault. He came at them like an angry rhinoceros, blinking bolts of lightning from his eyes.

The students scattered, trying to evade. Raza put a hand over the cup to stop its precious contents from spilling. She felt the liquid splash against her fingers as she dodged one of the bolts.

Karanora got hit. The girl's demonic shape was tall, pale, and ropy, like a humanoid maggot. It turned black in the fire and fell to the ground.

Raza looked back as she heard Kara scream. She was just in time to see Zenneff trample her corpse as he came barrelling toward them. The rest of the teachers came after, blasting Karanora's corpse into pieces. A bolt of lightning shot past Raza's head as well, whipping her hair.

*Looks like they're playing for keeps,* thought Raza. *Or at least the Vision is!*

She sprinted for a bend in the corridor, feeling the cocktail splash against her hand as she ran. Some of it splashed through the gaps in her fingers, sticky and warm. If she kept this up soon there'd be nothing left of the stuff. How many of those precious motes of god's blood had already been lost? She needed to stop and drink the cocktail, now, before it was too late.

She rounded the corner with the others, earning a moment of reprieve.

*Looks like it's now or never!* she thought.

She came to a stop and slathered her tongue across her sticky fingers, lapping up tiny flakes of ichor. She passed the cup to Zester and turned back towards the bend in the corridor, just as the teachers came charging into view, infused with the angel's murderous anger.

Raza stepped between them and her friends. There would be no more running now. She had to bet everything on the power of the ichor. But would it even work? She stood there as the teachers closed in, heart hammering, waiting for a sign that the god's blood was having its promised effect.

For a moment nothing happened.

*Oh fuck,* thought Raza.

Was the Grail a dud, just like in all those Arthurian legends? Perhaps the ichor was withered, inert, devoid of its potency. Or maybe her father and the other demon generals had quaffed it already, taking the power for themselves and replacing the ichor with raspberry juice or cabernet sauvignon? That would explain why the Cup had been cast so carelessly aside.

She sighed as the teachers closed in, and got ready to face annihilation.

Then time slowed down before her eyes. The world became a crawling kaleidoscope, turning upside-down and inside-out. She no longer knew whether she was standing up, sitting down, or floating in the air. Images cascaded from the ichor inside of her, memories straight from the Demiurge's mind. She saw the Celestial Fire at the heart of the void, bubbling and boiling in its Chaotic majesty. She saw the Demiurge's power taking shape, his patterns of Order weaving their way across the cosmos. Those patterns were hers now, she knew, as familiar as the back of her hand. Not to create, but to destroy.

She opened her eyes. Barely a moment had passed. The teachers were still barrelling towards her, albeit moving in slow motion, like insects in amber. She could see the strings that surrounded them, invisible chains that stretched back to the angel.

Raza's eyes filled with crimson fire. She unleashed it at the teachers, tearing not through their bodies but through their invisible chains. The puppeteer's strings snapped apart and caught fire. The teachers stopped running. For a moment Raza saw the relief that flooded their faces. Then their eyes filled up with hate as they turned back to face their tormentor.

The angel froze, still wearing its disguise. A moment later the teachers were upon it. The hallway exploded with motion as the demons unleashed their revenge, falling on the angel like a pack of rabid dogs. The details were hard to make out. Raza was reminded of a cartoon-style brawl, in which a horde of combatants combine into a whirlwind of violence that rolls along the ground. They smashed through a wall in a frenzy of smoke, fire and blood, leaving Raza suddenly alone.

And yet she wasn't alone. Beyond the smoke stood the captains and athletes of Our Lady's sports teams. Half of them were demigods in disguise, including Gogorizel, captain of the football team. She could see their true forms beneath their fake bodies. Information flooded her mind—their strengths, their weaknesses, even their family trees, though the latter in truth were more like shrubs, incestuous and stunted, their branches looping back to the trunks that had borne them. For a moment she was shocked by the wealth of information provided by the ichor. But then again, they were the descendants of the Demiurge, the spawn of his creation. She knew them now as he did.

But she did not love them as he did. She reached out and tore off their disguises, flaying them down to their deific cores. False skins flew off like jumpsuits discarded, leaving them naked and bloody. They all bore aquiline features and gleaming gold hair. Despite their uniformity, still she could make out Gogorizel's presence among them. She knew his true name now—Adagar. He looked remarkably the same as he had in the shower block, his body handsome and athletic. And yet she no longer viewed him with lust, but with utmost hatred.

She bared her teeth and strode towards him through the fires of the hallway.

For a moment the demigods stood there, naked and shaken, their demonic counterparts just as confounded. Then the two groups turned on each other and started brawling in the corridor.

Raza helped her peers as she strode towards Adagar, blasting the demigods with bolts of red lighting. Stunning blows they were not. She had the architect's eye for destruction now. She saw their bodies like a series of anatomical drawings by Da Vinci. Saw their muscles, organs, and bones, the reservoirs of power that flared in their bodies like sunspots. Her eyebeams shot out like surgical lasers, *unmaking* their forms with neon-red fire. They screamed as she tore them apart. She knew their names as they died, but didn't really care. There was only one she had a personal grudge against—Adagar.

He turned and ran from the hall as his colleagues came undone. Raza gave chase, holding back her beams. She was gonna tear him apart with her own bare hands!

Sketh watched as the angel's false flesh fell away, revealing its horrible, heavenly form. Bolts of light shot forth from its sapphire eyes, burning Bambexa to a crisp. Suddenly the art teacher looked a lot like one of her own charcoal sketches, albeit three-dimensional.

Zenneff rushed at the angel, punching it clean through a wall. He'd been an angel-killer during the war, and knew his craft well. Before the Vision even landed he leapt through the air and landed on top of it, bringing an armoured boot down upon its chest as it crashed to the ground.

The angel coughed up a mixture of blue blood and eyeballs. Zenneff reached down and tore off its wings. The Vision screamed. To Sketh's ears it sounded like the sweetest music imaginable.

She and the rest of the demons rushed into the room. Her very own classroom, it seemed, though the place was so ruined and swirling with dust it was hard to determine exactly where they were. And the demons were too busy to notice, piling on the angel and venting their wrath.

Kellikassey reached the Vision just after Zenneff did. The demoness' beautiful body had grown massive and terrible. Her tail whipped up and plunged down the angel's oesophagus, slithering deep into its guts. The tail was covered with barbs, like those of a harpoon. When it withdrew, the Vision's viscera came with it, dotted with sapphire eyes.

A moment later Belzoa rushed in, plucking out eyeballs and crushing them, unleashing miniature explosions of angelic power. They burned his flesh, but he seemed not to notice.

Sketh followed suit. She transformed into a multitude of serpents and crawled across the angel, biting its eyeballs and injecting it with venom. Its alabaster skin became black with necrosis. Its eyeballs exploded with energy, frying dozens of the serpents that made up her essence. Sketh was too enraged to care. She'd tear this thing apart, even if she died in the process!

The air filled up with blood and howls of demon laughter. Sketh laughed too, a sibilant chorus from dozens of mouths. Revenge had never tasted so sweet—even if it did taste like heavenly fire.

Suddenly the angel started glowing. Its chest was tearing open, revealing a massive sapphire eye.

"Look out!" shouted Zenneff as the light flared out to engulf them.

Smoke came pouring from Our Lady's interior, accompanied by sounds of destruction. The crowd grew alarmed. Restless students gathered at the entrance to the hallway, trying to peer through the smoke. They drew back as Adagar rushed into their midst, naked and covered in blood. Close at his heels came Raza. She caught him in a flying tackle that sent both of them shooting through the air. They overshot the stands and crashed down in the hockey field below, rolling through the grass in a tangle of limbs. Assuming her demon shape, Raza got on top and started beating his face to a pulp.

The crowd looked on, not sure what was happening. Murmurs of surprise shot through the ranks, arising from demons and demigods alike. The murmurs were joined by shouts of alarm as a figure came crashing through one of Our Lady's exterior walls. It was the angel. Wingless it flew through the air in a shower of dust and crashed down in the hockey field a dozen feet from Raza. Its sapphire eyes had all been gouged out, leaving its body a bleeding mess of hollowed-out sockets. Only its beady black eyes remained, fluttering in agony as the angel looked up to see a hulking figure come flying through the wall in its wake. Zenneff had just been able to absorb the angel's last attack. His armour was battered and hanging off his body, his skin charred and blackened beneath. He landed a few feet from the Vision, punching it down as it tried to stand up.

The murmur of the crowd grew louder as students from both schools looked on in confusion, still not quite sure how to react. Then Zester, Vogg, and Skiddix emerged from the smoke of the hallway, their eyes now blazing with the power of the god's blood.

"Students of Our Lady!" shouted Vogg, his voice at megaphone volume. "We've all been tricked. This whole Championship was fixed! Divinity College is cheating. It's time for a RIOT!"

For a moment the stadium was still. Then a wave of violence rippled out through the stands as Our Lady's demons began to clash with the prefects from Divinity.

The atmosphere exploded with insults. Gouts of blood laced the air, like crimson ribbons in a ticker tape parade.

Demons shifted up into terrible, death-dealing battle-shapes. Demigods unleashed bolts of deific fire, their bodies blazing with radiance. Cadaverous hall monitors appeared from the doors of the school to join in the battle, while the surviving teachers emerged from the ruins to take part in the slaughter and fight by the sides of their students.

Team Naked Badass leapt into the mayhem. Filled with the knowledge to unmake the demigods, they dealt out death wherever they landed. Vogg tore through god-flesh as though it were tracing paper. Skiddix's eyebeams turned prefects to ashes. Zester's pussy churned up bones like a wood chipper.

All the while Raza was beating Adagar like the rented mule of a red-headed stepchild. His handsome face was a welter of bruises. She picked him up by the neck and glared into his eyes.

"What happened to Vel?" she growled.

"She's . . . dead . . . " he said, struggling to breathe.

"And the others?"

"All dead," he said. "They died . . . to bring forth our children . . . "

"Sick fuck!" she yelled, just before she punched him clear across the field.

She rushed on after him, slashing his face as he rose. His nose came off and hung there, suspended by a sliver of meat. For a moment she wondered why he wasn't fighting back. Was he a masochist? Consumed with guilt? Did he have a martyr complex, like those arseholes from ISIS?

He stretched his arms wide. His face took on a look of maniac ecstasy. Maybe he *was* getting off on the beating!

"Arise," he yelled. "Arise, my spawn. Daddy needs you!"

The stadium shook. From under the ground came the sound of infantile screaming, albeit horribly amplified, like a rousing jet engine. Raza watched as a part of the field began to tremble and subside into a massive, yawning crater. A smell of foulness whipped up from below, a mix of rotten flesh and pungent waste.

*Smells like the world's biggest, fullest diaper!* thought Raza.

Other craters opened up around the stadium, swallowing tiers of seating. Students abandoned the rioting and fled for their lives. A moment later the creatures emerged from below, a quartet of giant, floating foetuses, the biggest the size of a three-storey building. Most of their bulk was made up by their heads, which sat huge and misshapen atop babyish bodies. Umbilical cords the size of fire hoses hung from their bellies, bearing the likeness of dragons and devouring worms.

# CHAPTER 29:
## ABOMINATION

"**FUCK ME!**" shouted Raza as one of the things loomed above her.

It was the biggest of them all. Part of its malformed face was transparent and purple. It must've been Velazelza's child.

The rest of its body was a riot of mutation. Raza could *see* the forces fighting inside of it, the blood of Chaos clashing with Order. The supernatural energies of demon and deity, warring in a cage of embryonic flesh. The creature must've been in a state of constant agony. Every time its deific cells tried to make it bronzed, blond and symmetrical, its demonic DNA would rebel, throwing up scales, tentacles, fangs, or extra heads. Then its divine inheritance would strike back, devouring and subsuming the mutating matter. Would the frenzy ever cease and give way to a stalemate?

Raza didn't have time to contemplate the possibilities. The creature's umbilicus whipped out towards her like a wingless dragon. She leapt back as it tore its way across what remained of the hockey field, throwing up dust in a billowing curtain.

She scanned its giant body, searching for signs of weakness she might be able to exploit. But the knowledge she'd gained from the ichor was useless against it. This thing might've been one of the Demiurge's descendants by blood, but it definitely wasn't a part of his design.

From a dozen feet away came a horrified cry.

"What have you DONE?!" shouted the angel, staring at Adagar with a look of abhorrence.

It didn't get to say any more. Zenneff's eyebeams burnt the Vision to ashes. He leapt across the field and landed next to Raza.

"I don't think I'll ever be able to thank you enough, kid," he said. "But right now we've got work to do!"

He was right. The infants were rampaging, attacking anything and everything in sight. Rainbow fire shot out from their eyeballs, blasting whole sections of the stadium to ruin. One of the creatures launched a tantrum at the towers that overlooked the sports ground, sending them crashing down to earth. Another flew up and swallowed the miniature sun that blazed above Our Lady, plunging the place into darkness. There was only the light of the nebulas and that of the infants' blazing eyes.

The brawl between the two student bodies was definitely over. Demons and demigods alike were fleeing from the stands as the place became an obstacle course of stark, sudden death.

In the shadows of his children, Adagar was laughing.

"That's it, my spawn," he said. "Today Our Lady, tomorrow creation itself!"

He reached up his arms, as if offering praise to his very own godhead. One of his children took notice. It reached down and picked him up. Its baby-like hand was the size of a horse.

"That's it, my child," he said, his voice getting lost amidst the screams. "Carry me on your shoulders!"

But the kid wasn't listening. With a childish laugh it tore him in two and shoved the sections straight into its mouth.

"So much for big daddy!" said Raza.

She and Zenneff nodded to each other, then turned towards the largest and closest of the infants, blasting its body with their eyebeams. The thing was Velazelza's child.

The infant roared, and struck back instinctively. Raza's

beams were swallowed by a blast of rainbow light that shot out from its eyes. The light filled her vision—

And was suddenly eclipsed. It took her a moment to realise Zenneff was in front of her with his back toward the monster, shielding her body with his massive, armoured form. His face was a grimace of agony. Terrible heat shot past his shoulders and sizzled her skin.

"Zenneff!" she cried.

A moment later the light was gone. Zenneff tumbled over, his back scorched down to the bone.

"I'll be fine," was the last thing he said.

Raza glared at the creature with a look of utmost hate. She leapt through the air, landing on its giant, egg-shaped brow. Gripping its skin she pummelled its skull and punched through the bone. Brain tissue exploded from the wound and transformed into a cloud of pink bats. They swarmed her, biting at her flesh as she tore out more brains by the fistful.

*How'd you like a frontal lobotomy, you little shit?* she thought.

The infant roared and swiped in her direction, but its chubby little arms were too small to reach. It blinked out bolts of fire, but she was just above its eyes, and therefore outside of the blast zone. Others weren't so lucky. Raza saw a whole section of the stands get immolated, demon-spawn and demigods alike reduced to stick figure statues of disintegrating cinders.

The infant vomited acid, but she was likewise too high up to get hit by it. Maybe she could manage to kill it—if the bats didn't eat her up first!

But she'd forgotten about the umbilicus. It whipped her aside like a bug on a windshield, hurling her down to the ground. She skidded on her arse and clawed at the grass to stop herself passing the brink of a yawning abyss on the edge of the field.

She came to a stop with a groan just inches from the brink. Her skin was roasted and torn off in strips. She was healing fast, but it might not make a difference. The infant was coming, spurred by some instinct for revenge or self-preservation. Fire was brimming from its eyes; acidic bile bubbled up from its mouth.

*At least nothing's coming from the back end!* thought Raza as she rushed to her feet.

The rest of Team Naked Badass stood in what remained of the stands. They'd just managed to dodge a succession of cave-ins and stampeding students. They caught sight of Raza below, locked in battle with the monster.

"We've gotta do something!" shouted Zester.

Skiddix scanned for weaknesses with his newfound knowledge—but he wasn't scanning the infant. He was scanning the fabric of the cosmos. The Demiurge's ancient equations flowed through his mind, showing him the secrets of time, matter—and space.

"I think I've got the answer," he said. "Go help Raza!"

Raza stood with her back to the edge of the chasm. The infant's eyebeams came sweeping towards her, carving troughs across the ground through which the toxic bile flowed in the wake of the beams. She waited as the beams got closer, closer—

Then darted aside. The beams shot past her and into the chasm, carving more furrows that channelled the following bile into the darkness below.

Raza ran. The beams followed after, eating up the ground in her wake. The crater expanded behind her, torn wider and wider by the force of the beams and the bite of the ever-flowing bile. Soon there wouldn't be any ground left for Raza to stand on, much less to run across.

Then Vogg and Zester appeared, leaping at the creature from what little remained of the stands.

Vogg landed on its shoulder and sheared off its arm. Zester took a tip from Raza's playbook and went straight for the head, smashing her fist into its brains. The infant let out a terrible cry and shook its body wildly, casting off the teenagers like ticks.

They landed near Raza on what remained of the hockey field, a ledge of earth surrounded by an ever-expanding abyss. Our Lady's upper towers were falling down into the darkness in front of them. The stadium above them was collapsing. The infant was moving in fast, acid tears flowing down from its eyes. It looked about ready to spit the dummy—big time.

Raza watched as the thing flew towards them, head-first, intending to ram them like a *kamikaze* aircraft. With the crater all around them and the stadium collapsing above, they had nowhere to go that didn't equal death.

"Guess this is it," said Vogg. "It's been a blast!"

"Team Naked Badass forever!" shouted Zester.

"I love you guys!" shouted Raza as she, too, prepared to get annihilated.

The infant's head bore down on them like a crashing Boeing aircraft, eclipsing the world. Raza waited for the impact—

But it never came. The creature disappeared. She glanced around the ruins of the stadium, watching as the infants started vanishing, one after the other.

"What the fuck?" she said.

"I don't know what's going on," said Vogg, "but it looks like we're saved!"

"Don't speak too soon," said Zester. "This place is coming down like a house of cards!"

She was right. The infants might've been gone, but the danger remained. The chasm was expanding like a giant, yawning mouth, while chunks of debris tumbled down from the school's crumbling towers.

"We've gotta move!" yelled Raza, trying to scramble up the side of the stadium.

No use. The structure was coming apart, unleashing an avalanche of stones that threatened to sweep them all down into the pit.

"At least we won't be a big baby's chew toy!" said Zester.

Then a giant eye looked down at them from the edge of the stadium, and the world disappeared.

But only for a moment. They emerged from the darkness of the space between dimensions, finding themselves inside of one of the towers. Luckily this tower wasn't falling. They looked down upon the chasm as it yawned far below them, devouring the rest of the stadium, then finally halting its ravenous expansion. Reverberations travelled through the campus, but they were already growing less and less violent. Debris was still falling, cascading past the window, but the pieces were smaller and smaller now. It looked like Our Lady would survive, albeit in significant need of refurbishment.

They saw Kellikassey fly past the window on a pair of black wings, carrying Belzoa in her arms, Sketh clinging to her legs in the form of rainbow snakes.

*They survived!* thought Raza excitedly. It looked like the school, as ruined as it was, would still have teachers to staff it.

Suddenly Skiddix emerged from the interstice beside them. It was his giant eyeball they'd glimpsed a few moments earlier, hovering above the fallen wall of the stadium.

The four of them shifted down into human form.

"Dude!" shouted Vogg. "That was you, wasn't it? You sent the monsters away and saved our butts! How the fuck did you do that?"

Skiddix shrugged. "It was actually pretty easy. I just used a bit of demon magick, coupled with the demiurge's knowledge of temporal mechanics. The technique was basically the same as using a teleportation circle, only faster. I didn't need any runes or special ingredients. I was able to send the monsters to any of the spatial coordinates I was familiar with. I sent one to Hester's Hollow. I figured if the Hollow itself wouldn't crush it to death, then Hester's descendants would murder it anyway. Another one I sent to the Chasm of Kirrible. I figure she'll eat it. The third one I sent into the heart of Orlum, the fifth Star of Rubex. I watched it burn to ashes with my very own eye."

"Holy shit that's fucking awesome!" said Vogg. "Come here, you beautiful genius!"

Vogg ran up and gripped him in a bear hug. Zester ran in and hugged him, too. So did Raza, giving him a kiss on the cheek. He blushed bright red, then looked away sheepishly.

"Maybe you shouldn't thank me so fast," he said. "I'm afraid I might've fucked up a bit. The fifth monster came at me, and I panicked. I sent it to the first set of coordinates that popped into my head—a desert in Iraq. I'm sorry, Raza, but I sent that monster to Earth—your home!"

Raza paused for a moment, then shrugged. Somehow she didn't care all that much. Let the people of Earth deal with the problem. Her home was here at Our Lady, amongst all the glittering stars.

# EPILOGUE

**R**AZA STARED INTO the scrying mirror. Her father's image was clearer this time, and even more painful to look upon. She could just make out the coils of his manifold horns, the twofold slithering of his serpentine phallus.

*Can't the guy cover up?* she thought. *He's like one of those hippy parents who's always going around naked!*

She tried to focus on his eyes. They were blazing and yellow, orbs of solid light. Staring into them was painful, and she quickly looked away. Such brightness might blind someone, maybe even give them a dose of melanoma.

"Hello, Raza," said her father.

His voice was booming. From somewhere behind him came the rhythmic grinding of a blade on a whetstone. He was sharpening his axe, the same one he'd used to decapitate a god.

"Hi Dad," she said. "To what do I owe this unprecedented honour?"

"I heard what you did at the school," he said.

Of course he had. Everyone had—everyone in the loop, at least. Demons, angels, gods, and anyone else who was plugged into the cosmic community. It wouldn't air on FOX News, or CNN, or Donald Trump's Twitter feed, but the events of Our Lady had made serious waves. The Demiurge had violated the Treaty of Zelen, and broken the peace. The demons had been forced to use their WMD. The dregs of the god's blood had been mixed up like cordial and handed out to demons far and wide. The party that resulted had been bigger than Woodstock, and fraught with apprehension. Everyone thought another war was coming, for sure. But the big dogs at the top had had some serious talks, and renegotiated the Treaty. The demons came out with a grab-bag of goodies, including a heap of new territories, as well as enough reparations to rebuild Our Lady a dozen times over. As one of the heroines who'd foiled the angel's plot—of which the Demiurge himself denied any knowledge, of course— they'd even let Raza make a personal request. It was a simple one—for the Demiurge to keep his hands off the Earth. After all, it was bad enough that humans now had to deal with a rampaging, monstrous foetus, let alone a narcissistic deity.

The condition was granted without much complaint. After all, the Demiurge had a whole heap of other planets and dimensions to mess with. Why would he care about losing just one of them? Raza wondered if all the religious people on Earth had even noticed the change. Did they feel the terrible shadow of god passing away from their lives, like a storm cloud dispersing? Did their prayer mats feel dusty? Did the words in their bible no longer ring true? Somehow she doubted it.

"You did a good job, Raza," said the God-Killer.

"Thanks, Dad," she said.

"Did you like the taste of the god's blood?" he asked.

His voice was mischievous. The implication was clear— he'd tasted it long before now, probably on the very first day it was acquired, breaking the rules of the Treaty immediately.

Raza shrugged. "I guess it tasted all right. Mixed with Coke, of course."

"Well, it is an acquired taste," he said. "But who knows? Maybe you'll learn to appreciate it neat. You keep on going like this, I might even ask you to help with the family business."

"And what is the family business, Dad?" she asked, though she already had quite an inkling.

The image on the mirror started to fade.

"Looks like we're breaking up," said the demon. "Stick to your studies, Raza. And never forget—Do What Thou Wilt Shall be the Whole of the Law!"

Raza waved as he vanished, then shot a glance at the stars outside. The Crone Sun was starting to ebb.

*Shit,* she thought. *It's almost time for Cosmic History Class!*

For FREE stories, reviews, images, and more,
visit B.J. Swann's website,
www.aeonofchaos.com

# About the Author

B.J. Swann is the mortal incarnation of a demon who shall not be named. Which makes him sort of like Jesus or the Dalai Lama, only not lame. He has come to earth to bring about the advent of the Aeon of Chaos, an age of madness, mayhem, and pleasures undreamed of. He likes boneless fried chicken, comic books, and bubble tea.

Feel free to get in touch with him—he loves to correspond!
www.aeonofchaos.com

CPSIA information can be obtained
at www.ICGtesting.com
Printed in the USA
LVHW021558180121
676808LV00012B/1416

9 780645 068719